Through the Chakras

A TALE OF ADVENTURE IN THE SEVEN GOLDEN PYRAMIDS

by Nayaswami Savitri Simpson

Cover and book design by Surya Crisman

Cover image retouching by David Jensen

Back cover photograph by Barbara Bingham

Edited and proofread by Sudarshan Simpson, Bob Stolzman, Lakshman Heubert, and Punita Greenberg

Many thanks to all who helped bring this book to completion!

ISBN: 13: 9781565893146

Printed in the United States of America

Dedicated to my spiritual teacher

Swami Kriyananda

(1926-2013)

We miss him greatly, but he is always with us.

Contents

INTRODUCTION TO
THROUGH THE CHAKRAS

By the Author

In 2011, after the completion of my first novel, *Through Many Lives: A Tale of Time Travel Through the Yugas*, many readers asked me if I would write sequel to it. After three years of trying to get the first one written and published, I couldn't even *think* of writing another novel, even though I generally enjoy writing very much.

"Why are they asking for a sequel?" I asked myself. Of course I was glad if they enjoyed the book, and hoped that was the reason they wanted the story to continue. I admit that I left my readers dangling at the end, not knowing whether the hero and heroine ever fell in love and got married. Did everybody live happily ever after?

Sorry about that! I didn't do it because of any plans for a sequel. It was because, while writing the novel, I discovered that the main characters seemed to come alive and tell me how they wanted things to happen or not happen. I found myself following their suggestions, even though I felt this process to be somewhat disconcerting. Later, I was consoled to learn that many authors of fiction have described the same thing happening to them, with good effect on their writings.

After four busy years, circumstances in my life conspired to offer me a year-long sabbatical, in 2015.

One thing I was sure of was that I didn't want to write another novel unless I had a large chunk of time and the space in which to do it well. Because I was working full-time, the first novel had been written piecemeal, late at night, on weekends, or on short vacations or retreats. I'd write for a while with great enthusiasm, and then have to drop it for days, weeks, or even months at a time. That is a very difficult way to write anything, but most especially a novel!

Then the sabbatical came along, offering me an opportunity

to write without interruption. I realized then that: a) I really was inspired to write another novel, and b) I might have enough time, the right environment, and sufficient energy to write it as a continuous flow of inspiration. And that is what happened. I'm grateful to say that the whole process was filled with joy!

The theme of *Through the Chakras: A Tale of Adventure in the Seven Golden Pyramids* makes it a stand-alone book and does not require that you read my first novel to understand it. Nevertheless it is a sequel to the first novel in some ways. It contains many of the same characters. It also takes place, as the first one did, on earth in Ascending Treta Yuga, approximately 3900 years in the future.

If you are unfamiliar with the yogic time-theory of the yugas and the way time moves in great cycles, please see, "What is a Yuga?" at the back of this book, for a simple explanation.

We are told that in Treta Yuga people rarely communicate with their voices, but instead, with their thoughts and projections of mental images. So please note that when I have written, "He said," or "She said," I mean that communication is happening by mental telepathy.

If you are unfamiliar with information about the chakras, I believe that this novel will clearly explain what they are and what they do. Even though the chakras can be a complex subject, they are essential to the teachings and science of yoga.

As in my first novel, in which I tackled the subjects of karma, reincarnation, and the yuga theory of cycles of time, I tried to present these deep and complex concepts in a lighter, easy-to-read, fictionalized form. My motivation for this book is the same and is similar to Mary Poppins's idea that, "...a spoonful of sugar helps the medicine go down . . . in the most delightful way!"

In this case, the chakras really *are* a delightful subject! I have been giving classes and seminars on the chakras for over forty years. After all this time, I never get tired of teaching, discussing, reading, and writing about the chakras. I find them endlessly fascinating and very important to know about and experience on many levels. Understanding them helps your meditations improve and shows you how to have a happier life in general.

Also at end of the book, I've added more information about the characters from the Indian epic, the *Mahabharata*, who appear in the novel (please see: "The *Mahabharata* and the Pandava Brothers"), two chakras charts, and a bibliography.

In this novel, you'll also find numerous references to my guru Paramhansa Yogananda and his path of Kriya Yoga. If you would like to learn more about him or his teachings, please begin by reading his *Autobiography of a Yogi*, First Edition, available from Crystal Clarity Publishers: crystalclarity.com. You can also find out more about Kriya Yoga and many other inspiring topics at ananda.org.

Finally, I offer my deepest love and heartfelt thanks to Yogananda's direct disciple Swami Kriyananda. After I told him I would try to write a "spiritual novel," he encouraged me all along the way, as I flailed about, faltered often, and sometimes considered giving it up entirely.

After he made this challenging request of me, he wrote and published several inspiring novels himself (see "Recommended Bibliography"). Swamiji left his body on April 21, 2013. How I miss him, though I often feel his sweet smile in my heart.

Once my first novel was published, Swami took the time to offer me his valuable insights. He did not spare me from the "sting" of his truthful evaluation. At first I was sad to think that I had not measured up to his very high standards of writing. Then I realized how blessed I was that he was willing to help me improve. Since that time, I've done my best to incorporate his suggestions into whatever I write.

The last time I saw him in person, his final words to me were: "I wish you great success with your novel. You have my blessings always." Those blessings have been more than I could have imagined.

I hope you enjoy *Through the Chakras*. If you have any comments or questions, I am most happy to reply. Please contact me at <u>savitri@ananda.org</u>

Nayaswami Savitri Simpson
Ananda Village, Nevada City, CA USA
316 Ascending Dwapara Yuga

Through the Chakras

A TALE OF ADVENTURE IN THE SEVEN GOLDEN PYRAMIDS

CHAPTER ONE

The mighty woman of peace keeps her soul a sea of contentment.
Instead of losing her peace through the rivulets of small desires,
She lets all the rivers of desires become absorbed within herself
And keeps her sea of peace filled to the brim.

Sabella walked slowly down to the Joyuba River, which flowed below her pyramid-shaped home, a lovely dwelling she shared with her husband, Thomas. She sat comfortably on a small sandbar and relaxed back against a sun-warmed boulder. It was twilight, her favorite time to enjoy the river-beach.

The softening sunlight brought the deeper colors of the river rocks and granite boulders alive, glowing as if from within. The crystal-clear river sparkled and danced with golden-green light patterns, and its fresh fragrance intensified with the coolness of the closing day. As she'd often noticed, the river began to change its gentle rustling daytime sounds into deeper, twilight tones, sounding almost like human voices laughing, singing, or talking together.

Sabella was one of the most respected musical talents of her day and often heard music within and around her. Even now, as she sat quietly by the river, a new piece of music was forming in her mind, calling itself "River Twilight." She enjoyed its inspiring melodies resonating as if between her heart and the music of the small river.

With some reluctance she stopped listening to the beguiling music. Sabella needed to focus her attention on something else this evening, which required her complete silence and communion with the inner Divine Presence.

She relaxed her body and mind into a meditative stillness.

Whenever she had a problem to solve, she first carefully outlined her main concerns. The challenge before her filled her mind with questions, and she prayed sincerely for help and guidance. Finally, using deep breathing and some of her meditation techniques, she quieted her restless mind and set aside all questions and uncertainties. She allowed her mind to relax into a place of deep silence, where superconscious solutions can be found.

Let us step back to understand this scene more fully: The year is 5952 AD, which is 1,852 years into Ascending Treta Yuga. While the Joyuba River sparkles with the last sunrays of the day, the little beach, surrounded by large boulders and small willow thickets, is shadowed by majestic pine, cedar, and oak trees.

A lovely woman carefully smooths the white sand beneath her and spreads out a golden silk cloth, upon which she sits for meditation. She is completely relaxed and unmoving, with her spine straight and tall. Her half-closed eyes are looking slightly upward, and an aura of peace surrounds her. You feel instinctively the desire not to disturb her inward focus.

At this time, Sabella is a mature woman—108 years of age. In Ascending Treta Yuga, when the average lifespan is 300 years, she is relatively young. Her three children are adults now; all of them have left home to pursue their own lives. She appears much younger than her age —even for a woman of Treta Yuga. Her golden hair is long and loosely curled, falling well below her shoulders. Her skin is peach-tinted and her eyes are an intriguing shade of dark turquoise. She is slim, in excellent physical condition, and of medium height (seven feet three inches, about average for a woman living early in Treta Yuga). Daily Energization Exercises, yoga stretches, long walks, and swimming in the river keep her fit.

Her husband, Thomas Timetraveler has always encouraged her to swim daily. Sabella has known how to swim since childhood, but had practiced very little. Before she knew Thomas well, she had not been enthusiastic about swimming, preferring to spend her time in the world of music. But now, thanks to her almost daily swims, she can keep up with Thomas and sometimes even win one of their impromptu swimming races.

Is Sabella a beautiful woman? Thomas frequently tells her that she is, but she knows better. Her face is pleasant and full of bright smiles, but is she the world-class beauty Sunitia had been? She knows very well she is not.

Sunitia and Sabella—the two women had much in common, even though they had never met in this lifetime. Thomas and Sunitia had been life-linked in a past life long ago, just as Thomas and Sabella were life-linked in the present time. Thomas and Sunitia had been together about 1,800 years before the close of Descending Treta Yuga—some 12,000 years earlier.

We might well ask: What is true beauty? Sabella possesses a radiant inner beauty—laughing often with great joy. Over the years she has helped bring out the sweeter side of Thomas, who has learned to leave behind his seriousness and enjoy the simple, childlike pleasures life can bring.

Sabella knows how to love with her full heart. Tuning in to the flow of Divine Love, she lets it pour unceasingly through her into everyone she encounters, as well as to nature and all its creatures.

Several years ago, her beloved spiritual teacher Simeon honored her by giving her the second name of Lovingheart, a gift-name she treasures.

What now disturbs this kind and loving lady? What new challenge has Sabella Lovingheart trustingly taken into meditation?

Just a few days ago, her teacher Simeon telepathically sent her the enigmatic words: "Sabella Lovingheart, now is the time for you to explore a new pathway in your life's journey."

Earlier he had explained that a project would be offered to her by the High Council. She would need to master a new discipline. Once having completed her initial studies for the project, she would facilitate an advanced learning degree in the Halls of Wisdom.

Sabella, now meditating in these lovely twilight hours, is preparing herself inwardly for the adventure coming her way. She knows that our lives are richest when filled with continuous growth and joyous adventures—even if those adventures take us beyond our present comfort zones.

Fifty years earlier, Thomas Timetraveler and Sabella Lovingheart had been asked by Simeon, their guide in the Halls of Wisdom, to take his place as the primary instructors for the Levels Four and Five Seminars focusing on training qualified students in the science and practice of time travel. With much trepidation, they accepted what they perceived to be a huge responsibility, even though Simeon had reassured them often that they were both well-suited and well-trained for these positions.

Nevertheless, several years passed before they felt completely comfortable in their new roles. At the time, they had been quite young to take on such an important responsibility. Thomas had been 63 and Sabella, 58 when Simeon had resigned from his position in the Halls of Wisdom.

The subsequent years brought challenges, joys, and sorrows, as life always does. In serving together, Thomas and Sabella fell deeply in love and asked Simeon's blessing on their wish to become life-linked. With his silver eyes twinkling brightly at them, Simeon performed their simple life-linking ceremony.

They rarely saw Simeon these days. As they grew more comfortable in their teaching roles, they no longer felt the need to seek him out with questions quite as often.

Recently Simeon had hinted that he might soon be leaving his honored position on the High Council and possibly be departing the material plane entirely, to live on an advanced astral planet called Hiranyaloka.

This was both happy and sad news for the couple. Simeon's impact on their lives had been enormous; he was their teacher and mentor, certainly, but really much more like a spiritual father. Their grateful love for him remained steady and unchanging; he had been the polestar of their lives. Without Simeon's wise and careful guidance, they would not have found each other and discovered that being linked together in this lifetime could be a joy-filled completion for both of them.

Though they would miss him greatly, they could only be happy for Simeon's well-deserved "promotion" to a higher plane.

In their harmonious relationship, Sabella and Thomas never kept secrets from each other. He had told her in detail about his first time-travel experience, during which he had visited Descending Treta Yuga.

During his visit to Descending Treta Yuga, he had re-lived a portion of his life with his then wife, Sunitia. That experience had sent Thomas into a long and agonizing period of depression. He explained to Sabella that he had never known such a depth of connection with another human being as he'd experienced with the beautiful Sunitia.

When Sabella heard Thomas recount his experience with Sunitia—who might well be his true soul mate, she assumed there could never be room for anyone else in Thomas's life, then or in the future! This was a sad realization for Sabella, who had been attracted to Thomas for a long time, though she had never expressed this to him. Carefully she stuffed her sorrow into the deepest recesses of her heart, promising herself never to let Thomas know of her love for him. She vowed, and kept her vow for several years, simply to remain his good friend and co-instructor in the Halls of Wisdom.

But Simeon knew all about her hidden heartache. She had never tried to hide anything from her teacher, because it never worked. Amazingly, he had very little to say about Sabella's sorrow, counseling her only: "Wait calmly, Sabella. You are young, and your life's path is still forming before you."

Sabella had experienced many time-travel adventures of her own, all of which she had revealed to Thomas. But never, during the times in which she had intensely relived portions of her past incarnations, had she encountered a relationship that felt comparable to what Thomas seemed to have had with his long-ago wife, Sunitia.

What could she make of this? Perhaps she'd not traveled to the right time and place to locate her own soul mate—this was possible, of course, for she had lived through millions of past lifetimes and only time-traveled to a few of them. She had promised herself to ask Simeon about this someday, but over the years, somehow she had never actually asked him this question. She found this interesting, since she knew that Simeon was able to temporarily "mind-blank" his students if he knew they wanted him to reveal part of their past or future he felt were better left unknown.

Sabella had grown proficient in the thought-transference and mental communication skills she'd struggled with in her early student years. She noticed that her friends and fellow students had also become more skillful in these talents. She attributed this to their moving more and more into Treta Yuga, the "mental age."

Time travel to her former lives in past yugas, too, had become almost second nature to her. These were skills which she and Thomas now helped teach the younger students in the Halls of Wisdom.

What great adventures in time travel she and Thomas had helped their students experience! Much could be learned about one's present life from careful observation of one's past lives.

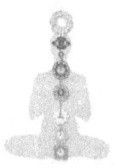

CHAPTER TWO

Simeon welcomed Sabella quietly into the outer courtyard of the High Council Pavilion. She felt honored to have been invited for her first visit here. When Simeon had initially told her and her classmates of his new assignment to this place, he said they would not be able to visit him there. Now she realized he meant they would not be able to visit him until they had grown deeper in their spiritual lives.

Sabella was enraptured by the unusual beauty of the structure. The massive opaque walls swirled with colors. Countless colors moved slowly into ever-changing patterns. It was, by far, the most stunning building she had ever seen, and she wasn't sure that it was actually a structure at all. It seemed to be floating lightly in the air, instead of built upon a foundation. Simeon enjoyed the curiosity and wonder playing on her features, though he himself had grown quite accustomed to the structure's magnificence.

While they waited to be summoned into the inner sanctum, Simeon suggested that they meditate together. Sabella agreed grudgingly; she would have preferred to pepper Simeon with dozens of questions about this place and their purpose in being there.

Last night, she'd tried to invite Thomas's advice about what to expect, but all he would say is, "You'll just have to keep your appointment and find out what they want of you."

"Why don't you join me when I go to the High Council Pavilion?" she'd said to Thomas as a thought-request. They were enjoying a quiet evening together on one of their decks, drinking their favorite Thyme-Travel tea, and enjoying the cool, evening breezes.

"I was not invited," he thought back to her with a chuckle. "But don't be so concerned, Sabella! You know Simeon always has your best interests in mind."

"I know," she sighed, "but he enjoys making meetings like this seem mysterious and a little bit scary, don't you think?"

"Perhaps he does. I'll admit he has interesting ways of adding surprises and drama to all of our lives. But I think that's part of his calling and his gift. When you are with Simeon, there is never a dull moment!"

"Simeon once invited you to the High Council, but you never told me what happened to you that day. What was it like there?"

Thomas gave Sabella his familiar quirky smile and continued to drink his tea and watch the stars. She knew he could not be coaxed into revealing anything more at that point.

"Please, God, help me deal with these headstrong and way-too-silent men in my life!" she thought peevishly.

"I heard that!" Thomas spoke the words aloud—something he rarely did—and she jumped with surprise. They laughed together, and Thomas gave Sabella an encouraging hug.

Simeon's soft thought-voice interrupted Sabella's reverie: "They are calling us to come inside, my child."

Together they stood and walked through shimmering curtains of glittering, silver strands of light.

In the High Council chambers sat four men, five women, and two children. They rested comfortably under a large tree that grew inside the building. They seemed to be in the middle of an indoor rain forest; it dripped around them, but no one was getting wet. Tropical birds shrieked; the air was cool, fragrant with the smell of tropical flowers.

"Welcome, Sabella," said one of the Elders, a woman who looked remarkably like Simeon. "My name is Issoweet, and I have been asked to be the primary spokesperson today."

Sabella joined the seated group and breathed slowly to

calm herself, striving to keep her overly inquisitive mind under control as each council member welcomed her with an introduction. One of the children said her name was Nila-Nightingale. She explained that she and her younger brother were included in the Council to help introduce the childlike quality of nonlinear thinking, whenever it might be needed, into all Council decisions.

Sabella wasn't sure she understood what the girl meant by these words, but she did not ask for clarification. She saw Simeon smile fondly at the boy and girl, who had big smiles and hugs for him in return. Simeon always had a special way with children.

Issoweet mentally addressed Sabella, "My dear Sabella, my brother Simeon has kept the members of our High Council apprised of your teaching career in the Halls of Wisdom. We want to thank you for the integrity and compassion that you have brought to your position, and we are also great admirers of your musical accomplishments."

"*Brother*?" Sabella thought to herself—she sincerely hoped it was to herself only. It felt unusually difficult to "shield" her thoughts from these obviously highly advanced souls! But her thoughts continued. "Could this woman addressing her be a blood sister to Simeon?"

There certainly was a strong physical resemblance between them. However, Simeon had never mentioned having a sister—in fact she was sure that Simeon had never mentioned *anything* about his immediate family members to Thomas or her, having more or less indicated that he was all alone in this world. They had often wondered between themselves why this was so, but they had never had the nerve to pry. Simeon was a very private person!

Issoweet continued, "We have a request for you, Sabella. You have been chosen for this project for many reasons. First, we know the depth of your meditations and how much spiritual progress you have made in this present lifetime. And you are uniquely talented in the world of vibration— especially color and music."

At that time in her life, Sabella was the world expert in "photism," the ability to see a sound or to hear a color. At her famous "Cosmic Photism Concerts," music was played, sung, and projected into the environment and into the minds of the audience in the form of shapes and colors. Each musical note corresponds to a particular vibration within the color spectrum. The shade and intensity of the colors depend on the octave and volume in which the notes or chords are sung or played. Shapes also spring from the vibrations of music, forming themselves into abstractions or actual scenes, according to the type of music performed.

These concerts, which she wrote, produced, directed, and sometimes performed in herself, always to capacity crowds, were truly exquisite. Though completely uninterested in her worldwide fame, she had learned to wear her fame gracefully. While Thomas had sometimes produced the performances with her, composing and playing some of the music himself, Sabella was the one the public recognized as the "star of the show" and the driving force behind this amazing form of entertainment.

"It has come to our attention," Issoweet continued, "that many of our students in the Halls of Wisdom are lacking in sufficient awareness and experience of what the chakras are, and how fundamental their influence is upon the lives of human beings. We want to create a new Level in the Halls of Wisdom, dedicated to the subject of the chakras and astral anatomy. We would like you to be its founder and director."

Sabella's mind reeled! Simeon had never even hinted that something of this magnitude would be asked of her. She felt his soothing voice in her mind: "Be at peace, my child. This is a wonderful opportunity for you. It is the next important step in your life!"

She shot a thought back to Simeon, "I can't imagine what is being asked of me or what is needed here or how to go about it!"

"I'll let Issoweet explain this project to you in more detail. She is the one who formulated the idea. I highly approve of what we are asking you to do and have full confidence that you'll be able to do it very well!"

"Will Thomas be involved?" she wondered, "So far, we've been an effective team in all our major endeavors in the Halls of Wisdom." Sabella realized that her insecurities and her lack of self-confidence were obvious, but she needed to know the answer to the question.

Simeon replied, "Thomas and I will certainly support you, as will Issoweet; but primarily it will be *your* project to pursue and develop!"

Because Simeon's resounding mental words reassured her very much, Sabella bowed her head in respect to the Elders and Council Members and broadcast this thought to them, "I am humbly grateful for your confidence in me. I don't yet understand this mission and all that it entails, but I do accept it. I will do my best to do whatever is being asked of me."

Smiles and twinkling eyes abounded among the Council Members. The indoor rain forest birds sang more beautifully, and the light grew brighter all around them.

"It's thrilling to us to hear your positive decision, dear Sabella! You are a brave and true adventurer to agree to do as we are requesting, with so little advance information about what it involves." Issoweet beamed at her.

Brave? True adventurer? So little advance information? Oh dear! To *what* sort of adventure had she so quickly said yes? Was she going to live to regret her quick decision?

Issoweet's voice chimed in her head again. "The Council will disperse at this time, but please linger here with me, Sabella, so that you and I can further discuss your project privately. Simeon and our council members have discussed most of my preliminary ideas, but we realize that you know very little."

"I know absolutely nothing!" Sabella thought wryly to

herself. "But I also am completely committed now, so I'd better find out all that I can about this 'new adventure' as soon as possible."

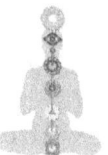

CHAPTER THREE

Issoweet guided Sabella out of the Council Hall into a small pyramid-shaped chapel nearby. She asked Sabella to sit with her for meditation. Her request pleased Sabella very much, for she knew that it was always best to begin important endeavors by first praying and then meditating. Due to her natural feelings of slight anxiety about her forthcoming adventures, she knew it would be best to use several effective mind-quieting techniques. Soon she was in a state of deep peace and non-attachment to whatever might be coming next.

Sabella was surprised to notice that several hours had passed in inner communion with God and the Great Ones. Issoweet was gazing at her out of familiar silver eyes.

"Sabella, my child, your meditative state is inspiring to behold. I hesitated to interrupt you, but felt I must do so, because we have much to discuss."

Sabella looked into Issoweet's hauntingly familiar eyes and simply could not prevent herself from asking a question, "Issoweet, this is our first meeting, but I feel I have known you forever. Is this a past-life connection or . . . ?" Here she paused, realizing that perhaps she was being disrespectful or "too familiar" in asking Issoweet personal questions only a short time after first meeting her. But she wanted to know if Issoweet was Simeon's blood-sister.

"I know the question in your mind, Sabella, and, yes, Simeon is my birth brother—in fact, he is my *twin* brother. We were separated at birth, back in the tumultuous early years of Ascending Treta Yuga, when the deadly Mantric Wars were still going on. I never even knew that I *had* a brother until

Simeon came to join us on the Council several years ago. Our first meeting was startling to both of us. It was like looking into a mirror and seeing a male version of myself, or the other way around, in his case." Issoweet smiled.

"The mental bond between us was instant and profound. We both knew that it had to be based on more than mere physical resemblance. So we began a small time-travel research project together, to understand what our connection really was and is. Going back in time, we learned of our twinship, and of the harsh circumstances surrounding our birth and infancy, which separated us completely and left us with no knowledge of each other's existence.

"It is a sad tale, Sabella, as I'm sure you can imagine, but all the past unhappiness has melted away in the unexpected happiness of our reunion. We are now able to help each other in many ways. What a great blessing this is for both of us now, in the last stage of our present lifetimes!"

Sabella was saturated in the blissful vibrations Issoweet was emitting. She was very glad to hear of Simeon and Issoweet's good fortune, for she loved Simeon very, very much. Still she wondered why Simeon had never mentioned Issoweet to her or to Thomas.

And what was this about, "the last stage of our present lifetimes"? That was a frightening idea. As hard as she tried to get used to the idea of Simeon's leaving the physical plane—and he had hinted at it often enough, lately—the thought of it still caused her great pain. Simeon was her beloved teacher and spiritual father. She had been his student for most of her life!

Sabella caught herself up short. She knew better! Life follows death and death life, again and again and again—in almost endless rounds. Surely she could understand this fact completely, from firsthand experience? Besides, in the final analysis, there is no separation of souls—we are all forever one!

"Your mind may know a fact very well, but your heart often lags behind your mind and can cause you great sadness. Do not be unhappy, my child. Simeon and I will still be around for a while—at least for long enough. . . ."

Sabella heard Issoweet's comforting words in her mind and knew that she had not been able to shield her curiosity or her troubled thoughts from this obviously very wise woman. This fact embarrassed her, as it should not have happened now, at her present level of mental maturity; but she also felt waves of soothing love fill her heart, satisfying a hunger within herself that she had not even known was there. It was a feeling so sweet, so feminine, so similar, and yet so different from what she felt from Simeon, which, though very powerful, was still, at times, extremely masculine and quite impersonal.

"Ah-ha," she thought. "I begin to see what is going on here. Issoweet is a balancing force for Simeon. She was brought to me now, in this stage of my present lifetime, to help me move into a new life-direction—into a journey of the heart."

"Well, you'll have to use your mind also, and every other talent and facility you have, and some you don't yet have!" The thought came to her like a golden fist, smacking her on the forehead. This feeling was so familiar after all her years under Simeon's tutelage that she turned to see if Simeon had entered the chapel.

He had not. Startled, Sabella looked back at Issoweet, who was laughing softly. "Simeon is not here, my child, but I want you to understand fully that you are right in thinking that he and I are very different, but also very much alike in *many* ways. We are all always going for 'the great balance'; do you understand what I mean?"

"But, of course!" Sabella reasoned inwardly. She reflected on all the "male-female balancing lessons" she had learned throughout the years of her life-link with Thomas and on all the important lessons, which she sincerely hoped that he had learned from her also. Is this not the primary purpose of a spiritual relationship, along with the help and comfort one can offer one's mate along the way? Life-linked couples must strive to learn and grow together spiritually, helping each other to find a happy balance between mind and heart.

Nevertheless, Simeon had never seemed lonely to Sabella. He had always seemed so complete in himself—so calm, so detached from the world. The thought that he needed anybody for anything was a startling one.

"Ah, how little we know about those we think we know the best," reflected Sabella.

Issoweet caught the thought and nodded in agreement, "Very true, my dear, but now we must move on to other subjects. We have *much* to discuss and many new things for you to learn."

CHAPTER FOUR

"Sabella, I will speak frankly to you now of an important and personal event that I know you know about very well; I suspect it might be something which could be somewhat uncomfortable for you to review. But for reasons I hope you will come to understand better soon, it is necessary. . . ."

Issoweet paused for a moment in her thought transference, and then continued, "Actually I think it would be better for you to 'see' all this in mind-pictures, rather than merely hearing me tell you about it in words. Will you agree to let me show you these scenes? Thezzy are from one of your husband's past lives."

"Uh-oh!" thought Sabella to herself, she hoped, "I think I know what *this* is going to be about! Nevertheless, I think I'm ready. I do feel inwardly stronger and also very secure in Thomas's love for me and in our life-link together. I will *not* let what I think I'm going to see now throw me off center in any way."

With only a moment's hesitation, Sabella, gathered up her courage, nodded to Issoweet, sending her a strong thought: "Let's begin—I'm ready!"

"Really, my dear, this is *not* going to be a violent situation that I'm going to show you! I'm not going to have you shot with a deadly projectile. I'm only going to show you a true mind-movie. You young people are often so abrupt with your emotional responses!" Issoweet mentally teased Sabella with a wry smile. But she could read Sabella well enough to know that she was emotionally mature and would be able to accept what she was going to show her.

Sabella had experienced mind-movies before, many times, but only with Simeon's assistance. He was a master of this kind of information-transference to his students through sight, sound, feeling, and even smell and taste. Happy memories of her student days with Simeon in the Halls of Wisdom came to her now. But she quickly put all these memories aside and readied herself to receive Issoweet's instructions.

Issoweet spoke softly, "Sabella, I will now show your mind an unusual place, which Thomas visited only once during his first time-travel experience. I know he told you about it."

"Yes," thought Sabella, "I was reasonably sure that is where we must be headed."

Immediately Issoweet and Sabella were standing beside each other on a hilltop, or so it seemed to Sabella. She knew that they were actually back in the little chapel in the High Council complex. She had opened her mind to Issoweet and to the mind-movie that Issoweet wanted to show her. Nevertheless, this type of mind-movie had a way of dissolving one's present reality and bringing a feeling that you are actually "there."

Sabella also knew very well that "mind-movie" was not the perfect term to use for this sort of educational experience. What she was seeing was completely true to the way it had happened—even though the events had taken place a very long, long time ago.

Issoweet said: "Be mentally still, Sabella. Observe and learn."

"Open your eyes now," a stunningly beautiful woman said to Thomas, holding his hand tightly in her own.

"Wait, wait!" Sabella said to Issoweet with unexpected anxiety. "Please remind me again. Can they see us? Hear us? Can they in any way sense that we are here with them? Suddenly I'm not sure that it's right to eavesdrop or invade my husband's private past life without his permission!"

"My child, you do understand what is going on here, don't you? This is just a scene from the distant past. It's not even your own past. The plays of shadows and light are being projected on the screen of your mind right now. These long-ago events are very much *over and done with* now, though the memories still remain in the ether. We are just observing what happened; we're accessing the cosmic memory patterns.

"I know it might seem quite real to you. You know how our ancestors would watch a movie being projected onto a 'real screen' and become completely caught up in the action," Issoweet laughed.

"I'm told that sometimes those ancient movie-watchers would become so engrossed in what they were watching that they thought it was really happening, right then and there. They'd screech in terror or even cry out to the actors in the movie, something like: 'Look out! The monster is sneaking up behind you!'

"Sabella, what we are seeing is just a mind-movie, a 'cosmic past-events movie,' simply being re-played now before your inner vision."

"Yes, yes I know this. But that's Thomas! Thomas Timetraveler, my dear husband!" thought Sabella. "What is he doing holding the hand of this gorgeous woman? This is *my* husband, after all, not hers!"

Sabella paused and prayed for help. Then she commanded herself sternly, "Oh, for Heaven's sake, Sabella! Get a grip on yourself. Watch the movie. You already know what is going on here! Thomas told you all about it. And there must be something important to learn from this 'mind-movie,' otherwise Issoweet would not have wanted you to experience it in this way."

Sabella took a few deep breaths and reminded herself that Thomas was her faithful and loving life-mate, in *this* present lifetime—and also in some others that she knew about through her own time-travel experiences.

Sabella was self-aware enough to perceive the main source of her discomfort. Thomas had casually described his many-centuries-ago wife, Sunitia, as a very lovely woman. Seeing her like this—she seemed very real, in full living color—it wasn't easy. But actually observing her now—she seemed so very real.

Sunitia had been described to Sabella by other time-travelers, who also knew or had seen her in that long ago lifetime, as a "world-class beauty." Well, so what? What did *that* mean? Now, Sabella knew *exactly* what it meant. Sunitia seemed to shine like the sun, with inner and outer beauty. Her obvious love for Thomas sparkled out of her eyes, as did Thomas's love for her.

Issoweet mentally whispered to Sabella, "Yes, she was a great beauty in that lifetime, I know. But let's get past that part. It is important for you to see what happens next."

Sabella, still slightly stunned, agreed, and the movie continued. It was then that Sabella realized she could not only see and hear them very clearly, but also she could know their thoughts.

CHAPTER FIVE

Thomas was slightly uneasy at not being sure about exactly where his wife, Sunitia had transported them, or even if they were still on earth. He saw, not far below them, a huge, golden pyramid.

They were standing on a high hill overlooking a lush green valley with a large river flowing through it. As Thomas looked farther down the river, he could see that there were several other similar pyramids, located at intervals along the river, stretching out in the distance as far as he could see.

"Thomas, there are seven of them!" Sunitia thought, reading his wonderment at what they were seeing. "They represent the seven chakras, the centers of energy along our own inner river, the astral spine."

"They are magnificent! Where are we? What is this place?"

"We are here on earth, in Descending Treta Yuga, of course! Where else would we be?" Sunitia teased him. "But we are in a very remote and secret river valley, ancient and unknown to almost everyone on this planet at this time."

"How did you find out about it?"

"This place was revealed to me in a dream only today. While I was taking a nap this afternoon, I was told in my dream how to get here. I immediately came to see what we are seeing now. I then decided to wait until you returned home to share it all with you. I want to be sure I'm not still dreaming." She beamed her bewitching smile at him.

"You're not," he thought to her, "unless we are both dreaming the same dream. So what shall we do now?"

"Let's explore—and I think we may be expected!" She grasped his hand and teleported them to the edge of the river, near the closest pyramid.

Sabella and Issoweet, unobserved, followed right along with them.

Thomas and Sunitia (and Sabella also) were awed at the sight of the first golden pyramid. It was huge, but more than that, there was a magnetic radiance and energy that it was emitting. They seemed to be transparent and made of sunbeams or some kind of mysteriously vibrating light. This place was holy and very powerful.

At that moment, they noticed a white-robed figure sitting nearby. He had just materialized himself there. He sat very still and was meditating.

Walking quietly to where he sat, Thomas and Sunitia sat down on either side of him, and assumed their own meditative poses. Intuitively they knew that he would speak to them only when he was ready to do so. Perhaps he needed to "read" their thoughts or feel their energy patterns. His vibrations were benevolent and extremely powerful.

Soon they were lost in the silence, calm, and uplifted. After a time, the man began to sing a song in a language unknown to them—it was glorious and soothing, a lovely way to end a meditation. At its close, he opened his eyes and smiled at them.

But before beginning his conversation with Thomas and Sunitia, Sabella was very startled to hear this man's voice in her head. "Sabella, hello! It is nice to meet you. I know you are watching this mind-movie from the future and you are welcome to do so. I also know why Issoweet is assisting you. Hello, dear Issoweet—it's been a while since we conversed."

"Hello, Brother Solonar." Issoweet offered him a small mental bow. "I am very glad to see you also."

"I thought you said they couldn't see or hear us, Issoweet!" Sabella said in a near panic.

"*They* can't, but Solonar can. It's all fine, Sabella. I'll explain later. All is well."

Brother Solonar turned his attention to the couple, who were oblivious of his brief acknowledgment of Sabella and Issoweet. "Sunitia, thank you for coming here and for bringing Thomas with you. You are a very receptive dreamer. I am happy to be able to show you the Valley of the Seven Golden Pyramids."

Sunitia smiled at the stranger who seemed to know all about her, and transmitted this thought: "We are honored to be here, kind sir. Please tell us, who are you? And exactly where are we?"

"I am Brother Solonar," he said simply.

"Are you the creator of these shining pyramids or temples or whatever they are?" Sunitia asked in eager awe.

Sabella now remembered that Thomas had told her that Sunitia was one of the most famous architects of her time. Naturally she would want to know all about these amazing buildings.

"They were co-created by the Great Ones, with help from the Divine Presence, and many others—both material and astral beings," Solonar said quietly. "You are blessed to be able to come here and see them. They are known to very few people on this planet. The pyramids were created eons ago as a reminder of certain important inner realities, the knowledge of which is gradually being lost to most human beings, as the present age of Descending Treta Yuga moves towards Descending Dwapara Yuga.

"In their material form, the pyramids will exist much longer than the memory of how they were made or why. The sands of time may blow over them or they may even cease to exist and be forgotten by most. But someday in the distant future, their message will once again be revealed to those who crave the knowledge they can offer."

"May we see them? May we enter and explore them? Can you tell me how long ago they were constructed, architecturally speaking?" Sunitia was very enthusiastic. "They are beautiful, so magnificent and perfect in symmetry and form! How long have they been here? They appear to be transparent, but surely there is something inside them."

"Be calm, my little sister. I will be your guide here, and eventually I will tell and show you everything you want to know about the pyramids. You will enjoy your tour, I'm sure."

With these thought-words, Brother Solonar stood up and guided the couple closer to the first golden pyramid.

Issoweet stopped the mind-movie and returned herself and Sabella to the chapel. After a few minutes of meditation and a little time to refresh themselves with an energy potion made with fresh mango pulp and liellia blossoms, Issoweet looked penetratingly at Sabella: "Well, what do you think?"

"I think Sunitia is the most beautiful woman I've ever seen. How can I go home and face Thomas after I've actually seen what she looked like? Having seen Sunitia, whom he had for a wife in that lifetime, and comparing her incredible beauty to the way I look—not to mention seeing their obvious deep love for each other—how do you think I must feel? I feel inadequate and very sad!"

Issoweet sighed, "I had anticipated that you might feel that way, but I'm sorry that you do. Sabella, you must rise above these thoughts! You are wiser and more spiritually mature than your present behavior implies. Besides, there is no need for you ever to see her again—she will not be involved in what you will be learning during your own pilgrimage through the seven chakra pyramids.

"But perhaps I shouldn't have transported us back to that particular time-scene. Somehow I thought it might be a good way for you to acquaint yourself with this fascinating place."

Sabella deliberately calmed herself as much as she could and thought to Issoweet, "No, no, it was exactly the right thing to have happened. I had often thought of time-traveling there myself, but truthfully, I was afraid to see her. No doubt, you have helped me face some lingering fears.

"However, before you show me what my next step in this quest will be, I feel I need to speak with Thomas about my strong reaction to 'seeing' Sunitia. I'd like to clear up this matter with him, lest remnants of my self-doubt remain to cloud my ability to do whatever is needed for this new project. Would that be acceptable to you?"

"Perfectly acceptable and understandable! I was going to suggest it myself. Take as long as you need. Then send me a message about when we can meet again." Issoweet smiled her wise smile at Sabella. As they parted, she prayed deeply that Sabella Lovingheart would find her way quickly to a place of peace within herself.

CHAPTER SIX

Thomas Timetraveler knew something very serious must have happened to his life-mate. Sabella's face was flushed and her usual peaceful demeanor seemed to have fled. Her aura was filled with patches of gray mist. Her mind, which was usually completely open to him, was closed and guarded.

"Shall we share about this matter here, or do you want to sit by the river," he thought to her. He knew that the river was, for her, a place of solace and meditation.

"River," was her one-word reply. Without further words or thoughts, they walked the short distance together to the banks of the Joyuba.

"Let's meditate together," they both smiled as this idea was transmitted from one to the other, at exactly the same moment. Almost always it was this way between them, for which they were very grateful.

Three hours later, the stars sparkled brightly in the moonless sky. Thomas and Sabella completed their meditation by singing a beautiful and ancient chant together, one of their favorites:

> *O God beautiful; O God beautiful;*
> *At Thy feet, oh, I do bow.*
> *In the forest Thou art green;*
> *In the mountain Thou art high;*
> *In the river Thou art restless;*
> *In the ocean Thou art grave.*

The sounds of their beautiful voices intertwined and flowed upward until they reached the stars above them; the stars and all of nature seemed to join together in blissful harmony. The river sounds added grace notes to the music, which expressed freedom and utter joy.

"Why is the river 'restless'?" thought Sabella. "And why is the ocean 'grave'?"

Thomas: "I think that is their nature. The word 'grave,' in this context, means very deep, wise, and solemn. You too seem both restless and grave tonight, my dearest Sabella. May I ask why?"

"Yes, my love." With these simple words, she opened her mind to Thomas, and he quickly saw all that had happened to her today, including her unusually strong emotional reaction to seeing Sunitia for the first time, even though they had often talked about her and about that long-ago lifetime.

"Ah, I see," was his simple comment.

"Do you really?" she asked. "Do you *really* know how I feel right now? I love you with a love that feels pure and God-given. We are life-linked in this lifetime, and life has been very good for us together. We've brought children into the world and raised them well, I think. But Sunitia was so very important to you then and so stunningly beautiful, in that lifetime with you among the golden pyramids.

"I am very disappointed in myself, because I placed so much value on her physical beauty—I really do know better than that—but there is more to it. When I 'saw' you together today, life-linked together in Descending Treta Yuga, you seemed to be . . . ," here she hesitated, looking for the right word or concept. "You seemed to be *one* with her.

"Thomas, was/is she your soul mate? If she is, and if you know that without question, how and why do you put up with me?"

"Dearest friend, wife, and companion of this lifetime, have I not convinced you of my love for you, which to me feels pure and God-given? Have we not grown together in inner-communion and learned many lessons from this and many other lifetimes? Does it truly matter to you who my soul mate may be? I've never asked you who you think *your* soul mate is." Thomas couldn't resist giving her this little mental dig, and Sabella couldn't resist poking him in the ribs with her sharp elbow.

"Ouch, that hurt!" and they laughed together.

Sabella thought, "The truth is that I don't know. I have wondered, of course, and have made some guesses."

Thomas thought back to her, "Simeon talked at length to us about what soul mates are—it's been many years ago, but I *know* you remember those teachings!"

Sabella, nodding ruefully: "My head remembers, at least somewhat, but tonight my heart is being very slow to catch up. Remind me again."

"Anything for you, my love. Here's the short version to jog your memory:

"In its essence the soul has no gender. But when the soul is first manifested in the physical world, it is as part of a dual, just as everything else in creation exists in duality, in opposites—for every 'up' there is a 'down,' for every 'out' there is an 'in,' and so on. Thus, every soul has its own dualistic counterpart, which might be called its twin soul.

"Throughout the soul's long journey through time and space and through its almost countless incarnations, one of these two souls generally and more fully manifests the more masculine side of duality and the other, the more feminine side. And whether they physically inhabit human bodies as males or females, they still basically have a particular way of expressing themselves in somewhat more masculine or feminine ways.

"Eventually these two souls must reunite. A soul mate need not be of the opposite sex in any particular incarnation. It could be your mother, brother, spiritual teacher, friend, even a stranger, or brief, chance encounter. This person might be a person you don't even meet in this lifetime, or if you *do* meet, you might not even *like* him or her very much. But there is always something connecting the two of you on a deeper level, and *only* when you are on that deeper level, will you be able to benefit from this tie. Otherwise, on an outward level, there might be all sorts of misunderstandings and difficulties.

"Also it is possible that one's soul mate could even be on another planet in a faraway galaxy; and in that case, you could unite yourself in vision in a lower yuga or through trans-space teleportation as we know it now, in the higher yugas.

"Remember that our truest soul mate is God alone. We seek union with God first and foremost. We know that it is *not* helpful to run madly about looking for one's soul mate. That union will come naturally when the time is right and when one has attained the highest state of spiritual consciousness."

Thomas continued, "Meanwhile, let me remind you of the words to the song we sang to each other in our life-linking ceremony."

Sabella's eyes brightened with happy tears as she remembered the joy-filled occasion. They joined hands, gazed into each other's eyes, and sang in harmony:

> *Dearest friend, in the blend,*
> *Of your life's path with mine,*
> *I have found Love is crowned,*
> *With freedom's vine.*
> *Sorrows all disappear,*
> *When friendship's gaze is clear,*
> *May our sight, shunning night,*
> *Toward God incline.* ©

"I am sure that is what we are, Thomas—spiritual friends in the best and deepest sense, helping each other along the journey to oneness. Thank you for reminding me in such a kind and gentle way. I promise to set aside my silly worries and be grateful for who I am in this lifetime and for what God has given me through our union with each other."

Then Sabella smiled mischievously at Thomas and sweetly said: "So now will you tell me? Do you know if Sunitia really is or is not your twin soul?"

"Sabella, are you serious? After all I have just said—and given that I have said emphatically and repeatedly that *I don't know*; and I believe won't know until the time comes—isn't that all you and I really need to understand right now?" Thomas looked a bit miffed.

"Sorry, sorry, just kidding!"

With this, Thomas scooped Sabella up and tossed her into the river. He dove into the water, where they laughed and splashed like joyful children under the starlit skies of Ascending Treta Yuga.

CHAPTER SEVEN

Sabella sent a mental message to Issoweet, saying that she was ready to continue her training and asking when it would be convenient for them to meet.

Issoweet came into her mind almost immediately, suggesting that they get together the next morning in the same small pyramid chapel where they had last met.

At the agreed-upon time, Issoweet asked that they sit quietly for a while to attune themselves with the Divine Presence. After a short meditation, she gently asked Sabella, "How are you? Were you able to speak with Thomas as you had planned? Did you come to a place of understanding and peace around this matter?"

"Yes, thank you Issoweet for your patience. I know that my 'meltdown' delayed your plans for our getting started with my training program. Thomas was able to help me resolve my fears and doubts about my not being able to measure up to Sunitia's great beauty and his love for her in that lifetime so long ago. I feel confident that I am steady and ready to proceed."

Issoweet smiled: "Steady and ready is good! I also want to mention that your aura is looking very bright today, my dear. So let us begin."

Issoweet explained that they'd be visiting the first golden pyramid in a slightly different way than through the time-travel or mind-movie technique to which Sabella had become accustomed.

Issoweet carefully explained: "You see, the chakra pyramids exist both on a physical plane, which is what we were observing in our most recent visit there through the mind-movie technique, and also on the astral or energy plane.

"It may be best for you to learn the things you need to know by being more on an astral level, since the chakras exist more dynamically on the astral level of our inner beings than on the physical level. Or perhaps a combination of physical and astral awareness will work best for you. We shall have to see how it goes and make adjustments as necessary.

"But before we visit the area of the first-chakra pyramid, I want to ask you to explain to me briefly the basics of what you know a chakra to be."

Sabella was happy to comply: "The chakras, seven in number, are the whirling, spinning balls of energy which are part of our astral anatomy. They are located along the *sushumna* or astral spine. Their function is to distribute *prana* (conscious cosmic energy) to all parts of our brains and bodies. In addition, they store information of our past karma, in the form of *vrittis*.

"Each *vritti* is 'deposited' in the chakra which vibrates most harmoniously with the action or thought which created the *vritti*. There are many techniques which increase the flow of *prana* through the astral spine and chakras, in order to clear and purify them. Thus, the energy we need for happiness, health, and most of all, for spiritual progress, becomes much more available to make these things possible. The chakras, therefore, hold the key to a person's well-being on every level."

"Amazing, Sabella. I had made a small wager with myself that you couldn't precisely define and explain the chakras in less than 200 words and you did it with 138 words! Well done! I am even surer now than ever before that you are the perfect candidate for this project!"

"Thank you, Issoweet. The subject of the chakras has always fascinated me, and I'll be very glad to learn even more! But first, let me say a few more words about my relationship to the chakras. I know that I explained succinctly what they are and what they do. Still, there's something of a more personal nature that I want to tell you about.

"I began to go much deeper into a direct experience of the chakras when I began to practice the higher Kriya Yoga techniques. Simeon gave me the amazing second, third, and fourth Kriya Yoga initiations when I was only 24 years old—a very long time ago! And I have practiced them daily and regularly for all these years, without fail. As you know, the higher Kriya techniques work very dynamically with each chakra, stimulating them, opening them, awakening them, and clearing them of all the obstructions which prevent the free flow of life-force through the whole chakra system.

"As time went on, I began to understand the chakras much better and actually, as I (perhaps quaintly) express it, 'to make friends with them.' Indeed, they became so real to me that I felt I actually could *see* them. And even more than seeing them, I felt them to be—don't laugh, Issoweet—little 'joy factories' inside me." Here Sabella couldn't help herself and laughed out loud. Issoweet joined her.

"Joy factories?" Issoweet said, still laughing with delight. "I've never heard the chakras called *that* before! The chakras do hold the keys to our inner and outer joy, our health and well-being or lack of it, and the speed of our spiritual progress. But the word 'factory' to me suggests an ancient, grim place of manufacture of a product of some kind. The chakras don't manufacture joy. Joy, or bliss is perhaps a better word, is already present within them, waiting to be uncovered, released, and expressed; isn't it so?"

"Well, yes, I suppose you are right, but they still feel like little joy factories to me! The more I tune in to their presence in meditation and in daily life and allow them to work for and with me, helping me to channel all my energy into an inward and upward flow, the more they churn out the true happiness, joy, and unending bliss that I now feel in every aspect of my life."

"Yes, perhaps I do see what you mean." Issoweet agreed.

In an abrupt change of topic, for which she was infamous, Sabella asked, "But tell me more now about exactly *how* we will travel to the valley of the golden pyramid-temples that we saw in the mind-movie. Will we teleport, time travel, astral travel, or what? And what or whose chakra will we be visiting, anyway—mine? Yours? Or just a generic chakra belonging to nobody in particular?"

Issoweet laughed again. "Simeon warned me about your rampant impatience, especially when your curiosity is fully engaged. He said that sometimes you can be a 'rapid-question machine.'"

Sabella blushed. "I apologize. It's something I've worked on for years—seemingly to little avail!"

"Don't apologize. Really, in essence, I'm the same way.'"

"You are?" Sabella's eyes got wide. "You seem so calm and unruffled all the time, just like Simeon—but then again, I have not known you for very long."

"It is an appearance which I have worked hard to cultivate. But when I was your age, often I was not fully in control of myself when faced with new situations and most especially when I felt highly motivated to learn more about a subject. So you see, I empathize with you, and I want to tell you frankly that I do enjoy your enthusiasm and your company. So many people I know are too 'buttoned down.' Your personality is very refreshing to me. I feel it is much better to be over-enthusiastic than under-enthusiastic.

"Did you know that the word "enthusiasm" comes from the root words *en* meaning 'in' and *theos* meaning 'Divine Spirit'? So when you are enthusiastic, you are in a divine energy flow."

"Thank you for your encouraging words. Perhaps I will learn someday to be more as you at least *appear* to be—calm and unruffled. Meanwhile, can you answer my questions?" Sabella's eyes sparkled with enthusiasm.

"As you wish. Today we will use the method of astral travel to reach the first golden pyramid."

Issoweet continued with her explanation: "There is no need for us to travel back in time, for the place we are going to still exists in the present time on this planet.'"

Sabella was startled to hear this news. "Are you saying that the valley of the golden pyramids—the exact place which you showed me in that mind-movie—has continued to exist on this planet in material form for many thousands of years—ever since the last Descending Treta Yuga?"

"Yes! And even longer ago than that." Issoweet beamed at her.

"Then how have they remained a secret—so well hidden and relatively unknown—for all this time?" Sabella asked.

"The Great Ones, who brought them into physical manifestation eons ago, have their ways of keeping them hidden from prying eyes, while *not* being kept hidden from the eyes of those who would benefit from experiencing them. If you like, you can ask Brother Solonar more about their history after we arrive there."

Issoweet went on: "You asked about traveling astrally? As you know, astral travel is very similar to the way you have learned to travel back in time. Basically speaking, the difference is that when you arrive at a destination (which can happen as fast as a thought), you'd not inhabit your physical body, but rather would be in your energy or astral body.

"And unlike time travel, in this case you will not inhabit a past-life body, or watch a mind-movie of past events. It is not necessary for what you need to experience at this time. However, later when you begin to go deeper into each chakra pyramid's subtle essence, you may need to be in your astral body more fully, at least for a while. This is because the chakras, as we have said before, while manifesting in all three of your bodies, physical, astral, and causal, may sometimes be perceived more clearly in their astral aspect."

"What will I look like in my astral body? A wisp of steam? A ghost of my present self?" Sabella laughed at her own joke.

"Sabella, you are joking with me again. I know you've experienced your astral body countless times, dwelling in the astral world in the periods between lifetimes. You do have memories of that, don't you, Sabella?"

"Well, now that you mention it, yes. But unless I'm time traveling, I tend to be more of a here-and-now, down-to-earth sort of person. Simeon often cautioned me about the spiritual dangers of too much astral travel while still inhabiting a physical body."

"Of course, Simeon was right." Issoweet again smiled. "But I know you know that your astral body is your energy body, a body made of light, ethereal and yet with shape and color, at least to a certain degree."

"I think this is going to be fun!" Sabella mused. "As a child, I experimented with flitting around the material cosmos in my astral body. Simeon used to say to others, 'I'm going to have to put a leash on that child!'"

Issoweet, trying not to appear shocked at this little revelation from Sabella, speculated that she might have her hands full in guiding this energetic soul. Issoweet had found that this was often true of people who possessed a great deal of creative energy.

"Sabella, you know as well as I do that astral travel should not be practiced simply 'for fun.' It is a serious matter."

Sabella sighed: "Yes, yes, I know, Issoweet. Dabbling in astral travel is similar to prematurely awakening the *siddhis* or spiritual powers, which naturally develop as one makes spiritual progress, but which also can become an ego trap. That is why Simeon had to be very strict with me and my astral travel proclivities.

"For example, I remember my first experience in astral traveling, when I was about ten years old. I noticed my mind saying, 'This is not only fun, but see how my friends can't do this. What a great and powerful being *I* am.'"

Issoweet chuckled: "What happened when you had that thought, Sabella?"

"Oh, you know the answer to that question very well, Issoweet—I can tell you do! I was abruptly thrown back into my physical body. Simeon patiently helped me to realize that my thoughts must be much purer and more ego-free, if I was to be able to continue with astral travel. Plus, I began to understand that astral travel must become something that I did only with divine guidance and for a higher reason than simply for the fun of it or to prove I was more advanced than others. I suspect that most young astral travelers have had similar experiences."

"Yes, you are right. But I'm glad to know that you understand the principle well." Issoweet was relieved.

"I do understand. Simeon will tell you that I was a rebellious and sometimes sneaky little astral traveler, but I learned fairly quickly. I am at least somewhat reformed now. I'm ready to go anytime, using any method you may choose to get us to our destination."

But Sabella couldn't help it. Privately (she hoped) she thought, "I still think astral travel is a lot of fun."

CHAPTER EIGHT

"We've arrived!" Sabella thought. "We're at the base of the first-chakra pyramid, aren't we, Issoweet? Can we go inside? I don't see a door."

A deep voice resounded within her mind, but from . . . whom? She didn't see anybody nearby. "Yes, you have arrived in the astral aspect of the Valley of the Seven Golden Pyramids, Sabella. A very joyful welcome to both of you!"

"Issoweet, did you hear that?" She looked in Issoweet's direction and gasped at what she saw. "I know it's you, Issoweet, floating there beside me. But how do I recognize that it's really you? To me you appear to be a brilliant rainbow butterfly or something like that."

Then it occurred to her to wonder what she looked like herself. "Do I look like you, now?" she reflected. "Are we dead? Are we between lives in the astral heavens? Did our physical bodies die *en route*?"

"No, dear, we are very much alive. We are in our astral bodies, and yes, you are now a very beautiful vibration of light and color. To answer your first question, what you heard was Brother Solonar's thought-welcome to us. He will guide us into the first-chakra temple and explain what happens next."

Issoweet patiently continued, "And how did you know it was I? Because my vibrations are as particular to me as yours are to you. There's no mistaking the identity of a person when he or she is in an astral body."

"Brother Solonar," Issoweet said. "I feel it would be best for us to take on our physical aspects again, at least for a little while, so that Sabella can have time to get used to all these sudden shifts in bodies, locations, and energy fields."

"I agree. We can do that immediately." With a whooshing sound, a pillar of light whirled to the ground beside them; it then took on the material form of Brother Solonar. "Will this do? I can appear in whatever body or form you prefer, you know."

"That's fine Solonar, and I see that we appear to be our usual physical bodies now. Thank you," Issoweet said quietly.

As Sabella saw that this was true, she couldn't help feeling a little disappointed. She had liked the brilliant rainbow-light butterfly effect of their astral appearances.

Solonar caught the thought and smiled: "All in good time and at the *right* time, my dear little butterfly."

They laughed together.

Brother Solonar said, "Issoweet is right. I believe that we should take everything at a somewhat slower pace, here at the beginning of your chakras pilgrimage. It takes a little getting used to—this shifting from material form to energy form and back again so quickly. Let's have some refreshments and chat for a while."

Sabella noticed a beautiful little gazebo nearby, located on a high bank of the mighty river which seemed to flow both into and beyond the massive first-chakra pyramid. Within the pavilion, there were three chairs and a simple table. On the table were fruits and drinks, all ready for them to enjoy.

"Please join me, my dear friends," Solonar said.

They went through a fragrant and colorful flower garden into the little structure, which Sabella noticed was covered with what looked like twinkling fireflies, dancing about and creating beautiful, multi-colored patterns of light. The mighty river flowed nearby, and Sabella noticed it was unusually quiet for such a vast river. She was more used to smaller rivers, like the Joyuba River near her home, which was never quiet and often made musical sounds.

"Why is the big river so quiet, Brother Solonar? And what is its name?" She just couldn't help herself. Her curiosity, as always, got the better of her.

Solonar smiled in understanding. "This is the River Sushumna; and believe me, it is not silent when you listen to it inwardly. Would you like to try it?"

"I'd love to do that. But what should I listen for? River sounds?"

"Just listen inwardly, as you do in meditation. I think you'll enjoy it." With these words, Solonar gently touched her in blessing, at the point between the eyebrows.

As the three of them sat up straight and closed their eyes for meditation, Sabella remembered that the Sanskrit word *sushumna* designates the astral spine, a central core of energy within the human body, which is often called a "river of light and energy."

Sabella quieted her restless mind with some breathing exercises, then meditated and listened internally and very intently. In minutes she began to hear the lovely sounds of AUM, rolling through her consciousness. Certainly she had heard the sounds of AUM many times in meditation. But now she realized that never before had she heard them in such a clear way. The sounds were exceedingly loud and very powerful, but not unpleasantly so. The primary sound was less like a river and more like a mighty ocean's roar, yet it was very comforting—she felt like she was coming home from a long journey.

She soon realized that the ocean sound was not just one sound, but many sounds all blending together in a great symphony of sounds, lights, and vibrations. Ah, AUM! The music of the spheres! The loveliest sound in the universe! The great ocean of cosmic bliss! The Comforter! Her whole body began to vibrate with the all-encompassing sounds of AUM, the eternal and highest of all *mantras*. She became absorbed in its vibrations.

About an hour later, she felt a gentle touch at her spiritual eye. "Sabella, please rejoin us." Issoweet's voice softly spoke in her mind.

46

"Must I?" she queried.

Solonar replied, "It is very inspiring to perceive your deep state of meditating on the AUM sounds, Sabella. But yes, we have some important instructions to give you, and we should begin the process soon. Open your eyes and join us again. I think you'll enjoy this food and drink."

Sabella slowly opened her eyes and saw Solonar and Issoweet with blissful expressions on their dear faces. She knew that they too had been immersed in the great inner ocean of AUM and that they understood completely the joy she was feeling now.

She took some long slow breaths to help her fully reenter her physical body. She was very grateful for what she had just experienced and expressed her heartfelt appreciation to Brother Solonar.

Solonar transmitted to her: "It was not *I* who gave you this experience, Sabella. Remember that what happened within you came from God alone; you were simply ready to receive it. Now, please, have something to eat—it has been especially prepared to welcome you here to this holy place and to ground you in the present time."

They drank a sparkling liquid from crystal containers; it tasted like flower-filled nectar. They ate some plump and perfectly ripe cherrilingos and usha fruit. They were delicious, and partaking of them steadied her soaring spirit. Looking out from the pavilion to the great river Sushumna, she realized that now she could easily hear echoes of the deep AUM sounds coming from the depths of the river, as well as from within her own body.

Oddly enough, she realized that she could also smell the river as well as see and hear it. It had a very sweet but spicy smell, a little bit like ginger, roses, and gardenias combined. She then realized she could also taste what she smelled, in the nectar she was drinking.

"We are drinking Sushumna river water, aren't we?" She mused. No answer was expected from her guides. She knew it was true. It was amazingly invigorating to drink the sparkling water, which represented *amrita*, the blissful nectar of God.

After a time of eating, drinking, enjoying the view, and silently communing with one another, Solonar began to project into Sabella's mind words of instruction and encouragement for the great quest which lay ahead of her.

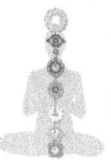

CHAPTER NINE

"Sabella, what do you understand about what you are being asked to do?" Solonar asked.

"I believe that I am being asked to enter and explore each of the seven golden chakra pyramids, from the first to the seventh, in order to understand the seven chakras within myself and within everyone. Then I will do my best to transmit what I have experienced to students in the Halls of Wisdom. Would I, at some later time, be bringing students here for their own similar pilgrimages?"

"That remains to be seen," replied Issoweet. In truth, we are not yet sure. It depends on how *you* respond to your adventures. These chakra pyramids are places of very high energy and not everyone is ready to deal with such energy at their present level of development."

"There's that word again: 'adventures.' The way you say it, Issoweet, it sounds a bit ominous. What do you mean by it?"

This time Solonar answered her with a smile: "All of life is an adventure—you know that very well, Sabella."

"Insufficient answer!" Sabella said back, with a wry smile. "I want to know exactly what I'll be facing upon entering these giant golden pyramids, such as the first one that I see close by!"

"Exactly, I can't say. For each pilgrim is different in the way he or she responds to a journey through the chakra pyramids. It depends a great deal on who you are, how strong you are in your spirit, and how your own chakra system responds. For in a very real way, this is both an inner and outer journey of discovery that you are undertaking. But please don't be overly concerned. We will offer you excellent guidance and information all along the way."

Sabella asked: "You say, '*each* pilgrim.' Have there been many people, in the past, who have done what I will be doing?"

"Not that many recently," Solonar replied. "But because we are moving closer to the highest age of Satya Yuga, pilgrimages like yours will become more and more important as ways to share the wisdom of the ages, to attain states of higher consciousness, and to participate in certain spiritual initiations."

"Initiations?" Sabella asked.

"Yes," Solonar replied. "In past higher yugas, the golden pyramids were used often as places of initiation and for teaching qualified students the highest inner science of Self-realization or union with God."

Sabella was curious about something else. "It seems to me I've heard of the existence of another such place, composed of temples located along the Nile River on the continent which I think was known as Africa. The last temple close to the mouth of the river was a large pyramid, perhaps similar to these. And if I recall my very ancient history lessons, it was called the Great Pyramid of Cheops."

"Yes, the ancient people who lived during the latter phases of the most recent Descending Treta Yuga were trying to recreate something vaguely remembered from past higher yugas. The country was called 'Egypt,' by the way," Solonar explained.

"They built temples and pyramids along the Nile River as places to train young priests and priestesses in the sacred ways of inner spiritual development. And there were seven locations also, indicating that they knew of the inner existence of the seven chakras, which are located along the *sushumna*, the astral spine/river of life."

"Amazing," thought Sabella. "Do these Egyptian temples and pyramids still exist on our planet?"

"Only in memory," Issoweet replied. "The sands of time have erased their physical existence. Of course it is possible to time-travel back to ancient Egypt, that is, if you have had a past lifetime during which you lived in that time and place.

"Where we are now is on earth, as I told you, but not near the Nile River."

"Oh yes, of course! Now I remember." Sabella was very enthusiastic. "Thomas told me about one of his past lives in which he served in ancient Egypt. That must be why all of this seems somewhat familiar to me. He said he was the head priest at one of the major temples of initiation along the sacred Nile River in late Descending Treta Yuga. I don't remember which of the seven temples he served in, but I'll ask him when I see him again. This time I'll pay closer attention to listening to all he can remember about that lifetime.

"There have been so *many* time-travel experiences, for both of us, that it is difficult to keep track of the specific details of any one particular past life. It's one of the complications of traveling through time, as you know."

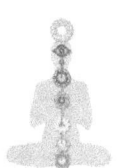

CHAPTER TEN

"Sabella," Brother Solonar said, "It will soon be time for you to enter the first-chakra pyramid, but first, there is a special person whom I'd like you to meet. Come with me now."

Sabella was surprised as he turned away from the first pyramid to face downstream. Here she noticed something she'd missed seeing before. It was a big lake, and it looked as if it was the source of the Sushumna River—yet the water was somehow *not* flowing out of the lake into the river. This seemed to defy the laws of physics as she understood them.

"What is this big lake?" she queried her hosts.

"Do you want to take a guess at its name?" Solonar teased her.

She thought for a few minutes and surprised them both by saying: "Lake Kundalini?"

"Exactly!" Solonar and Issoweet both exclaimed with admiration.

"You *really do* know your astral anatomy well!" Issoweet beamed at Sabella. "But now look more closely at the lake."

Out of its still, dark waters there slowly emerged a woman with straight black hair, which fell down her back to below her waist. She was dressed in a luminous black robe of some sort. The robe had a silver coiling design in it, spiraling around it from the hem to the neckline. It seemed to come alive when she moved even slightly; and it did that now even more so as she walked forward to meet them.

Her skin was dusky and her eyes looked like fathomless jet-black pools of dark water. Her face was still and composed, but her whole aura radiated a very strong, and yet somehow dormant power. She looked at Solonar and said in a soft, low voice: "Why have you called me, Brother Solonar? As you know, I sleep most of the time, and I don't like to be disturbed, unless it's exceedingly important that you do so."

"Please excuse me, my lady, but it *is* important for you to meet my new friend and pilgrim, Sabella Lovingheart."

The lady nodded in acceptance of his words. She took Sabella's hand in a very gracious way and said, "It is nice to meet you, Sabella. Forgive my lack of hospitality. It's been a long time since we've had a pyramid pilgrim come here, but I do wish you well in your adventures."

"That *word* again!" thought Sabella ruefully. She said, "And what is your good name, my lady?"

"I think you must know my name, Sabella, for you knew the name of my lake, didn't you?"

Sabella stepped back in awe. "The Goddess Kundalini—is that who you are? Well, that must be your name, if this lake is your home!"

"Yes, but please call me Draupadi, if you don't mind. It was a name I had in ancient India and within the fables of the great spiritual epic called the *Mahabharata*. Do you know of this epic, Sabella?"

"I do know it well, and I know your part in that wonderfully inspiring story. You were a very powerful woman, and I have always admired you greatly! And I can see that the *Mahabharata*'s claims of your being 'the most beautiful woman in the world' are justified."

"You are kind to say that. But then you must also know that I was, at that time, a princess of the house of King Drupada. When I was at the proper age to marry, I chose for my husband the greatest of all warriors, Arjuna, of the royal house of the Pandavas. Then circumstances conspired for me to become the Pandava Queen not only as Arjuna's wife, but as the wife of his four brothers, Sahadeva, Nakula, Bhima, and Yudhisthira as well!"

"Yes!" Sabella mentally projected with great wonder, "I remember the story, but I really thought it was some kind of ancient, though important, symbolic myth! Did this really happen to you back then? I can't imagine being married to five king-warriors all at the same time! I can barely manage to be successfully married to one man!"

They both laughed.

"I like you, Sabella," Draupadi said. "You speak what is on your mind, as I always did in that lifetime. But yes, it is true. Although it really did happen as it was written down and captured for the ages by the author Sage Byasa, the *Mahabharata* is also deeply symbolic. The five Pandava brothers represent the five chakras. I represent the Kundalini power, which must be united with *all* of the chakras, and not with just one of them.

"In truth, I loved Arjuna very much; after all, he was my first choice. But his mother, Queen Kunti, whom I soon grew to love and respect very much, somehow knew that it was important for this *very* unusual sort of marriage to take place. Her word was law in that family, believe me, second only to Lord Krishna, whom I worshiped and who. . . ."

"Tell me, Queen Draupadi, how you worked out such an unusual marriage to five husbands in your living arrangements—I mean, how did you . . . ?" Here she broke off in embarrassment, realizing that she was interrupting a queen, not to mention asking a very private question!

"Don't be embarrassed, Sabella. I know what you are asking. I wondered about this myself at first, of course! But we worked it out with my mother-in-law, Queen Kunti's help. I spent one year living with each husband. And believe it or not, I grew to love each one of them equally. We united ourselves deeply, on every level, even though they had personalities which were *very* different from each other, just like the chakras they represent.

"But you'll soon understand all of this much better when you see them in their respective pyramids. I had sons with each one of them also. My son with Arjuna was—well, never mind, you can review all these old stories again any time you like."

"Are you saying that I actually will meet and talk with each one of the five Pandava brothers?" Sabella thought excitedly.

"Why yes, of course! I see that Solonar has not told you yet what is going to happen as you enter each pyramid. But please do remember that I will help you always on your pilgrimage, whenever you call upon my power. I'll let Brother Solonar explain all this to you, for I am sleepy again. Do you mind if I return to my lake, dear? Have a wonderful time and say hello to each of my five husbands, who will be your hosts. Tell them that I miss them."

While still maintaining a large aura, which projected rays of vast amounts of potential power all around her, Queen Draupadi sighed drowsily and reentered Lake Kundalini, whose dark waters lovingly enclosed her. There was not even the slightest ripple to show that she had just been there.

Somewhat flustered, Sabella said out loud, "That was intense! Perhaps I need to sit down and drink some more of that Sushumna nectar."

CHAPTER ELEVEN

Back in the quiet pavilion by the river, Sabella sat thoughtfully for a few minutes. Her mind was afire with unspoken questions. She was sure that Solonar and Issoweet knew this, but they remained quiet also, letting her catch her breath and return to her inner center.

Finally, feeling steadier and refreshed by the nectar, she calmly thought to both of them, "Could you explain to me what just happened? What did all of that mean?"

"What do *you* think it meant?" Issoweet said. Sabella recognized Issoweet's closeness to Simeon's style in answering a question with another question. She knew it was to help her think it through for herself, but sometimes this tactic got a little annoying.

Issoweet went on, "What do you know about the *kundalini* energy and how it relates to the chakras?"

"Ah, the back-in-school mode again," she thought to herself (she hoped).

"Well, I know that the *kundalini* power is—wasn't Queen Draupadi amazing? So powerful and yet very subdued! I really liked her and—Oops, sorry. Getting back on track now. . . .

"*Kundalini* is a Sanskrit word literally meaning a coil or coiled-up potential energy. It is sometimes described as a coiled snake or a dragon coiled about its treasure—though really these are just symbols. *Kundalini* is a vast reservoir of *prana* or conscious, cosmic energy, which lies dormant (mostly sleeping, like the dark lady whom we just met) at the base of the astral spine or *sushumna* in the area at, or just below, the coccyx chakra, near the base of the physical spine."

She paused in her recitation and glanced over at the Sushumna River flowing nearby. She then looked in the other direction at Lake Kundalini, with its brooding, mysterious appearance.

Sabella continued: "*Kundalini*, more specifically, is the magnetic pull or tension which keeps us in a state of matter consciousness and makes possible our involvement in the material world. It is the pull away from our highest aspirations for unity or oneness with God. It is the furthermost pole of outward-moving Divine energy within our astral bodies. *Kundalini* represents the soul's being blindly pulled into inertia or unknowing; it also represents matter as balanced against spirit.

"Even though, for spiritual progress to take place, it is essential to awaken the *kundalini* energy, nevertheless *kundalini* is a very great power, which, like fire, if misused or mishandled, can be harmful. Care, knowledge, prayer, and humility are necessary to awaken the *kundalini* power within ourselves, naturally and safely. The Goddess Kundalini, as this power is sometimes called, is a force never to be feared, but whose dormant power we must always respect."

Sabella paused to catch her breath.

Issoweet and Brother Solonar both gave her a small round of applause. Issoweet conveyed to her with obvious approval: "Once again, well done, Sabella! You are a good 'explainer,' of what is often a difficult-to-understand subject. You are quite accurate in all you have said about *kundalini*, including what exactly it is and how it functions."

Sabella was grateful to feel their encouragement, but now she had a question: "I've never understood why *kundalini* is always referred to as 'she.'"

"I'll answer that one." Solonar smiled at Issoweet and Sabella and said, "It's nothing personal, of course, dear ladies; it's not gender related. It has to do with the subtle magnetism in all our bodies. The astral spine is like a great magnet, with the north (or masculine) pole in the two upper chakras and the south (or feminine) pole being located at the base of the spine. The laws of duality make it necessary for this sort of magnetism to exist, in order to keep the great 'show' of creation happening.

"A marriage or union of the south and north poles within our beings is necessary for complete soul liberation to happen, to be free of all duality and to return to our oneness with God, who is neither masculine nor feminine, and who is beyond all duality—that great oneness of all that is. As you know, this final union is the goal of all meditation and yoga practices. It is the ultimate home we are all seeking."

Sabella looked thoughtful. "I thought Queen Draupadi (aka Lady Kundalini) just told us that she 'married' or somehow became united with each of the chakras. Surely that is not the same 'marriage' of the north and south polarities we are talking about right now?"

Issoweet laughed and said, "Well, there are the 'little marriages' within each of the first six chakras, which come before the 'big marriage' of the bottom and top aspects of the spine. But I suggest we get away from the word 'marriage' and use the word 'union' instead; that makes it clearer, I think."

Solonar interjected, "Before we leave the fascinating subject of *kundalini*, which we should soon, I'd like to ask Sabella if she understands what it is that awakens the *kundalini* power within us and causes it to rise up in the spine, uniting itself with all the chakras. How does that happen and when?"

Sabella once again put on her "explaining hat" and took a big breath. "This is how I understand it. Please correct me if I am wrong. We create a strong field of magnetism in all of the chakras, but especially in the devotional aspects of the heart chakra and in the spiritual eye, which is where we focus our attention in meditation. There are several specific techniques of Kriya Yoga which help with this process.

"Gradually we learn to magnetically *draw kundalini* upward from above, rather than force it upward from below.

'*Kundalini*'s rise' should be a gradual process; it is best that it not happen suddenly or all at one time. For example, each time we have a devotional, positive, or uplifting thought, *kundalini* rises upward, like an 'advance scout' who safely clears the way, accustoming the nervous system a little at a time, for the full flood of the *kundalini* power.

"Working with *kundalini* successfully and safely means *never* to force it to rise within us, but to draw it upward lovingly, devotionally, and above all, gradually. Nevertheless, it will happen for everyone, without question, for our destiny as children of God is to reunite ourselves with God. It's not a matter of if; it's only a matter of when! The astral spine with its chakras is a part of the inner 'highway' upon which this transformational journey takes place. As Paramhansa Yogananda clearly taught, 'The astral spine constitutes *the one and only* pathway to spiritual enlightenment.'"

Brother Solonar stood: "Excellent, really! I am certain that we've covered the topic of *kundalini* sufficiently for now. It's time to quit talking and start *experiencing*. I suggest that we enter the first-chakra pyramid without further delay.

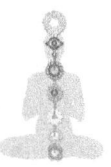

CHAPTER TWELVE

Sabella thought to herself. "It seems like *they* think I'm ready; so I guess I must be. Here we go!"

Saying a quick prayer, she stood and courageously faced the golden first-chakra pyramid towering in front of her.

Issoweet rose from her chair and embraced Sabella. "I leave you in the capable hands of Brother Solonar, and will return to teleport us both back home when you've finished here. Blessings to you, my brave child."

Solonar transmitted, "Sabella, we should take on our astral forms again, for as we've mentioned, these temples exist in a physical form, as you see before you, with your physical eyes. But they also exist more perfectly, for your learning purposes, in an astral or energy form. Is this acceptable to you? I will explain more as we go along. I think this will make things easier and better for us both."

"Brother Solonar, I trust you completely. Do as you will."

"It must be *your will* also, my dear Sabella. I will never do anything to you or even for you. I will simply show you the way, and try to explain things to you, when explanations seem to be needed."

Sabella nodded in agreement.

Solonar transformed them both into beautiful patterns of colored light. As he did so, Sabella noticed that she now had 360-degree vision; she could see in all directions simultaneously, not just in front of her, as was usual. As she looked at the first pyramid, she realized that she now could see *through* the walls into what looked like a large palace.

As quick as a thought, she and Solonar were inside the transparent walls and in the presence of another astral being; it was a man, she thought, but she wasn't quite sure.

"Welcome, Sabella," an obviously male voice boomed within her mind. "And welcome, once again, Solonar! Welcome to *Muladhara-loka*, the kingdom of the first chakra. I am King Sahadeva, but don't call me that, it's too formal. 'Sahadeva' will do nicely. I will be your host here.

"I represent the first chakra, as well as the first quality of the eightfold path of Patanjali, which is *yama*, or the power to avoid harmful attitudes."

Sabella bowed her head toward him and said politely: "It is good to meet you, Sahadeva. I was recently speaking to your wife and she told me to say hello to you, and that she misses you."

"Which wife was that?" Sahadeva chuckled. "I had more than one, you know, as did all my brothers. It was the custom back in those days."

Startled and embarrassed, Sabella answered: "Excuse me, sir. I meant Queen Draupadi. I believe you were one of her five husbands. How many wives did you have?"

"Not *that* many, but pardon *me*. I was just having a little fun with you, Sabella. I knew to whom you were referring. Queen Draupadi told me that she had met you recently."

"And *Muladhara-loka* means . . . ?" Sabella inquired.

"*Loka* means location, or the place of. *Muladhara* is the Sanskrit name of this location, that is, the first chakra. Literally it means 'root' or 'support.' It is a place of great strength and security, an excellent attitude with which to begin a pilgrimage like yours. The Earth Element has the power to keep us secure and grounded in our inner strength," Sahadeva explained.

Sabella gazed at the pattern of light which was "speaking" to her and called itself Sahadeva. It was very beautiful to behold, but she couldn't help wondering what he looked like as a human being—or *was* he a human being now? "Better not ask," she thought.

"Too late—I caught that thought." Sahadeva gave a mighty laugh and instantly took on his physical form. Following his example, Brother Solonar and Sabella did the same.

Sahadeva was about ten feet tall and, like the Lady Kundalini, he had dark, dusky skin, black eyes, and long black hair. Sabella tried very hard to shield her thoughts from him, because he was, without question, the handsomest man she had ever seen. Absolutely stunning to behold—she couldn't stop staring at him in admiration.

A great and noble warrior, Sahadeva was strong and as firm as a rock. He stood perfectly still, like the big boulders which were placed all around him.

He smiled at her and said: "Best drop the thought-shielding thing while you are on this pilgrimage, Sabella. I caught that thought too, and I thank you, even though physical appearance doesn't mean that much in the long run, as you know.

"Let me tell you a little more about myself. Nakula and I were born as twins to our mother, Queen Madri, having been magically sired by our fathers, the twin gods of healing and knowledge, the Ashwini Kumaras. We were the youngest of the Pandava brothers, half-brothers to Arjuna, Bhima, and Yudhisthira, who were the sons of Queen Kunti.

"As you'll see when you meet Nakula in the second-chakra pyramid, we really don't look or act alike, at all. Nakula is very fair-skinned and light-complexioned. We are like 'yin and yang,' or the light and the dark, so to speak—opposite but complementary. We are a very good balance for one another's particular energy patterns and qualities. Nakula and I were also known as 'physicians to the gods.'"

Brother Solonar interjected, "Sahadeva is being modest. In his time on this planet as King Sahadeva, he and his twin, King Nakula, who was just a few minutes older, were said to be the handsomest men on earth. Like his four brothers, he was formidable in war. He was an absolute observer of all the laws of morality. He was heroic and supremely intelligent—in fact, there was not another person equal to him in intelligence or in eloquence. He offered his wisdom in the assemblies of the wise ones of his time, and they frequently consulted with him when important questions arose.

"One quick story about Sahadeva: A very great devotee of Lord Krishna, he was one of the few kings of his time who realized that Krishna was actually the almighty God, now come to this world as an *avatar*. He often performed loving ceremonies for Krishna, declaring openly among contemporary kings and princes, in the face of *great* opposition, that Krishna deserved their highest respect.

"Krishna once asked Sahadeva what should be done to stop a great war that was coming. Sahadeva told him that he (Krishna) must be tied down and imprisoned. When Krishna smilingly challenged him to try to do just that, Sahadeva started meditating and envisioned Krishna as a small baby. Thus he was able to tie him down firmly. Krishna, unable to free himself from the bondage created by Sahadeva in his meditative state, blessed Sahadeva with divine vision. Sahadeva then released the very impressed Lord Krishna."

Sahadeva interrupted: "Ahem! I think that's enough of the old fables. Please let me show you more of *Muladhara-loka* now. What would you like to see first?"

Sabella was completely at a loss about how to answer. She looked at Solonar for guidance, and he rescued her by saying. "Sahadeva, first please explain to Sabella what human qualities you represent. You mentioned *yama*, the power to avoid harmful attitudes. What exactly are the *yamas*?

"Please, my friends, let us sit down first; it may take a little while to explain. I'll try to be brief, Sabella, for I know you have studied Patanjali's *Yoga Sutras* and have tried to live by the highest moral principles of *yama* and *niyama*." Saying thus, Sahadeva manifested three chair-shaped, granite boulders.

Sabella looked at these unusual "chairs" a little warily, but Solonar sent a private mental thought to her to try one out before passing judgment. She sat down and was very surprised at its feeling of comfort; it was perfectly molded to her physical shape and not cold at all, as boulders sometimes can be.

She loved the feeling of sitting on the sun-warmed boulders near the river at home, but not for too long because boulders could start feeling very hard after a while. The sandy beach was more to her liking for sitting, than were the boulders. Then she got it: the symbols for the first chakra include rocks, boulders, soil, sand, or any other part of the mineral kingdom. Her boulder-chair was just another part of her learning process.

"I'm glad you are enjoying your earth chakra chair, Sabella," Sahadeva teased her. "I thought you might like it, but you never know how pilgrims are going to respond to new experiences like these. Why don't we sit and meditate briefly before we continue."

Closing her eyes to meditate, Sabella began to feel a great sense of firmness and immovability, unlike anything she had ever felt before while meditating. It was as though she couldn't have moved even if she had tried! Oddly enough she enjoyed this feeling very much. Her granite chair seemed to give her great bodily strength and steadiness in her posture, especially in her spine.

A first-chakra affirmation came into her mind, and she repeated it mentally several times: "I am firm, steadfast, determined, and unshakably loyal to truth. I endure all things with calm faith in God."

After a few minutes, Sahadeva quietly transmitted: "Sabella, please offer all the energy of your first chakra, up your astral spine to the spiritual eye, at the point midway between your eyebrows."

Sabella did as he asked and began to behold a great light, golden-yellow in color, shaped with four angles—a beautiful diamond shape. She realized that she had glimpsed this light before in her practices of the sacred second Kriya Yoga technique. But now it was clearer and brighter than she had ever seen it.

A great motor sound, like the hum of a giant bumblebee, was heard throughout her body. This sound, too, was familiar from her practices of the Kriya Yoga technique of listening to the inner sounds of AUM. She understood it to be the inner sound of the first chakra, one of "the baby AUMS," as they were sometimes called. *Baby?* Perhaps, but now this very loud sound engulfed her being completely. Her whole body was vibrating with it. It was a beautiful and powerful sound to hear and feel.

Sahadeva said softly, "Enough meditation for now, dear ones. I want to honor Solonar's request and tell Sabella more about my *yamas*."

"Thank you for that meditation experience, Sahadeva," Sabella softly said, for she sensed that she'd been greatly helped and blessed by his presence.

He smiled but made no reply.

Sahadeva continued, "As you know, in the ancient sage Patanjali's teaching about the yoga sciences, there are five *yamas*: non-violence, non-lying, non-stealing, non-sensuality, non-greed. These are moral restraints and to work on perfecting them is a good way to remove negative human impulses from your life, to clear away the 'energy-drains' and also to cleanse your first chakra, so that it is able to function better in the purity and joy for which it was created."

Sabella said: "I've always thought that the *yamas* involve many 'non's' and 'don't's' to work on in our lives. Don't do this; don't do that . . . huff-puff, huff-puff!"

Sahadeva chuckled. "Yes, it could seem that way at first glance, but to perfect a *yama* is, in a way, to perfect them all. It lightens the burden of being alive when we become free of negativity, bad attitudes, and heavy attachments to harmful behavior patterns, as you know. As Paramhansa Yogananda once said: 'You have to live anyway, so why not live rightly?'"

Sabella glanced quizzically at Sahadeva and thought to him: "I've always wondered why they are called 'non-somethings,' such as 'non-lying.' Why not simply call it 'truthfulness'?"

"There is a subtle but very good reason for these names, Sabella. The *yamas* are often called the 'don'ts' of the spiritual path. By *removing* harmful attitudes from our lives we acknowledge that the 'holes in the milk pails of our beings' must be 'plugged up' before the pail can hold the 'milk' of divine bliss—otherwise it leaks out almost as quickly as it is being poured in.

"It may seem strange at first to hear these principles stated negatively; but in that way, the *yamas* can be revealed clearly as great virtues which begin to shine forth from within ourselves once the opposite, negative quality which is hiding them is removed. Each principle of *yama* serves the purpose, similarly, of permitting an innate virtue, such as truthfulness, which *already* exists within us, to blossom forth, when the harmful quality that is keeping it from flowering is removed.

"For example, when we strive to remove from our lives the tendency to lie to others or even to ourselves, then the great virtue of truthfulness, which is a powerful soul quality, can emerge in fullness and beauty. Figuratively speaking, every *yama* removes the 'dirt' of negative attitudes which is covering the true gold of our essential nature. What is left, once a negative tendency has been removed, is revealed as a part of the soul's true nature."

Solonar looked pleased and said, "Beautifully stated, Sahadeva. Sabella, is this explanation clear to you?"

"The clearest I've ever heard!"

"Do you mind if I offer you another small reminder, before we leave the subject of the *yamas*?" Sahadeva asked. "When a *yama* is perfected, a power is attained by the truth-seeker. Do you remember what these powers are, Sabella?"

"Yes, I do remember them well, for this aspect of Patanjali's *Yoga Sutras* has always fascinated me! They are:

Non-violence or *Ahimsa*'s perfection brings the power of causing all wild animals, all people, and even criminals to become tame or harmless in one's presence.

Non-lying or *Satya* brings a power that causes whatever

66

one says to come to pass—it must happen! And even one's thoughts become binding on the universe.

The resulting power of non-stealing, *Ashteya*, is that wealth comes whenever one needs it; all one's needs are automatically taken care of.

Non-sensuality, *Brahmacharya*, means not dissipating one's energy through the senses, allowing the freed-up energy to give one the greatest possible physical vigor and mental clarity.

Non-greed, sometimes more correctly called non-attachment or *Aparigraha*, grants one the perfected ability to remember, learn from, and let go of all of one's past-life experiences.

Sahadeva said, "Sabella, I am pleased to see that you understand Patanjali very well, and also I can feel that you have moved far along the pathway to the perfection of many of these qualities."

CHAPTER THIRTEEN

Solonar said, "This information has all been very helpful to review. I'm sure Sabella will agree, but aren't there some other qualities of human behavior that you and the first chakra represent?"

"Yes, Solonar, but in this case, it would be much better for Sabella actually to experience these qualities, than merely to talk about them. Please follow me now."

Once again they assumed their astral forms, and Sahadeva instantly transported them into a different area of the first-chakra pyramid. He said, "Look around you now at the many symbols for the first chakra."

Sabella used her all-around vision to see, and what a surprise it was! They were looking upon a natural setting, filled with rocks, stones, giant boulders, pebbles, sand, crystal, and shining gemstones of all colors—it was an incredibly beautiful place. There were even some small, rocky hills and larger mountains around the edges. She smelled the fragrance of the earth, soil, clay, and minerals of many types. Lovely flowers, grasses, and trees grew here too.

"Ah yes," she mused. "The Earth Element theme is appearing again. It is not only beautiful, but it also feels solid and very comforting to me."

"Yes," Sahadeva said, catching her thought. "But always remember that the wise person builds his house upon the 'rock' of faith in God alone, and the foolish person builds his house on the 'shifting sands' of the material world. In this chakra, we ask an important question: 'What is it that makes me absolutely secure and safe from all harm? What or who do I trust the most?'

"If your answer is money, family, friends, your body, this material thing or that, or even the earth upon which you stand, then you have 'built your house' in the wrong place and it is sure to be destroyed sooner or later by life's continuous and ever-changing storms. But if you have built your 'house' on, or put your faith in, the 'eternal rock' of God-realization, you find that absolute, unshakable, unchangeable security is yours forever.

"We are seeing some of the many symbols for the first chakra, which people have around themselves almost every day of their lives—sadly, they often go unnoticed. But I don't want to linger here. Come with me a little farther along this way."

They soon entered a corridor of giant, standing granite pillars, which had been positioned in a row extending out far into the distance. Half of the pillars were on the left side of the corridor and half were on the right. It reminded her of pictures she had seen of a very ancient place on the earth called Stonehenge.

As they grew closer and began to walk down the long stone corridor, she noticed that each pillar had a kind of "scene" or "five-dimensional movie" projecting out of the top of it; each scene was different, alive, and very clear. As she looked closer, there could be no question about what she was seeing. These were scenes *from her own present and past lives*, right up there in full color for anyone to see!

On the left of the giant corridor, she could see herself doing or saying things which were embarrassingly negative. Each individual scene had to do with one or more of her negative attitudes. As a matter of fact, she now noticed that the name of the harmful quality was written in big, capital letters on each pillar, in titles such as: STUBBORN (she *knew* that attitude was a huge challenge for her), FEARFUL (another very disturbing quality), CAUGHT IN OLD WAYS OF THINKING, OBSTINATE, STUCK IN A RUT, JUDGMENTAL, UNYIELDING, and UNWILLING TO CHANGE WHEN CHANGE IS NEEDED.

Sabella cringed as she watched the scenes. She saw the disastrous results of taking a quality to its harshest manifestation, in one past lifetime or another.

"Don't be dismayed by your negative past actions or attitudes, Sabella," Solonar sternly reminded her. "Remember the powerful words of that great *avatar*, Swami Sri Yukteswar: 'Forget the past! The vanished lives of all men are dark with many shames, but everything in future will improve if you are making a spiritual effort now!' This you *have* done, Sabella, and are continuing to do, even now."

Almost as if she hadn't heard him, Sabella thought: "But what exactly can I *do* about all the harmful things I've done to others and to myself? I've hurt others, as I can clearly see that now. The memories, the karma—much of it is still inside me. How do I rid myself of all this negativity? It's got to be clogging up my first chakra! How can I move along my spiritual path while dragging weights such as these along with me?"

Sahadeva replied firmly, "Sabella, it is time for you to take action and find your own answer to the important question you have just asked. Solonar and I will leave you for a while, and you must remain in this place *alone*. Bless you, my dear child. We have great confidence in you. Here and now is where your inner adventure really begins, courageous pilgrim!'

Sabella was instantly all alone, confused, and wondering what she was supposed to do *now*.

"Observe and figure it out," she thought to herself. "I guess I can start out by moving closer to the giant pillars. I think I'll sit down here and enjoy the column of pillars on the right, which seem to be projecting my good first-chakra qualities. Let's see, their names are LOYALTY, COURAGE, STEADFAST DETERMINATION, GROUNDEDNESS, PERSEVERENCE, STRENGTH, TRUST, ENDURANCE, and FAITH IN GOD. Yes, I know that these good qualities are within me also, but. . . ." She paused to think it through.

". . . I suspect that it is more important for me to deal with the harmful ones first, the ones being displayed here on my left. I know that I should get rid of them or destroy them somehow. But how can I do that? I have no weapons or tools, and these columns are massive and obviously very strong!"

Nevertheless, she decided to assume her regular physical body and walk over to a pillar, the one entitled FEAR. Carefully not looking at the scene it was projecting—an embarrassing episode in a past life in which she had been completely consumed by her fears and was psychologically crushed as a result—she slowly leaned forward to touch it. Instantly she was 'absorbed' into it. Almost as quickly, she felt herself become petrified; she was completely frozen and paralyzed by nameless fears.

If she had been able to move, she'd have run away immediately, but that was not an option. And besides, where could she go? She realized that she was seeing realities within her own self, so where *was* there to go?

"No matter where you go, there you are." She thought ruefully. At this point, if she had not been completely paralyzed, she'd have cried bitterly.

"Cry?" she thought. "I obviously can't do that, so I must think, instead! I was just talking to King Sahadeva, one of the wisest souls who ever lived. What would he have done? Not wept in frustration, surely. He would have taken appropriate action immediately. But how can I take action when I can't even move?"

"But you *can* move," a soft voice said to her. "Even now you are 'moving' your thoughts about quite rapidly."

Sabella tried to "see" who was talking to her, but she was surrounded by darkness. "Who's there?" she said. "Solonar? Sahadeva? Have you come back to rescue me, I hope?"

No answer.

Then again softly the voice came, "You've forgotten me already?"

"Lady Kundalini, I mean, Queen Draupadi, my lady, where are you?"

71

"I'm within you, as always."

"Wonderful! Then tell me how to free myself from the paralysis of fear. I can't move at all, and I am terrified. What should I do?"

"Ah, yes, one of the greatest 'attitude traps' of the first chakra: being unwilling to move, grow, learn, change, thus succumbing to the fear of failure. Well, as I said, your mental powers still seem to be undiminished. Use them!"

"Think my way out of this mess?" Sabella was incredulous.

"Perhaps cogitation will help, but meditation, prayer, and calling on those who can help you, might be better for you just now." Draupadi's soft, dark voice came again.

"How can I meditate? I can't even breathe!" Then Sabella realized how utterly ridiculous that sounded. One of the goals of deep meditation is to attain breathlessness. She'd certainly met at least a part of that goal now; this thought almost made her laugh until she realized that she couldn't even smile, much less laugh.

"In times past, when I reached a breathless state in meditation, my thoughts were still also. Obviously they are not still now. I do trust you, Draupadi. Will you help me?" Sabella offered her sincere plea to her friend.

"But of course!" the dark lady answered intensely. "All you needed to do was ask me. It is for this purpose that I exist!"

Sabella didn't need to close her eyes to meditate. It was already completely dark, and she couldn't move her eyelids anyway. She didn't need to control her breath; it was already "controlled." But she knew without question that she *did* need to control her thoughts and, most of all, her fears. She quickly turned her mind to what Draupadi had suggested she do. She asked God, her guru, all the Great Ones to be with her now.

Firmly controlling her thoughts and letting go of all her fears, she let her consciousness relax into a state of acceptance and deep inner peace.

In only a moment, she found herself outside the pillar, looking back at "herself." The pillar she had touched was no longer a sheer, tall block of stone. It had formed itself into a statue of Sabella! Its eyes were wide with fear. Its arms were thrust forward as though to ward off some great danger and its mouth was open in a silent scream.

"Oh, poor thing," was her immediate thought. "I must help her, I mean me!"

Draupadi whispered to her again, "How will you do that? May I make a suggestion?"

"By all means!" Sabella was happy for all the help she could get.

Draupadi continued, "Together, you and I, with God's help, can dissolve this fear-created statue of Sabella into its smallest components. We can transform them into light and offer them first to a comparable positive first-chakra quality. Then we shall offer all your first chakra's qualities, harmful and beneficial, into the great River Sushumna, to be released, purified, and moved upward into the Divine Light within you."

"What do you mean, 'smallest components'?" Sabella asked.

"You tell me," Draupadi said.

"Ah, the *vrittis*, I remember now. One *vritti*, a tiny whirlpool of committed energy, is an increment of *karma*. *Karma* is the sum total of every action, activity, or thought that I or any human being has ever had in this or any other lifetime. There are uncountable *vrittis* in our chakras, because the chakras store our *karma*. You are saying that this statue is made up of my past 'fear *vrittis*'?" Sabella asked.

"Yes, dear one, that is right. Just as a human being's physical form is, in the material plane, made up of billions of swirling atoms, so the astral spine contains countless *vrittis*, which primarily congregate in a chakra with similar vibrations. Like attracts like.

"'Fear *vrittis*,' though they may be located to a small extent in other chakras, as you'll see later, tend to congregate in the first chakra. *Vrittis* clog things up in the chakras, especially the most harmful *vrittis* which tend to be very 'sticky' and to clump together—in this case, your fear-based *vrittis*. When that happens, the *prana* can't flow smoothly in a spiritually beneficial inward and upward direction. This condition also causes the chakras to lose energy, allowing it to leak into a downward or outward flow. This makes a person lose massive amounts of life-force to addictive behavior, harmful habits, likes, dislikes, and attachments.

"Sabella, do you know what fear really is?"

Sabella thought, "I know more about it now, after my very recent experience of being solidified into a 'fear statue' of myself. I know fear to be the greatest of all paralyzers. But simply put, I think that being fearful is being afraid that something will happen to hurt or harm me. It also involves my wanting things to be different from what they are or might become."

"Yes, you are right. Ultimately 'fear *vrittis*' are like all *vrittis*, and thus like all *karma*, which is composed of countless *vrittis*. *Vrittis* are the seeds of committed energy within you. By clumping together tightly, they deplete your energy and hold you back from your highest destiny."

"Well, let's start dissolving these *vrittis*!" Sabella said.

"Are you sure you are ready, Sabella? Do you realize exactly what you are about to dissolve?" Draupadi asked softly.

"Some part of me? Will I be destroying parts of myself?" Sabella said. "Then I must be honest. I'm not sure I want to do that!"

"'Destroy' is not the right word. The blocking, negative *vrittis* stored in your chakras are made of energy. You are going to *transform* this harmful energy and to release it into a better, more helpful pattern of energy. Energy cannot die or be destroyed. But we can change its direction of movement."

"Yes, I understand. I'm ready to try." Sabella felt very calm.

Draupadi asked Sabella again to pray and then meditate. "I will help you!" she said. "Tune in to my power, which is very close to your first chakra at the base of your spine. Feel it begin to rise in a loving, gentle way, being magnetized by your devotional heart. I know you can do this, for your full name is Sabella Lovingheart, is it not? At that point, the great power of the *kutastha*, your spiritual eye, will help draw your energy ever more inward and upward in the process of transformation.

"Sabella, feel my great *kundalini* power beginning to flow within you now."

Sabella became aware of the first-chakra AUM sounds manifesting themselves. She watched in awe as the large statue, an amazing likeness of her fearful self, quickly crumbled into tiny shards of blue crystal.

"Do the crystals represent my 'fear *vrittis*, Draupadi'?"

"Yes, dear one. What do you want to do with them?" Draupadi asked her.

"I feel I should let them go, transform them, give them to God, or something like that, and—" She caught herself as she remembered the teachings.

"Oh yes! I remember that *first* I should offer these harmful energy patterns into the more beneficial energy patterns, for energy cannot die. It can only change directions."

"A transmutation of energy—that is what is needed now!" Draupadi agreed.

Sabella glanced to her right at all the Beneficial Pillars of Light, standing in a great row. She was immediately attracted to the one labeled COURAGE. She thought, "That surely is the perfect place to offer these crystals representing my fear *vrittis*."

Draupadi gave Sabella one of her dark veils. With it, Sabella gathered up a large bundle of the tiny blue crystals and took them to the COURAGE pillar.

While doing this, Sabella began repeating an affirmation,

with all the power she could bring forth from within herself: "I offer all my fears into my vast resources of courage-energy. I am safe, I am sound. Henceforth, I live without fear!"

The bundle was drawn gently away from her and absorbed by the COURAGE pillar, which soon began to blaze with a great inner light. Sabella saw that all the harmful pillars of stone were being dissolved and absorbed into the beneficial ones. The positive pillars began flowing upward, as though they were as light as feathers, instead of behaving like the huge chunks of stone they were. Sabella could hear the great, triumphant symphony of all the AUM sounds and see the colorful lights issuing from each of the rising pillars.

Inwardly, she felt very light and free; her spirit was uplifted into a place of perfect peace and joy. She had a feeling of having accomplished something *very* important for her future well-being. But Sabella was becoming a wiser woman these days. She understood that she had not done it alone; therefore she immediately gave thanks for all the help she had received, seen and unseen.

Finally, everything around her became empty and silent, and Sabella was alone in the first-chakra pyramid.

CHAPTER FOURTEEN

"Sabella?" Solonar said quietly. "We are here. Sahadeva and I have seen all that happened to you. Your chakra quest has begun very auspiciously."

Sabella looked up at Solonar and Sahadeva and thought: "One down and six to go?" She felt exhausted.

Sahadeva laughed joyfully. "Almost, Sabella. Just a little more to do here, but I think you'll enjoy this part. We have a small ceremony prepared for you. Please join me."

He extended his energy toward her and "lifted" her into his massive arms. "I know you are somewhat energetically depleted from your recent adventure. Relax now."

Instantly, they were transported to the topmost chamber of the first-chakra pyramid. She could see the whole first-chakra pyramid spread out below her. She saw the great Sushumna River flowing inward and upward through the pyramid.

"Rivers don't flow upward," she thought tiredly.

"This one does, or should, for best results," Sahadeva said to her.

He placed her on a feathery soft divan and said, "Rest now, dear one."

"What? No more hard-rock chairs for me now?" Sabella teased. "Not that I didn't enjoy the other one."

Sabella noticed that she looked and felt different. She stood up to inspect herself, intrigued to see that she was dressed in a radiant garment of colored lights. The colors were interwoven in ever-changing patterns of blue, gold, and red. She also saw that Solonar and Sahadeva were similarly robed.

"Come to the altar, Sabella." Sahadeva made a gesture toward a large altar behind her. "Please kneel."

She did so, drawing her palms together at her heart center to honor the Divine Presence represented by the sacred altar. She wanted to close her eyes, but couldn't. At the moment, she was awed by the magnificence of all the colors, lights, and music dancing all around her. The Earth Element altar was a giant, perfectly round boulder, studded with gemstones and crystals. It sat firmly on the ground, which seemed to rumble a little ("Earthquake?" Sabella wondered). But this altar looked ancient, strong, and completely unmovable.

Sahadeva touched her at the point between her eyebrows and said: "Sabella Lovingheart, your labors today within the first-chakra pyramid will be blessed with a gift. From now on you possess the first-chakra yogic power: that is, the power to assume absolute rock-like stillness and immovability, mentally or physically, and the ability to become extremely heavy whenever you choose."

Sahadeva moved to a standing position behind her. She felt him place something around her neck. Looking down she saw it was an unusual pendant about an inch and a half in diameter; it was suspended from a small red ribbon.

Sabella was surprised to see that the pendant appeared to be made of lead. It was not at all unattractive, but it looked as though it might weigh heavily around her neck. Amazingly, however, it seemed to weigh almost nothing at all. It settled itself lightly on her chest, resting near her heart chakra. Upon it was an emblem of a red lotus blossom with four petals. Imbedded within the red lotus was a large, deep-blue sapphire with tiny reddish lights flashing out from it, set in such a way that it touched her skin. In the center of the sapphire was a much smaller four-sided figure, diamond-shaped and golden-yellow in color.

"With my greatest blessings," Sahadeva conveyed to her simply.

Sabella looked at him with tears in her eyes. "Thank you, King Sahadeva. I am honored. I don't know what else to say, except, may I ask if this means that my first chakra is open and cleared of all *karma* forever?"

Laughingly, Sahadeva said, "Would that it were so easy, Sabella, but please rejoice in the exceptional progress you've made so far. Later Issoweet will explain to you more about what has happened to you inwardly. She will also tell you about the symbols on your first-chakra pendant. I'm sure you'll soon notice several changes in yourself, for you are a very sensitive person.

"Meanwhile, it is time for me to introduce you to my twin brother, Nakula, and let him, in turn, guide you into his second-chakra pyramid."

Sabella looked at Sahadeva and Solonar in alarm. "Wait, wait! I need a pause in this pilgrimage. Sahadeva, I mean no disrespect to you or your brother. But I think it would be best for me to return to my home now and be with my husband. I need some time to process all that has happened to me here. I have many questions, as you can imagine, and I know that I need to be in a familiar place in which to rest and more fully integrate everything that has happened to me here. King Sahadeva, Brother Solonar, please, would this be acceptable to both of you?"

"Ah, these mortals," Sahadeva sighed in resignation. "I keep forgetting that they tire easily—but don't take that personally, Sabella. I know you are doing your best. I'm not going anywhere; I'll be here whenever you are ready to return and have me introduce you to my twin brother."

"I *am* immortal," thought Sabella indignantly. "But," she conceded, "I also know I have not yet fully *realized* my immortality."

"Your request is acceptable, Sabella." Solonar said. "Let it be so."

"King Sahadeva, guardian of the first-chakra pyramid," Sabella said as she knelt to touch his feet. "Thank you for everything you have showed, offered, and taught me here! I'll see you again very soon. I am very happy to have met you and to know that, in a very real sense, you always live within me—in my first chakra."

"Yes, that is true. I am with you always. I will see you again very soon, dearest Sabella. And from me personally, here is a tiny parting gift." He slipped a small folded piece of red velvet cloth into her hand.

"May God's perfect peace dwell within you always!"

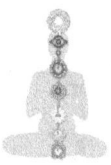

CHAPTER FIFTEEN

Sabella was instantly transported to the pavilion by the Sushumna River. She found Issoweet waiting for her there, smiling kindly at her. "Well done, my child, very well done! I know you are ready for a rest. I am here to take you to your home and husband. Are you ready to go?"

Tired as she was and very ready to be at home with Thomas, Sabella sent a thought to Issoweet, "Before we leave, I'd like to have a brief moment alone to look at this little gift Sahadeva just gave me."

She excused herself to open her gift in private. Somehow she felt it was a very personal gift and should be seen by her eyes alone. As she unfolded the red velvet cloth, she beheld a beautiful gemstone. It was a smooth, round, deep-blue star sapphire, with a mysterious white star suspended within its depths.

She'd seen pictures of this kind of very rare gemstone, but certainly had never held one in her hand before. It glowed with inner light, and Sabella knew that it was a real treasure from her friend and guide Sahadeva, to be cherished forever. With all her heart, she inwardly thanked him.

"Now," Sabella said as she returned to Issoweet's side, "I want to speak to Queen Draupadi. Is this possible?"

"Let's walk over to Lake Kundalini and see if we can summon her," Issoweet replied.

They arrived at the dark, still lake, and even before Sabella could call her name, the night-clad lady rose up from the waters and walked toward her.

She kissed Sabella on the cheek and said to her in her low, mellow voice, "I know why you are here, child. You want to thank me for my help. It is completely unnecessary. As I told you, this is what I do. I am always ready and happy to assist you on your quest through the chakra pyramids. Now I return to my sleep. Farewell until we meet again."

And she was gone.

Sabella turned to Issoweet with a question. "Issoweet, why does she seem to need to sleep most of the time?"

"Sabella, remember she is a *symbol* of the *kundalini* power which lies 'sleeping' within us at the base of our astral spines. Our spiritual pursuits awaken her a little at a time, until she is able to move upward, unobstructed, and in possession of her full power, along the purified *sushumna*. It is very important to remember that she should never be forced to do this. Kundalini should be *invited* gently to rise through the power of love and devotion. When her power grows stronger and stronger within you, she is drawn upward in a natural and loving way, helping to assist you all along your way until you attain final union with God. In your recent time of need, was she not drawn to be present with you in a very timely fashion?"

"If you say so, but truthfully, at that moment, I wasn't thinking of her, or of calling to her specifically in a loving, or in any other way that I knew of consciously. I was gripped with fear," Sabella sadly related.

"That is how we all learn, Sabella—through experience! Nevertheless, she felt your loving heart and came to you just when you most needed her help."

"She certainly did, and I am very grateful. Issoweet, I'm ready to go home now."

Thomas awaited her return on their outdoor patio overlooking the river. Beside him sat Simeon, smiling his welcome. Issoweet was there also.

Sabella was astonished to notice that Issoweet and Simeon were dressed in robes identical to the red, blue, and golden-yellow one she had received at the time of her first-chakra initiation. Around their necks were identical platinum necklaces with nine colorful pendants hanging vertically, in order and one beneath the other, down the center of their bodies.

Sabella was amazed again at how much Simeon and Issoweet looked like each other, especially now that they were identically dressed and adorned. She admired their long silver hair, silver eyes, and noble faces—twins, indeed!

Sabella's mouth fell open in wonder. She stifled any exclamation, but privately thought, "More and more twins in my life these days; I wonder what that means?"

Thomas interrupted her thoughts, saying, "Welcome home, my love! Nice outfit! Do you want to celebrate or take a nap? I've made us all some tea—your favorite."

Sabella embraced Simeon and Issoweet, kissed Thomas fondly, and finally collapsed on a nearby lounge chair. "Please sit down and join me for tea. I need just a moment to orient myself to where I am. But I am so glad to see you all here together at my home. Simeon, especially you! I so rarely see you these days. I miss you very much and. . . ."

"Yes, Sabella, I miss you, too. And I know you have a thousand questions about your experiences in the first-chakra pyramid." Simeon, as usual, seemed all-knowing; he never minced his words. "I am here to greet you only briefly, as I am needed elsewhere, but I wanted to reassure you of my love for you and to congratulate you for what you are doing with this new project. Issoweet can answer all your questions as needed."

With these words, her beloved teacher faded away into the ether.

Sabella sighed and looked at Issoweet. "Forgive me. I know you can help me as much as Simeon. I just miss him these days. He was my teacher and spiritual father for such a long time."

"Don't worry about it, dear. I completely understand. But

I want to say that your questions can be answered more effectively *after* you have rested for a while. Therefore, I, too, will leave you alone with Thomas. If it's convenient for you, I'll see you in the High Council Chapel tomorrow at noon. If you need to rest longer, just send me a mental message, and we'll arrange something else."

Issoweet also disappeared from the patio.

"Drink your tea and tell me what you'd like to do now, Sabella." Thomas was the embodiment of tenderness and understanding.

What *could* she have done in the past to deserve to be life-linked in this lifetime with such a great soul as Thomas? Instantly she remembered a few past lives in which she had saved his life, in several different ways, and how she had been his wife or husband or mother or father or friend or. . . . But all this was much too complicated to think about right now.

Instead, she looked lovingly into his eyes and thought to him, "It's wonderful to be at home with you now, Thomas. I think I'd like to take a nap."

Several hours later, Sabella awoke in her own bed, which seemed unusually soft and comfortable. She smelled something delicious and realized she was ravenously hungry. When was the last time she'd eaten anything? A very long time ago, it seemed: sitting with Issoweet and Brother Solonar in that pavilion by the Sushumna River, before all her adventures began.

Thomas must be preparing dinner for her. What a treat! He was gourmet cook, but rarely had time to create wonderful meals in the way he thought they should be prepared. She felt relaxed and refreshed by her nap. "How long was I asleep?" she wondered, as she bounced from the bed and into their kitchen.

"What's that I smell?" she queried Thomas, almost drooling.

"Specialty of the house, dearest. Your favorite dinner and dessert!"

The meal was truly delicious, and because it had been prepared with love and blessings, it was even more satisfying. After they had eaten together quietly, they returned to the patio to enjoy the evening breezes. Sitting in a double swing and holding hands, they were silent for a while. Thomas knew not to prod Sabella; she would communicate with him when she was ready.

Sabella began with a question that surprised him. "Thomas, as Brother Solonar was preparing me for the beginning of my chakra pilgrimage, I remembered that there was another place and time to which you had traveled, during your early time-travel experiments. You called it Egypt and mentioned that it was along the Nile River in Northern Africa. I believe you told me that you served there as a high priest in one of the seven temples of initiation. Am I remembering this right?"

"Your memory is accurate; I did describe to you my time-travel experience for that lifetime."

"I don't remember the details. Could you tell me more about what you did there, and what it was like?"

"Of course, and I can see why you are asking. The seven chakra pyramids were 'copied' by certain people who lived in those ancient times. Living as they were in a descending yuga, they felt strongly that they should create temple complexes and pyramids—places designed to teach young people about the inner spiritual path and to serve as sacred pilgrimage/initiation locations. It was hoped that in this way they could help preserve some important inner teachings. A great deal of this knowledge was being lost at that time; they hoped somehow to hold on to portions of the knowledge for as long as possible.

"In that lifetime, I served in the fifth temple complex—a lovely garden-like place, located on the banks of the Nile River; it represented the fifth chakra. As a high priest, I was responsible for instructing the young aspirants who had made it that far, to prepare them for the fifth level of initiation. After receiving that initiation, they could travel up the Nile River to the all-important sixth and seventh temples, the seventh being in the Great Pyramid."

"Was it a good lifetime for you, Thomas? What did you learn from it?"

"Yes, it was a blessed lifetime, even though I always felt somewhat frustrated to feel important spiritual knowledge slipping away from the earth at that time. It was a good way to learn non-attachment. As high priest, I had completed six out of the seven temple initiations and was almost ready for the final initiation in the Great Pyramid. I enjoyed training the young initiates in what was called a 'mystery school'—here they learned spiritual truths in preparation for becoming priests and priestesses themselves."

"But I thought the ancient Egyptian pyramids were merely tombs for the great rulers of those times: Phadrons, I believe they were called?"

"Pharaohs," Thomas corrected her with a smile. "But no, the Great Pyramid was not built to be a tomb, though many of the pyramids were later used for that purpose. They were great storehouses of spiritual energy."

"What was it like when you finally visited the Great Pyramid?" Sabella, curious as always, asked her husband.

"I didn't tell you that part, did I?" Thomas thought to her.

"No, you did not! Why not?" she asked

"It was too sacred an experience for me to talk about then or even now after all these centuries. And I was told never to reveal any part of it to anyone, ever! I'm sure you understand." Thomas was grave, as Sabella looked at him with disappointment.

"But I'll give you a hint. Centuries later, a great spiritual teacher visited the King's Chamber, the holiest and most powerful location in the Great Pyramid. About it he said: 'It was a profound place to meditate. I was able to bring all my inner energies to a focus in the sixth and seventh chakras, just as the shape of a pyramid brings all energy to a sharp focal point at its peak. I intuitively knew that the pyramid shape could not be used very effectively in our present age.' He was speaking in early Ascending Dwapara Yuga.

"'The dome-shape,' he continued, 'is a more useful shape for Dwapara Yuga.'

"He also explained how the power of the pyramid shape was understood well and used effectively during Treta Yuga."

"Where we are in this lifetime!" Sabella said. "But back in Dwapara Yuga, didn't they try to learn more about the purposes for which the Great Pyramid was built and used—that it was much more than just a tomb?"

"They could only speculate, Sabella. It was a place of great mystery during the lower yugas. No one back then could figure out even how they were built!

"But here's a little more information for you, my curious wife. Many other spiritually minded people who visited the Great Pyramid in Dwapara Yuga reported that it greatly affected their consciousness while they were inside it. One well-known truth-seeker arranged to spend a night in the King's Chamber, during which he had a profound and life-changing experience, wherein great spiritual truths were revealed to him.

"One woman author claimed to have memories of being a spiritual initiate in ancient Egypt. She maintained that the Great Pyramid was used to help spiritual aspirants make a 'breakthrough' into higher levels of consciousness—especially those who were very close to achieving those levels, but were still not able to do it on their own. She also said that the initiates prepared carefully for this experience. Even to enter the sacred pyramid, they needed to have refined their physical bodies, especially their central nervous systems, in order to be able to absorb safely the much higher frequencies of subtle energy which were present in the Great Pyramid.

"Initiates also needed to have prepared their minds, through various mental disciplines of concentration and meditation, so that they would not be overwhelmed by the pyramid's powerful vibrations. She described the entire Giza Plateau, where the Great Pyramid was located, as a home both for those in training to receive initiation and for those who had received it in the past. At that time, these priests and initiates were understood to be among Egypt's most precious possessions.

"I remember the woman author from that time. She was a very interesting person," Thomas mused quietly. "But please, Sabella, don't ask me any more about that particular lifetime. I've told you all that I feel comfortable revealing."

Seeing a familiar look on his serious face, she knew it was best not to question him further. Changing the subject she asked: "Thomas, why were Simeon and Issoweet wearing exactly the same type of colorful robes that I just received at my first-chakra initiation?"

Sabella was now dressed in her favorite old blue t-shirt, which said "Plain Living and High Thinking" on the back of it in faded gold letters, and an equally old, but very comfortable, pair of blue yoga pants.

"You'd better ask Issoweet that question tomorrow, Sabella. But as a guess, I'd say that they both received their robes in the first-chakra pyramid, in the same way you received yours. They probably were wearing them as a way of offering you loving support for your present quest and to show that, in the past, they too, had completed their own pilgrimages though the chakra pyramids.

"I noticed that their necklaces are somewhat different from yours. May I look at your new pendant more closely?"

She removed it from around her neck and placed it carefully in his hands. "It is unusual and very beautiful," he said. "I assume it represents your accomplishments in the first-chakra pyramid?"

"Brilliant assumption, my dear detective husband," she teased. "But shall I tell you more about how I got the pendant, the robe, and all that led up to my initiation?"

Sabella was off and running, projecting to Thomas mental pictures of all of her adventures, as clearly and as quickly as she could.

"Whew," said Thomas, "Stop a minute. I want to ask you a little more about King Sahadeva, whom you called 'the handsomest man in the world' and about how he carried you in his giant warrior arms to a divan and . . . ." He laughed at the look on her face.

"Don't be silly, Thomas. "He was just being kind to me. I'd been through a great test, as you have heard."

"Sorry, dear, I just couldn't resist teasing you a little. After all, it wasn't too long ago that you were quizzing me about Sunitia, who, according to you, was described as the most beautiful woman of her time."

Sabella interrupted him. "Thomas, I have seen someone even more beautiful than Sunitia. I first saw her emerging from the dark waters of Lake Kundalini. It was Queen Draupadi, who, as I have told you, helped me when I was in great need."

"More beautiful than Sunitia? I don't know if that's possible!" Thomas said with a straight face. "Show me your mind-picture of Queen Draupadi again. And when can I meet her?"

Sabella laughed, "OK, OK, Thomas. I know how I can get distracted by physical appearances."

Thomas became serious as he changed the subject. "Sabella, is this pilgrimage going to be dangerous for you at times? I can't help worrying about you. As you know, I met Brother Solonar in a past lifetime, but only briefly. I don't know him well. He seemed like a competent pyramid guide at that time, but will he intervene to help you, if you need assistance?"

"Perhaps that is not his assignment, Thomas. I felt that he was there only to guide me into the various pyramids, and that there would be other entities upon whom I could call for help as needed. I will admit to you that suddenly becoming an inert statue made of my own fear-*vrittis* was not pleasant. For a time I was very frightened. But I always felt that things would turn out well for me; and as you can see, they did.

"It has been explained to me that my pilgrimage is to be a powerful learning experience and a great adventure. And yes, it will include various tests of my abilities to overcome inner obstacles. Still, I don't sense there is any grave danger, though I am very pleased that you are concerned for my welfare." She gave him a big hug.

Thomas sighed in relief. "I hear the truth in what you are saying, and I trust that you will be safe. Congratulations on all you accomplished in your first foray into the valley of the pyramids. I think we've talked enough for tonight. Though you napped for a long time today, I didn't, and I'd like to go to bed now. It's late."

"I want to meditate down by the river, but I will join you later."

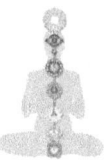

CHAPTER SIXTEEN

The next morning Sabella felt rested and ready to visit Issoweet, for what she knew would be a time for her debriefing and a chance for her to ask questions. She sent Issoweet the mental message that she was on her way.

Wearing her new colorful robe and pendant, Sabella entered the small pyramid chapel—the place from which she first had been teleported to the valley of the pyramids. She was surprised to see that Issoweet was not alone. Joining them were the two children who were members of the High Council, Nila-Nightingale and her younger brother—what did he say his name was? She searched her memory.

The little boy appeared to be about nine years of age; he smiled at her and mentally said, "Greetings, Sabella Lovingheart. It is nice to see you again. I am Notea-Nightingale, and we are here to enjoy some chakras chanting with you."

Nila-Nightingale was sitting in front of an ancient musical instrument which Sabella, being an extremely experienced musician, knew had been called a harmonium. She had never played one herself and was intrigued to see one in use here. Notea-Nightingale had a lupoodjra drum in his lap, and Issoweet had a small pair of silver cymbals on her fingers.

Issoweet motioned for Sabella to join them in sitting on the soft carpet and said, "We thought you'd enjoy a musical chakras tune-up this morning, beginning with a first-chakra chant. I asked the children to join me because I remembered that this chant was originally composed *for* children, but more truthfully because, young as they are, they are excellent musicians. Your fame as a musician is well known to them, so they are very grateful to be here to play and sing with you. After we finish the chant, we'll practice AUM-ing the chakras exercise, with which I'm sure you are familiar, and then we'll meditate together for a while.

"The chant, though very old and one you may not have heard sung before, is in perfect attunement with the earth chakra, which you were exploring recently. Here are the simple words—I know you'll catch on quickly:

> *Nothing on earth can hold me;*
> *Rise, O my soul, in freedom:*
> *Nothing to fear anymore.* ©

With a quick mental signal from Issoweet, the children closed their eyes and began playing, swaying and singing with great gusto. Issoweet joined in, keeping the rhythm with the tiny cymbals on her fingers. Notea-Nightingale was very proficient on the drums, especially for one so young, keeping a perfect, though not overly loud beat going. But it was Nila-Nightingale's playing and singing which most profoundly moved Sabella. Nila was well named, for her high, sweet voice was like the lilting song of a nightingale; it soared up to the top of the little chapel and returned to envelop them all with love.

Sabella quickly learned the words and melody, closed her eyes, and, in great joy, joined in chanting with the small group. They sang loudly at first, then more softly, then whispering, then silently, and mentally only. Entering the superconscious state of chanting, Sabella realized that she had stopped chanting the chant and the chant was chant-ing her. Going even further into it, the words manifested as truth; she felt her soul rise in inner freedom.

The chanting session lasted for a little more than an hour. Sabella concentrated on her first chakra's feeling of purity and openness and her newly found inner reservoirs of strength, courage, and freedom from all fear. Yes, devotional chanting was always very inspiring to do, and without question this was the perfect chant for her today.

They sat quietly after the instrumental music and all outer and inner chanting had ceased, absorbed in inner bliss.

Next, Nila-Nightingale began to lead them in the familiar practice of chanting of AUM at each chakra, using these musical notes:

First chakra –   the G note, below middle C
Second chakra –   A
Third chakra –   B-flat
Fourth chakra –   D
Fifth chakra –   E-flat
Medulla, receptive aspect of the sixth chakra – F
Spiritual eye aspect of the sixth chakra – G, above middle C

Up and down the chakras they sang the AUM-notes at length, letting the M-mmmmm sound linger at the end of each AUM. Finally they stopped with a final long AUM-m-m-m-m-m-m at the spiritual eye. After a moment, Nila-Nightingale began to play a G-minor chord (G-B-flat-D-G), and they began to chant "Waves of AUM," with each one chanting different musical notes, moving them around, sometimes lingering longer on one chakra or another.

"Waves" of beautiful AUM-chords began to circulate around the chapel. Sabella was astonished to see how closely this sound resembled what she had heard in the last moments of her first pyramid experience. It was uplifting and awakening on every level!

Hearing a new sound now, she watched as little Notea-Nightingale beginning to play a large gong, set to the side of the chapel, which she had not noticed when she entered. And how he played that gong: softly, then louder and louder, but always very sensitively—it was amazing for such a small child to be able to do this, for the gong stood taller than he did!

Closing her eyes again, she began to feel her heart chakra and her spiritual eye opening. She felt her whole being become part of the great internal ocean-roar of AUM. The waves of AUM chords and the gong's vibrations slowly died away. There was nothing to do but meditate; Sabella couldn't have done anything else, even if she had tried. It was blissful!

An hour later, Nila-Nightingale played the threefold AUM very softly on her harmonium, to lead them out of their time of meditation.

As she opened her eyes, Sabella saw the children gazing at her with admiration and love. Nila-Nightingale summoned up her courage and said, "Notea and I are honored to have been invited by Issoweet to chant with you today, Sabella. We know of your musical accomplishments and have attended a few of your concerts. We also wish you all the best for the remainder of your chakras pilgrimage. We hope to learn more from you in the Halls of Wisdom someday, when your pilgrimage is finished and you are able to share with us as your students your newfound knowledge of and experience with the chakra mysteries."

"The honor is mine, dear little ones. Nila, you sing like the nightingale whose name you carry. The words of a great saint describe you well: 'The Cosmic Nightingale emerges from the darkness of the unknown, perches on the branches of our inner perceptions, and sings for our enjoyment songs of eternal wisdom.'

"And Notea, your drumming and gong-playing were superb—especially the drumming, which was exceptionally well done. Drums are often played too loudly when accompanying chanting; their sound can overwhelm the melody instead of supporting it.

"Perhaps you know what a great yoga master once said about drumming in relation to chanting. One of his disciples was not used to hearing a drum accompaniment to religious music and didn't particularly like it. The Master chided him, saying: 'You *must* get into it! Rhythmic drumming loosens the karma in the spine and helps us to release it more quickly.'"

"I also sincerely thank you, Issoweet, for asking the children to join us here today." Sabella was glowing.

Issoweet graciously accepted her thanks. She turned to the children, and mentally addressed them. "Perfect in every way, Nila and Notea. I know you have other duties to attend to now, so we'll say farewell."

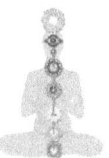

CHAPTER SEVENTEEN

With the children gone, Issoweet asked Sabella if she was ready to begin the debriefing session. "Would you like any refreshments or a brief rest before we begin?"

"Thanks, but no, I feel invigorated from the chanting and meditation. I'd like to get started."

Issoweet began, "Please show me, in mind-pictures, *all* that you experienced and felt during your time in the first-chakra pyramid?"

Sabella did so skillfully and succinctly.

Issoweet was pleased and said, "Wonderful! Your inner strength prevailed, even as you were passing through the darkness of your own fears. Now let's address your questions."

"Issoweet, I see you are wearing your red, blue, and golden-yellow robe, which looks exactly like mine. Where did you get it? And the necklaces with the many chakras pendants on it—I noticed you and Simeon wearing them yesterday. How many pendants are there and what do they symbolize? I'd love to look at your necklace more closely and ask some questions about it. Is that possible?"

Issoweet shook her head. "Sorry to decline, Sabella. You must earn each pendant by successfully completing your journey through each pyramid in succession. Each new pendant will be added to your necklace when you receive that chakra's initiation ceremony. But for now, please take off the pendant you are wearing, and I will explain its symbolism to you."

Sabella lifted it from around her neck and gave it to Issoweet.

Issoweet continued. "As you see, the pendant reflects the colors of the robe you received. And yes, Simeon and I received the robes we wore yesterday in exactly the same way as you. Our pilgrimages happened many years ago. We wore them to show you that we understand, from firsthand experience, the nature of your upcoming adventures, and to reassure you that you have our complete support in the trials of your future journeys.

"Did you notice that the blue, red, and yellow-gold colors matched the color scheme of the altar where you had your initiation ceremony with King Sahadeva?"

"Yes, I did. I also noticed that Sahadeva was dressed in a similar robe.

"Another question—when Draupadi was helping me to dissolve my first chakra's negative tendencies in the form of that frightening statue of me, the statue dissolved into tiny blue crystals. Were they sapphires?"

Issoweet smiled, "Very observant, my dear, even during that stressful and dramatic moment of your pilgrimage. Yes, they were very tiny blue sapphires, the 'reigning precious gemstone' of the first chakra."

"Why a blue sapphire instead of another kind of gemstone?" Sabella asked.

Issoweet explained, "One of the more esoteric aspects of the chakras connects them with our inner astrology, the zodiac, ruling planets, gemstones, and so on. I'll list for you the gemstones for each of the chakras, from the bottom to the top. There are nine of them."

"Nine gemstones? How could that be?" Sabella was curious. "There are only seven chakras!"

"Patience, Sabella, I *will* explain!

"The first chakra's helpful stone is a blue sapphire. The second chakra's is a yellow sapphire. The third is red coral. Fourth, diamond; fifth, emerald; sixth, pearl, and the seventh is ruby. The other two are hessonite (cinnamon garnet) and chrysoberyl (cat's-eye). These 'extra' two gemstones represent, respectively, the upward-moving current in *iḍa* on the left side of the astral spine and the downward current in *pingala* on the right side of the astral spine. In Vedic astrology, they are called *Rahu* and *Ketu*.

"In times past, there have been substitute stones for those who could not afford the more expensive gemstones. For example, one could use a lapis lazuli stone instead of a blue sapphire, though it was suggested that the substitute or semi-precious stone be of a size larger than two carats, perhaps five or six carats.

"A blue sapphire, a yellow sapphire, and a red ruby (for the first, second, and seventh chakras), are not all that different from one another in their basic chemical components. It was the exact *color* of the gemstones, whether precious or semiprecious, that was most strongly emphasized.

"In the ancient system of Vedic astrology, a person's natal or birth chart was carefully read to determine which chakras were in a weakened state due to astrological influences. The prescription was a flawless-as-possible gemstone of two carats or greater. The gem was worn in a piece of jewelry (pendant, bracelet, or ring), set so that the gemstone touched the skin. Notice, Sabella, that the blue sapphire was placed in your pendant to achieve that end."

"I did see that! Thomas commented on the unusual nature of my new pendant."

"It is more than a piece of jewelry," Issoweet mentally projected. "By wearing it, you strengthen the energy of your first chakra."

"Are you saying that my first chakra still *needs* more energetic help?" Sabella felt slightly disappointed.

"Not exactly. *Your* chakra pendant is more of a *symbol.* In time, if all goes well, you will receive the other eight chakra pendants. Together, they can be a kind of *navaratna* for you. A *navaratna* is a nine-stone astrological bangle, which symbolizes and strengthens each of our seven chakras and the two spinal currents which pass through them."

"I've heard of *navaratna* bracelets or bangles. Would it be a good thing to wear one? Do you have one? Come to think of it, I don't recall ever having seen one on anybody that I know. Why not?" Sabella asked.

"In the present age of Treta Yuga, energy aids such as astrological gemstones are not needed for most people. They were much more useful during the lower ages, especially in Dwapara Yuga, the age of energy. No, I don't think a *navaratna* bangle would be especially helpful for you at this time."

Sabella took the pendant from Issoweet and examined it carefully. "Please tell me why the pendant's disc is made of lead. Lead seems an odd metal to use in a pendant. What does it symbolize?"

Issoweet smiled, "I knew you were going to give me a mental workout today through your many questions. And I appreciate that quality in you, for I am also a curious person and am ready to answer your questions as best as I can.

"Each of the chakras is associated with a different metal. Again, in order: first chakra, lead; second chakra, tin; third chakra, iron; fourth chakra, copper; fifth chakra, mercury; sixth chakra, silver; and the seventh chakra, gold.

"Paramhansa Yogananda often recommended that his students wear a bracelet or arm-band, which he called an 'astrological bangle.' It was made of gold, silver, and copper, and it was designed to strengthen the aura and the fourth, sixth, and seventh chakras. In order for the bangle to be effective, there is an exact formula for the weight and purity of these three metals. Many people wearing the bangles report that they definitely feel the bangle provides them special protection and energy.

"Anyway, here are a few items of interest about lead: It is a very heavy metal, and in the past it was used to weigh things down, like fishing lines. That was back when people were barbaric enough to catch and eat fish.

"In the ancient English language of Dwapara Yuga, there was a phrase, 'get the lead out!' It was a rather vulgar directive indicating that a person should quit being slow or lazy and get to work! I think you can see how the characteristics of lead make it a good symbol for the first chakra.

"And finally, there was an unusual episode in the life of Paramhansa Yogananda. As a young man, he was told by his guru, Swami Sri Yukteswar, one of the greatest astrologers of all times, that he should begin wearing an astrological bangle made of lead and silver, to help him overcome a very serious illness that would be coming to him soon. One wonders why a great *avatar* like Yogananda would need *any* sort of chakra-strengthener, especially a bangle containing the metal representing the lowest chakra. Can you guess why this happened to him?"

"I remember that story in Yogananda's *Autobiography of a Yogi*, but never stopped to wonder why Sri Yukteswar recommended that Yogananda wear lead, the first-chakra metal. Let me guess. Yogananda, the great *avatar* that he was, came to earth fully liberated, but with a large mission to serve as a savior for millions. He offered them the life-giving techniques of Kriya Yoga and taught all who would listen about how to live in the material world, while still striving to make rapid spiritual progress.

"Perhaps it was as hard for him to stay 'rooted' to the earth (a very first-chakra quality) as it would be for most people to rise above the earth's downward-pulling energy fields. Thus he needed the grounding and therefore (for him) healing quality of lead. Could this have been the explanation for the lead bangle, Issoweet?"

"I think you may be correct, Sabella. That is what I surmised from the story. Unfortunately, the metal and gemstone prescriptions given by Sri Yukteswar were never fully explained—at least, in any records that we know of. But it seems to make perfect sense. You have an excellent understanding of the first chakra's qualities. I can see that now."

Sabella had another question. "Does astrology rule our lives? Are events, such as a serious illness, fated to happen to us—are they 'written in the stars'? I thought free will and will power were much more important than blind fate!"

Issoweet answered, "To a very great degree, karma rules our fate, but not as most people understand it. We created karmic debts for ourselves in the past. Impelled by karma, the soul chooses to be born into a human body at just the right time, astrologically speaking, to offer the ideal circumstances to allow these karmic patterns to emerge and hopefully allow us to learn the needed lessons. Once learned, we are free of that particular karmic pattern. However, due to the overwhelming number of past lives, we have created massive amounts of karma. It takes many lifetimes to work it all out. And yes, free will and will power are very important in this process."

Issoweet went on to add: "Here is what Yogananda said in *Autobiography of a Yogi* about the subjects of astrology and free will:

I had been prejudiced against astrology from my childhood. . . . Occasionally I told astrologers to select my worst periods, according to planetary indications, and I would still accomplish whatever task I set myself. It is true that my success at such times has been accompanied by extraordinary difficulties. But my conviction has always been justified: faith in the divine protection, and the right use of man's God-given will, are forces formidable beyond any the 'inverted bowl' [the stars in the sky] can muster.

The starry inscription at one's birth, I came to understand, is not that man is a puppet of his past. Its message is rather a prod to pride; the very heavens seek to arouse man's determination to be free from every limitation. God created each man as a soul, dowered with individuality, hence essential to the universal structure, whether in the temporary role of pillar or parasite. His freedom is final and immediate, if he so wills; it depends not on outer but inner victories.

"Thank you! Reviewing and clarifying all this information is great fun!" Sabella sparkled! "And now, please explain to me the meaning of the stylized red lotus blossom with its four petals on my pendant. What does it symbolize?"

"Lotus blossoms, with their many petals, are ancient symbols for the chakras. It is interesting that for each chakra, the lotus blossom has a different number of petals. The first chakra has four petals; the second chakra, six; third chakra, ten; fourth chakra, twelve; fifth chakra, sixteen; sixth chakra, two; and the seventh chakra, a thousand petals.

"These petals symbolize the number of 'rays' of energy emanating from each chakra, each petal representing a ray of energy. The first chakra has four rays: one ray imparting the ability to walk, another giving the power to excrete bodily wastes (through urination, bowel movements, etc.), and the remaining two influencing other first-chakra abilities. I won't describe them, but I think you get the general idea."

"I think so," commented Sabella, "But there does seem to be a numerical progression of some sort, from four to sixteen. Then it jumps down to two petals at the sixth chakra, and finally it takes a huge leap up to a thousand petals in the seventh chakra. What is the meaning in all those numbers?"

"Yes, there is a lot going on with the chakra symbols. I'm glad you are so enthusiastic about understanding this information. I think it is fun, too.

"The two petals at the sixth chakra represent the way energy originally enters the body through the receptive part of the sixth chakra, which is a part of the brain called the *medulla oblongata*. The life-force enters our body as a spiritual oneness, not existing in the 'two-ness' or the opposites of duality, until that moment when the sperm and ovum meet. At that point, the one Spirit bifurcates (splits) into two channels of energy, representing duality. From that moment forward, as human beings we exist always in duality, until we reclaim our oneness with God who is the universal ONENESS.

"These two currents, which we mentioned when talking

about *Rahu* and *Ketu*, are also called the *iḍa* and *pingala* *naḍis* or *prana* channels. They are an important part of our astral anatomy, as are the chakras. They create the rising and falling currents of energy which cause us to inhale and exhale. These two currents remain dormant in a baby while still in its mother's womb. At the moment just after birth, when the child first inhales, currents of energy begin their movements up and down the astral spine; they remain active until our last exhalation, right before death. Thus, these currents keep us locked in duality.

"Regarding the different numbers of 'petals' in the chakras, the two very important central *naḍis* 'bifurcate' or split again and again as they move into the chakras. This bifurcation creates rays that distribute the life-force needed to sustain the many functions of our physical and energetic beings. The lower chakras need fewer petals or bifurcations because their essential life-functions are less complex and sophisticated than those of the upper chakras. The most complex center, the brain, is said to have a thousand petals. This is not necessarily an exact number, but indicates the large number of rays of energy that are needed to keep the sophisticated mechanism of the human brain functioning."

"Fascinating!" thought Sabella. "Utterly and absolutely fascinating."

"There's another bit of esoteric information you might like to know about the lotus petals of the chakras. If you add the number of petals in the first six chakras (4, 6, 10, 12, 16 and 2) you'll get fifty petals."

"Fifty? What does that number mean?" Sabella was puzzled.

"Fifty is the number of characters in the Sanskrit language. Sanskrit is often called the 'language of the gods.' No other earthly language has been able to capture the subtleties of the inner sounds, spiritual vibrations of the astral body, and *mantras* as thoroughly and accurately as Sanskrit. That is why so many words, terms, chants, and *mantras* that we use in the yogic sciences are in Sanskrit."

"Whew! So much to absorb!" Sabella contemplated. "Perhaps I do need a little time to regroup and assimilate all we have discussed."

"I agree!" Issoweet said. "Same time and place tomorrow?"

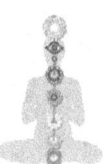

CHAPTER EIGHTEEN

Sabella spent her free time relaxing and indulging in her favorite activities. These included swimming at her favorite river-spot, talking to Thomas, and enjoying one of his incredible back rubs. Inspired by all that preceded, she carefully recorded all her thoughts, including plans which kept coming to her in great waves—creative ideas about how she might effectively share what she was learning with students in the Halls of Wisdom.

She kept returning to the concept of *experience*. She knew that while discussing and reading about the chakras provided a base for their understanding, they needed direct, active, inward, and outward experiences of them. These things she vowed to do her best to provide for them.

Sabella mentally contacted each of her three children. She was eager to update them on her latest adventure and see how life was going for them. Their replies indicated all was well. No news of potential life-linking or grandchildren. But never mind. They were still young and there was plenty of time.

The next day, she met Issoweet in the High Council's small pyramid-chapel.

"Issoweet, I've been thinking that I should learn more about Vedic astrology. It seems an important subject to understand, especially the ways in which it relates to the chakras."

"It's not necessary to know as much as you might think, Sabella, unless you want to become a Vedic astrologer yourself. However, there is one aspect of the subject which is very important to understand, especially for those who practice Kriya Yoga."

"What is it? I think I know, but can we review it anyway?" Sabella asked.

"I'd like to make an agreement with you, Sabella. Vedic astrology is a huge and complex subject. After you complete the next portion of your pilgrimage, we'll discuss the several aspects of Vedic Astrology's connection to the chakras, astral anatomy, and Kriya Yoga.

"At this time, we need to finish talking about the colors of the chakras. I believe that is where we left off yesterday?"

"I agree to wait until a later time to discuss Vedic astrology," Sabella said.

"And yes," she continued, "you are right. We discussed the numbers of petals or rays of the chakras. We were examining my first-chakra pendant, but I didn't get to ask why the lotus blossom on my pendant, and I assume on yours and Simeon's also, is red in color."

"The different color references in the chakras can be confusing. We have the colors of the gemstones of which we have spoken, the rainbow spectrum, the inner colors, and even the colors of the metals, all different, all representing certain aspects of the chakras.

"On our pendants, the four petals of the lotus blossom are red because of the ancient tradition of tying the chakras to the rainbow spectrum. Red for the first chakra; orange, second; yellow, third; green, fourth; blue, fifth; indigo, sixth; and violet for the seventh chakra.

"We sometimes call these the 'outer colors' of the chakras, because they relate to the colors we see, wear, or want to have in our environment. They do seem to influence us outwardly. The lower chakra colors are warmer and more energizing. The upper chakra colors are cooler, more soothing, and spiritually uplifting. Green, the beautiful color of nature, is healing in many ways. The colors we wear are important, because they influence our auras and the ways people relate to us when we wear them. Wearing brightly colored clothing and having bright, light-filled colors in our environment are important. Dark or muddy colors are to be avoided.

"Often, whether we recognize it or not, we experience what might be called a 'color hunger.' On certain days or in certain periods of our lives, we seem to crave one color over another. It is fun to play with color in these ways—after all, we need to have fun in our lives! We've prepared some colored waters for you to play with today."

Issoweet led her to a table outside the small pyramid where they had been meeting. On the table were seven large colored bottles, in the seven rainbow colors Issoweet had mentioned. The sun was shining brightly on the bottles. It was a very colorful sight to see!

Sabella heard giggling behind her and turned to see that Nila- and Notea-Nightingale had just arrived. "We want to play with the colored water, too!" they said happily. "May we join you?"

"Yes, of course, children," Issoweet said. "Please explain to Sabella how we make and use the colored waters."

Nila said, "The colored bottles are clear enough to allow the sun to shine through them into the water inside, irradiating it with that specific color's vibrations. First we put fresh, clean spring water into each colored bottle and then cork them. Then we leave them in the sunlight for at least two hours, soaking up the color vibrations. We prepared these for you earlier this morning, didn't we Notea?"

Notea nodded, his big blue eyes sparkling.

"And a very good job you did, too," Issoweet praised them. "Thank you!"

Nila continued, "Sabella, if you have a particular color hunger today, take that colored bottle and pour out a little to sip." Nila put a tray of small, clear glasses on the table for them to use.

"Very well." Sabella smiled at the children's enthusiasm. "I choose to drink red water now." She poured from the red-colored bottle into a glass.

"Yum," Sabella said. "It doesn't look red to me, but it tastes very red, perhaps like ripe cherries."

"Really?" Notea asked. "Does it really taste like red cherries to you?"

"Try it and tell me what you think." Sabella beamed at little Notea.

He rushed to do so, then stopped and looked at Sabella disapprovingly. "You are surely teasing me, Sabella. I don't taste cherries at all!"

They all laughed.

Nila said to her little brother, who was blushing—his cheeks like cherries—"Silly, it doesn't taste red in *that* way. It's only a vibration of the color red, you know."

'Notea, I'm sorry, I was teasing you," Sabella said. "I really didn't taste anything but fresh water, but I'm going to try again." She closed her eyes to concentrate and lifted the glass to take another drink.

Nila was bouncing up and down with excitement. "Wait, Sabella, let's try an experiment. Turn your back and let me pour you a different glass of colored water. I don't want you to see which color I'm pouring. Then drink it and see if you can tell me what color it is!"

She did as instructed. "Yellow," she said after a few sips.

"Wrong," the children laughed, "it was green, but you were close!"

"Let me try, I want to try it!" said Notea. Taking his turn, he immediately shouted: "BLUE!"

"Correct!" said Nila, proud of her brother. "Try again."

One by one, he unhesitatingly got every one of them right, even when Nila tried to trick him by giving him the same "colored water" three times in a row.

"How are you doing that, Notea?" Sabella was astonished.

"I don't know," little Notea said, a bit embarrassed. "I just tuned in somehow and. . . . I can't explain it. They just vibrated their colors to me."

They spent some time experimenting with each other. Although as time went on, Issoweet, Sabella, and Nila became more proficient at accurately identifying the color of the water, no one could come close to Notea's accuracy. He correctly identified every one of the colored waters he was given.

"That's an amazing talent you have, Notea," Issoweet said. "I'm glad we discovered it today. Thank you, children, for taking time to prepare and play with the colored water with us. Sabella and I must get back to our discussion now."

Offering a charming farewell, Nila and Notea happily skipped away, hand in hand. Sabella and Issoweet went back inside the pyramid-chapel.

"They are such delightful children, Issoweet. Thank you for asking them to be with us again. It was wonderful—amazing, really! I plan to get some of those bottles and show them to Thomas and to my children when they visit. I want to have them available to drink, especially when I feel a particular 'color hunger' or when I can identify a need for a specific sort of energy lift. And why drink regular water when we can drink colored water?"

Issoweet said, "I thought you'd enjoy that little experiment and some more time with the children. So you see, the rainbow colors in relation to the chakras have their place in our lives. However, in truth, it is the inner colors and shapes which are most important to us, spiritually. Now, look at your pendant again."

Sabella looked at the golden-yellow square or diamond-shape in the center of the pendant and asked, "This yellow-golden shape must represent what we see at the spiritual eye in deep meditation when the first chakra awakens. Refresh my memory—what are the other inner colors and shapes?"

Issoweet replied: "When we raise the *kundalini* energy in the spine, thus awakening the chakras more fully, the greater the upward flow of energy, the clearer the light at the point between the eyebrows becomes. It reveals a specific colored light at each chakra. These lights and shapes are perceived in the spiritual eye. They are as follows:

A yellow square for *muladhara* [1st chakra]
A white half-moon for *swadisthana* [2nd chakra]
A blood-red triangle for *manipura* [3rd chakra]
A ball of palpitating blue for *anahata* [4th chakra]
Smoke color with luminous specks of light for *bishuddha* [5th chakra]
The spiritual eye [6th chakra] is seen as a ring of gold surrounding a field of deep blue-violet, with a silvery-white five-pointed star at the center.

"The rainbow colors are comparable to the seven chakras, especially because of their gradual change in hue from a more materialistic red, through orange, to yellow, green, blue, and indigo, to the highest vibrational rate of violet. But the inner colors we've just discussed are the actual chakra colors that we can see in the spiritual eye in meditation. In this way, we can say that, spiritually speaking, the inner color system is much more important to us than the rainbow spectrum colors."

"Yes," Sabella thought softly, "I've sometimes seen those inner colors and shapes while meditating—now I understand much better what I saw and what it means."

Issoweet continued, "This information is a lot to take in, Sabella, I know—all the many different chakra symbols, sets of colors and shapes, and the many reasons behind them. While it can be a little overwhelming, I believe you can understand now why our first-chakra robes are blue, red, and yellow-gold and perceive how the first-chakra pendant is designed with the symbol, metal, stone, color, and shape that are related to the first chakra."

"I understand and I thank you, Issoweet. I find the many colorful aspects of the chakras to be very interesting, helpful, and entertaining. So, what will we do now?"

"Why, go to the second-chakra pyramid, of course! Are you

ready?" Issoweet inquired with a smile.

"Awake and ready!" Sabella said joyfully.

"Then let me send you on your way today with these words from a great sage: 'To seek God requires a bold and adventurous spirit. Anyone who, instead, clings timidly to trivial worldly advantages and to dimly glowing earthly delights is both short-sighted and a coward. O devotee, be brave! Fear not to invest your last coin to discover the fabled treasures of your soul. Success will come to that one who summons up the courage to hurl everything he or she has and is into the divine expedition.'"

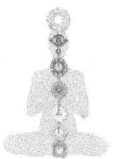

CHAPTER NINETEEN

Brother Solonar was waiting for them at the table in the same small pavilion by the Sushumna River. Sabella greeted him lovingly and took a moment to gaze again at the great river stretching out into the distance, with the giant golden pyramids shining brightly in the sunshine—it was a beautiful sight to see. Sabella could relate to the pyramids a little better now, after having traveled through the first one with Sahadeva and Solonar.

"I will leave you now, Sabella. You have my prayers and blessings for the next portion of your pilgrimage." Saying these words softly, Issoweet disappeared.

"Welcome, Sabella!" Solonar said. "I trust you are rested. You are looking very well and exceedingly colorful in your first-chakra robe."

"Yes," she replied, "I am color-saturated in many ways and very happy for it."

Brother Solonar surprised her by saying, "I am not accompanying you on your visit to the second-chakra pyramid, my dear. I believe you are much more accustomed to the pilgrimage process by now and that you are strong enough to proceed without me. You will be well guided and cared for by Nakula, your second-chakra pyramid host."

Solonar transported her to the beautiful first-chakra altar, where she encountered King Sahadeva standing where she had last seen him.

"Greetings, dear child, and welcome again to you. May I introduce you to my brother Nakula?"

Sahadeva's twin brother King Nakula, ruler of the golden second-chakra pyramid, suddenly appeared at Sahadeva's side. Even though she felt she had prepared herself for this moment, she was astonished nonetheless. How could they be twins and yet look so different from each other?

Nakula was ten feet tall as was his twin, and he had similar facial features and body type—both were obviously mighty warriors. But there, all resemblance stopped. While Sahadeva had dark hair, eyes, and skin, Nakula was blazingly blond, blue-eyed, and light-skinned. And equally handsome? Absolutely!

"Oh my!" she said and knelt in his presence, reaching out to touch his sacred feet in the ancient traditional way of showing respect. Meeting these great beings could be overwhelming, but she quickly felt comfortable with Nakula. He looked at her with such kindness, sweetness, and love, whereas Sahadeva had been a little stern at first.

Nakula took her hand and lifted her to her feet. "It is a great joy to meet you, Sabella. My brother told me all about you. Come with me now, and we will enter my kingdom, the second-chakra pyramid. It is called *Swadisthana-loka*. The Sanskrit word *swadisthana* means 'sweetness' and I believe you'll find it to be a sweet experience in many ways."

Sabella glanced back to say good-bye to Solonar and Sahadeva, but they had already melted away into the ether.

In the twinkling of an eye, Sabella and Nakula were standing in what appeared to be a gigantic lower chamber of the pyramid that looked and felt different from *Muladhara-loka* in every possible way. Sabella was astonished to see that they were underwater. Sunlight streamed through the pyramid's transparent walls making the water appear to be bright azure in color.

Looking more carefully at herself and Nakula, she could see they now were in their astral bodies. She thought, "I suppose I'll get used to these quick shifts soon enough. I guess I'd better. And I suppose it is a good thing to be in my astral body now. I am reasonably sure that my physical body would drown being underwater like this. How lovely I feel in this watery place, and how sweet it all seems to me!"

Nakula transmitted to her, "I agree, Sabella. Water is the Element of the second chakra and a wonderful element indeed! All the great masters agree on this subject. Even your physical body is primarily composed of water and fluids of various kinds.

"Water has always been a bit of a mystery. It has the beautiful quality of an almost absolute adaptability and the ability to flow and change, fitting perfectly within its surroundings. Water also responds immediately to our thoughts and attitudes, good or bad.

"The Great Ones have said that when you come to a body of water, be it a small spring, a tinkling brook, a larger stream or river, a placid lake, or even the mighty ocean itself, you should sit down and meditate on the beneficial qualities of water: flexibility, fluidity, openness, adaptability, creativity, and embracing growth and change."

Sabella was happy to hear this, for she was a great lover of water and had been so all her life. Her favorite meditation place was right beside the Joyuba River. Nevertheless, she had not spent a lot of time completely *submerged* in a body of water as she was now. Still, she felt no fear, only a sense of floating freedom and joy.

"Is this pyramid completely filled with water?" Sabella thought this question to her host.

"No, only at its lower level. But I thought you might enjoy seeing and feeling it in this way in the beginning of your visit. It is a way of completely 'saturating' you, so to speak. I also knew of your great love for water." Nakula laughed quietly, a sound which reminded Sabella of water gurgling over stones. "Would you be comfortable meditating with me for a while, here underwater? I think it might be a new experience for you."

"Sure!" Sabella replied. "What do I do?"

"What you always do!" He vibrated a smile to her.

She understood and turned her energies inward. She could hear Nakula's fine voice, rippling and singing inside herself. He sang a beautiful old chant, which she knew well:

> *I am the bubble, make me the sea,*
> *Make me the sea, Oh make me the sea!*
> *Wave of the sea, dissolve in the sea*
> *So do thou, my Lord,*
> *Thou and I, never apart.*

Sabella mentally joined him in the liquidly lilting chant and gradually merged her consciousness into a large sea of bliss, until there was no separation between herself and the Cosmic Ocean of Spirit. She also began to hear inner watery sounds; at first it sounded like the tinkling music of a little brook. As she meditated on that sound, it took her deeper, and she realized that the soft water-sounds were changing into the sound of a flute being played within her—played with surpassing beauty.

"Krishna's flute!" she thought. "Never had I hoped to hear it this clearly." Inwardly she bowed to the Lord Krishna and let herself be filled with the sweetest flute music and the perfect "baby AUM sound" of the second chakra.

"This *is* a very sweet chakra!" This was her last thought before she allowed the heavenly second-chakra sounds to lead her deep into her astral spine, to become absorbed in the great oceanic thunder of AUM.

CHAPTER TWENTY

Sabella resurfaced from this matchless watery meditation to find herself completely dry and in her physical body, sitting comfortably on a grassy knoll overlooking a vast, calm lake. The little hill was covered with fragrant white flowers, each individual blossom shaped like a tiny half-moon. Nakula sat quietly beside her.

"Thank you for that experience, Nakula." She took a deep breath of fresh air.

"Sabella, you must be aware that, although we are here to guide you, it is truly your own higher Self that is leading you along your journey through the chakras to Self-realization.

"We have some other subjects to discuss," he continued. "One part of your pilgrimage in the second-chakra pyramid is to understand one's need to perfect the *niyamas*. You remember discussing with Sahadeva the five *yamas*, which are an important aspect of his domain? In mine, we focus on the five *niyamas*, the 'do's' of the spiritual path. Please tell me what you know of them, as you told my brother about the *yamas*.

Sabella began: "The *Yoga Sutras* of the great sage Patanjali present the *niyamas*, which in Sanskrit means 'non-control.' They are the five moral requirements necessary to make spiritual progress. They are cleanliness, contentment, austerity, self-study, and devotion. Like the *yamas*, when any one of them is perfected, the spiritual seeker begins to see the outward manifestation of its perfection in their life in the form of a power. These are their names and a short description of the gifts they bestow:

Cleanliness or *saucha* brings freedom from the body, and a

disinclination for its pleasures.

Contentment or *santosha* offers unceasing inner joy; realization of bliss in every atom of creation and beyond creation.

Austerity (self-discipline, sacrifice) or *tapasya* develops many or all of the various yogic powers called *siddhis*.

Self-study (introspection) or *swadhyaya* gives us the ability to commune with beings on higher spheres and to receive their help.

Devotion to the Supreme Lord or *Ishwara Pranidhana* allows us to enter into the sacred ray of divine love, the dwelling place of Infinite Consciousness.

"One memory comes to mind when I think about Patanjali's *yamas* and *niyamas*. As a child and somewhat new to meditation, I complained to Simeon that I was having trouble meditating as deeply as I wanted. I really hoped he would offer me a fantastic new meditation technique that would allow me to dive deeply, quickly, and easily.

"Instead, he surprised me by asking if I was working on my *yamas* and *niyamas*.

"I had to admit that even though I thought I understood them, I was not particularly focusing on them in my life—which, of course, he already knew.

"Still, I could not comprehend why he would say this to me! I thought to myself, 'I know they are good for us to work on, but what could these "do's and don'ts of moral behavior" have to do with my meditations?'

"As always, Simeon knew my mind's question, but this time did not answer me directly. He simply said, 'Perfection of the *yamas* and *niyamas* in your daily life is necessary if you want to perfect your meditative life.'"

Sabella continued, "It took me many years to understand more fully what he meant. But because I trusted him so much, I began actively to work on understanding the deepest aspects of each of the *yamas* and *niyamas*. I was diligent about practicing them in daily life. A helpful practice was to pick out one *yama* or *niyama* at the beginning of each calendar year and focus on that one for the whole year. It took ten years to cycle through all of them, but it was well worth it. This practice worked so well in deepening my meditations that I decided to continue it for the rest of my life."

"Sahadeva was right," Nakula said in a very pleased manner. "I, too, am impressed with your knowledge of Patanjali and your ability to state these principles clearly and succinctly. But more important is your dedication to putting these teachings into practice throughout your life. It is an often ignored fact that one's meditative life and daily life should not and *cannot* be kept separate from each other."

"Thank you for your kind words. But I suspect that you have other qualities or psychological attributes of this chakra, both beneficial and harmful, to show me," Sabella said somewhat warily.

"You *are* catching on quickly, and you have only progressed as far as the second-chakra pyramid. But yes, you are right. Please look carefully at the body of water you see before you."

Sabella saw the sunlight sparkling on the big lake. It looked oddly dark and somehow menacing on the left side and clear and still on the right side. Looking more closely, she noticed a mysterious force field beginning to generate ripples. The ripples grew into larger and larger waves, finally forming into one giant wave running straight down the center of the lake.

Astonishingly, the lake began to divide into two sections, left and right. Between the divided waters, the lake's bottom was revealed as a pebble-strewn walkway. The pebbles were clear and tinted a light yellow color. The pathway was wet and looked slippery from having been underwater.

"Let me guess, Nakula. You are going to send me to walk down the pathway between those large walls of water," Sabella said wryly.

"You are correct. It is time for you to walk along this watery pathway alone; in doing so, you will learn many things about yourself and about the important qualities and attitudes of the second chakra. Take care, Sabella. Go with God and with my love." His mental voice faded away, and then she was alone.

Sabella sighed and said a brief prayer for guidance and protection. She stood up and began walking slowly towards the strange pathway between the two walls of water. Once on the path, she observed the water towering about 30 feet above her, being held in place by some unknown energy field.

Looking into the left water-wall, she saw it was swirling, dark, muddy, and full of debris. On the right side, the water was as clear as glass and absolutely still. She walked on, being very careful of her footing, for the polished pebbles were partially covered with a slick slime. She stooped to pick up one of the cleaner stones. Based on her previous experience in the first-chakra pyramid, she surmised that these were really small yellow sapphires, the astrological gemstone of the second chakra. Placing the stone in her pocket, she wandered on, wondering what to do next.

She considered where she was, thinking, "This place feels very different from the avenue of the giant pillars in the first-chakra pyramid, but there must be some similarities. The left side probably represents the harmful qualities of the second chakra, and the right side, the beneficial ones."

Stopping, she tentatively reached out to touch the unpleasant-looking water-wall on her left. It was wet, and as she touched it she felt a tingle of energy in her fingers. An ugly, ancient plastic bag floated by, with the word INDECISIVENESS clearly written on it.

"Ah-ha! My second chakra's harmful qualities are revealing themselves to me."

Other pieces of trash, flotsam and jetsam, slime-covered debris began to float by also. They had other words written on them, such as: FLIPPANT, NOT GROUNDED IN TRUTH, INDISCRIMINATE, UNRELIABLE, UNABLE TO MAKE FIRM DECISIONS AND STAND BY THEM, FICKLE, WEAK-MINDED, PROCRASTINATING, and UNTRUSTWORTHY.

In her mind she heard Nakula's voice say, "Sabella, you must clean up this side of your lake."

"Yes, I see that," she mentally answered back to him, "but how, exactly, am I to do that? It is a large lake with a lot of very unpleasant stuff in it!"

Silence. No answer came.

"OK, so here we go again! Figure it out, Sabella," she told herself firmly.

No great ideas were coming to her at the moment. Her life's experiences had taught her that it was better to do *something* than wait around doing nothing. Even if that something turned out not to be the right thing, it often led to the next right thing or proved a valuable lesson.

Sabella reached out to touch the wall of water again. This time she applied pressure and extended her will power to reach a piece of debris floating by. The debris was labeled WISHY-WASHY. She was alarmed when she realized she was being violently pulled into the maelstrom of muddy, polluted water, filled with massive whirlpools of swirling debris.

At first she was merely surprised, but her surprise quickly turned to terror, as she began to be tossed about wildly underwater, not knowing up from down. She bumped against pieces of junk, which dealt her sharp, painful blows. She was holding her breath, and knew drowning was imminent if she couldn't make her way to the surface, and soon.

"Solution! Solution!" she prayed with determination. "I know there is a solution, and it is. . . ."

Just at that moment, Draupadi's voice came into her mind. "Drowning, Sabella? Don't know which way is up? Feeling painful jabs and blows to your body? Perhaps it would be better for you to have a different kind of body, right about now."

"Yes! Oh yes! I urgently need to be in my astral body. Can you help me, my lady, before I drown or am pummeled to death by all this turbulence and debris?"

"I will help you *this* time, Sabella, but you need to work on finding your own solutions in moments like these. Remember that the chakra pyramids and all that is within them exist, in many ways, more on the astral plane than in the material plane. It would have been better for you to attempt to make the transition *before* you entered this dangerous, watery place."

"Yes, I *will* learn, Draupadi, but for now, ..." Sabella thought as she began to panic, resisting the urge to helplessly breathe the murky water into her lungs.

Instantly her physical body melted away, replaced by the patterns of light and energy of her astral body—a body which was untouchable by the water or debris around her.

Calming herself, she remembered why she had gone into this polluted environment in the first place. Nakula had told her to clean it up. She began swimming about with lightning speed, feeling none of the usual resistance of water.

She found she was able to gather up most of the junk and debris. As she did so, the waters around her became calmer and cleaner. Feeling she had done her best, she moved toward the right water-wall.

Still in her astral body, she easily exited the left water-wall and penetrated into the right water-wall. As she did so, Sabella saw beautiful rainbow bubbles floating all around her. Within each bubble there were words describing the second chakra's beneficial qualities, such as: FLEXIBLE, WILLING TO CHANGE AND GROW, FREE-FLOWING, CREATIVE, MALLEABLE, OPEN-MINDED, PERFECTLY DISCERNING, and ADAPTABLE.

She carefully offered each piece of negative debris that she had gathered up, one at a time, into a positive-quality bubble that expressed its opposite quality. Each bubble drew the negative quality into itself and dissolved it away, like sugar being stirred into hot tea. Soon enough, her dark attitude-burdens had been transmuted into positive, light-filled second-chakra qualities.

As she completed the mission, she saw that the bubbles were being caught up in a powerful, upwardly spiraling current. As the bubbles moved rapidly upward, she was swept along with them in a glorious flow.

Happily, she thought, "I believe I did the right thing here, because this feels somewhat like my experience in the first chakra's corridor of granite pillars."

"Perhaps," she thought to herself, "there will be similar patterns among the various tests that I may encounter on the rest of this pilgrimage—situations which might repeat themselves in each pyramid. Let me learn from my experiences so far, the better to be prepared for future chakras adventures.

"First it seems necessary to offer the harmful qualities of each chakra into the beneficial qualities of that same chakra, in order to transmute them energetically into more positive or beneficial energy patterns. Once the transmutation process is underway, the positive qualities are able to move much more quickly into an inward and upward stream of energy—and the *kundalini* power is then able to move things along much more quickly, once it is not obstructed by sticky, clumping, negative *vrittis*. God bless my ever-dearer friend and ally, Queen Draupadi-Kundalini!

"The currents of the river of life, enhanced and made stronger and swifter through the power of *kundalini,* are no longer being impeded or leaking outward through harmful habits, bad behavior, and negative thought patterns. At last they can flow freely and powerfully, with fewer and fewer obstructions to keep them from their divinely ordained central channel. They can flow inward and upward to their final, glorious destiny.

"Good or bad, with a great outpouring of energy, every quality is eventually drawn upward along the River Sushumna and into final liberation at the crown chakra."

As Sabella thought through these crucial concepts, she realized she was learning that there were (thankfully!) some very efficient tools to use and procedures to follow that would help her to advance more easily on her journey.

She allowed herself to be drawn along by the water's increasingly strong and upwardly moving current. How wonderful it felt to be here! She did not worry at all about where she was going or how quickly. She simply relaxed and enjoyed the lovely sensation of going with the flow.

Sabella felt herself dissolving in joy as the river of life within her, like a mighty river rushing towards the sea, merged its watery second chakra energy into the great ocean of bliss. AUM thundered around her like the sound of a swelling sea, and all was ONE.

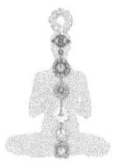

CHAPTER TWENTY-ONE

"Sabella?" Nakula's sweet voice in her mind softly called her back to herself.

It was early evening and she was with Nakula on a beautiful barge, floating along the Sushumna River. She was reclining comfortably on a plush couch and he was sitting on a cushion nearby. As she stirred and began to sit up, she sensed the couch gently sloshing about beneath her. It was not a regular couch; it was rippling, like an old-fashioned waterbed!

"A water-couch! How appropriate for this ultimately watery place," she laughed to herself.

She saw that she was back in her physical body. How and when had that happened? She guessed that King Nakula and Lady Kundalini were responsible.

"What an amazing experience!" Sabella thought. As Nakula smiled lovingly at her, she noticed that his twin brother had appeared at his side and joined in, offering her his big identical smile.

"Greetings, Sabella! Nakula asked me to join the two of you on this barge. I admit that a rocky mountaintop would have been my first choice for the best place for us to meet. I like to keep my feet on solid earth, you understand. But after all, *Swadisthana-loka* is Nakula's domain, and it is his right to choose the backdrop. He always goes with the water motif, which is understandable. In any case, it is good to see you again, dear one. Congratulations on what you have accomplished in the second pyramid."

Once again she was startled to see the Pandava twins together, looking so alike and yet so different: Nakula with his light complexion, and Sahadeva's much darker skin, both tall, powerful warriors, and the handsomest men ever to live on this earth, or so the legends go.

Sahadeva was dressed in his shining robe of red, blue, and golden-yellow. Nakula's glowing garments were orange, yellow, and white.

Remembering the different chakra color systems that she and Issoweet had discussed recently, she understood that Nakula's robe symbolized the orange in the rainbow-spectrum system of chakra colors. Yellow was for the yellow-sapphire gemstone which influenced the second chakra beneficially, and white was for the white half-moon that was the inner light and shape of this chakra. She then noticed a beautiful half-moon hanging in the night sky above them, just behind Nakula's head, casting its pale yellow glow over everything around them.

Nakula mentally spoke. "Sabella, before we offer you the simple initiation celebration to mark your successful passage through this pyramid, we want to give you an experience which involves both Sahadeva and myself, symbolizing the first and second chakras' close connections to each other, and the ways in which they balance and help each other.

"By extension, you'll soon begin to experience how *all* the chakras help and support one another, through their holistic nature. You'll better understand the important connections between and among the chakras as you move through your pilgrimage and meet all our brothers and teachers.

"But here, in the first two chakras—the 'twin chakras' they are often called—this balancing/connecting principle is most clearly revealed and easily understood.

"As you know," Sahadeva continued, "the two lowest chakras are located very close to each other in the astral spine, only about an inch and a half apart. In relation to the physical body, the first chakra is located very near the base of the physical spine, in the area of the anus or rectum. It influences the feet, calves, knees, thighs, anus, and rectum, and the abilities to walk, remain grounded, and excrete waste from the intestines.

"The second chakra influences the area of the reproductive organs and human sexuality, a small part of the lower intestines, and the hip joints."

Nakula chimed in, "The second chakra's greatest beneficial qualities, as you well know by now, are creativity and flexibility. These traits offer balance for the first chakra's beneficial qualities of strength, firmness, and groundedness. Helping each other, they form the perfect foundation for truth-seekers as they begin their inner spiritual journeys."

Sabella asked: "What do you mean by 'help each other'?"

Nakula gave Sahadeva a knowing and somewhat mischievous look. "The perfect question for what we want her to experience next!"

"Indeed it is," Sahadeva replied. "Sabella, please join us on a short excursion to a nearby island. Stand between us, and we will guide you."

Sabella saw that the barge had come aground at a small island in the river. She followed Sahadeva and Nakula as they came ashore and walked directly into a flowery, moonlit meadow.

She stood confidently between the twin warriors, facing the half-moon in the sky. They began to instruct her, speaking softly and in unison: "Sabella, stand up straight, close your eyes, and remain perfectly still."

For the first time, Sabella inwardly called upon her first-chakra power, that is, the rocklike ability to remain absolutely unmoving and unmovable.

The twins continued: "Excellent! Now, place your feet very close to each other and hold your arms tightly along the sides of your body. Imagine that you are a giant tree. Spread your toes and feel them to be like the roots of this tree. You, the tree, are sending your roots down deeper and deeper into the earth beneath you, enabling you to hold yourself firmly in place and to draw water and nutrients up from within the earth into the rest of your tree being. The trunk of your body feels like a giant pine tree: strong, steady, powerful, and unmovable."

They mentally projected to her, "You are doing very well, Sabella—you have 'become' a tall tree, straight and solid. But what would happen to you if a huge storm came along and you remained in this rigid condition?"

Sabella could sense what he was asking. "It might snap me in half because of my rigidity!"

"Correct!" They instructed her further, "Now, lift your hands and arms up above your head. Spread out your fingers to represent the tree's leaves or needles. Feel the top part of your body begin to sway with the constantly moving air currents all around you, while the lower part of your body stays firmly rooted and unmovable. You've surely noticed how, even on a seemingly wind-free day, the tops of the trees still sway about gently."

Sabella did as she was told and began to feel more and more treelike, swaying in the gentle wind, but firmly rooted to the earth beneath her. Soon, she felt the gentle breeze strengthen until it was evident that a big storm was upon her. The top of her "tree-self" began to whip and whirl about violently, bending low, left, right, and all around. The trunk and roots held firm.

Firmness and flexibility danced together, bringing victory to both qualities, each helping the other to cooperate in perfect balance and wholeness. What a feeling! Sabella understood to the core of her being, and as never before, how the first- and second-chakra Elements of Earth and Water were designed to help each other weather the storms of life.

Then all was still and peaceful again. She very much enjoyed being a tree and thought she might like to continue for a while, but the twins instructed her to lower her arms, come back into the awareness of her human body, and return with them to the magnificent river barge.

Back on board the barge, they led her to the bow. The barge moved up the river, and she enjoyed the cool evening breeze on her face. She saw a shining Water Element altar near the front of the deck. It looked very different from the Earth Element altar in the first-chakra pyramid.

It was not a solid thing at all, nor was it bedecked with rocks, jewels, and minerals like the Earth Element altar. Instead, it flowed and swayed and moved, like giant kelp beds under the sea. It grew larger and smaller, changing from moment to moment, sending forth ripples and rainbow bubbles of light in all directions. Water sounds and sweet flute music filled the air around it, along with the tangy scent of the ocean. She stood and tried to take it all in, but it was not easy—the altar was mesmerizing and almost beyond comprehension.

She saw that she was adorned in a new robe, very similar to the one she'd seen Nakula wearing when she first entered his pyramid. It was orange, yellow, and white, and it shone with remarkable radiance under the evening's half-moon–lit sky. When she moved or breathed, it rippled like a moon-lit lake.

"Do one's garments change colors magically when one is on a chakras pilgrimage?" she wondered.

"Yes, they tend to reflect the environment both within and all around you," Nakula replied. "But remember that most of what you see and experience on your pilgrimage is primarily symbolic of inner realities.

"It is time for your second-chakra initiation ceremony and blessing."

King Sahadeva stood to one side, extending his hands toward her in blessing.

Sabella knelt before King Nakula who prayed deeply with soft words; although tender, they also roared with power like the ocean. "Sabella, you are blessed by your experiences in this holy place of water and sweetness. Henceforth, you possess control over the water and fluids within your physical body, the power to walk on water, and the power to be underwater indefinitely, when needed. Most importantly, from now on you will manifest the quality of creativity and the ability to grow, flow, and change throughout all of life's turbulent challenges and circumstances."

Rising to her feet, she felt quite different; within her lower body, her first and second-chakra powers were dancing together in harmony and perfect balance. As she faced Nakula and the unusual rippling altar, he asked her to close her eyes. He touched her at the point between her eyebrows with a cool drop of holy and healing water.

The drop of water stayed in place, reminding her to lift all that she was feeling and experiencing up her astral spine to that point.

Sabella felt a light mist blowing across her face and body. The mist burst into diamond sprays of liquid light. She swayed on her feet, feeling ecstatic, almost unable to stand. She felt a twin on either side of her steadying her. Nakula softly asked her to open her eyes.

Standing before her was Draupadi, robed in the night-winds, dark and mysterious. "Sabella, you have navigated the early stages of your chakra pilgrimage with courage and creativity. Have you enjoyed meeting my handsome twin husbands?"

Sabella watched with amusement as the powerful warrior-twins quickly left her side and knelt before Queen Draupadi like little children. No words were spoken, but their loving, inward union and communion was unquestionable and inspiring to behold.

Nakula rose and added another beautiful pendant to Sabella's necklace. Just above the first-chakra pendant, there now was a disk made of tin. On it was a glowing orange lotus blossom with six petals, within which was a large yellow sapphire. In the center of the gemstone was a small, white half-moon shape. It was lovely, and complemented the first-chakra pendant suspended just below it.

"Thank you," she said humbly to Nakula and Sahadeva. "I will treasure these pendants always, as remembrances of my time spent with both of you."

She looked at Queen Draupadi. "And once again, thank you, my lady, for your help when I was being so badly battered by my harmful second-chakra attitudes in that scary 'soup,' in which I found myself drowning earlier today."

She bowed to the dark goddess, who acknowledged her

with a soft smile and said, "Remember, I am always within you, ready to help you remove any obstacles on your inner journey."

Suddenly the barge disappeared as did everyone and everything else, except for the River Sushumna, which rushed along in its unusual way. Without hesitation, Sabella let herself be swept away by the river's powerful upward current.

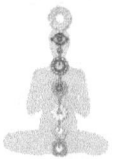

CHAPTER TWENTY-TWO

Because Sabella's guides had not suggested that she begin the next part of her pilgrimage immediately, she decided to do as she had last time and return to her home to rest, record her experiences, and spend time with Thomas. Sabella always enjoyed his perspective on whatever was going on in her life—and at the present time, spectacular events were happening, to be sure.

She knew that Issoweet would contact her soon, but in the meantime, she enjoyed resting in her small home, walking, and meditating alone by the river.

Never again would she look at water in the same way. It was such a powerful symbol of creativity, growth, and change within herself, and in everyone and everything around her.

Thomas admired her new robe and the new medallion on her chakras necklace. She told him of her recent experiences and asked his opinion about a few of them. He hesitated to say much, feeling sure that Issoweet would share with Sabella the specific wisdom needed to guide her through her pilgrimage adventures.

Soon Issoweet sent Sabella a mental message with a time and place to meet. Sabella was surprised that Issoweet had not suggested their usual spot in the High Council Pavilion's small chapel, but rather on a beach.

Issoweet knew that Sabella often preferred to be in a natural setting, and Sabella was beginning to notice how Issoweet tuned in to her most subtle or even subconscious desires. She happily agreed to meet her where she'd suggested.

They sat together on a woven straw mat on the pristine white beach, watching and listening as luminescent, turquoise blue waters lapped softly nearby. Gazing at towering, green-clad mountains across the lagoon, Issoweet sighed in contentment. Together they enjoyed the magnificent scenery, the tropical winds, and the shade of several palm trees.

Issoweet said, "I don't take the time to visit here as often as I'd like. Many, many years ago, this island paradise was called Bora-Bora. People still agree that it is the most beautiful beach on this planet. Have you visited here before, Sabella?"

"Not in this lifetime. I did visit once, on a time-travel expedition. The year was 316 Ascending Dwapara Yuga. While the scenery was beautiful then, too, it was spoiled, to my thinking, by the scores of tourist bungalows, near the beach and even placed on stilts out in the lagoon. The many visitors caused an increase in pollution to the degree that it harmed the underwater flora and fauna. I'm glad that era has long since passed away, and that places like these are preserved now in an ecologically clean state."

"Why did you choose to visit that past lifetime? Who were you then, Sabella?"

"No one of consequence. I was a young man who made his meager living entertaining tourists by being a 'fire twirler.'

"Why did I visit that lifetime? It was Thomas's suggestion. This was a few months before our formal life-linking ceremony, and he thought it would be instructive for me to see how I felt about being someone who lived a whole lifetime near the 'world's most beautiful beach.'" He knew how much I enjoyed being near water—as I do in this lifetime also.

"I learned a good lesson by observing and reliving a small part of that particular past life. There I was in a place of unsurpassable earthly beauty, and yet people who lived there were not especially happy—neither the natives like me, nor the visiting tourists.

"You'd think that in an earthly paradise like that, happiness would be something that came naturally to everyone, residents and guests alike. But no, it was not so. I saw petty human desires, negative emotions, and much meanness of spirit manifesting all around me—and worst of all, in my own behavior.

"I remembered an old saying: 'No matter where you go, there you are!' We take ourselves with us, no matter where we live or travel. We can be in the most beautiful place in the whole universe, but even so, there can be no running away from our negative thought patterns and the *karma* that we carry with us from lifetime to lifetime." Sabella sighed wistfully.

"I was relieved to return to Treta Yuga and did so with a renewed determination to gain freedom from all *karma* and to help others to do the same. Thank you, Issoweet, for suggesting that we meet here today. It *is* an exceedingly lovely place; the lagoon and beach are very peaceful. I appreciate it even more now, after my second-chakra experiences. But as I'm sure you are aware, I have questions to ask about what went on there and about some of the deeper aspects of the chakras."

Issoweet smiled at the younger woman: "That is what we are here to do. But first, do you remember what Nakula's first and very important suggestion to you was?"

"I do! He said, 'Whenever you are near a stream, river, waterfall, lake, ocean, or any body of water, take some time to meditate on the Water Element of the second chakra and especially the beneficial inner qualities of water.' If you are suggesting that we meditate here for a while, I'm all for it!"

Sabella and Issoweet sat up with straight spines. Issoweet began softly chanting AUM at each chakra. Sabella joined her. After a few rounds, they chanted the blended "Waves of AUM" chord until their voices naturally became quieter and merged into the soft sea sounds nearby and the AUM sounds within.

Three hours passed in deep inner communion. Concluding their meditation, Issoweet softly chanted the three-fold AUM *mantra* several times, and they returned their consciousness to the beautiful beach setting.

"A dip in the Infinite is better than a dip into water of any kind," Sabella said. "Thank you, Issoweet."

"No need to thank me, dear child. It is always a joy to meditate with you. Now let's get on with your observations and questions about the second chakra. As I promised, I will explain a bit more about Vedic astrology and its relationship to the chakras. Should we begin there?"

"Yes," thought Sabella. "I had almost forgotten that I wanted to know more about this subject. A lot has happened since the last time we talked about Vedic astrology. But first I want to ask this question. Is astrology based in truth? Is it a provable science? It seems so 'mythological' or something. Can the stars and planets truly influence us?"

Issoweet explained, "It is most certainly true that they exert a measurable force on the energetic aspects of our physical bodies, and to a certain degree sensitive people can feel their effects. But it is much more important to see them as characters, as it were, in the stories of our lives. And it is more helpful yet to make friends with them. It is like the way you are getting to know the Pandava brothers in each of the chakra pyramids. They symbolize inner realities, which greatly influence us."

Sabella happily thought of her budding friendships with her hosts in the first two pyramids, Sahadeva and Nakula. "Yes, I see what you mean. But I would still like to know more about astrology and its connection to the chakras, for the purpose of helping students. I realize it is a vast subject, but please help me gain at least a rudimentary understanding."

"As you wish," said Issoweet. "I will do my best to condense this complex subject into a clear and concise account."

"Vedic astrology is an ancient science devoted to understanding the movements of certain energy patterns *within the human body*, especially among the chakras. In its essence, it is *not* primarily a study of the movement of the stars of the zodiac and of the planets seen in the night skies; however there is an important link.

"When a child is born into this world and takes its first breath, the planets and constellations are in specific locations in relation to our planet. This configuration is unique to the moment and location the child takes that first breath. The soul, while still residing in the astral world between lifetimes and before its next birth, has chosen an *exact* time and place to take its first physical breath, in its new incarnation. That first breath is tied to the advent of the movements of *prana* (life-force) up and down the *iḍa* and *pingala* energy channels or *naḍis*.

"The movement of *prana*, from the moment of our first breath to our last, causes us to breathe physically—it causes every inhalation and exhalation for the entirety of that incarnation.

"This is why most astrological charts are *natal*, meaning they are based on the moment of a baby's birth, specifically when it takes its first breath. It is a very important moment for every human being, to say the least! At that point, out in the heavens, the planets and constellations are perfectly aligned to create the perfect life-conditions and environment for this unique person in this unique incarnation, to learn his or her specially needed lessons.

"Remember that nothing in the sky or in our inner lives ever stays still! There is always movement. Therefore, from the very instant of a baby's first breath, life-force begins moving up and down the inner astral spine while the planets are moving through outer space, revealing information about the lessons a soul has come to learn in this particular incarnation.

"Simultaneously there is a movement of 'planets' through the inner 'zodiac,' consisting of the astral spine and chakra system, which also reveals clues to help us understand karmic patterns in our lives. The effects of these vibrational patterns, especially if they are difficult or harmful, can be mitigated with certain aids, like the gemstones and metals we've discussed, *mantras* (words of power), or most important of all, meditation techniques.

"Sabella, what is your birth date? At what time and where were you born?"

Sabella was taken aback, for in Treta Yuga, these questions were considered impolite. But because she trusted Issoweet and was anxious to learn all she could, she complied willingly by replying, "I was born on January 15th, 5744 AD, at 7:42 in the evening, in Luissia, Indulsia Sector, planet Earth."

Issoweet smiled. "Interesting! I was born on that day also, though many years before you and at a different time and place. But I think that a shared birthday enhances the harmony we feel with each other!"

"I am delighted and honored!" said Sabella. Then it suddenly dawned on her. "That means that my spiritual teacher, your twin Simeon, was also born on that day! All the years I have known him—to imagine we've shared a birthday, and he never told me about it!"

"I think you know him well enough by now, Sabella," Issoweet said with a dry smile. "Any one birthdate in any lifetime would seem trivial to him."

"So true!" They laughed together. "Still, this is good news for me, if for no other reason than that I now have something to tease him about."

"Back to the subject at hand." Issoweet liked to stay on topic and did not like to waste time.

"On the day that you were born, the sun in the sky over planet Earth was passing through the constellation Capricorn; 365 days later, the sun would be in the same place in the sky, and we call that date your 'Sun-day,' better known as your birthday. The sun is an important heavenly body for us on earth, but not as all-important as some ancient astrologers used to think.

"It is only one of seven heavenly bodies which represent the patterns of energy movements in our astral bodies and the seven chakras. For example, while the sun's cycle is 365 days. It takes only 28 days for the moon to return to its original natal position. It takes 12 years for Jupiter to make its return cycle and 29 years for Saturn to do the same.

"Jupiter, sometimes called the guru planet, rules the second chakra, and influences a very important life-cycle, which manifests every 12 years at the ages of 12, 24, 36, 48, 60, 72, and so on. Look back on your own life and see how major shifts, especially spiritual ones, often take place on or around those times."

"It is true!" thought Sabella. "Adolescence usually happens for humans close to the age of 12. The age of 24 is typically close to the time which we move away from home and parents into a new phase of adulthood. I was 60 sun-cycles-old when I married Thomas, and that was *certainly* a big change for me. So yes, I can see the influence of the Jupiter cycle on my own life clearly. But what does this have to do with the chakras?"

"As it takes the planet Jupiter twelve years to cycle through the outer zodiac, so also, it takes twelve years for the 'inner Jupiter' to come back to its natal position in our chakras system."

"Is that why we practice the Kriya Yoga breathing technique in increments of twelve?" Sabella inquired.

"You are a smart one, Sabella Lovingheart! Yes, it is symbolic of the guru's accelerating influence on our spiritual lives, by means of the most powerful of all yoga techniques, Kriya Yoga. This offers us a clue to what great masters mean when they speak of 'shortcuts' to final liberation. By practicing certain yoga techniques, we speed up our natural evolution.

"Paramhansa Yogananda said that the practice of one Kriya breath, done perfectly, is equal to one year of normal, human evolution. A whole year's worth of past karma released in about 30 seconds! Think about it: I'd call that a dynamic speeding up of our spiritual evolution! Shortcut, indeed—I say, 'Hurray for all shortcuts!'"

Sabella wholeheartedly agreed.

Issoweet continued enthusiastically: "What the sacred practice of Kriya Yoga does is help you consciously direct your "inner sun" around your "inner zodiac" in 30 seconds instead of taking a whole year. A Jupiter cycle which would normally take twelve solar years to elapse can be completed in about six minutes of Kriya practice.

"But let me quote Yogananda directly, because he explains it so simply and beautifully: 'One who practices Kriya Yoga correctly mentally directs his life energy to revolve, upward and downward, around the six spinal centers (medullary, cervical, dorsal, lumbar, sacral, and coccygeal plexuses) [chakras 6, 5, 4, 3, 2, and 1, respectively] which correspond to the twelve astral signs of the zodiac. One-half minute of revolution of energy around the sensitive [astral] spinal cord of man effects subtle progress in his evolution; that half-minute of Kriya equals one year of natural spiritual unfoldment.

"'The astral system of a human being, with six (twelve by polarity) inner constellations revolving around the sun of the omniscient spiritual eye, is interrelated with the physical sun and the twelve zodiacal signs. Everyone is thus affected by an inner and an outer universe. The ancient *rishis* discovered that man's earthly and heavenly environment, in twelve-year cycles, push him forward on his natural path. The scriptures aver that man requires a million years of normal, disease-less evolution to perfect his human brain sufficiently to express cosmic consciousness. The Kriya short cut, of course, can be taken only by deeply developed yogis, those who have carefully prepared their bodies and brains to receive the power created by intensive practice.'"

"I see it clearly now!" Sabella cried. "Through Kriya Yoga, we speed up our evolution by sending energy (*prana*) much more quickly and deliberately through the chakras and astral spine, our own inner zodiacal system. That's amazing and incredibly motivating information, Issoweet. I now under-stand much better how we can clear away those millions of lifetimes of past karma in an efficient and relatively quick way! I love it! I think I'm going to drop everything and do nothing but practice my Kriya Yoga techniques night and day until I'm free of all karma and ready to merge into the Infinite."

Issoweet laughed. "Sabella, I love your enthusiasm, which

happens to be a major positive quality of the third chakra, the next destination on your quest. But the truth is that a human body, both astrally and physically speaking, is not yet ready to receive that much energy. It would overload our nervous systems. The inner quest must be approached in a gradual and scientific manner.

"You remember how we talked about the dangers of *forcing* the *kundalini* energy to rise prematurely, before the way is cleared for it to rise in a natural and safe way? The Kriya Yoga shortcut is valid, indeed, but in the beginning it must be coupled with intense work on changing our attitudes from those which are harming us, that is, impeding the flow of *prana* through the chakras, into those which help us, and therefore enhance the flow of *prana* through the chakras. Perfecting ourselves in the *yamas* and *niyamas* and *all* the stages of Patanjali's eightfold path to enlightenment and final liberation is also necessary in order to allow a stronger upward flow of energy."

"Yes, I remember. And I do understand that there is both inner and outer work left for me to accomplish." Sabella sighed. "I just like that word 'shortcut' so much!"

"Sabella, take heart, for even to want to know about deep spiritual truths shows that you are very close to final liberation; that is, of course, relative to the millions of lifetimes you've already lived.

"Before we leave the subject of inner and outer astrology, I want to review with you the names of the planets and zodiac signs associated with each chakra. They are as follows:

Chakras	Ruling Planets	Zodiac Signs

(-negative and +positive polarities, respectively)

Chakras	Ruling Planets	Zodiac Signs
Seventh Chakra	Sun	+Leo
Sixth Chakra	Moon	-Cancer
Fifth Chakra	Mercury	-Virgo and + Gemini
Fourth Chakra	Venus	-Taurus and +Libra
Third Chakra	Mars	-Scorpio and +Aries
Second Chakra	Jupiter	-Pisces and +Sagittarius
First Chakra	Saturn	-Capricorn and +Aquarius

Issoweet continued: "In conveying this information to your students, Sabella, always caution them not to fixate, as people sometimes still do, on their zodiacal sun sign and say things like: 'I'm a Capricorn!' Saying this indicates a misunderstanding of the system, an assumption that one's sun sign is the dominant factor influencing personality characteristics.

"Similarly, we'd be wrong to look at a Capricorn's ruling planet, Saturn, and say: 'I've heard that Saturn is a very *bad* or *negative* planet, and now I find it's my personal planetary "ruler!" That can't be a good thing, can it?'

"I strongly suggest you tell your students that if they want to understand and act on information revealed in Vedic astrological charts, they must have a reading with a qualified Vedic astrologer. It takes a great deal of knowledge of this special inner astrology to understand the planetary periods we go through. The Vedic astrologer also can prescribe beneficial gemstones to alleviate the challenges in their lives.

"Finally, be sure your students understand that the plus and minus signs (+ and -) do not mean good and bad. They indicate the dualistic nature of each chakra's positive and negative polarities. Taking our shared birthdate as an example (January 15), one born on this date might look at a chart of ruling planets and zodiac signs and say: 'I'm doomed. I'm a Capricorn, which puts me on the negative side of the lowest chakra! There's probably no hope for me'!" Or Leo folks might say: 'Wow, I'm as high as you can get—right up there right at the positive side of the peak of human evolution. No problems for me'!

"No, Sabella, it's just not that simple! All the planets and their cycles, movements, and relationships to each other, throughout the dynamic and ever-changing star systems and the chakras system, *must* be taken into account."

Issoweet paused, thought a bit, and added, "I believe we've discussed Vedic astrology sufficiently for now. You understand the essence of it. At a later time if you feel the need, you may study the subject more thoroughly on your own. If ever you have further questions, I can refer you to an excellent Vedic astrologer who can give you more information.

"I suggest that we rest a while and then swim together in this beautiful azure lagoon."

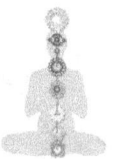

CHAPTER TWENTY-THREE

They took some time for a leisurely swim among the brightly colored fish and coral in the azure and turquoise lagoon near their chosen spot on the beach. After enjoying a snack of tropical fruit, they relaxed on the sand, looking up at the cloudless blue sky and listening to the soft sounds of the water lapping close by.

Issoweet asked Sabella, "You said you had some questions about your recent experience in the second pyramid. Would you like to ask those questions now?"

Feeling very relaxed and refreshed now, Sabella said, "Yes, I do have some questions for you." Sabella paused to organize her thoughts, for it was a sensitive issue.

"Issoweet, the second chakra is sometimes called the 'sexual chakra.' What exactly does that mean? I never felt any sort of sexual energy while visiting the second-chakra pyramid. Was there something I missed? And is it appropriate that I am asking you these kinds of question?"

Issoweet smiled and said, "Even though you have been life-linked to Thomas for many years, a union that produced three beautiful children, and I have chosen a life of celibacy, there is no reason why we shouldn't discuss sexuality. In fact, it is good that we do, because it is almost inevitable that the subject will come up whenever the second chakra is taught or discussed.

"The second chakra's location near our sexual organs is, of course, the reason it is thought to be the sexual chakra. However, the power of procreation is only a small part of its psychological impact on human behavior. The primary qualities of the first chakra are security and self-preservation, while the second chakra's main qualities are creativity and flexibility.

"Human beings have the power to draw souls from the astral world into the physical world—which is no small power!—by means of sexual union. A higher aspect of creativity is the power to manifest *whatever* one needs. An attitude of creativity is necessary to achieve anything in life, especially progress on the spiritual path. A great saint once described this type of creativity as 'the willingness to do something new or to think some new thought every day, something that you've never done or thought before.'

"In lower ages, people were limited to producing children through sexual union and the merging of sperm and ovum. In this era we are able to avoid physical union and produce children in other ways, manipulating hereditary traits and genes. But coming to terms with the sexual aspect of the second chakra and of our sexual natures in general requires a clear understanding of the creative impulse within us all. In order to mature spiritually, we need to expand our view of this impulse to mean much more than just the ability to create children.

"Sometimes sexual motivation has been called 'the urge to merge.' There is some truth to this term, for it indicates that we do not feel complete within ourselves and therefore wish to expand ourselves to *include* others, and in this case even to *produce* others.

"The truth is that we are *not* complete within ourselves until our souls achieve union with God. It is no wonder that through the fog of delusion, this urge to merge gets misdirected, and that in our confusion we think that what we are longing to merge with is another person. That sort of merging can be fulfilling, but it can *never* satisfy us completely. Unfortunately, it takes a long time to realize this truth.

"Sexual union, or even simple physical affection, is a natural part of being human. Affection can become increasingly beautiful if it is spiritualized. It can also become selfish and demanding, when it is not based in a giving, selfless love, but rather in a taking, selfish, 'what's-in-it-for-me' attitude. No sense pleasure, including sex, can continue to be enjoyable if it is overindulged. Every sense pleasure is enhanced by moderation.

"The best way to approach sexual union is to beautify and spiritualize it by seeing it as a communion between hearts and souls, rather than merely a coming together of two physical bodies. Eventually a spiritualized union can offer each partner a sweetness, mutual respect, and deep connection that will be a source of joy for themselves and for everyone around them."

Sabella was deeply impressed and said, "Issoweet, I've never heard anyone speak about sexuality, creativity, and this aspect of the second chakra as purely and clearly as you have done just now. Your words ring with truth. I am very grateful, and I shall carry these thoughts within my heart and mind forever!"

Issoweet nodded, and in her quiet way said, "I've truly enjoyed spending the day with you in this tropical paradise. I think it is time for us to depart now. You need time to reflect and prepare yourself for the next phase of your pilgrimage. You'll be visiting the third-chakra pyramid tomorrow—a very dynamic place, as you'll soon see!"

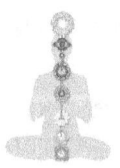

CHAPTER TWENTY-FOUR

The next day, Sabella transported herself to the river valley of the seven golden pyramids. She found Brother Solonar waiting for her just outside the third pyramid. He had a big smile on his face and welcomed her, offering a slight bow with his palms folded in front of his chest. She bowed and returned his smile.

Brother Solonar said, "Welcome back, dear child. I am glad to see you in such good spirits. Issoweet and I agree that you are making excellent progress in your pilgrimage and that you are ready for your next adventure in the third pyramid. Before we enter, do you have any questions?"

"I thank you for your gracious greetings, sir. I'm curious, what do you do when you are not with a new pilgrim helping them as they enter the pyramids? I wonder also why I have not yet seen any of the other seekers of truth who come here."

"Nor will you, my dear, for you have been designated as one who needs to have a very special pilgrimage experience—one which you must have *alone.* Yes, others do come here from time to time, sometimes alone, sometimes in groups, and I help them as best I can. Unless there are prearranged group pilgrimages, we make sure that there are no overlapping visitors. This keeps me busy enough for my tastes, and I get to meet dear and great souls like you; otherwise my time is my own, and I spend it primarily in prayer and meditation. It is a good life for me. Is there anything else you wish to know?"

"Yes, I'm feeling some trepidation about meeting Arjuna, the prince of devotees. I've long been in awe of the amazing stories of his life as the general and leader of the Pandava brothers on the battlefield of Kurukshetra.

"He was the greatest archer and warrior who ever lived and the one to whom Lord Krishna related one of the most inspiring scriptures of all times, the *Bhagavad Gita*. And more than this, I know that in that lifetime he was already a fully liberated *avatar*, who later reincarnated as Paramhansa Yogananda. How am I to behave in the presence of such a lofty being?"

"Sabella, just be yourself—no need to do or be anything else. Great though he is, he will put you at ease immediately, as you'll soon see. In many ways you are like him, with your wonderful enthusiasm and zest for life."

With no further words, Brother Solonar took Sabella's hand and guided her to the third-chakra pyramid. Immediately, great waves of bright light, warmth, and dynamic power washed over her.

Instead of seeing Arjuna as she had expected, Sabella saw the handsome twins Sahadeva and Nakula, standing on either side of a huge bonfire just outside the pyramid's entrance. Although briefly taken aback, she was pleased and comforted to see them again, for by now they felt like good friends and allies. She released Solonar's hand and went to kneel at their feet. As they lifted her up and blessed her, she could see in their eyes that indeed these two brothers not only loved her, but had become a living part of her, in a way that no mere mortals could ever be.

In unison, the twins said, "Sabella, welcome! We are here to introduce you to our brother, King Arjuna, ruler of *Manipura-loka* and keeper of the Fire Element within us all."

They gestured gracefully towards the fire, in the midst of which stood Arjuna. His countenance was blazing with energy and power, shining like a million fiery diamonds. In his right hand he held the sacred conch *Devadatta*, meaning "the gift of the gods, which gives joy." He lifted it to his lips and blew through it like a mighty horn—four times, while facing in each of the four cardinal directions in turn. The tremendous sounds vibrated throughout creation.

Almost overwhelmed with joy, Sabella knelt before Arjuna to touch his radiant feet. She was grateful for this customary greeting, for she doubted that her trembling legs would have held her up much longer anyway.

Arjuna placed his hands on top of her head to bless her. Sabella expected them to be hot or perhaps even to burn her, since he had just stepped out of the fire; but no, his hands were only slightly warm, and they gave her a tingling feeling of energy. He offered her his strong right hand and helped her stand.

"Welcome, Sabella, to *Manipura-loka*. The word *manipura* means 'blazing, shining jewel.' Sahadeva, Nakula, and Queen Draupadi told me about their time with you and your experiences in the first- and second-chakra pyramids. It is my great joy to meet you and assist you on your pilgrimage through this sacred third-chakra pyramid."

Sabella stood before Arjuna, who was indeed a magnificent being! She gazed at him in wonder. He, like Sahadeva and Nakula, was a very tall and strong warrior. She found herself looking at his giant arms and understanding why one of the many titles by which he was addressed in the *Bhagavad Gita* was "Strong-Armed." Not quite as physically handsome as the twins, still he was pleasing to look at. His hair was reddish-gold and his tan skin glowed in the sunlight.

Everything about him seemed alive, warm, vital, and energetic. There seemed to be fiery sparks radiating from his whole body and especially from his eyes, so much so that she couldn't say what color they were. Later when Thomas asked her this specific question, she could say only that "Arjuna's eyes were like blazing jewels of fire; such radiance and depth were surely not of this world!"

Sabella felt rather foolish when the first words that came out of her mouth were: "King Arjuna, how is it you stood in the fire, but were not burned?"

Solonar took this moment to say, "As I warned you, Arjuna,

you have a feisty and curious pilgrim here. I will leave her in your capable hands and be on my way."

Nakula and Sahadeva also said goodbye and slipped silently into the ether.

Arjuna gave an electric smile to the now embarrassed and red-faced Sabella and beamed energy and joy to her by saying, "Be at ease, dear one. 'Feisty and curious' are both good qualities. I have them myself!

"In order to balance those qualities, you will need to add another important third-chakra attitude into your life: FIERY SELF-CONTROL. First, please join me in a special chamber of this pyramid. The way is right through here."

Arjuna pointed at the fire, took her hand, and began leading her directly into it.

Sensing her fear, Arjuna whispered into her ear, "Don't be afraid, Sabella. Call upon your newly acquired qualities: courage and determination from the first chakra and, from your second chakra, willingness to do new and creative things.

Immediately Sabella was surrounded by a protective energy field. The fire burned all around her, but it did not hurt her at all. Instead it was invigorating, oddly cooling, and spiritually uplifting—purifying her internally and exter- nally. After passing through the fire, she felt as though she had been transformed into a new person: pure, clean, and innocent.

She saw that they were standing in a natural setting, with the sun shining brightly through the transparent walls of the pyramid. Before her was a huge, cone-shaped mountain, apparently of volcanic origin. As she looked more closely, she saw it was actually an *active* volcano, for bright reddish- orange lava was streaming down its sides.

"Ah, another fiery symbol," she thought. "But what else should I expect in the Fire Element chakra pyramid?"

"What else, indeed?" Arjuna laughed. "Let's sit here and

contemplate this magnificent volcano. It has lessons to teach you, Sabella."

They sat together on a pleasant, sunlit hillside, and Arjuna asked her, "In Pantajali's eight-limbed yoga system, what is its third 'limb,' and what does it represent?"

"That limb is *asana*," Sabella replied. "In its deepest definition, it means one's ability to sit absolutely still and unmoving. It takes a great deal of self-control to do that successfully, as anyone who has begun to earnestly practice meditation can attest.

"In ancient times, many systems of Hatha Yoga, the physical branch of Raja Yoga, were developed to help people to do so, by means of bodily stretches and positions called *asanas*. It also included breathing exercises, and in more advanced types, such as Ananda Yoga, included mental affirmations designed to reprogram the practitioners' minds to receive maximum benefit from the *asanas*."

"What would that maximum benefit be?" Arjuna asked.

"The mind cannot be stilled when the body is filled with restless energy. Hatha Yoga is an effective tool to re-channel restless energy through movement and stretching. The ultimate goal of *asana* is to be able to sit up straight without moving or even breathing. In this way, one can reach much deeper states of meditation.

"Oddly enough," Sabella continued, "in ancient times, Hatha Yoga, as helpful as it is for yoga students, was mistakenly thought to be an end unto itself. Some teachers professed that students needed to perfect 1,008 distinct yoga postures before they were ready to meditate. Some of these *asanas* required extreme flexibility and many years of discipline and practice.

"Fortunately for most truth-seekers, it soon became evident that the true meaning of *asana* was achieving the ability to sit perfectly still, in a quiet place, being comfortable, but not too comfortable, with the spine held upright and the body relaxed, but not too relaxed, and the mind under one's control, still and peaceful. Eventually, even the heart and breath become calmer or even cease completely. It is so blissful. . . ." She paused and looked at Arjuna.

"Shall we try this truest form of *asana* right now, Sabella?"

"Gladly!"

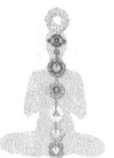

CHAPTER TWENTY-FIVE

Hours later Arjuna chanted a soft AUM to close the meditation. Sabella felt relaxed, recharged, and simply wonderful. She also felt more comfortable being with Arjuna now, even though there was a part of her that still remained in awe of this shining Great One.

The volcano stood before them in the distance, ablaze with rivers of fiery lava flowing slowly down its sides and plumes of fire, smoke, and gas coming out of its cupped peak.

"Sabella," Arjuna said quietly, "All of the first three chakras are represented in this active volcano. Can you see and understand the important symbols represented here?"

"I think so," she said. "First, the mountain is made of rocks, minerals, and earth, representing the first chakra and the Earth Element. The streams of molten lava, as well as the steam and vapor produced by the volcano, represent the ever-moving and changing liquidity of the second chakra's Water Element. And finally there is the great heat and fire which liquefies rock to create lava, which obviously represents the third chakra's Fire Element."

"Your perceptions are correct!" Arjuna approved. "Now, can you guess this volcano's name?"

Sabella thought for a moment, but could not remember any spiritual teachings that referred to a symbolic volcano with a specific name, so she shook her head, and simply said, "No."

"You are right—forgive me for the trick question." Arjuna smiled at her. "It does not have a name yet, because it was created for you alone. It is yours to name now, if you like."

Sabella was completely taken aback, for she had never been asked to name a volcano. After a few minutes of thought and a quick prayer for guidance, she stood, raised her hands toward the volcano, and spoke formally: "I name thee Mount Sah-nak-arjun. I thank you for your beauty, power, and glory. And I am grateful to you for showing me how the first three chakras are perfectly represented here by the elements of earth, water, and fire, dancing together in power and in perfect harmony."

Within her mind Sabella heard the voices of Sahadeva, Nakula, and Arjuna saying: "Beautifully said! We are honored that you have given the volcano our combined names and are happy that you understand how the first three chakras harmonize in these elemental ways."

Arjuna continued, "We have discussed how the chakras work together to move each truth-seeker towards Self-realization. This is another good example of how Sahadeva's first-chakra qualities of firmness, strength, and immovability work in harmony with Nakula's second-chakra attributes of flexibility, growth, and change—each providing exactly what the other might lack in times of challenge and also creating a perfect environment for transformation.

"Another important relationship among the chakras involves the triad of the first, second, and third chakras, which are called the 'chakras of our humanity.' The upper three are the 'chakras of our divinity,' and the heart or fourth chakra, located as it is in the middle of these two triads, is the pivotal point between them. A truth-seeker learns to offer her human nature into her divine nature for further purification.

"Being the oldest of the three younger Pandava brothers, I represent the quality of LEADERSHIP, specifically the ability to lead our more human qualities inward and upward, to be offered into our more divine qualities. Our humanness imposes a strong downward pull upon our spiritual nature. It takes fiery self-control and other warrior-like qualities to reverse the downward energy flow and turn it around, to rise upward along the inner road to freedom.

"Remember that the spiritual path is not for cowards and weaklings!"

"I see that much more clearly now," Sabella mused. "Arjuna, I always wondered why you were made the supreme general of the Pandava forces in the battle of Kurukshetra. No offense, but why was that honor not given to your eldest brother, King Yudhisthira? You and your brothers always offered him deference in every decision. Or to Bhima who was by far the largest and strongest warrior among the five of you?"

"Good question! I often wondered about it myself," Arjuna laughed. "I think it may have to do with my very close friendship with Lord Krishna. As you know, just before the beginning of the great battle, everything paused, and Krishna offered to me, on behalf of all mankind, the highest of all yoga teachings and the science of God-realization, which came to be the *Bhagavad Gita*. He also revealed himself to me in his highest God-like form. In that moment, in greatest awe and being almost completely overwhelmed by the vision, I begged him to return to his familiar human form, as my friend, cousin, and charioteer—which he graciously did.

"And frankly, I believe that I was the Pandava warrior who most needed his divine help at that time, representing as I did, in the sacred dialogue between Krishna and myself, 'Sadhu Everyman.'

"In the divine scheme of things, I was designated to ask the questions which, eventually, every human asks his Creator. What's really going on? Why am I here? And most of all, what do I do about it? You see, Sabella, like you, I always wanted to know the truth about everything. I had a strong and enthusiastic drive to understand the deepest realities of life at any cost."

"Thank you for your candid answer, Arjuna. I have another question. Sometimes the lower three chakras are characterized as being bad or evil, to be ignored or excluded from the truth-seeker's life altogether. Instead, it is sometimes taught that we should focus on the heart and the chakras above it. Why be human when one can be divine instead? Is there any

153

truth to this idea?"

Arjuna smiled. "Those who attempt to hasten their spiritual progress by ignoring the lower chakras, or any chakra for that matter, always find that it is an approach that *never* works. That is because the chakras are a holistic system, with each chakra divinely designed to contain specific energy patterns that enable humans to function physically, mentally, emotionally, and spiritually. Each of these patterns is tightly interconnected with the energy patterns of the other chakras. They work together cooperatively and beneficially.

"In short, the first three chakras *cannot* be ignored without consequences.

"To focus excessively on only one or two chakras in order to 'unblock' or heal whatever you think is wrong with you, never works either. Again, they are too intimately and dynamically connected to be held separate from one another. They are divinely designed to help each other.

"Queen Draupadi's story of her marriage to us, the Pandava brothers, is symbolic of the fact that all the chakras must function together in a very intimate way. Although she chose me to be her husband, circumstances conspired to have her become the wife of my four brothers, as well."

"I hope this is not an inappropriate question, Arjuna, but did you ever feel short-changed having to share your beautiful wife with your brothers, especially because, as you say, she had chosen you *first*?" Sabella sincerely wanted to know.

"No, never, for our unusual marriage was all a part of the symbolic 'divine play' manifesting through our lives as the Pandava brothers. And because we all loved each other very much, we found ways of working it all out. Draupadi is a woman of great power, and she linked us all together as nothing else could." Arjuna smiled at the memories.

"Before we leave this subject of the relationships among the chakras, I wanted to clarify something. The more people live in a worldly way, the lower what might be called their spiritual 'center of gravity' or place of primary energy-focus will be. The more spiritually inclined a person is, the higher within the chakras system one's energetic focus will tend to be. To spiritualize your consciousness, it is best to increasingly focus your energy in the upper three chakras."

Sabella was confused and asked, "But how can the lower chakras be awakened, if one's concentration is directed exclusively to the higher chakras?"

Arjuna answered, "One's concentration should not be focused *exclusively* on any one chakra, except when the energy of that chakra is being offered up to the sixth chakra in meditation. Nevertheless, maintaining a stronger focus on the higher chakras generates a magnetism that attracts the energy upward, *through* the lower chakras into the higher chakras.

"It is this upward flow of energy within each chakra that constitutes its awakening. By paying excessive attention to the lower chakras, especially in their outer aspects, which is the normal focus of worldly people, their life-force flows downward and outward, through the chakras and the senses, and out into the world. In this case, it is the *outer* rather than the *inner* aspects of the lower chakras that create a greater magnetism, drawing the energy of the upper, more spiritually inclined chakras downward into the outer aspects of the lower chakras and even further outward into entrenched worldly attachments.

"In any case, it is not a question of *exclusive* concentration. In relation to one another, and spiritually speaking, the upper triad of chakras deserves more attention than the lower, especially in meditation. Nevertheless, please remember that *no chakra should be neglected*! Each chakra can and should be spiritualized through a concentrated focus on its inner, more beneficial aspects. This is preferable to allowing the chakras to 'leak' energy continuously outward into the world.

"Another excellent and effective way of spiritualizing the chakras is to practice chanting 'AUM' mentally three times at each of them, moving up and down the spine several times. This withdraws the energy from the outer body into the inner centers. Once you feel the energy in the chakras, draw it upward by concentrating at the sixth chakra, the point between the eyebrows, and the symbolic dwelling place of Lord Krishna.

"May I guide you through this practice now, Sabella?"

Sabella was honored to have Arjuna lead her in chanting AUM for each chakra. His voice was so vibrant that it seemed to light up each chakra in turn, up and down her astral spine. His voice drew her mind increasingly inward with softer and softer AUMs. On the final round, he stopped at the sixth chakra, and they sat in perfect silence for a while.

After a short time, Arjuna asked Sabella to open her eyes. On the glowing, golden lawn in front of her, a small *homa* or sacrificial fire had appeared. Arjuna used it to lead her in a sacred fire ceremony. They chanted together in Sanskrit, first the *Gayatri Mantra* and then the *Mahamrityunjaya Mantra*, seven rounds of each: one round for each chakra.

While chanting the *mantras* Arjuna spooned a little *ghee*, or clarified butter, into the fire, which represented devotion. He then tossed a few grains of rice into the flames, which represented the seeds of all past bad karma, which is holding back our spiritual progress. At the close of the ceremony, he led her in an affirmation several times, first loudly, then softly, then whispering, then mentally—going deeper and deeper within:

I cast my thoughts, desires, and all past karma into the flames of joy. I am whole, I am pure, I am one with Thee!

Arjuna, who was sitting beside her on a golden silk cushion, said: "Sabella, I'd like you to join me now in a simple ceremony of purification.

"Fire is a symbol of cleansing, purification, and release of all past karma and unwanted habits and tendencies. Please think of a few harmful third-chakra attitudes which may have troubled you in the past or which you feel may still be holding you back from spiritual progress in this lifetime."

Sabella thought carefully, and began her list: "LACK OF SELF-CONTROL, TRYING TO CONTROL OR MANIPULATE EVERYONE AND EVERYTHING AROUND ME, BEING TOO INTENSE, FEELING GUILTY, LACK OF DISCIPLINE, HAVING TOO SEVERE A SENSE OF SELF-DISCIPLINE, SELF-ESTEEM ISSUES, SELF-HATRED, RELENTLESSNESS, MERCILESSNESS, CRUELTY, and a DICTATORIAL ATTITUDE."

Arjuna was surprised! "That's quite a list and more than a few, Sabella. It's hard for me to see all these harmful qualities in you."

"Well, you said, '. . . either now *or in the past.*' After visiting many of my past lives, I can assure you that I manifested all of these negative qualities and more at one time or another; fortunately I was able to observe their consequences in later lifetimes. I feel that with God's help, I have left most of them behind me forever."

"Most of them?" Arjuna inquired, lifting an aristocratic eyebrow.

"I'm still working on a few CONTROL issues here and there. I sometimes give in to feelings of GUILT for not measuring up to the high standards I set for myself. Or I feel disappointed in my students at times and perhaps try to push them harder than they are ready to be pushed. I think you could call that MANIPULATION. Lately I am finding that I can recognize these qualities quickly when they show up in my life, and I do my best to correct them immediately. In any case, I am glad to offer all of them now for purification."

"Excellent!" Arjuna said. "Please come kneel before me. I believe you are familiar with the simple words we say as a part of this ceremony."

Sabella knelt before Arjuna with her palms folded at her heart. With eyes closed, she deeply and sincerely prayed, "I seek purification by the grace of God."

After a few moments of silence, during which she felt great waves of blessings and healing flowing through her, she heard Arjuna say to her, "The Master says, 'Open your heart to me, and I will enter and take charge of your life.'"

Arjuna gently touched her at the center of her chest and continued to pray that she be released from all the harmful qualities she had mentioned. Then he said softly, "By the grace of our Masters you are free!"

He asked her to turn and bow before the *homa* which was still burning brightly.

With a fiery power flowing through her unlike any she had felt before, she complied. Looking into the fire, she felt its warmth and purifying energy. She mentally cast all that she was, had ever been, and ever hoped to be, into its bright, mesmerizing flames. As the fire burned more and more brightly, it seemed to call to her to enter into it completely. She looked at Arjuna questioningly.

"If you feel ready," was his only reply.

Without hesitation, she stood and walked into the flames. Amazingly, the fire was only comfortably warm. She walked with bare feet on live coals and understood that neither the fire nor the coals could burn or hurt her in any way. On the contrary, she felt comforted and blessed by the fire's bright light, crackling and sparking all around her.

The sounds of plucked stringed instruments—harps, vinas, and sitars—droned loudly in her right inner ear, gloriously vibrating in heavenly harmonies, intricate and completely new to her ears. She was hearing the AUM sounds of the third chakra as she had never experienced them before.

The whole experience was joyful, healing, cleansing, and other-worldly. She felt all the negative qualities of the third chakra melting away and the beneficial qualities taking their place: FIERY SELF-CONTROL, ZEAL, ENTHUSIASM, DYNAMIC ENERGY, ZEST FOR LIFE, LOVING LEADERSHIP, PERSONAL POWER, SELF-ACCEPTANCE, and the greatest INNER JOY she had ever known. She watched as these positive qualities swirled around her, entering her being, and uplifting her spirit.

Overwhelmed with joy, Sabella decided that the purifying fire of the third-chakra pyramid was a perfect place to be, and that she should remain here, now and forever.

In the instant she had this thought, she felt a cool arm wrap around her shoulders, and she heard a familiar whisper, "Sabella, remember that this is only the third chakra pyramid. Yes, I know it is very powerful and joyful here, a great blessing for you to experience, but please let me remind you that you have another four pyramids to visit before your pilgrimage is complete."

It was Lady Kundalini, of course—who always seemed to appear just in the right place and at the right time.

With a sigh, Sabella stepped out of the fire. King Arjuna and Queen Draupadi were standing near her, arm in arm, smiling blissfully at each other. The ceremonial *homa* on the ground and the active volcano Mt. Sah-nak-arjun in the distance had vanished.

They were now in an initiation temple at the peak of the third-chakra pyramid. Its altar held many large yellow, red, and coral-colored candles, with a large iron lamp in the middle, beaming glorious, golden light rays out the top of the pyramid into the night sky. A miraculous wall of living fire burned behind the altar, without a visible source of fuel. It glowed brightly with all the colors of the rainbow, as well as a few she was sure she had never seen before.

Queen Draupadi, alias Lady Kundalini, beautiful beyond description and dressed in her usual dark veils, came to Sabella, kissed her gently on her cheek, and said, "I will see you again soon." She vanished before Sabella could say another word.

Arjuna wore the fire-colored ceremonial robe of the third chakra—golden yellow, deep red, and glowing coral. As he touched Sabella at the spiritual eye in blessing, she realized that she, too, wore a similar robe. Their garments shimmered with firelight; they were certainly the most beautiful garments she had ever seen.

159

Arjuna said quietly: "Dear one, you have my blessings and my love, now and always. Remember never to misuse the great power of the third chakra. This power can easily harm others or yourself unless it is offered inward and upward to God. It can also be harmful if it is not balanced by the cooling, flowing water energy of the second chakra below it and the loving, soothing energy of the fourth chakra above it.

"We see how fire, when under control, is valuable for cooking our food, lighting up a dark night, warming our bodies, and cheering our spirits. But a raging forest fire will show you the painful and destructive danger of fire out of control. So it is with the third chakra's Fire Element within us—it demands our respect, and it requires our control.

He added a new pendant to her chakras necklace to hang above the two medallions she had already received. It was a small disk made of iron, the appropriately strong metallic symbol of the third chakra. On it was a yellow lotus blossom with ten petals, and a large piece of polished red coral with a blood-red triangle, its tip pointing upward in the center. "Like a little two-dimensional pyramid," Sabella happily observed.

Arjuna, catching even this tiny, fleeting thought, said, "When you return home, ask Issoweet to give you more information about the chakra shapes—it is knowledge that will be beneficial to you in the future."

Asking her to kneel for initiation, Arjuna said formally: "My child, you have acted wisely and well in this sacred and fiery pyramid. May the Divine Light burn brightly in you now and forever, and may we be one in that light someday."

He placed both his hands on the top of her head and blessed her gently, just as he had done when she first entered his pyramid. He said quietly, "I am King Arjuna of the Pandava brothers, son of Indra, king of the gods and all the heavenly realms. Henceforth, you possess the power of control over all fire, to be in it unharmed, and to manifest it or quench it, as you will. You have its healing, purifying blessings within you now, and you may also offer these blessings to others."

As she stood, she felt tears spring to her eyes at the thought of leaving Arjuna.

160

"I am your friend forever, Sabella! I truly live inside you, as do all my brothers, my wife, the Goddess Kundalini, Lord Krishna, and another great being whom you have not yet met."

Comforted, Sabella bowed before him, palms folded. She said enthusiastically: "What's next on the agenda? I'm ready!"

"Soon enough, you'll visit the kingdom of the heart in the fourth-chakra pyramid. I know that you feel prepared and greatly energized by your visit here, for that is part of the dynamic power bestowed on us through the awakening and purification of the third chakra.

"My suggestion is that you continue the pattern you have already established for yourself. Go home, rest, meditate, pray, and let yourself integrate these unique, fiery energy patterns. It is possible for the newly enhanced fire of your third chakra to burn you out quickly, so be with it peacefully for a while and let your system become accustomed to this dynamic power.

"Talk with Thomas and Issoweet, too. Then in a little while, when the time is right, you'll meet my elder brother King Bhima. He'll take a little getting used to at first." Arjuna smiled mischievously and vanished.

CHAPTER TWENTY-SIX

Arriving home, Sabella was delighted to see that once again Thomas had prepared a meal for them to enjoy together. As she smelled the luscious aromas coming from their kitchen, she found herself to be ravenously hungry—hungrier, actually, than she remembered ever having been in her life!

"What is going on inside me now?" she wondered.

Thomas answered her thought-question, "As you are just now emerging from your third-chakra pyramid experience, and the third chakra influences everything having to do with your stomach and your physical body's digestion and assimilation abilities, it stands to reason that you might be unusually hungry."

"Ah, dear life-partner, you may be right about that! Thank you for being so thoughtful. All the cooking that you have been doing for me lately is surely going to spoil me! When can we eat?"

"Step out onto the patio, and I'll serve you in style, my dearest." Thomas smiled at her affectionately. She looked as energetic and joyful as he had ever seen her, and he looked forward to hearing about her meeting with Arjuna and the rest of her most recent adventure.

The next day, still energized and refreshed, she mentally contacted Issoweet and asked when and where they should meet. Issoweet got back to her immediately and transmitted that if it was convenient, she'd arrive at Sabella's home early the next day, and they'd take it from there.

Sabella was grateful for a day off, and spent her time in domestic duties, recording her third-chakra experiences, and then taking a thoroughly enjoyable swim in the river, followed by a short nap in her hammock.

Early the next day, Issoweet appeared on Sabella's upper deck just as she was finishing her morning meditation.

"Sabella, you look absolutely radiant," Issoweet said. "The third-chakra pyramid certainly did recharge your energy patterns!"

"Hello, Issoweet, welcome to my home! Yes, I am feeling perky and full of fiery energy. Meeting King Arjuna and my adventures in the third pyramid were amazing experiences for me, to say the least! And I have questions, of course. Are we going somewhere new today?"

"Yes, there is a place I'd like you to see. It will be very different from our visit to the tropical beach, but I think you'll enjoy it also. Hold my hand, and I'll take you there."

Immediately they were transported to a most unusual setting. Sabella hoped it was a friendly setting, for she found that they were enveloped in absolute darkness. She could sense that they were underground, deep within the earth, with rock walls all around them. Except for a few pleasantly musical dripping sounds, it was absolutely silent.

Issoweet said, "Are your eyes open, Sabella?"

"I think so."

"Then close them for a moment. I don't want the light to dazzle your vision."

After a moment, Issoweet said, "Now, dear Sabella, open your eyes and look around you."

The first thing Sabella saw was a small fire, like the *homa* by which she and Arjuna had sat recently. She looked around and gasped in surprise and delight at what she saw. They were sitting in an underground ice cave, on a small, flat boulder in the middle of a frozen lake.

The ice in the lake was exceptionally clear, except for what seemed to be frozen bubbles captured inside it. It appeared to be bottomless. The flickering fire illuminated stalactites and stalagmites made of ice in all sizes, some as tiny as threads, others as large as a temple column, and all sizes in between.

In the past Sabella had visited limestone caverns and seen formations which looked something like these. But never had she seen formations made entirely of silvery, sparkling ice! They were the source of the dripping noises she'd heard when they arrived in the cave. Now, the firelight made them sparkle, flicker, and glow in amazing ways. It all shone like a fairyland, and was cool and pleasant.

"Issoweet, this is lovely! Are we on or in the earth?" Sabella asked.

"Very much *in* the earth! We are in a lava tube in a volcanic area in the north-central part of ancient California."

"What is a lava tube? And will there be any more lava coming through it any time soon?"

"Sabella, I love your quick wit! But, no, this area is part of a shield volcano that is inactive."

"And what about all the ice formations and the ice lake? Where do they come from?" Sabella inquired. "This place is unusual and very beautiful—unlike anything I've ever seen before!"

"A lava tube is formed when lava flows smoothly beneath the hardened surface of an earlier active lava flow. As it cools, it forms cave-like channels, like this one. The icy formations occur when rainwater or melted snow flows into the lava tube. In an area like this one, where the winter temperatures drop below freezing, the ice formations freeze around the entrance to the tube, creating a trap for the cold air, which sinks further into the underground tube. These conditions preserve the ice formations well after the spring and summer temperatures rise, sometimes allowing them to remain as year-round cave decorations.

"The formations are all quite fragile. We won't stay long, lest our fire, small as it is, adversely affect the beauty of this place. In any case, I thought you'd enjoy feeling the first three chakra symbols all around you, in slightly different forms. And while we're here, I'd like to ask you to participate in a brief ceremony of purification, just like the one Arjuna did for you, except that now I'd like you to purify me."

Sabella was momentarily speechless. "But am I qualified to perform such a ceremony for you, Issoweet? You are my mentor and. . . ."

"Yes, child, it is time for you to become a Lightbearer in a more formal way—to act as a channel for inner purification for anyone who seeks it from you. You have earned this honor.

"I know you are thinking that I, as your mentor, don't need purification." Issoweet laughed and continued. "This is not true. I am still a mortal, and like all mortals I err in my actions and attitudes. So, please let us proceed." Issoweet knelt before Sabella and said the familiar words: "I seek purification by the grace of God."

"Thank you, Issoweet. I humbly accept the honor and the responsibility." She offered Issoweet the brief Ceremony of Purification. She could feel the grace and energy pouring through her and out through her hands, in purification and healing. What a blessing to be a channel of light in this way! She remembered the words of one of the Great Ones: "The channel is blessed by what flows through it."

After a few minutes of silent meditation in the cool ice cave, Issoweet transported them to a spot above ground, near the ice cave's entrance. They were standing in the midst of an ancient black lava flow. The lava, molten rock at one time, had solidified into fantastic shapes.

Sabella asked, "The 'volcano motif' again?"

"Yes, Sabella. I know how Arjuna asked you to name the active volcano he showed you in the third-chakra pyramid. Mt. Sah-nak-arjun is a somewhat unusual but lovely name, and it was thoughtful of you to choose that name in honor of the first three Pandava brothers. Look behind you now."

Sabella turned to see a sight that, although she had seen it

165

in another lifetime, still took her breath away. There in the distance, completely covered in shining white snow, was Mt. Shasta and her smaller sister volcano, Mt. Shastina. At the summit of Mt. Shasta they could see large cloud-streams being blown southward, looking like whipped cream being blown off the top of a giant scoop of vanilla ice cream.

It was early morning on a spring day, sunny with a little chill in the fresh, spicy-smelling air.

"Let's have a picnic and enjoy the view." Issoweet's mental voice sounded like that of a happy child.

Instantly, they were transported closer to the mountain, away from the rugged black lava fields. They sat in a flower-filled meadow near a tiny brook tinkling over colorful stones. Spread before them on the ground for their enjoyment were a red-and-white–checkered tablecloth, a picnic basket, and some comfortable cushions to sit on.

Following Nakula's reminder always to meditate in the presence of water, they sat for a few minutes, listening to the brook's pleasant murmurings, appreciating the beautiful day, and taking it inside themselves in grateful thanksgiving to God.

They thoroughly enjoyed both the picnic and the magnificent view of Mt. Shasta. Resting after their meal, Sabella said, "Is this a good time to ask a few questions, Issoweet?"

"Fire away!" Issoweet laughed at her fire pun. "Did you find the third-chakra pyramid to be an exciting place?"

"Nice pun, Issoweet, and yes, it was truly amazing. The best part was getting to meet and spend time with Arjuna. What a privilege—I don't think there are words to express what I felt in his presence. I know I'll never be the same.

"Arjuna asked that you explain more about the shapes that represent the chakras, which leads me to my first question. We discussed earlier that the inner shapes and colors for the first three chakras were a yellow square, a white half-moon, and a blood-red triangle.

"I understand that these are the shapes and colors we see in the spiritual eye when the *kundalini* energy begins its rise through the innermost astral spine. But my question is this: Why are all the places I am visiting to learn more about the chakras shaped like pyramids? Wouldn't it make more sense for them to be shaped like a square, then a dome, then a pyramid and so on, to correspond with the inner chakra shapes?"

Issoweet answered: "These chakra pyramids were created in our planet's most recent Descending Treta Yuga and have endured for many thousands of years into the present Ascending Treta Yuga. The perfect architectural shape for Treta Yuga is a pyramid, as evidenced by the fact that you and I, and most of the people of our era, live in one. These shapes are related to the yugas and the ways in which time moves through the cycles of ascending and descending energy.

"For each of the four yugas, there is an appropriate architectural shape, which corresponds to one of the first four chakras and its inwardly perceived shape. The square or diamond shape is connected with the lowest age of Kali Yuga. That is why people living in Kali Yuga often built cube-like structures—square buildings with many sharp angles.

"The dome shape is better suited to the energy of Dwapara Yuga. During this age, there were many buildings with soft curves, arches, circles, or, at the very least, elevated ceilings. As people became more sensitive with the advancing age, they didn't care for flat ceilings 'pressing' on their heads. The dome, a beautiful shape which resonates with the second chakra's sweetly curving energy, is shaped like the top of your head or the 'bowl of the sky' above you. In the most recent Ascending Dwapara Yuga, the dome eventually became the predominant shape for living spaces and places of worship.

"In Treta Yuga, our present age, the dome shape extended further upward to a point of focus, evolving into a pyramid. The pyramid is the ideal shape for the present era and a very powerful tool for deep meditation, as you've seen.

"The final evolution of this form, appropriate for the highest age, Satya Yuga, is the sphere."

"How can people live in a sphere?" Sabella asked. Thinking about it a little more, she speculated. "Perhaps they will live in spherical space stations. Outer space has no gravity, so it might be feasible."

"Possibly so, but think a little more about it, Sabella. What is the shape of the planet you live on?"

"A sphere, of course! That would be the perfect shape for Satya Yuga, when the climate is always perfect and there is no need for any sort of shelter to protect you from bad weather. The whole sphere of our planet would be your home. I've heard life in Satya Yuga described as living in an earthly paradise."

Issoweet was pleased by Sabella's astute observation. "You remember ancient myths and stories of earthly paradises such as the Garden of Eden or Shangri-La. These myths were born out of dim memories of a past Satya Yuga."

"I vaguely remember something about the story of the Garden of Eden," Sabella said. "Wasn't it about people who lived in a beautiful garden but were driven out of the garden by God, because of their sinful actions? What was *that* all about?"

Issoweet smiled. "This is an effect of the rising and falling of the ages. In a descending yuga, knowledge, and especially spiritual awareness, is gradually lost. Human beings definitely feel and mourn the loss. The wise ones alive at that time understand and adapt as well as possible. The chakra pyramids you are visiting on this pilgrimage were manifested at such a time. Through creating the seven golden pyramids, they hoped to preserve important spiritual wisdom through the darker ages to come.

"When the ages again began their ascent, this wisdom blossomed forth. We can see this happening in the current Ascending Treta Yuga. So although it seems that the shapes of initiation temples in a chakras pilgrimage should have been represented more correctly by a square, a dome, or a sphere, our wise ancient ancestors felt that the pyramid was the best shape for preservation of powerful spiritual knowledge. The pyramid shape helps to bring wisdom to a sharp focus for us, just as the pyramid has a sharp point at its top. Does this answer your question, Sabella?"

"Yes, I see the logic of it. I have another question. I know that chakras five and six have inner colors and shapes associated with them. So why is there no corresponding architecture for the yugas that represent the upper chakras?"

Issoweet said, "Because on this planet, there are only four yugas: Kali, Dwapara, Treta, and Satya. Their energy corresponds with the qualities of the first four chakras. Perhaps in other yuga cycles on other galaxies or planets, there may be more yuga divisions. But for now, these higher chakras are not represented architecturally on earth. I doubt that humans could live comfortably in something made of 'smoke with specks of light,' which are the inner colors and shape of the fifth chakra.

"I'm not sure how to even imagine a place shaped like the gold, blue, and silver-white spiritual eye, but my best guess is that when the energy of a planet moves beyond the fourth chakra, no architectural forms are necessary. At that point, people's consciousness has advanced enough spiritually to go beyond the need for buildings or physical forms of any kind. Formlessness, most likely, would be the 'shape' for such advanced souls. Wrap your head around that idea, if you dare, Sabella." Issoweet laughed with delight.

"I love it, Issoweet! I enjoy all your interesting speculations. It is such a joy to let my mind flow freely into unknown realms, with you as my guide."

"It is my joy also. You are a bright and shining star among all the students I've had the privilege to guide over the years."

"One more little question before we leave this subject, Issoweet. Why do the chakra pyramids appear to be golden instead of some other color?"

Issoweet sighed, "Why do *you* think this is so, Sabella? I'm sure you must have speculated on this matter at least somewhat, or you wouldn't have asked me."

Sabella paused and thought more about her question, "Gold is the color of the metal representing the seventh chakra. Does that mean that even though the pyramid shape is related to Treta Yuga and the third chakra, our goal in moving through the chakras is always to lift the consciousness toward the highest chakra? Perhaps this is one reason why, on our planet, gold often has been treasured above other metals."

"Basically, you are correct, Sabella. We are 'going for the gold.' Remember how Oceana Lumina won a gold medal in the 'sustained right attitude' event during the last Olympic Games?

"But as usual, there is a more subtle aspect to the metals associated with each chakra. If you don't mind, let's discuss the chakra metals later. Right now, I have another important subject we need to cover, before we can call it a day."

CHAPTER TWENTY-SEVEN

Twilight was descending over the flowery meadow, coloring Mt. Shasta's snowy, white shoulders with shifting shades of orange and pink. It was stunning to watch!

Issoweet said: "We must leave soon, but let's discuss the subject of the chakra's elements quickly. People often wonder what is meant by the term, 'the traditional *elements* of the chakras,' thinking that the word 'element' might refer to the chemical elements in nature, such as oxygen, hydrogen, or carbon.

"In this case, an 'element' is meant to be viewed as a spiritual symbol. There are five such 'elements' in all: earth, water, fire, air, and ether. In the yoga teachings they are always given in that sequence, relative to the first five chakras.

"On a cosmic level each of these 'elements' represents an elemental stage of creation. The consciousness of Spirit, when it becomes condensed enough to enter into gross material manifestation, first becomes the cosmic energy, or the Ether Element, out of which the physical universe appears. This energy condenses into cosmic gases, or the Air Element, which in turn condense to form the fiery stars, or the Fire Element. As fiery matter cools, it becomes molten, representing the Water Element of cosmic manifestation. As it cools still further, it becomes solid; thus it reaches its final, elemental stage of material manifestation, the Earth Element.

"The elements also describe the stages of the soul's descent into matter, and, when reversed, the progressive stages from matter into its final liberation. In the process of entering the physical body, the consciousness hypnotizes itself into thinking that we have *become* the solid matter of our bodies. To break this hypnosis, we must identify ourselves with our souls.

"We will find it easier to retrace our steps Godward if we also, instead of denying God's presence in the lower elemental manifestations, draw divine understanding from every manifestation. For God truly has become everything. It is our growing ability to perceive this fact clearly, which eventually allows us to behold God perfectly, everywhere and in everything.

"By ever-deepening realizations, we 'de-solidify' ourselves and gradually climb back up the 'elemental staircase' by which we descended into delusion—from earth, to water, to fire, to air, to ether, and beyond into what might be called 'super-ether,' which is pure thought or consciousness."

"O! Upward climb the living tree!" Sabella enthused, quoting a line from one of Paramhansa Yogananda's metaphysical poems.

The twinkling stars were adorning Lady Shasta's darkening, but still slightly glowing slopes. Sabella didn't feel ready to go home yet. Issoweet, sensing this, said, "What else is on your mind, my dear?"

"I was *very* inspired by being with Arjuna. Before we leave, would you tell me a story from his life?"

"There are many, Sabella, and I'm sure you've heard most of them at one time or another. But I will tell you two of my favorite stories and, in my opinion, the most important ones.

"In the *Mahabharata*, Lord Krishna, representing God in an inner conversation with the soul, offers two choices to the primary protagonists in the upcoming battle: Arjuna, who represents the sincere devotee and his cousin King Duryodhana, who represents material desire.

'You must choose,' Krishna said, 'between me and my army. If you choose me, I will be with you in battle, drive your chariot and offer my blessings and advice, but I will take no personal part in the battle. If you choose my huge and powerful army, you will have a vast force fighting on your side, but you will not have me.'

"Arjuna, given first choice, replied, much to Duryodhana's surprise and delight, by saying: 'I choose you, Krishna. For wherever you *are*, there is victory!' Duryodhana was overjoyed to receive the gift of Krishna's entire, vast army. In the end Arjuna, his brothers, and the Pandava army won the war, even though greatly outnumbered by Duryodhana and the Kaurava forces.

"Never forget, Sabella, in every one of life's choices, if you choose to have God and guru at your side and *on* your side, helping and guiding you, then victory and final liberation are assured."

"The second story happened much earlier in Arjuna's life. He and his brothers and cousins were being trained in the arts of weaponry and war by the greatest master of those skills, Dronacharya. To test his students' archery skills, Dronacharya placed a target shaped like a bird at the top of a very tall pole, located a long distance away. Each of the cousins and brothers were asked to shoot at the bird-target.

"Before being allowed to proceed, each student was asked by Dronacharya: 'Tell me what you see before you shoot.'

"Several answers were given, such as, 'I see the sky, the pole, the bird, the clouds, my teacher, my bow, my arrow,' and so on. Each one of them, although highly-trained archers shot their arrows, but did not hit the target. Finally Arjuna was asked to come forward to shoot at the bird-target. When asked what he saw, he said calmly, 'I see the eye of the bird.'

'And what else do you see?' Dronacharya asked him.

'Nothing! I see only the eye of the bird.' Arjuna said.

'Go ahead and shoot; I know you will not miss.' And it was so."

"Arjuna's perfect power of self-control and concentration would not let him fail. This story is symbolic of the great concentration necessary to reach our spiritual goals. We can look at nothing else but the 'single eye' in meditation and try

173

to absorb ourselves deeply enough to actually *become* it."
Issoweet stood to indicate that it was time to leave.

"Don't give me that little frown, Sabella. I know what's on your mind. You want to know more about King Bhima, ruler of the heart chakra, whom you will meet tomorrow at the fourth-chakra pyramid. In many of the stories about him, he is depicted as being bigger than life and often frightening in his actions.

"It is said that when he became passionately angry at his enemies or those wanting to harm him or his family, he would rip a giant tree out of the earth with which to slay them. But please don't fear this ferocious side of his nature; he is also a 'king of hearts.' I predict that you will soon appreciate his great loving spirit, and I know he will love you also.

"Now it's time to return to our homes!"

CHAPTER TWENTY-EIGHT

Early the following morning, Sabella transported herself to the small pavilion beside the River Sushumna. Faithful Brother Solonar was waiting for her, smiling in welcome.

He said, "Issoweet tells me that you have a few concerns about meeting Bhima. Is this true, and if so, how can I help?"

Sabella replied, "She assured me that I have nothing at all to fear. All of my hosts so far in this sacred river valley have offered me only love, support, and encouragement. I felt they wanted me to have the best possible experiences on this pilgrimage. Still. . . ."

"Yes, still what?" Solonar asked. "Let me know your concerns."

"I would if I could, but, that is my problem, I think. I'm not really sure *what* my present concerns are. Perhaps it is the thought of Bhima's giant size or the rumors of his ripping trees out of the ground to use as weapons, when he was angered. May we meditate together for a while? Surely meditating with you will bring me inner peace."

"Of course!" Brother Solonar was happy with her request. He suggested that they move a little closer to the Sushumna River and sit under a large, inviting shade tree. The air was still, and except for the rushing sounds of the river, all was quiet and peaceful.

Sabella prayed deeply at the beginning of her meditation for courage, peace of mind, and openness of heart. After all, it was the heart chakra pyramid she was about to enter. She also practiced many rounds of deep, cleansing breaths, which seemed appropriate—the heart chakra being responsible for the lungs and the ability to breathe. Soon she was completely still in body and mind, in a breathless state, the ultimate goal of all yogic breathing exercises. Even her physical heartbeat was barely discernible.

Solonar prayed for her, as he meditated beside her.

After about an hour, Sabella heard a deep gong or bell-like sound, drawing her even more deeply into her heart chakra. She recognized this sound as the AUM-sound of the fourth chakra. It was lovely, playing upon her heart-strings and opening her spirit to divine love. She felt enveloped in that love and strengthened in every way.

As she was closing her meditation, she was very startled to hear the sound of giant church bells pealing through the air. This time, she was sure the sounds were not coming from inside herself.

She looked at Solonar who smiled back at her and nodded toward the fourth pyramid, gleaming golden in the sunshine. "That's Bhima's way of inviting you to join him. Do have any further questions or concerns before proceed?"

Sabella searched her mind and realized that all her questions or fears had either been answered or had vanished altogether—in fact, she wasn't even sure what they had been! Wondering at the change in herself, she realized that she had been depending on her intellect without consulting the deeper feelings of her heart. She had let her mind roil itself up into waves of restless doubts and questions. She had neglected to consult her heart, where all true answers can be received, if we but ask.

Answering Brother Solonar, she said, "No more questions, my friend. I am ready!"

In an instant they were standing inside the fourth-chakra pyramid. There was Bhima, the fourth of the Pandava brothers, renowned in song and legend. Sabella fearlessly moved forward to touch his very large feet in greeting, but he quickly gathered her up in his giant arms for a big, Bhima-type hug.

Bhima had often been cautioned by his brothers and mother to go easy on the hugs, where regular human beings were concerned. Crushed ribs could result if he did not exercise care.

Sabella felt embraced by his energy which was surprisingly gentle and loving for such a powerful warrior. His booming voice said, "Sabella Lovingheart, I am so glad you have arrived at *Anahata-loka*, the airy realm of love and joy. My brothers have told me about you. Welcome, welcome! I love you!"

Sabella, even in her state of awe at being held in the arms of King Bhima, felt he was being somewhat presumptuous. "I thank you, sir. But how can you say that you love me when you don't even *know* me yet!"

"Ah, but I do, dear one, I do indeed! For I dwell in your heart and in the hearts of all. But forgive me. I forget that my energy can be a little overwhelming at first. My younger brother Arjuna chides me for being that way, saying that sometimes I can 'out-enthuse' even him, who is the epitome of zest, zeal, vigor, and enthusiasm for life. Then again, he is a master of perfect self-control, which I sometimes lack. I often need to call on his energy to balance my own. The powerful emotions of the heart can really get out of control, as you may have noticed in your own life, yes?" He laughed loudly and contagiously.

Sabella laughed too—she doubted anyone could have resisted sharing a great belly-laugh with Bhima. He placed her softly on the ground, and she stepped back to get a better look at the huge being standing before her. He was about twelve feet tall and exceedingly muscular—amazing to behold. She could see why he was called "the strongest warrior who had ever lived." He reminded her of one of the giant redwood trees that still grew on earth.

His smile was full of light, like welcome sunshine appearing after a rainstorm. His laughter boomed throughout the pyramid, causing flocks of colorful birds to rise up from the trees and fly in formation over his head. A few of them landed on his giant shoulders, singing in happiness as he gently crooned back to them.

Solonar sent a thought into Sabella's mind, "I can see that

you are feeling more comfortable now, so I will leave you. Be happy—I know you will!" And he was gone.

Bhima wasted no time. He took Sabella by the hand and said, "Do you like to fly? I hope so, because the best way to see *Anahata-loka* is by air!"

Without waiting for an answer, Bhima launched them into the air, and they soared above the treetops, with brightly colored birds, butterflies, and dragonflies flitting all around them,

"You are quite light on your feet, Bhima, for such a big man. Where are we going?" Sabella laughed, a little breathless, but very much enjoying the feeling of flying, something she had rarely experienced, except in her dreams.

Bhima roared again with joyful laughter. "The heart chakra has a huge and often unwieldy energy field, so it takes a big man to oversee it. And this is the chakra of the Air Element!" Bhima said. "You'll see where we're going soon enough, and flying is the easiest way to get there."

It was an amazing sensation—to feel so light and free. Clouds blew by them as she enjoyed the exquisite landscape below them.

After a time, Bhima said: "Let's sit and chat for a while."

Assuming they were going to land somewhere, Sabella looked down below her.

"How about right there," Bhima said, smiling at her startled face as he pointed to a large, brightly colored rainbow coming down from one cloud and then curving upward to another, making a colorful swing-seat for two.

"I've never tried sitting on a rainbow before," Sabella said. "Is it possible to do that?"

"Again, this is the Air Element kingdom, my dear little one. Many new talents become available to those who visit here. If you don't find it comfortable, we can sit on that big puffy cloud—over there in the distance—your choice." Bhima said.

"Let's start here," Sabella said. "But I'd like to try the cloud later, if you don't mind."

"Ah, a woman who appreciates variety—I like that! My wife, Queen Draupadi likes to ride the winds of change also—I believe you know her?"

They relaxed on the gently swinging rainbow and began to talk about airy subjects.

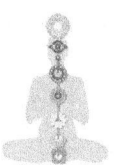

CHAPTER TWENTY-NINE

Sabella began by asking the meaning of *Anahata*, the Sanskrit name for this chakra.

Bhima answered, "It means 'un-struck.' Imagine a huge bell (which, as you know, is the inner sound of the heart chakra) waiting to be struck or rung. It implies the vast store of potential energy in the heart chakra, waiting to be unlocked."

He continued, "Let's discuss the important qualities of the heart chakra, both helpful and harmful."

Though he had mentioned earlier that "...it takes a very *big* person to control the often unruly energy of the heart chakra," she was curious about why this was so. But she felt it might be impolite to ask Bhima this question right now.

Immediately she saw that Bhima had caught her thought—would she ever learn to remain mentally silent on this pilgrimage? It was obviously impossible to shield her thoughts from the God-like Pandava brothers. Sabella mentally apologized for her thought-leak.

Bhima continued with a mischievous smile. "Apology accepted, and it's perfectly fine. I'm used to it. And I want to reassure you that my uprooting-trees days are in the past. As a young warrior, my emotions were often out of control, to say the least. I bested many demons in my time as a warrior, but the greatest achievement of all was conquering the 'demons of emotion' in my own heart. This happens for every soul who consciously makes an inner chakra journey—which is, of course, *everyone*, sooner or later!

"Before we explore the subject of the heart's emotions, let me ask you about the 'limb' of Ashtanga Yoga, which corresponds to the heart chakra."

Sabella replied, "Yes, that would be *pranayama*, which fits well with the fourth chakra, because it influences not only the heart, but also the lungs and our ability to breathe. It is not correct to define *pranayama* as breath control or breathing exercises, as many people did in the past. Back then, the word *prana* was often misunderstood at its deepest level.

"*Yama*, in this context, does mean control. But *pranayama*, in its highest sense does not merely refer to control of the breath, but means control of the life-force—that living force which animates us as human beings and keeps us alive, awake, and moving about in action and thought.

"The definition of *prana* I like best is: 'conscious, cosmic energy.' *Prana* is conscious and absolutely aware. It knows where to go and what to do, if we give it a chance and are willing to work on clearing away the impediments to its free flow, especially in the astral spine."

"And what is the best way to do that, Sabella?"

"There are many ways! In essence, all of the techniques of the yogic sciences are designed to enhance the free flow of *prana*. But the most powerful are the techniques of Kriya Yoga. Paramhansa Yogananda stated emphatically and repeatedly, 'Kriya Yoga plus devotion work like mathematics. They cannot fail!'

"My exceptionally wise brother Sahadeva recently told me that this Sabella-human, whom I would be meeting soon, was very knowledgeable—not equal to him, of course, but impressive, nevertheless. I see that he was correct in his evaluation of you!" Bhima said.

"Me, I'm more of an action-oriented and heart-motivated guy. As you are learning, all the chakras eventually balance each other perfectly. And each chakra plays a unique and important role in the great drama of life."

"Thank you for telling me what Sahadeva said." She blushed and changed the subject. "Can we move over to sit on that puffy cloud now? This rainbow swing is lovely, but I want to experience everything!"

181

After a sudden surge of wind, they found themselves sitting on a soft, white cloud. It was the most comfortable 'seat' she had ever experienced, although she realized it wasn't fully material and perhaps that was why it was so comfortable! It was gliding through the blue sky as clouds do. Its slow movement produced a cooling breeze, which kissed her cheeks lovingly.

"Don't get *too* comfortable, Sabella. We have many other subjects to talk about. Do you remember my mention of the 'demons of the heart'?"

"Yes, I do, and I must admit that the word 'demons' sounded a little ominous!" Sabella sent this thought back to Bhima. She was getting used to his great size now. He was so tender and considerate—he always arranged where they sat or stood so that she could look into his eyes while they spoke. And what wondrous eyes they were—soft, brown, and radiating divine love from his heart to hers.

But now he looked more serious as he transmitted these concepts to her, "Unfortunately, these demons are real and numerous. I will list a few of them for you now, but first, please understand that they *all* come under the heading of emotions out of control."

Sabella asked, "What exactly *are* emotions? Are they always bad? What about love?"

"We'll talk more about love in a while. And no, emotions are *not* all bad. Think of them as energy flowing or 'e-motion,' meaning 'energy in motion.' Energy is neither good nor bad. It is neutral, but it becomes harmful or helpful depending on the direction of its flow. If it's moving downward and outward through the chakras, it is harmful. If it's moving inward and upward, it is helpful."

"A few of the harmful emotions or qualities would be JEALOUSY, LUST, ANGER, SELFISHNESS, GREED, ATTACHMENTS, DESIRES, LIKES AND DISLIKES, HATRED, RAGE, PRIDE, ENVY, CONCEIT, COMPLAINING, and A JUDGING OR CARPING SPIRIT.

"When Lord Krishna complimented my brother Arjuna on 'having overcome the carping spirit,' his words were meant to be a very high compliment.

"Yogananda's guru Swami Sri Yukteswar pointed out many of these qualities and called them the 'meannesses of the heart.' These are the 'demons' of which I am speaking."

"You said you would list only a few of them. How many are there? And why are they demonic?" Sabella asked.

"I cannot give you an exact number, for they are legion—almost impossible to count. On the ancient battlefield of Kurukshetra, King Material Desire's forces were far more numerous than our army. But they fought on the side of darkness of spirit, and we fought for the inner light. It may take time and great effort when greatly outnumbered like that. And it is urgently important to recognize our need for the help and grace of God and our guru on the battlefield of life, but the inner light eventually prevails—always!

"They are demonic because they promote darkness and confusion in human beings, causing them to lose sight of their own divine nature. Have you ever seen the face of someone who has *fallen* into what might be called a 'red rage?' He or she barely looks human. I know this state well, as I spoke of earlier. In the past, I would act in destructive ways, reacting violently to my feelings of anger.

"And notice that I emphasized the word *fallen*, for it is very important to understand that harmful emotions are simply energy moving in the wrong direction. Change an emotion's direction of flow from downward and outward to inward and upward, and the energy of that emotion becomes helpful instead of harmful. Energy (*prana*) is never a bad thing—it is neutral—it just is. But it can be, and often is, misdirected, causing suffering for ourselves, as well as for others.

"Here, in the heart chakra, the battle of light and darkness escalates, which is good, because it becomes easier to notice and allows us the opportunity, *finally*, to do something about it! Since we mentioned anger and rage, which everyone experiences at one time or another, let me offer you an efficient way to deal with anger energy.

"Anger is always caused by thwarted desires, or wanting things to be different from what they are. And this is tricky, for many times conditions seem very bad and *should* be changed, if at all possible. Nevertheless, as sincere truth-seekers, our job is to deal with anger energy in ourselves by channeling its flow in constructive rather than destructive ways.

"Merely to say, 'I'm not attached to anything, therefore I'm never angry about anything,' is simply not true. Letting go of *all* attachments, thereby purifying the heart chakra completely, can take many years or even lifetimes of intense effort. Desires are sneaky. Let go of one and you may find ten more springing up to take its place in your heart—desires that you didn't even know existed!

"There are three ways to deal with anger-energy. These are: suppression, expression, and transmutation.

"Suppression is saying or thinking, 'No, no! I am *not* angry!' when everything about you, your voice, your face, your body language, betrays that you are angry. This is never a good thing. Suppressing anger can cause a person to become seriously ill in body and/or mind.

"Expressions of anger (being violent, cursing, yelling, screaming, hitting, or in other ways acting out) have been thought, in the past, to be a better way to deal with anger than through suppression. This is true, but only to a small degree. It is somewhat better than suppression, but expressing anger outwardly is still problematic because it creates harmful 'boomerang' karmic patterns.

"Violent words or energy hurled at someone because of perceived displeasure or pain, or being angry about a situation of which we don't approve, have a way of giving birth to more anger and violence. Inevitably this negative energy will come back to us to hurt us.

"Anger energy has the potential to hurt others, which is something we should avoid at all costs, if for no other reason than to avoid reaping the *karma* that is created. We must understand that, sooner or later, expressing negative emotions always causes repercussions, which inevitably return to plague the one who expressed them."

Sabella nodded in agreement, "How well I learned that lesson reviewing past lives. Even in my present lifetime, the laws of action and reaction have revealed themselves to be true and exact. So obviously transmutation is the best way to go. But what does that mean? How do we actually *transmute* the demons of negative emotions in our hearts into angels of positive emotions?"

Bhima said: "It's not so hard to do, believe it or not. First, recognize that anger, or whatever the negative emotion may be, actually is happening—don't turn away from it because you don't like it or think it should not be happening.

Second, carefully observe what is causing the harmful emotion. It's always the same thing: attachment or wanting things to be different from the way they are.

"Third, remind yourself that it is neither helpful nor healthy for you to continue to remain in the grip of such negativity.

"Finally, go inside and become centered in the astral spine, especially in your heart chakra. Offer the negative energy pattern inward and upward to the spiritual eye, the sixth chakra, to be transformed into positive and helpful energy. Find and tune in to the positive attitudes of your heart. With the emotion of anger, for example, these would be COMPASSION, FORGIVENESS, and UNCONDITIONAL LOVE.

"Remember that meditation is the most helpful tool for accomplishing this transmutation process. In a way, it can even be practiced 'in the thick of it.' It is just a matter of remembering to internalize your energy flows and thus to become uplifted in inner calmness, even if only for a moment.

"And the most important point of all is to ask for help and guidance. Never try to do it all alone!

"The fire ceremony and purification ritual you performed with Arjuna is symbolic of this process. Remember that he touched you at the heart chakra and said, 'Open your heart to me, and I will enter and take charge of your life!' We need all the help we can get to transmute negative energy patterns into positive ones—it's a big job.

"The Purification Ceremony ends with these words: 'By the grace of the Masters, you are free." Freedom of heart, purity of heart, this is our heart's natural state. Instead, out of ignorance, most people remain heart-bound by their negative emotions, causing them great suffering.

"The great Master Jesus Christ summed it up beautifully by saying, 'Blessed (which should be thought of as *blissful*) are the pure in heart, for they shall see God.' What a promise!"

"Yes, it is!" Sabella said and then stifled a yawn. "Excuse me, sir. I think this cloud seat is becoming a little too soft for me. I find I am becoming sleepy!"

"You are right," Bhima said. "What we both need now is more action and less talk."

"Uh-oh," thought Sabella. "What does that mean?"

"It means enough theoretical talk about the demons of the heart. It's time for you to face your *own* demons fearlessly and deal with them appropriately."

Having forcefully uttered these words, he drew a large, gleaming knife from his belt and handed it to her. "You'll need this soon."

The long, sharp knife was nicely proportioned for Bhima, but in her small hands it looked more like a sword.

"I'm not particularly proficient with knives or swords, but I'll do my best to carry on and overcome whatever is in store for me," Sabella thought courageously.

"That's the spirit!" said Bhima.

Instantly, they were transported to a breeze-filled meadow, with colorful wildflowers everywhere, dancing happily with wind-blown energy. The flowery meadow was surrounded by tall trees, their branches swaying wildly and joyfully. She could hear tinkling, bell-like music coming from hundreds of wind-chimes in all sizes and shapes, hanging from the limbs of the trees. In the center of the meadow was an old-fashioned hot-air balloon. Though tightly tethered to the ground, it was completely inflated and seemed to be straining to rise up into the air.

"Soon you will learn to ride with the winds. But first please sit here beside me and close your eyes. Sabella Lovingheart, I will leave you now to face your test alone, as you faced the challenges in the three lower chakras. May God bless and keep you!" And he was gone.

Sabella felt a slight tugging sensation in her heart chakra. To her astonishment, she saw many strings emerging from the center of her chest.

"Oh yes," she laughed to herself in embarrassment, "These must be my heart-strings."

She saw that each string was attached to something in her life that she liked or didn't like, wanted or didn't want. This was not so bad, until she noticed that the small heart-strings were being joined by thicker ropes and then by steel cables. These bindings became heavier and heavier, weighing down her heart. Her first thought was to find out what each one was attached to, especially the largest and heaviest cables. She noticed that one of the thickest was attached to AMBITION. Another was tightly wrapped around THOMAS. Another held firmly to MY HOME.

"I think I can disengage from my personal ambitions, but how am I to let go of my dear husband and my lovely little pyramid-home by the Joyuba River?"

As she thought these words, she realized that she was bound up, restricted, and very upset about her state. It seemed that she no longer inhabited her own body. Instead she was living outside herself, more specifically at the ends of each of the cables, ropes, or strings—dwelling *in* her attachments, identifying with them, and feeling sure that these things defined her happiness. She knew she was no longer calmly centered in herself or in her heart chakra—or anywhere else in her physical or astral bodies.

Suddenly, Sabella was horrified to see the MY HOME attachment explode into a million fragments, causing that heart-cable to "twang" and yank powerfully on her heart chakra. Deep in her heart, she felt a huge wave of grief and loss began to overcome her.

She stooped forward with her hands and arms covering the front of her chest, falling deeper and deeper into physical and mental pain. She began weeping uncontrollably. Her emotional state was so intense that she had the fleeting thought that it was a heart attack and she might soon die. She desperately wanted to run from what she was witnessing, but was too despondent to flee and so bound by all her many *other* attachments, that she was paralyzed—unable to move at all.

A soothing voice said, "Sabella, is losing the home that you and Thomas created, lived in, raised your children in, and obviously love very much—is it truly worth all this paralyzing pain and anguish?"

"My Lady Kundalini," Sabella sobbed, for she instantly knew the soft voice. "Have you come to rescue me from my troubles yet *again*? Is this really happening, or am I dreaming? My grief at the loss of my home and everything in it feels unbearable."

"This is not the time to discuss what is real and what is not real, Sabella. It feels real enough to you right now, no doubt. But that is not the most important question now. The question should be, 'How can I find the best way to alleviate this intense pain?'

"So, what should you do, Sabella? I suggest that you calm yourself, get centered, and remember the important spiritual principles you have been taught all your life. I will help you get through this, as will God and the Great Ones."

Sabella did as Draupadi suggested, closed her eyes, and prayed for assistance. With the force of her will power, she blocked out all thoughts of attachments, likes, dislikes, wants, needs, habits, and anything else which might define or limit her. Instantly, an affirmation she learned as a child came to her:

*With the sword of devotion I sever the heart-strings
that tie me to delusion.
With the deepest love, I lay my heart at the feet
of Omnipresence.*

After repeating the affirmation several times, she felt freer and lighter in every way.

Achieving a state of inner calmness, she recalled that she was holding a real sword in her right hand. Well, it was really King Bhima's big knife, but it could serve as an ample substitute for a sword, which she knew she desperately needed now. With her right hand, she lifted it high in the air and unhesitatingly brought it down in front of her in a single sweeping arc.

Sabella triumphantly cut through all the heart strings, cords, ropes, and cables which had been tightly binding her heart chakra. At the end of each of the bindings, there were many forms of emotional attachments, which were being transformed into small, colorful balloons filled with helium. They all rose higher and higher into the sky.

"Good-bye!" she called out, watching them ascend and waving to them happily. Soon they had all disappeared from view. Somewhat surprisingly, this left her with no regrets at all.

She looked at her heart area to see that it was completely free of all attachments. What a feeling! Oh, if only she could be sure she would never, never forget this feeling of complete inner freedom.

Sabella saw that she was now wearing a new robe of colorful light. This one was patterned with shimmering green and blue and was covered with tiny sparkling diamonds. She noted with a small sigh that the beautiful dark lady, Queen Draupadi/Kundalini, again had slipped away undetected.

She walked toward the hot-air balloon, tugging at its tethers. Its bright colors matched her new robe, and she knew that she would be boarding it soon.

Intuitively she understood that severing the tethers of the

hot-air balloon symbolized letting go of even more binding attachments. With Bhima's knife she slashed through all the ropes tying the big balloon to the earth and preventing it from soaring upward, as was its nature. She levitated herself into its passenger basket, and noticed quite a bit of ballast in the basket, each piece of which was labeled "old *karma* stored in your heart chakra." She threw it all out and the basket began to rise.

As the balloon gracefully lifted itself up above the meadow, her whole being felt light as air—completely pure and free; in freedom she offered all her energy inward and upward to her higher chakras.

Sabella relaxed in the comfortable basket suspended under its giant balloon. It rose quickly and silently, carrying her up into the freedom of the vast blue sky, and her heart sang a line from the chant the children had sung with her:

Nothing on earth can hold me! Rise O my soul in freedom! ©

Sabella's attention was so firmly focused on the freeing, lifting effects of the Air Element of the fourth chakra, that she soon felt herself becoming the air itself. She affirmed to herself quietly and joyfully:

My soul, like a weightless balloon, soars upward through skies of eternal freedom!

Unseen by Sabella, Bhima sat on a nearby cloud and watched as she floated upward past him in the basket of the lighter-than-air balloon. He smiled with delight to observe the lovely, wind-blown woman gazing triumphantly upward, rising rapidly through the clouds, rainbows, air currents, and far, far beyond.

CHAPTER THIRTY

Somewhat later, Bhima guided Sabella into a chapel which appeared to be constructed of vapor and light. It was floating close to the peak of the pyramid, commanding a view of the whole fourth-chakra kingdom spread out below them. A giant gong was ringing as they entered the chapel, resonating with Sabella's heartbeat, bringing tears of joy to her eyes.

"It's difficult to contain all the pure love and expansive joy that I am experiencing now. My heart feels like it might burst and overflow. Bhima how does one deal with such joy?"

"I understand. When a truth-seeker's heart begins to open fully, it can feel emotionally overwhelmed at first. You'll soon learn to work more calmly with your emotional responses, even the sweetest ones, such as your present tears of joy. You'll understand how to transmute all your emotions, bad or good, into pure, divine devotion.

"In the beginning, tears like these can wash away many sins. Still, they are emotionally rooted. In the kingdom of the heart we must learn to transmute *all* emotions into devotion. I will show you a simple technique to help you do this whenever you wish."

Sabella sat on a small cloud-chair and Bhima sat cross-legged before her, instructing her, "Sit up straight and tall with shoulder blades drawn together in back. Uplift your chest and let your heart chakra feel as though it is wide open. Bring your hands up to the center of your chest, letting them cover the center of your chest, so that your right hand covers the top of your left hand. Take several very deep breaths."

Sabella did this.

Bhima continued, "Feel the beating of your physical heart. Notice your chest rising and falling with each breath. Now mentally go beyond these two physical manifestations of the heart into the heart chakra itself. Feel it to be a spinning, whirling sphere of energy in the center of your astral spine.

"Take another deep, slow breath. Move your hands away from your heart center, resting them in your lap with the palms facing upward, close to the junction of your thighs and abdomen. Draw your shoulder blades together in back and again, lift your chest up, so that you can breathe deeply. Release all awareness of the physical manifestations of this chakra—especially the heartbeat and breath.

"Bring your right index finger up so that its tip is touching the center of your chest. Mentally say, 'Every emotion of love and joy that I feel at this moment, I offer inward and upward for transmutation at my spiritual eye.

"Now lift your finger from your chest and move your hand slowly up the front of your body and face until you can touch the point between your eyebrows with your finger. Lift all your heart's energy up and focus it at that point. Mentally say, 'I transmute all my emotions into devotion!'

"Pause there for a moment, and then lift your hand slowly up toward the sky, look up and affirm mentally, 'I offer all this love and joy back into the hands of God from whence it came.'"

Sabella sat very still, eyes closed, with her right hand lifted skyward. Her heart chakra became as light, free, and pure as it had ever been. Breezes of DIVINE DEVOTION and INNER BLISS wafted through her physical and astral bodies—very purely and soothingly, so different from the turbulent winds of emotion that brought tears to her eyes. She realized that her breath had ceased flowing and her heart had stopped beating.

"Am I dead? I must be, for I seem to have neither heartbeat nor breath now," she wondered curiously, but without a care in the world for these things. Such is the state of supreme bliss and divine love! In this sacred moment, she knew that she was not dead. She was very much *alive*, more alive than she had ever been before!

A beautiful song briefly glided through her mind:

> *I can't breathe for Love*
> *All the stars above*
> *Call to me, "Come home!*
> *Life's waves all end in foam."*
> *Only Love can heal.... ©*

Sabella sat unmoving, unthinking, un-breathing, her eyes slightly open and uplifted, completely detached from the world and from herself. Deeply meditating, she became united with her joyful and completely still heart.

Through her inner vision, her heart appeared to have been polished by powerful light rays; it was perfectly clean—shining brightly. In her new state of heart-awareness and pure open-heartedness, she entered into the great un-beating heart of God.

CHAPTER THIRTY-ONE

The heart chakra bells and gongs began to ring within and all about Sabella, bringing her expanded consciousness back to the cloud-seat high in the Air Element pyramid. She was reluctant to return, but could inwardly feel Bhima calling her to be fully present in her body.

"Your deeply devotional state of meditation is inspiring to behold, Sabella," Bhima thought to her. "But before you complete the fourth-chakra pyramid experience and receive your initiation, there is one more matter I wish to discuss with you, and that is human love."

"Human love?" Sabella was mystified. "How can there be anything more important than Divine Love?"

"While you are fresh from your joyful experience of the perfect Love of God, I want to ask if you know how to express it perfectly in everyday life?

"Tell me, Sabella. How do you love your husband Thomas? Is it Divine Love or human love that you express to him? Do you love him unconditionally, no matter what he does or does not do, no matter what he says or does not say, and no matter how he behaves? Do you love him more than anyone else?"

"You have asked several important questions, Bhima. I'll do my best to answer them all. Truthfully, sometimes I love Thomas *with* conditions and sometimes, without conditions. I am *aspiring* to love him always, not with human love, but with unconditional, Divine Love. I certainly fail from time to time, because, great soul that he is, occasionally Thomas can act in ways which deeply annoy me.

"Do I love Thomas more than anyone else? That's a tough

question! I love my spiritual teacher Simeon. I love my three children. There are many people whom I love. And I try to love everybody and everything.

"Nevertheless, I understand why you are asking. There is a strong tendency in every human being to *particularize* his or her love toward a certain person or persons—to think, if not to say, 'I love this person more than that person. And that person over there, I can't stand her. Look how she is behaving! Do I have to love her also'?"

"Yes," Bhima replied, "We eventually come to a place of spiritual advancement wherein we love *all* beings equally, with unconditional Divine Love. But that does not mean you have to love their *actions*, especially when they are acting badly. We must learn, in our hearts and minds, to separate people from their actions.

"We can love a person's divine essence and not approve of his or her actions. Relating to a person's *soul*, that deepest essence of God within them, even if *dharma*, or one's righteous duty, requires intervention of some kind to control or stop the person's bad actions.

"One of the greatest demons of the heart is a JUDGEMENTAL attitude. It's imperative that it be recognized and destroyed, if the heart is to be truly free and pure! One way to accomplish this is to see everyone and everything as one. Paramhansa Yogananda clarified this principle succinctly and beautifully explaining that when Jesus Christ said, 'Love thy neighbor as thyself,' it should be understood to mean, 'Love thy neighbor, for he *is* thyself.'"

"We must learn to respond unhesitatingly: 'Who or what is this person, thing, or situation that I am judging? Why, this is me! We are all *one. Everything is one!'*

"Of course we can get in trouble by judging ourselves too harshly and not feeling God within us, in everything, and that we are a part of all that is. We need to recognize this as the truth and act upon it, by honoring our own Divine Natures."

Sabella agreed, "I know the attitude of SELF-NEGATION very well. When I was young, I suffered greatly from low self-esteem and a lack of self-acceptance.

"One day, a few months after we had been life-linked, Thomas asked me if I would mind if he told me about a harmful quality that he had noticed in me. What could I say to that? It frightened me, for I loved him very much and desperately wanted him to have a good opinion of me. But of course I also wanted to hear what he had to say.

"Thomas said to me, 'Sabella, I have been watching you closely. You are a lovely and loving person! You are forgiving, kind, and generous. But I think you would never treat anyone as badly as I see you treating yourself. Don't you realize that you are being disrespectful to God who dwells within you—who *is* you?'

"These simple words changed my life forever, because finally I was ready both to hear and act on them.

"Oh, how right he was, and how grateful I will be to him always, that he was able to find the right time and words to show me this truth about myself. For most of my life, I had been striving to please God, gurus, my spiritual teacher, and everybody else as well. And here I was, offering love to everyone *except* myself. Somehow I had missed the point in a big way.

"What's more, then I could see how much my ego was reinforced by the thoughts, even subconsciously, 'I am no good, I am not worthy, I am not capable, strong enough, smart enough, and on and on.'

"I finally understood how an attitude like that puts all the focus on *I, I, I,* and *ME, ME, ME!*

"With every ounce of energy that I could generate, and asking for Divine help, I renounced the harmful attitude of SELF-NEGATION. Whenever, over the years since then, I noticed it creeping back into my heart—and I've found it to be a very sneaky 'demon,' indeed—again and again I worked to let it go immediately. To aid in this process, I often repeat this affirmations to myself:

Sabella reflected further: "I think it might be impossible to understand all the subtleties of love or to understand the many different *kinds* of emotions which we make a part of the word 'love.' Isn't this true Bhima?"

Bhima replied, "It is very true, dear one. Most people who say or think, 'I love you' to another human being are implying a missing word at the end of that phrase. The word is *if.* 'I love you *if*. . .,' really meaning I love you IF you behave in a certain way, and IF you don't, then I don't love you as much, and perhaps I'll withdraw my love altogether.' That is *not* Divine Love but conditional and selfish love. If we really want to be truthful about it, it is not love at all: it is attachment and nothing more!"

Sabella laughed, "By all means, let's be absolutely honest about love, and while we are at it, let me relate a true story about Thomas and me. This also happened while we were still new at being life-linked. I learned that he occasionally liked to tinker with weird contraptions, puzzles, antique motors—that sort of thing. I thought it was a little strange that a man with his towering intellect would bother himself with such mundane, material things, but he claimed it relaxed his mind.

"One day I was sitting on our new patio composing music, and he called out to me from our bedroom 'Sabella, do you love me?'

"I replied instantly, 'What did you do?'

"Thomas came to where I was sitting and looked sheepish. He saw that I was glaring at him. He wiped some black motor-grease from his hands onto a filthy rag and said with a twinkle in his eye, 'Now what kind of love is that? Is that unconditional love?'

"His cute half-smile was contagious, but I tried my best to keep a serious look on my face. I asked again with more emphasis this time. 'What did you do?'

"'Perhaps you should come and see, my love,' Thomas said.

"I followed him into the bedroom where I immediately noticed, to my shock and horror, that there were several small greasy motor parts lying haphazardly on our bed, on the beautiful hand-made quilt, one of my favorite wedding gifts. It had been crafted carefully and with love by a dear friend of mine."

"'Thomas!' I shouted, 'Look at what you've done!' And then I understood why he had asked me if I loved him unconditionally, despite *what* he had done to my beautiful quilt!

"Sadly he looked down at his feet and thought these words to me: 'I was walking through our bedroom to go out the back door, while balancing a large tray of motor parts. I somehow stumbled, and a few of them tumbled onto the bed. I think I can clean the quilt without damaging it, and it will be as good as new.'

"There were a few more moments of heated discussion between us, but to shorten the story, I knew that he was truly sorry for what he had done. After all, it was an accident! Later, he *was* able to clean the precious quilt to my complete satisfaction. It still covers our bed and is a constant reminder of what I learned that day.

"Thomas was right to ask if I loved him unconditionally just at that moment; because the truth was, I *didn't*. When I remember that event—I can *still* feel the pain in my heart as I saw my new quilt, ruined by splotches of black grease. Obviously I had created some very strong heart-string attachments to the quilt.

"'TWANG!' went those heart strings, as Thomas showed me what he had done. 'OUCH!' went my heart chakra. I was obviously not living in my center. I was living 'out there' *in* that quilt. To hurt it was to hurt me directly, or so it seemed. What foolishness! I was *not* my quilt. It was just a thing!"

Bhima smiled at her, "Sabella, that is a poignant and deeply inspiring story. Very few people can see their attachments for what they are—limitations to freedom and perfect joy—let alone detach from them so quickly."

Sabella smiled back at him, "I bless Thomas for helping me to see this attachment and how it was keeping me from experiencing unconditional love. I doubt that I would have been able to do it alone. And it took more than a few minutes to come to a place of peace within myself. It was an excellent lesson and I am grateful for the incident, because it enabled me to see what unconditional love is and what it is not. I know that is the way that God and the Great Ones love us—unconditionally! And that is how we must strive to love each other, although it is not always easy."

Bhima replied, "Would you like to know the secret of how to make it easier?"

"Absolutely!"

"We must realize that when we love, it's best not to love with our *own* love, but instead, tune in to the great river of Divine Love. The flow of love is always there, ready to be tapped into. We can become a channel of love to everyone.

"This is the secret of the saints and masters who love everyone so completely, unconditionally, and magnetically. When we truly become channels for Divine Love, it opens and heals our *own* hearts, for the channel is always blessed by what flows through it."

Sabella shared another memory saying, "Bhima, as you know, I work with music. There's a lovely old song that I asked to be sung at Thomas' and my life-linking ceremony. I believe that these few lines from the song perfectly capture what we are saying." She began to sing the hauntingly beautiful melody:

> *What is love?*
> *Is it only ours?*
> *Or does love,*
> *Whisper in the flowers?*
> *Surely we, children of this world,*
> *Could not love,*
> *By our own powers.* ©

"I know the song well, but the deeply inspiring and heartfelt way you just sang it—I shall never forget this moment! Bless you, dearest Sabella!" Bhima said sincerely.

He continued, "Two more 'heart subjects' to touch on quickly. The first is healing.

"The heart chakra influences not only the heart, lungs, breathing, thymus gland, and everything located between the diaphragm and the top of the sternum; it also influences the arms, hands, and manual dexterity. That is why loving, healing energy can flow so easily from the heart chakra through the arms and hands. A healing touch or prayers for others are magnified when we are aware of this connection.

"Our hands, especially, can be filled with heart-healing energy and the power of Divine Love. Many techniques of healing involve channeling energy through the hands, either in person or at a distance. You know many of them—the basics are taught to children in the Halls of Wisdom. Healing is an important function of the heart chakra, so I felt I should emphasize it now."

"I agree, Bhima," Sabella said. "I recognize the healing power of the heart chakra, especially when it is channeled through the hands. Many years ago, I once saw my teacher Simeon act as a channel for divine healing for one of my fellow students, Loralon.

"While we were on a class field trip, Loralon was showing off foolishly, climbing about on a large, slippery boulder. He had a bad fall, and it was obvious that he had broken a bone in his lower right leg; we could see that the injury was severe and that he was in great pain.

"Simeon immediately closed his eyes and prayed to be a channel of healing. He placed his hands on Loralon's leg. We could actually see the bone moving back into place, resetting itself, and finally fusing perfectly. All signs of pain vanished from Loralon's face.

"Simeon looked intensely at Loralon and then at all of us, and said, 'Always remember that it was *not* I who healed Loralon, but the power of Divine Love flowing through me. All of you can learn to offer healing energy to others in this way. But please understand that this sort of miracle *only* happens through the alignment of your own will with the Divine Will.'

"In later years, I came to understand more deeply what he meant," Sabella smiled in remembrance.

Bhima continued, "The next and final subject I want to discuss with you is the term 'broken-hearted.' We hear this term used freely, especially when referring to romantic love. But the heart chakra *cannot* be broken. It can only malfunction temporarily. As in all the chakras, the flow of energy through our hearts can become impeded and choked by the debris (*vrittis*) of our present attachments or past karma.

"We must understand that the heart chakra stands at *the pivotal and central point* of the astral spine—right in the middle, with three chakras below (the chakras of our humanity), and three chakras above (the chakras of our divinity). It is the half-way point in our inner journey to freedom. The energy here is easily agitated through the power of both positive and negative emotions, and can just as easily go down as up.

"I am an excellent symbol for emotions out of control. Yanking trees out of the ground and bashing my enemies with them is a perfect expression of this state. It was certainly not the best way for me to behave, even if they did have it coming."

Sabella and Bhima laughed together, as old friends do. How could she *ever* have feared this ultimately loveable being?

Bhima continued, "The heart is filled with powerful energy and when agitated or excited, has the potential to send that energy inward and upward toward spiritual freedom, or downward and outward into stronger entanglement with the world of suffering. While this is true to a more limited extent in the first three chakras, you can see how the movements of *prana* would be especially dynamic here, in the kingdom of love.

"I recognize that I may be slightly prejudiced, but I sincerely believe that the heart chakra really is the most important of all the chakras, at least for a large portion of one's inner journey to freedom. It directs the flow of energy into positive or negative channels, which then settle into beneficial or harmful behavior patterns. It would solve just about everything if people lived with Divine love in their hearts and also letting that love flow through their hearts to others.

"The sixth and seventh chakras *ultimately* are the most important ones, representing as they do the goal of our enlightenment and final liberation.

"But I, Bhima, ruler of the heart chakra kingdom, stand firmly in the middle of the chakra system!" Bhima appeared to grow even larger as he spoke these words loudly and with great power.

"It is here I do my best to direct all emotion into devotion and send *prana* where it needs to go to be of greatest benefit— always inward and upward, toward bliss and oneness with God!"

After a moment he said more quietly, "Sabella, I want to give you your heart chakra pendant and the fourth-chakra initiation ceremony. Please come and stand before the altar."

As Sabella rose and faced the altar, she saw with great delight that Sahadeva, Nakula, and Arjuna, each in their colorful chakra robes, were standing quietly at the altar, ready to offer her their blessings, too.

Bhima showed her the fourth-chakra medallion and put it into place on her chakras necklace. It was a disk of brightly shining copper. Centered in the disk was a green twelve-petal lotus emblem. Set into the lotus, in the usual way, so that it touched her skin when she wore it, was a magnificent two-carat white diamond. In the middle of the diamond was a tiny blue circle, hypnotically whirling and spinning, drawing one into its mysterious depths.

As she looked at her amazing new pendant, she fought back a gasp of sheer delight, then quickly controlled herself, and gave it all to God, from whom all things come and to whom all things return.

Kneeling before the luminous cloud altar, floating in joy,

Sabella felt each of the first three Pandava brothers come to her in turn and touch his right index finger to the center of her chest. Ah, bliss!

But even in the midst of these sacred moments, she could feel that each brother's blessings held a slightly different vibration. Sahadeva's blessings were filled with steadfast strength and courage, Nakula's, with sweet creativity and flexibility. Arjuna's powerful touch conveyed fiery self-control and enthusiasm for life.

Finally Bhima came to her and indicated that she should stand. He placed his large index finger at her heart chakra, where it vibrated mightily and filled her with Divine Love. He then leaned over—a long ways over—and declared to her, while looking deeply into her eyes, "I am Bhima, son of Vayu, the god of the wind. In my youth, my brothers often teased me and called me 'long-winded,' or 'full of hot air.' Forgive me if I have talked too much during your heart chakra pilgrimage, but anyway. . . ."

He could not subdue a big chuckle, even though the moment was supposed to be sacred. Sabella stifled her laughter, realizing that the great and mighty Bhima was truly a loveable rascal and now such a dear friend!

"Ahem . . . anyway, I now bestow upon you, dear little one, the powers of the fourth chakra, which are levitation, flying, and control over every aspect of the Air Element. Use them wisely and well." With this he placed a tiny gift in her right hand and whispered softly for Sabella alone to hear, "May you always be a channel for Divine Love."

A little later, after she departed the fourth pyramid and the river valley of the seven golden pyramids, she took a moment to look at Bhima's little gift and was surprised to see that it was a tiny piece of candy, green in color, and shaped like a heart. She ate it then and there, for she intuitively knew it was important to eat it *now* and not just keep it on her altar as a memento. It tasted something like fresh limes. She was interested to find that the slightly sour taste satisfied her completely.

In her mind, she heard Bhima say in his distinctive booming voice: "Farewell for now, Sabella. When you see Issoweet next, ask her to tell you about the tastes of the chakras. My small gift was a sample of the heart chakra's distinctive taste."

She could feel his mischievous delight at her puzzlement.

"Each chakra has a taste? It seems there is always something new to learn!" Sabella happily thought to herself.

"Farewell for now, dear Bhima, friend of my heart. Is it permissible for me to *fly* home instead of teleport, as has been my usual practice?"

His laughter roared in her head, "Sabella, you are such a delight! Yes, go ahead, but keep a low profile. Don't startle Thomas when you come in for a landing."

"Good point," thought Sabella.

She immediately sent Thomas a mental message concerning her imminent and unusual mode of arrival. Off she flew soaring over the Sushumna River Valley, enjoying the cool evening wind on her face and in her long hair, all the while appreciating the magnificent vistas passing beneath her.

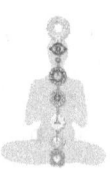

CHAPTER THIRTY-TWO

Thomas was standing on their home's highest deck, looking up at the sky awaiting the arrival of his "flying wife." He soon saw her, just as she had mentally warned him, soaring towards him like a graceful bird. She came down softly, her eyes shining with joy. She gave him a big hug, then asked him to wait just a moment while she looked around, appreciating that her home was all in one piece—with not a thing out of place, as far as she could see.

"What was *that* all about?" Thomas asked. "Did you expect either me or the house not to be here when you returned?"

"I am greatly relieved. I was afraid our home might still be in small pieces after—but I'll tell you all about it soon, dearest. First, can you tell me how long I've been gone?"

"Oh, about the usual amount of time, I think. You left early this morning right after your meditation, and it's now about eight o'clock the evening of the same day," Thomas thought to her.

"That is hard to believe. It feels like I've been away for several days, at least. The heart chakra pyramid was. . . . " Words and even thoughts failed her.

"Vast? Complex? Interesting? Absorbing?" Thomas supplied helpfully.

She agreed that each one of those descriptive words could apply.

"So quit levitating and sit down here with me in the swing. We can enjoy watching the stars come out, while you share your heart chakra adventures with me. I want to know all about King Bhima. When you departed this morning, I could tell that you were intimidated by his reputed size and boisterousness."

Sabella realized that she was floating about three inches off the deck. "Oops!" she said, and came down. "Bhima cautioned me to keep a low profile with my new flying and levitating abilities, and here I am already, not even noticing what I am doing. Sorry about that!"

She sat with Thomas in the comfortable porch swing and began to recount her adventures, "Bhima is not at all what I had expected. I think the best word to describe him is exuberant. He is a very large and majestic man, as the stories tell, and his heart is equally large. He is gentle, kind, childlike, funny, and. . . ." On into the night—and it did take most of the night—she enthusiastically shared everything with Thomas.

Dawn's colors were glowing in the east when Thomas yawned and said, "I don't know about you, dearest, but I need some rest, meditation, and breakfast before the new day begins. Fascinating as your stories are, and as stunning as you look wearing that diamond-sprinkled robe, can you hazard a guess how much more there is to tell me? Can we continue talking later?

"And by the way, your gown truly is stunning—it makes you look like the earth as seen from space, all blues and greens, with lights twinkling like diamonds. You look gorgeous!"

"I appreciate the compliment; I've never been told that I look like a planet!"

They both laughed a bit giddily, and Sabella said, "Of course, you are right, my love. I was very close to completing my story anyway. Thank you for letting me share it with you. It is very helpful when you listen so attentively. As you can see, the whole experience was deeply meaningful—particularly in the ways I hope I have learned to love differently and better.

"When I call you 'my love' now, those words feel much deeper. It's difficult to explain the new feelings of my heart using mental concepts."

"Yes, I can feel it, too, *my love*," his eyes twinkled with love-light.

After a day's rest and reflection, she caught up with messages, one of which was a startling note from her eldest daughter, Lalaree, who revealed that she was in love and considering life-linking with a young man named Juniper. This was a bit disconcerting because Sabella had neither heard of nor met the young man.

She sent a mental message to Thomas asking if he knew about Lalaree's plans, adding that personally, she thought her daughter was far too young to consider taking such a serious step.

Thomas replied, "I heard from her while you were away. I wanted to bring up this matter last night, but felt it was more important for you to have the time to discuss your experiences while they were still fresh in your mind and heart.

"We'll talk more about Lalaree and Juniper soon. To me it sounded like they were still in an 'only-talking-about-it' phase, so I'd say that there is still plenty of time to offer them our opinions, not that they necessarily would *want* our opinions, but still. . . ."

Sabella sighed at his answer. He was right, of course, but after learning more about "matters of the heart," she was not exactly sure how or even *if* she should answer her daughter's message. Eventually she sent Lalaree a mental message conveying her deepest love, explaining that she'd been out of contact recently while on her pilgrimage, and that she and Thomas would like to talk more with her as soon as possible.

Finally Sabella contacted Issoweet and asked about a convenient time and place to meet.

Issoweet suggested that they meet early the next morning. In keeping with the Air Element theme, Issoweet said that it might be nice to meet on the bluffs of a place once called the "Torrey Pines Wind Sanctuary," which overlooked the Pacific Ocean. The strong air currents there were perfect for observing gliding birdlife and gliding people, too. Sabella smiled at the message and agreed to be there on time.

Issoweet greeted Sabella with folded palms; Sabella replied in kind. They looked into each other's eyes for a moment. Sabella was conscious that Issoweet knew what divine, unconditional love really was—she was channeling it to Sabella today, in full force. Sabella staggered and almost began levitating, or was it the strong wind currents buffeting them in this beautiful, airy place?

The Pacific Ocean was wildly alive with white-capped waves and crashing surf, spreading out before them in all its majesty for as far as they could see. Dolphins were bounding through the waves not far offshore, whales were sounding further out, seeming to leap for joy, and sea gulls were soaring over the water and over their heads. Now that she knew more about the joy of flying, she longed to join them in their air dances.

"Maybe I didn't choose the best place for us to meet today," Issoweet transmitted wryly, picking up Sabella's small wish to soar with the gulls.

"No, it's fine! I love being here! Let's sit and talk and enjoy the fresh sea breezes. I have questions for you, dearest Issoweet."

They sat down, dangling their legs over the edge of the most prominent cliff in that area. Sabella began, "First, while I remember it, Bhima sends you his greetings and love. He asked that you explain to me about the 'tastes' which are experienced in connection with the chakras.

"As we were parting, he gave me a gift of a small piece of heart-shaped candy, which tasted a bit sour, like crushed limes. I've never tasted anything quite like it. I think it was not really a physical taste at all, but perhaps an astral taste, if that makes any sense. It was ultimately satisfying!

"I hope you brought another picnic lunch with you. Although I haven't been hungry since I ate Bhima's parting gift to me, I think I am going to be hungry soon."

"The large-hearted Bhima!" Issoweet laughed. "Isn't he the biggest dear-heart of all times? And he always does things a little differently.

"And no, I didn't bring a picnic lunch this time, but we needn't be long in our discussion this morning. When we are finished, I'll prepare you a good, 'hearty' meal at my home."

Sabella was thrilled. She never expected to be invited to Issoweet's home, though she often wondered what it might be like. A person's home often reveals much about her personality.

Sabella had not known Issoweet very long. Like her twin brother, Simeon, she seemed to be a very private person. Sabella longed to know her better—this kind, but somewhat reserved, sister of her most-beloved spiritual teacher, Simeon.

"To answer your question about the 'tastes' of the chakras: this is one of the more esoteric aspects of the chakra sciences, and one not often taught, except to advanced students. Here's how it is explained. When one nears enlightenment and the *kundalini* energy approaches the *Kutastha* (the spiritual eye and the positive pole of the sixth chakra), several phenomena begin to occur.

"We discussed the colors and shapes which can be seen in the spiritual eye and the individual chakra AUM sounds that can be heard inwardly. In addition to those experiences, there is a specific taste for each chakra that comes into the mouth and taste buds; this happens when a chakra is purified and awakened. Here are the tastes in order, as they have been revealed by the Great Ones:

1st chakra, Earth Element, a sweet juice taste
2nd chakra, Water Element, a mildly bitter taste
3rd chakra, Fire Element, a bitter taste
4th chakra, Air Element, a sour taste
5th chakra, Ether Element, an extremely bitter taste
6th chakra, Super-Ether, *amrita*, also called *soma*, the blissful nectar of God and the sweetest possible taste that can be experienced

"Fascinating!" Sabella exclaimed. "Tell me more!"

"Paramhansa Yogananda described the taste of each chakra. For example, here are his words describing the taste experienced in the first chakra: 'When the Earth Element's vibration in the coccygeal plexus [first chakra] is manifest in meditation and reflected in the *Kutastha* [sixth chakra], sweet juice is tasted in the throat and attachment for sweet juices accrues.'

"Yes, I know what you are thinking, Sabella. You are thinking, 'Wait a minute, I thought we were trying to get rid of all attachments to sense pleasures, not make them stronger! What's with this 'attachment-to-sweet-juices' thing'?"

Sabella laughed, "Issoweet, you are very quick to pick up on my tiniest mind-questions, but yes, that is exactly what I was wondering."

Issoweet transmitted, "I believe that Yogananda was using the word 'attachment' in a slightly different way than how we usually use it. He was suggesting that since we are attached to many things anyway, why not put our energy into the higher or more helpful attachments, those that will lead us to freedom on the inner pathway of the spine? Harmful attachments or addictions should be the first ones we work on letting go of.

"Attachment to the 'taste of sweet juice' would fall into the category of a helpful or at least benign desire. Or perhaps a better term than attachment would be 'a deeper *appreciation* of sweetness,' or something like that."

"Yes, that sounds right, and it is right on time, because I want to ask you more about the subject of letting go of all attachments."

"That's a big subject, Sabella, best addressed after we have a nourishing lunch. But first, I want to tell you more about the *amrita* taste, the blissful nectar experienced in the sixth chakra.

"In Yogananda's description of cosmic consciousness in his *Autobiography*: 'I cognized the center of the empyrean as a point of intuitive perception in my heart. Irradiating splendor issued from my nucleus to every part of the universal structure. Blissful *amrita*, the nectar of immortality, pulsed through me with a quicksilver-like fluidity.'

"The great masters of yoga explain how, in deep ecstasy, the tongue automatically turns upward toward the brain. They teach a yoga technique you have practiced, called *kechari mudra*. This *mudra* involves stretching the tip of the tongue upward and backward in the mouth, so that it touches the uvula, and then with practice, reaches further behind the soft palate into the nasal cavity.

"At the tip of the tongue is a positive magnetism which, when united with its negative complement in the nasal cavity, 'short-circuits' (in a manner of speaking) the flow of energy, preventing it from leaving the brain and flowing into the body. With this physical union, a kind of 'nectar' is created, described as having the taste of a blend of *ghee* (clarified butter) and honey. This nectar is able to sustain the body for long periods of time while fasting, or more importantly, while the soul remains rapt in superconscious union with God.

"When the positive and negative energies in the tongue and nasal passages are joined together, they create a cycle of energy in the head which generates a magnetic field that draws energy upward from the body and the base of the spine to the brain. It is said that when one attains *samadhi*, the tongue automatically turns backward and its tip enters the nasal passage. For this reason, assumption of *kechari mudra* hastens the advent of deep spiritual states of consciousness.

"Do you remember the words to a devotional chant which Yogananda translated from the Bengali language, called 'Satya Mangala' or in English, 'Thou Art My Life'?

"Oh yes," said Sabella, "It's always been one of my favorite chants!"

Spontaneously they sang the chant together, their voices blending in beautiful harmony together:

> *Thou art my life,*
> *Thou art my love,*
> *Thou art the sweetness which I do seek.*
> *In the thought by my love brought*
> *I taste Thy name, so sweet, so sweet!*

Sabella felt her heart open like an exquisite lotus blossom. She remembered once again the truth of Yogananda's famous admonition: "Chanting is half the battle." In her experience, there was no other kind of music that opened her heart in quite the same way as devotional chanting. This brought up a question that had been bothering her for some time.

"Issoweet, I understand that all of life is a battlefield, an inner battle between one's own forces of good and evil. I'm having firsthand experience in my pilgrimage of what it means to be a 'spiritual warrior.' But if 'chanting is half the battle,' what is the other half? Surely it must be meditation."

Issoweet replied, "I once asked a wise sage this very question. He surprised me by saying that the other half of the battle is devotion.

"I replied, 'But it is my understanding that chanting is a devotional practice—probably the best. I certainly would have guessed that meditation is the other half of the battle.'

'In a way, you are right,' he said. 'Meditation cannot be neglected. Nevertheless, it must be done devotionally, that is, with the heart fully open and receptive to God's grace."

"Oh, Issoweet, thank you for that most satisfying answer to something I've wondered about for many years! I can see how it is just one more way of emphasizing the importance of the heart chakra's purity and devotional tendencies as major components of our inner spiritual journey."

Sabella thought shyly. "I love this breezy cliff by the sea, but I must admit I'm very hungry. May we eat soon, or should I start practicing *kechari mudra* to keep hunger away?"

Sabella wanted to suggest that they fly to Issoweet's home, but since she didn't know how far away it was, she didn't say anything. Issoweet teleported them in the usual way.

"Sabella, we could have flown here as you wished. It wasn't that far," Issoweet said, picking up her thought, "but Bhima was right when he advised you to 'use discrimination,' or, as I think he said to you, to 'keep a low profile when flying or levitating.'"

"Yes, he did say that, and I've been wondering why? Can you tell me?"

"After lunch! I'm hungry, too. No fasting is necessary today!

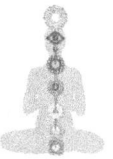

CHAPTER THIRTY-THREE

Issoweet's home was not far from the High Council pavilion, where she and Sabella had first met. Like Sabella's home, Issoweet's home was built in the shape of a pyramid. But unlike Sabella's, it was very large, with transparent walls, and was mostly empty!

"Why does she need all this empty space? And why is there no furniture to speak of? And why transparent? She seems to be such a private person." Sabella wondered to herself.

"Because I *prefer* the feeling of emptiness all around me. And because I like to see the stars at night." Issoweet smiled.

"I'll take you to my outdoor kitchen and dining patio in a few minutes, but first let me give you a quick tour of my home. Let's fly up to that round platform floating above you. Flying inside my home is allowed, especially if I say so, and now I *do* say so—to you," she laughed out loud, slightly startling Sabella. She loved seeing this playful side of her mentor.

"I know we are both hungry, but since we are here, I want to invite you to meditate with me for just a few minutes. You are one of very few of my friends whom I have ever allowed to see my home, much less sit with me in my meditation space."

Hunger vanished, and Sabella gratefully accepted the kind invitation.

Issoweet took her hand and they flew up to a space near the top of the pyramid where a large round, transparent platform floated. Sabella noticed that it had been carefully placed in the upper central part of the pyramid—the focalized power-point of all pyramidal shapes. This was Issoweet's private meditation space. It was stunningly beautiful, softly illuminated with colorful floating lights and infused with fragrant incense. It had holographic images of the saints and masters of many religions and times, carefully placed in the air all around the platform. Fresh flowers and fragrant sprigs of fresh herbs also tastefully decorated the sacred space.

Since her visit to the fourth-chakra pyramid, Sabella no longer needed a chair or cushion to sit on for meditation. She simply sat comfortably cross-legged, while levitating a few inches above the ground. It felt perfect and completely natural. She noticed Issoweet doing the same thing.

After meditating for a short time, Issoweet chanted softly to bring them out of meditation:

> *Door of my heart*
> *Open wide I keep for Thee. . . .*

She then prepared a delightful meal for the two of them, and they ate it outside, on Issoweet's small patio.

The meal consisted entirely of fresh herbs and vegetables, harvested earlier that same morning from Issoweet's garden, including a small dessert made of just-picked raspberries and sliced peaches.

The herb, vegetable, and fruit gardens and orchards surrounded the patio. It was refreshing to feel the fresh food entering her body, as Sabella gratefully ate the tasty lunch. She could feel that everything she was eating was saturated with larger-than-usual amounts of *prana.*

As she ate silently, chewing slowly, savoring each bite, it was only natural for Sabella to offer her inner and most sincere appreciation to the lovingly-grown food, to these plant-friends who she knew sincerely loved to give back to their human friends, as they were able. She also thanked Issoweet for preparing the meal for her.

"I have never eaten a meal that tasted quite this good, and I do mean that! Thank you and thanks also for inviting me to visit your unusual home and spectacular gardens. I am truly honored . . . words fail me."

Issoweet accepted the compliments graciously, "It has been my joy to have you as my guest! When I cook, I always try to include a little of each of the chakras' tastes: sweet, bitter, and sour. Could you tell? That sort of combination, along with a very small amount of pink-salt-crystal flavoring, makes for a correct *Ayurvedic* diet.

"But the real secret of good food is love. I love to grow and help nourish the plants. I give them care and love, and they give it back to me through what is produced, with God's and all the nature *devas'* assistance. I pray and sing as I prepare it, sending divine love and blessings into it.

"Love is the most important ingredient in *any* meal!

"And my dear Sabella, I must tell you that I am growing to love you more and more as a close friend, and not just as a student I am mentoring at Simeon's request."

Tears sprang to Sabella's eyes when she heard these words. Then she remembered Bhima's admonition to transmute emotion into devotion. Quickly she inwardly employed the technique he taught her. She was astonished how quickly and well it worked. The love was still present, but it had been transformed from human love into something much higher and finer. Divine love! Oh that the whole world could feel this kind of love!

"I do agree with that thought," Issoweet said happily.

Sabella said quietly, "And I love you also, Issoweet."

"Now I need to do Bhima's technique," Issoweet said, wiping a tear from her eye.

Issoweet, ever-practical, said, "Let's clean up from lunch and then we'll talk some more before you return home."

Sitting together in the garden a little later, Issoweet said to Sabella, "You asked about Bhima's instructions about flying. I agree with him that keeping this fourth-chakra power private as best as you can is wise—as a protection for *you*. As with all powers, it is critical to keep the abilty to fly from creating deeper ego attachment."

Sabella was surprised. "But how could *that* happen? To me, flying simply feels like an extremely enjoyable thing to do."

"Yes," Issoweet agreed. "I also enjoy flying. But watch your mind carefully, especially if you are seen, while flying, by people who don't possess the same power. They might become envious. But the biggest danger is that your mind might move into a downward spiral of self-involvement, by telling you, 'See how *I* can do something that other people can't. Great for me! Too bad for them, but obviously I am more spiritually advanced than they are.'

"And remember our discussion about astral travel? You told me how Simeon explained the pitfalls of the egotistical way you were experimenting with astral travel when you were very young. I believe the lesson Simeon tried to teach you then involved the same principles we are discussing now."

Sabella reflected on these ideas for a while and had to admit that ego entrapment could happen if one were not careful. She said, "This reminds me of when I was a child and was having many flying dreams. I would enjoy the dreams very much, until I began to think more carefully about what I was doing.

"In the dream, I'd realize, 'I'm flying! How wonderful this feels—but wait a minute. I can't really fly normally. How am I doing this?' And at that moment in my dream, I would sink to the ground and become unable to 'lift off' again, at least during that particular dream experience. How disappointed I would feel, especially after awakening and remembering how wonderful it felt to be able to fly.

"'Next time I have a flying dream,' I'd say to myself, 'I won't question my ability to fly. Perhaps that way I can continue flying, without sinking again.' But my doubts were relentless. Flying in dreams was very enjoyable, but it always ended when I began to question my ability to fly."

They laughed together, and Sabella said. "Yes, I do understand, and I promise to be discreet with my flying and levitating abilities."

Issoweet said, "I know you will, dear one. Always keep in

mind Sri Yukteswar's words to Yogananda after Yogananda's experience in cosmic consciousness. 'Spiritual advancement is not measured by one's outward powers, but only by the depth of one's bliss in meditation.'

"You said earlier that you wanted to discuss the aspect of the heart chakra concerning attachments. Please tell me what you would like to know."

"Yes, I do. Thank you. After I returned home from my experiences in the fourth pyramid, I received a message from my eldest daughter, Lalaree. She is considering life-linking with a young man. My first response surprised me. I felt very strongly opposed to their union, even though I've never even met her friend, Juniper!

"And I thought, 'Surely she can't mean to do this *now*. She is too young! She couldn't know him well enough. She is still learning about life and who she really is. . . .' And so on.

"I felt that particular attachment cord on my heart give a big TWANG, just as Bhima had so graphically described and had me experience firsthand. And it hurt! I immediately recognized the twinge of heart-pain, for I understand that attachment is the cause of all heartaches and heartbreaks. No one who has experienced a failed relationship would say, 'I'm suffering from a broken brain, knee, or any other part of the body.' No, the feeling is always in our hearts. Heart-string attachments are very real and powerful!

"What can I do with heart-pain like this? Should I not care about my daughter, my first-born child? How could I *not* love her and want the best for her? The heart chakra is such a 'tricky beast,' isn't it? And how can I explain this important concept to future students?"

"Oh, I agree! Our hearts are 'tricky beasts' indeed! In the fourth-chakra pyramid, you used Bhima's knife to cut through all your heart strings to feel free of all attachments—at least temporarily. This is a wonderful practice to begin all our meditations.

"Visualizing cutting away all ties and letting them go, at least for the time you are meditating, is very helpful for the truth-seeker. In this way, we *practice* getting rid of attachments.

"Ties like these don't go away immediately. Nor should they! A mother needs to be attached to her child to a certain degree, or else the baby might annoy the sleep-deprived mother so much with its constant demands that she might be tempted to throw it out the window!"

"Issoweet, that is so harsh! I am shocked that you would say such a thing!"

"Hear me out, Sabella! We can release all our attachments in meditation through prayer or visualization. But before we even realize it, they've jumped right back onto us soon after meditation ends, and we resume our mundane daily lives. So as I said, what is necessary is practice, practice, *practice*, until non-attachment becomes a natural state of mind. Then we can still lovingly perform all our duties, without attachment. It's really the only way to go!

"Please realize that we don't have to jettison our families, friends, homes, and so on, least physically or all at once. It can and *should* be a gradual process. It needs to occur in a particular sequence, with our first step being the letting go of obviously harmful attachments. A negative behavior pattern, such as constantly losing one's temper, is a good example.

"Remember that in the world in which we live, most of us have many responsibilities, such as taking care of business, finances, family, home, and so on. But we can learn, *gradually*, to carry on successfully with our lives and increasingly cultivate an attitude of non-attachment in the heart."

Sabella interrupted, "But isn't there some danger that a constant attitude of detachment could turn one into a cold, harsh, or unfeeling person? I pray never to be that way!"

"It could, but it won't, if you do it right, Sabella Lovingheart. It is very important to learn how to love in the *right* way, not with attachment, but by allowing yourself to be a channel of pure, Divine Love, which can then flow unobstructed through your heart to all.

"And with specific reference to your daughter, think of it this way. If Lalaree had died at an early age, I'm sure you would have mourned her loss and missed her greatly. But what if she had, unknown to you, been quickly reborn in the home of your next-door neighbors? Would you have loved her as deeply then?

She might even have returned as a bratty little boy who came over and trampled down your newly planted flower beds. Same soul, but in your mind and heart, he would not be *your* child. How would you feel about him or her then?"

"You are right, Issoweet. I wouldn't have felt the same. Intellectually I know that we are all one, and everyone deserves our unconditional love—it's just so *difficult* not to love certain people more than others. I can see that I still have inner work to do in order to accomplish equal, perfect, and unconditional love for all."

"In this respect, you are similar to almost everyone else who lives or has ever lived. This is a strongly ingrained tendency and it takes time and great effort, plus deep meditation to change it! Take *heart*!" she chuckled at her play on words. "You'll get there soon enough. We all will. It is our unfailing destiny. The only variable is how long it takes. And that is completely up to us to decide."

Issoweet continued, "I know that you and Bhima discussed many 'heart subjects' extensively, but have you ever wondered how a great saint or master is able to love *everyone* equally and without exception? It would seem to be a task which is massively heroic or even humanly impossible, which, in a way it is!

"But it is *divinely possible*. While the Great Ones love the essence of a person, they might not necessarily love the way they are acting. They love and relate to the 'God-spark' or the soul within each person. They feel their oneness with that soul and its connection with their own souls. If it could be said that they have any desire at all, it would be the 'desire-less desire' to help all souls, or as many as possible, to emerge from their cocoons of ignorance and bondage in not knowing who and what they really are! Each one of us is divinely free and one with God—we only have to realize it."

"Is the last desire to go the one of wanting to help others to become free also?" Sabella asked.

"So it would seem," Issoweet said quietly, with a twinkle in her eye.

"For now, dear Sabella, it is time for us to go our separate ways. Before we do, do you have any questions or concerns about your next adventure?"

"The fifth chakra!" Sabella exclaimed enthusiastically. "With the help of my gracious guides, I seem to be making progress—anyway, so far, so good. Although I am looking forward to meeting King Yudhisthira, the eldest of the Pandava brothers, it seems that just before I am to enter a new pyramid, I begin to feel overwhelmed by the idea of meeting yet another of these great personages But no, I don't think I have any more questions.

"I do want to say how much I appreciate the discussions we have after each portion of my pilgrimage. I have come to love and trust you deeply, Issoweet. I feel that I can ask you anything in the world, and you won't judge me for my faults, ignorance, or shortcomings. You are a blessed gift in my life right now."

Sabella knelt and touched Issoweet's feet in the ancient gesture of greatest respect. Issoweet slowly lifted her right hand to touch her own forehead, fingers pointed upward, symbolizing that she accepted Sabella's offering, but was giving it all back to the Source of everything.

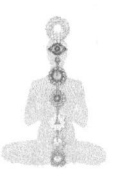

CHAPTER THIRTY-FOUR

At home that evening with Thomas, Sabella spoke to him about the next portion of her pilgrimage. "Thomas, what do you know about Yudhisthira, the eldest of the Pandava brothers? As you know, he will be my host tomorrow in the fifth-chakra pyramid."

"I know a little about him. Yudhisthira was the first-born son of King Pandu and Queen Kunti. Actually his 'real' father, whom Kunti invoked with a special magic *mantra*, was Lord Dharma, the God of perfect righteous action, absolute wisdom, and unfailing truthfulness."

"Thomas, what does it mean when we are told in the story that the five Pandava brothers were half humans through their mothers and half-gods through their fathers? I think I understand, but I want to hear your ideas about it."

"It seems clear to me that this is an important part of their nature as symbols for the chakras, which are both human and divine. The material parts of our beings are easier to know and relate to than our spiritual natures. This is because our physical bodies often seem very solid to us, being outward-oriented and as strongly influenced by sensory input as they are. Therefore, even though the constantly outward-moving energy patterns feel much more familiar to us, the subtle, inward-moving energy patterns of our divine natures are every bit as much a part of us.

"When a child is born, it possesses a powerful instinct to reach outside of itself for breath, food, a loving touch, and so on. The young child's initial and important self-preservation instinct becomes a habitual way of relating to the world, that is, relating only to what is outside of him or her. We invest greatly in the concept that we absolutely must get all our sustenance and input only from outside ourselves. And so these energy flows are quickly established and constantly reinforced.

"This is a natural part of our *humanness*. Nevertheless, humans also possess a divine nature. We are both children of God and children of this world. Our divine nature abides within us, often dormant for a long time, patiently waiting for us to become aware of it and to begin to awaken it.

"When our spiritual awakening commences, as it eventually must, we begin to perceive the need to relate to our divine nature. The divine part of us is like a seed in the ground that lives there quietly, remaining dormant until the rain and the warmth of the sun coax it to sprout, grow, and expand itself as a plant, reaching toward the light."

Sabella beamed at him in appreciation, "Thank you, dearest one, for explaining this concept so clearly. What else can you tell me about Yudhisthira?"

"Another of his names was Dharmaraj, which means the 'king of *dharma*.' *Dharma*, as you know, means right action. We behave in a *dharmic* way when our own human will is attuned to the will of God.

"Victory for the Pandavas in the great war of Kurukshetra was assured for two primary reasons:

"First, they chose to be divinely guided by God in the form of Lord Krishna.

"Second, although Yudhisthira was the eldest brother of both clans and the rightful king of the realm, he and his brothers were forced to reclaim their realm from the evil usurper, Duryodhana, or 'King Material Desire' through armed combat. It was a righteous war in which King Yudhisthira would prevail. He was the epitome of truthfulness and righteousness. He was always careful to do the right thing, under every circumstance. He was so exceptionally pure in heart and mind that his feet and the chariot he rode in never quite touched the ground.

"Not too long before the war began, Yudhisthira's father, Lord Dharma, came to him in disguise and tested him to see if he would remain *dharmic* under extremely trying circumstances. One by one, Lord Dharma killed each of Yudhisthira's four beloved brothers, to Yudhisthira's great dismay!

"Lord Dharma told Yudhisthira that he was sorry for what he had done and that he would relent slightly by giving life back to one, but *only* one, of his brothers.

'Which one of your brothers do you choose to be brought back to life?' Lord Dharma asked him.

"Without hesitation, Yudhisthira said, 'I choose Nakula.'

"Lord Dharma was astonished. 'But why would you choose Nakula? Arjuna is the greatest archer in the world, and it will be essential that he serve as your general in the coming battle. Bhima is the largest and mightiest warrior who ever lived. You'll certainly need his strength to assure your victory. Why choose Nakula from among all your brothers?'

"Yudhisthira calmly answered. 'As Kunti's son, I still live; therefore she will have one living son. If I asked for life to be restored to either Arjuna or Bhima, she would have two living sons, while my step-mother, Madri, who is Nakula and Sahadeva's birth mother and whom I love equally, would have no sons left.'

"Dharma was very impressed by his son's selflessness and wisdom. He revealed his true identity and gave Yudhisthira an *astra*, which is an invincible, supernatural energy weapon, to help him in the coming war. Lord Dharma also restored the lives of all four of Yudhisthira's brothers. He had passed his father's test with flying colors."

Thomas continued, "Yudhisthira also stands for 'calmness in psychological battle.' He is an *excellent ally* for all of us to have on the battlefield of life."

Sabella smiled at her husband, "I'm so glad I had the good

sense to become life-linked with you, Thomas. You are amazing!"

Thomas laughed, and said that he felt the same way about her.

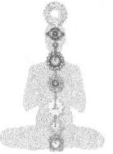

CHAPTER THIRTY-FIVE

Early the next day, after meditation and a light breakfast, Sabella teleported herself to the entrance of the fifth-chakra pyramid. Radiantly golden in the morning sun, from the outside it looked like the first four pyramids she had already visited. But even before entering, she could feel stronger and higher vibrations emanating from this pyramid.

As always, Brother Solonar was there to greet her, answer questions before they entered the pyramid, and offer his blessings for the next part of her pilgrimage. She thanked him graciously, and assured him that she was ready. In the twinkling of an eye, they were inside. Similar to her first four experiences, she saw that the walls of the pyramid were transparent, except in this case, they seemed to be floating in outer space, with suns, moons, stars, planets, galaxies, and comets all whirling and whizzing around them in perfect coordination. It was a breathtaking sight.

A quiet voice beside her said, "Sabella, what do you think of my kingdom of *Bishuddha-loka* and of the Element of Ether and all space?"

She turned to see a very royal-looking man—regal in every sense of the word. He was a mighty warrior, like his brothers, and was dressed in a gloriously lush, royal blue robe. He wore a small crown studded with deep-green emeralds, and his eyes were the same intense green color of the gemstone in his crown. His lustrous, dark brown hair was greying at the temples, making him look wise and distinguished.

Without hesitation, she knelt before him and said, "King Yudhisthira, it is my great joy to meet you. The cosmic beauty of this place is stunning."

After he had acknowledged her, Yudhisthira turned to greet Solonar, "Welcome, Brother Solonar. Would both of you like to join me in my private quarters for some refreshments?" Yudhisthira's voice rang with power, and yet was soft and kind.

Solonar replied, "Duties call me elsewhere, sir. May I have your leave to attend to them now? Sabella, do you need me for anything else before I go?"

"Thank you, my kind friend," Sabella said, "I am fine. I'm happy to be here and learn more about this amazing place, with King Yudhisthira guiding me."

In an instant, Sabella and Yudhisthira were sitting in a large room which looked like someone's very old, private library, for it contained actual *books*. Although printed, physical books were almost non-existent in Treta Yuga, Sabella had seen pictures of them. She was fascinated to see many, many volumes of such books, right here, in this room.

"I know you are surprised to see all these books, Sabella. Written language and the tiresome task of creating, writing, and then laboriously translating ones thoughts into written words, began to come into being shortly after my lifetime as King Yudhisthira, at the close of Descending Dwapara Yuga.

"Writing skills became necessary for the people of that age to develop, because human beings were quickly losing their ability to remember things accurately by means of an oral tradition—a result of the decreased mental energy of an increasingly darker age. So writing and books had to be created in order to help people remember what needed to be preserved.

That is how the great *Mahabharata* epic, including its core essence, the *Bhagavad Gita*, came to be written down and preserved. Thus it was able to survive the mental darkness of Kali Yuga. It is important to be reminded occasionally of momentous changes like these, no matter in which yuga you presently live."

He stood to show her the ancient books which were in a

prominent place on one of the bookshelves. She was honored to see them, for she knew that within them were presented, in story-form, a complete outline for the inner spiritual journey. And even more important to her, the epic's main characters were now her close friends and guides, the Pandava Brothers and their wife, Queen Draupadi.

He went on, "Somehow, it comforts me to have all these books around. Draupadi often teases me about this, calling me her bookworm. She also takes me to task for being too quiet, too inward, too enamored of intellectual pursuits, and for wanting to live a hermit-like life. Back in the *Mahabharata* era, Draupadi rightly demanded that I honor the duties as king and warrior that came with being the eldest brother.

"In any case, the books remind me and my visitors that human beings are continually struggling to find higher truths, and having found what they perceive to be true, to record it and act on it. It is a never-ending show, isn't it, Sabella?"

Sabella nodded in agreement. Yudhisthira indicated that she should join him at a beautifully set table nearby, which was laden with out-of-this-world desserts, delicacies, and beverages.

"Please sit down," he said simply, "We can chat while you sample the simple fare that I had prepared especially for you."

"If this is simple," thought Sabella privately as she filled a solid silver dessert plate, "I'd cringe to see what he would consider to be gourmet food."

Sabella stopped chewing a delicious morsel, when she noticed with embarrassment that Yudhisthira was not eating anything.

"I wanted to offer you a royal spread—kingly appearances to keep up, you know. On the whole, I prefer to fast and pray. But please go ahead, dear child," he smiled at her encouragingly, "and don't mind my abstinence. It's just my way."

She needed no further encouragement. Deeply satisfied, she finally sat back in her chair and thought of how grateful she was for her fifth chakra's part in enabling her to swallow.

Seeing that she had finished eating, Yudhisthira said,

"*Bishuddha* (sometimes spelled *vishuddha*) is the Sanskrit name for the fifth chakra. As you know, it means 'to purify.' By the time a truth-seeker's life-force has risen to the first of the three higher chakras, known as the 'chakras of our divinity,' great rays of light become available for the purification needed to help to complete the remainder of the journey.

"What else do you know about the fifth chakra and the Element of Ether, Sabella?"

Sabella replied, "The fifth chakra is located in the lower throat area. It influences the neck, throat, our ability to swallow through the esophagus which connects the mouth to the stomach, our ability to breathe through the trachea, which connects the nose and mouth to the lungs, and the ability to speak and sing, because of its proximity to the larynx and vocal cords.

"Which reminds me, Yudhisthira, if you don't mind my asking, do you sing? It would stand to reason that you would, because. . . ."

Yudhisthira interrupted her with his laughter, "Honestly, Sabella—and I am always scrupulously honest—no pilgrim has ever asked me that question! But I understand that with your talent as an excellent musician, composer, and singer, naturally you would be interested in that aspect of *Bishuddha-loka*. The answer is yes, but I'd rather show you firsthand than tell you. I have a special concert arranged for you a little later on. I wanted it to be a surprise, but you intuited it before I could even tell you! I'm impressed."

Sabella was delighted to hear this, but knew Yudhisthira was waiting for her to explain more about the fifth chakra.

"Using our speaking voices in a divine way, being conscious of blessing people with the tone of our voice, is a wonderful way to purify the fifth chakra. It helps to use our voices not only as a 'beast of burden' for our ideas, but as a channel for sending out calmness and love. I've found that by simply modifying the vibrations of my speaking or singing voice that I can beneficially influence my own and other peoples' levels of consciousness.

229

"If we listen carefully when we or others speak, we will notice when negative emotions are expressed. For example, if a person is feeling a lower emotion—anger, tension, egoism—a sensitive listener can hear it reflected in the speaker's tone of voice. One scripture puts it this way, 'Out of the fullness of the heart, the mouth speaketh.' This is true in a literal sense!

"We have all heard someone caught in anger forcefully say, 'I am not angry!' Even without the physical signs of clenched teeth and fists, the tone of voice is a dead give-away that the person is indeed very angry, even if they have been trying hard to suppress it. The anger-emotion arising from the heart chakra shows up clearly through the vocal aspect of the throat chakra.

"It's hard to hide our emotions when we speak. This demonstrates one of the many connections among the chakras, in this case, between the fourth and fifth chakras.

"One great saint said that it was easy for him to identify anyone's level of spiritual development by hearing their speaking voice. I too have noticed that a person's voice vibrates differently—sweeter, softer, and calmer—after they begin to meditate regularly.

"The fifth chakra is very important for all forms of communication and not just because it influences the physical ability to speak or sing. It is the bridge between body and brain—the place through which all messages must pass, that is, from the brain to the body and from the body back to the brain. It is 'Communications Central,' so to speak."

Sabella continued, "In Patanjali's eightfold path, the throat chakra corresponds to *pratyahara*, which means that in meditation one becomes able to interiorize the mind completely. It also refers to the withdrawal of life force from the five senses—which Yogananda often referred to as 'turning off the five sense telephones.'"

"Excellent, Sabella!" Yudhisthira complemented her. "I would only add one more item to your explanation. *Pratyahara*, or interiorizing the mind, is more easily perfected when it is connected with the practice of *pranayama*, which brings the energy-flows of our bodies under our control.

"However, working on any 'limb' of Patanjali's eightfold path will enhance our ability to perfect the other 'limbs,' just as working with our chakras is best done holistically. It is far better to *not* focus too exclusively on any one chakra, to the exclusion of the others. We must strive to see the whole in each individual part of the spiritual path."

"Yudhisthira, I know that this is the kingdom of the Ether Element, but I must admit that I'm not sure I understand what *ether* really is. I believe at one point, thousands of years ago, ether was a gas used to anesthetize people undergoing physical operations, in which knives were actually used to cut them open, in the hopes of healing them." She flinched at the thought of such a barbaric practice.

"The other chakra elements of earth, water, fire, and air are easy to relate to and are such perfect symbols for each of the first four chakras. But *ether*?"

"Yes, I understand that the word ether is difficult to comprehend. That's because *ether* is insubstantial and . . . well, *ethereal*." Yudhisthira chuckled at his small joke.

"Ether has very little material substance. In ancient scientific theories, light was considered to be a wave. Since waves are disturbances of a medium and light can travel in a vacuum without air, scientists invented the concept 'luminiferous ether,' a mysterious substance through which light waves were thought to travel. Further experiments showed that this was not true.

"*Ethereal*, in another sense, means 'that which is intangible, highly refined, delicate, part of the celestial spheres, or heavenly.' These terms more clearly define the true nature of the Ether Element of the fifth chakra; it symbolizes our ability to break through the final veils of delusion. It can help us to realize that there is something altogether beyond the ego and personality.

"Paramhansa Yogananda said that 'ether is the vibration that separates the material universe from the astral universe—the

231

vibration of space.' He also said that ether actually exists, even though it is a *very* subtle, and not an always fully understood, vibrational field."

"It seems like this chakra represents a kind of 'space station' or a 'jumping-off place' from which to leave behind all material things, including our physical bodies, and begin to merge into universal consciousness," Sabella reflected.

"Yes, that is the general idea," Yudhisthira said.

He continued, "The qualities of this chakra are subtle and often difficult to understand.

"On the beneficial side are deep CALMNESS, INNER and OUTER SILENCE, and EXPANSION OF CONSCIOUSNESS.

"The fifth chakra's harmful side includes RESTLESSNES AND BOREDOM, which expresses itself as being MERCURIAL and too CHANGEABLE. Its influence may cause us to feel that we are being mentally tossed about, back and forth, up and down. It can make us restless, with a tendency to run around and do things, and a desire to have experiences as a way of fighting boredom. It also may cause a FEAR OF EXPANSION OF CONSCIOUSNESS."

"Wait! Boredom? How could that be?" Sabella asked. "To me the fifth-chakra kingdom seems gloriously expansive, highly evolved, and filled with vibrations of cosmic light! Deep meditation is very calming—but it is not boring or threatening to all the things that we enjoy. Instead, it makes all of life better and offers us the ability to enjoy all things more sensitively and completely!"

Yudhisthira sighed and answered her, "What you have said is true, but even sincere truth-seekers sometimes grow tired of their continuous spiritual efforts; to them it seems like it is taking too long. Their efforts seem to demand unceasing, hard work, with too few tangible rewards.

"Even after experiencing great joy in meditation, I've heard them say things like 'I'm bored. I'm tired of the constant need for meditation, chanting, introspection, and working on perfecting my attitudes. I think I liked my old life better.

It was easier! I think I'll go back to my old ways. I want a hamburger! I want to get drunk and dance the night away. I need sex. I crave diversion and entertainment'!"

"Yes, I understand fully," Sabella said. "These feelings cause us to want to drop back into the downward and outward flowing energy streams of the lower chakras. I remember feeling that way several times when I was younger."

"May I ask what you did when this happened?" Yudhisthira enquired.

"Often I gave in and indulged myself in the things of this world—at least for a short time. But these experiences quickly grew empty and pale by comparison to the spiritual joy I was beginning to feel. I guess I just had to get a few desires out of my system. I never told anyone what I had done, thinking they might say I had 'fallen' from my high aspirations, or something like that. But I came to find out later that this sort of thing happens to almost every truth-seeker.

"I began to notice that each time it happened to me, these diversions evolved to a higher vibration. For example, instead of a hamburger and a highly-caffeinated beverage or an alcoholic drink, I was much happier and more satisfied with a bowl of freshly picked cherries and a glass of sparkling water. I knew that these *somewhat* 'higher' kinds of diversions showed that I was making at least *some* spiritual progress."

She continued, "It seems that the right thing to do, after something like this happens to us, is to say to ourselves, 'Well, I gave in and did it; now it's over and done with. I can more clearly see how indulging in such 'lower activities' are *not* part of what I want my life to be about in the future. I no longer wish to be attached to anything except divine calmness and inner joy.'

"Then it is best to turn our energies back to spiritual pursuits as quickly as we can, and never give into guilt for what we might have done or not done. Indulging in guilt is a complete waste of time and energy. A slip is not a fall! It's just one more step, even if it is a *misstep*, on our inner journey. And it can be a good learning experience!

"In certain ways, I knew I was a stronger person for having dealt with those temptations. They helped me to see that spiritual progress rarely moves in a straight line. When I began my teaching career, my previous missteps gave me great compassion for younger truth-seekers, for whom these sorts of lapses often happened.

"Another question please, if you don't mind. I'm puzzled by the meaning of a FEAR OF EXPANSION OF CONSCIOUSNESS?"

Yudhisthira said sadly, "You would be surprised at how badly a person can react to feeling her consciousness expand out of her usual comfort zone. Moving from living in the awareness of the little self as the *only* reality into the feeling of living in and being a part of the whole universe and beyond can be startling and even frightening.

"But let me show you what I mean in a clearer way. Would that be acceptable?"

"Yes, of course," Sabella said trustingly.

Her next moment of awareness showed her to be a little bird living in a cage. For a moment she was so startled by this transformation that she was unable to move or even chirp. But she soon grew more used to her "bird-ness," and she began to explore the confines of her cage.

It was a fairly large and comfortable place—it had nice perches, clean water in a cute little container, and plenty of fresh bird seed in another. She remembered that she had lived in this same cage since she was a nestling—it was all she had ever known! Looking through the bars of the cage, she could see that it was hanging from a small tree, under a starry night sky. She felt a pleasant breeze blowing through her feathers.

Something began stirring restlessly inside her breast, and her little bird-heart felt a strong, unknown longing. She was no longer comfortably at home in her small cage. She felt rebellious against what she now perceived was a life-long imprisonment. She squawked loudly and in her rising panic, fluttered wildly around the cage, throwing herself against its locked door.

"I want out! I want freedom! Let me go! Oh, let me out of here!" Her chirping grew weaker as she wore herself out.

It was then that she heard a familiar voice, coming from very close by. The voice said, "Sabella, I heard your call for help. Don't hurt yourself or waste time and energy battering yourself against the bars of the cage. Come over to the perch closest to the door and listen to me carefully."

"Who-o-o is there?" the little bird cried out in fear.

"I am your friend, Lady Kundalini. Sabella-birdie, don't you remember me? Please be calm. I am here to help you!"

Sabella's little bird-brain was not sure she understood what was going on, but she began to feel more at ease in the presence of the beautiful, dark lady.

"That's better, dear," the lady cooed to Sabella in soothing bird-tones. "Now I am going to open the cage door very slowly and invite you to hop onto the door's ledge and look around."

Sabella's little bird-heart felt happy. Her newly-awakened and fondest wish might be coming true. She hopped to the edge of the cage, and as instructed by the pretty lady, looked around in amazement. She was free!

The night sky twinkled with many stars which called to her saying, "Come to us. Be free with us."

She looked at her wings, fluttered them a little, and said to herself: "I have wings! I was born to fly!"

With that thought she flapped her wings joyfully and burst out of her cage in full flight. Lady Kundalini stood calmly beside the cage, and carefully watched the little bird, waiting to see what might unfold next.

For a few minutes, Sabella-birdie soared around in large circles, thoroughly enjoying being able to fly freely, unobstructed by her cage's confinement. Then she heeded the call of the night sky and flew straight up into the sky. It wasn't very long before her wings began to tire.

She had thought that the stars or moon would be close

enough for her to land on and rest for a while. She began to have a small inkling of the vastness of the universe before her—billions of stars, planets, suns, moons, nebulae, galaxies—all floating on the tides of space. The distances involved were beyond her comprehension.

Great fear clutched at her bird-heart, and she could barely breathe. She chirped loudly! "This is too *big*. The universe and all of space is much too large for me to endure. I'm just a little birdie, after all." With this thought, she turned around and flew as fast as her wings could carry her, back to her cage.

Lady Kundalini was there waiting for Sabella and said to her kindly, "It's big isn't it, dear?"

"Oh, kind lady, yes! I thought I wanted only freedom from this cage, but now I find I am afraid of that freedom. It's such a big universe. Perhaps I'm better off staying here, safe in my nice cage."

"You may do that, if you wish," Lady Kundalini said. "But I must warn you that since you've had a taste of flying freely, I suspect your sense of unhappiness with your confinement will rapidly return. I suggest that you rest for a while. We can leave the cage door open, so that after you are rested and your strength and courage have returned, you can begin taking short flights outside, traveling only as far away as you like, while always knowing that you can return here any time you wish."

And so it was that the little bird, over time, began to take longer and longer flights out into the sky. The comforts of the cage began to lose their attraction, when compared to the freedom and joy she experienced with each new flight.

One fine evening as she flew toward a particularly bright, silvery-white star, it occurred to her that she really did not need to go back to her cage ever again. All space, the entire universe, *this* was her true home! She knew that she was free forever and a part of the universe. With these liberating thoughts, her speed increased, and she focused *only* on the star. She soon merged into its bright light.

Lady Kundalini laughed joyfully and softly closed the door to Sabella's now useless cage. The brave little Sabella-bird had found her way to perfect freedom.

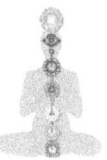

CHAPTER THIRTY-SIX

The light of the star was stunning, very bright and yet still soothing. Sabella felt completely free everything, especially her cumbersome body and restless thoughts. In freedom she floated through several universes, effortlessly one with all she perceived. No longer was it necessary to think or do anything—she could just be, and be, and be—forever!

She was startled to hear a voice in her non-existent ears, saying. "Sabella, please return to my presence. This is *not* the time for your final freedom. It will come, but there is still work for you to do. Your pilgrimage is not over yet!"

Hearing these words, she shrank back into her human body, which was comfortably seated in a dark blue and very plush reclining chair. Yudhisthira sat beside her, watching her calmly. The library walls had melted away and they were sitting together under the familiar stars and moon of the earth's night sky, all shining brightly above them.

Tears sprang to her eyes, for as beautiful as the sight of the night sky above her might be, she was unable to feel the same oneness and formless freedom she had so recently experienced.

Yudhisthira smiled gently. Wanting to help her become grounded in her ordinary state of being, he said, "Sabella, our Pandava queen, Lady Kundalini was quite helpful, wasn't she?"

Sabella smiled back at him gratefully. She knew what he was trying to do. She took a deep breath and answered, "Draupadi always shows up in the right place and at the right time. How does she do that?"

"It's easy. She is a part of you."

Sabella nodded in understanding and continued, "Her guidance was exactly what I needed. I can see now how the liberating shock of omnipresence could be too much for a truth-seeker to bear all at once. A gradual approach is essential. If we move too fast, without appropriate inner preparation and the guidance of our gurus and spiritual teachers, unnecessary difficulties are sure to follow.

"I offer my gratitude to you and Queen Draupadi for my experience as that little bird. I could not have fully understood the FEAR OF EXPANSION OF CONSCIOUSNESS until it happened to me, personally. The cage of the human body and mind are among the strongest limitations that we have created for ourselves. It's frightening to feel that you might be losing what you identify with so closely—it is like physical death, but even more so."

"Yes, on your chakra pilgrimage, you gradually begin to 'die' to your little self and awaken to your Higher Self," Yudhisthira agreed.

"In the fifth chakra, the inward and upward journey begins to escalate rapidly, and the purification process becomes intensified, because you are coming much closer to God-realization."

He continued, "Now, dear child, I promised you a concert, but first I want to mention a few things about chanting, music, and the voice, since it is such an important aspect of this chakra. To set the stage, I'd like to talk more about the human voice. Then we can chant together.

"Sincere truth-seekers should take special care with their speech and remember the powerful link between the fourth and fifth chakras. Always speak kindly and lovingly. Many great saints have said that one of the first things to change in a person who has taken up the spiritual path in earnest is the tone of his or her speaking voice—it becomes sweeter and calmer. The habit of harsh or loud speech drops away.

"Speak kindly and lovingly as much as possible. However,

in situations where firm words are needed, then speak with power, but never in rage or anger. If you are unable to control your emotions and therefore your speech, it is better to stay silent. In fact, one of the most powerful tools for beneficial change and the attainment of DEEP CALMNESS in the fifth chakra is the practice of consciously remaining in SILENCE for long periods of time.

"Isn't it true Sabella that you often take times of seclusion, during which you take a vow of silence and communicate only with God and guru?"

Sabella answered, "Yes, that has been my practice for many years. Once a year, I take a full month of solitude in a tiny cabin. I don't speak or even sing for all that time. After a few days, I notice that the energy in my fifth chakra changes direction, from flowing outward to flowing inward. Most of us chatter too much in the course of our daily lives!

"I found that as the life-force turns inward and my inner silence grows deeper, my ability to receive intuitive guidance becomes stronger and stronger. It's amazing—it feels like the static of my own and others' thoughts is gone or at least reduced; thus I can perceive Divine inner guidance much more clearly.

"Often I practice a partial or complete fast during part of my seclusion, but during one of my very first seclusion experiences, I had my meals brought to me once a day from a nearby group kitchen. One day I was sitting on my deck, when a young woman whom I had never met, but who had kindly volunteered to bring a plate of lunch to me each day, arrived at my cabin. She didn't notice me sitting nearby, and she placed the meal on a small table just inside the door of my cabin, before quietly leaving, respecting my desire for silence and seclusion.

"As I glanced at her, I suddenly knew everything she was thinking. I didn't mean to intrude on her thoughts. It happened spontaneously! Just because people can communicate via thought in Treta Yuga, it is clearly understood that we should never listen to others' private thoughts, unless invited to do so.

"Later, when my month of seclusion came to a close, I went to find her, to express my thanks for her faithfulness in bringing me lunch every day. Out of curiosity, I couldn't resist asking her if she remembered that day when she didn't find me at home. She said she did. I told her of my experience of spontaneously and effortlessly hearing what was in her mind. I then asked her if I could confirm with her what I had heard."

"Well, uh, yes, I guess so," she said warily.

"I assured her that there was nothing which would embarrass her. I certainly didn't want to do that, but I wasn't overly concerned because her thoughts that day were of simple things such as, 'I wonder where Sabella is today? She's usually here at this time to receive her lunch. I suppose it will be fine for me to leave the food here, just inside the door. I wouldn't want to leave it outside and have an animal eat it. Would any animal pilfer her food out here in the forest? What kind? A squirrel? A mouse? A bear? Anyway, I hope she's having a nice seclusion.'

"'Why yes,' she said. 'That was exactly what I was thinking. But I don't care for the fact that you read my mind when I had not given you permission. Henceforth I will have to watch what I'm thinking when I'm around you.'

"I sincerely apologized to her, assured her that I hadn't meant to eavesdrop on her private thoughts, and that it wouldn't happen again. Eventually we became good friends and often laughed together about what had happened on that fateful mind invasion occasion.

"This little episode taught me an important lesson. It is never acceptable, without previous agreement, to invade a stranger's mental privacy. Nevertheless, it showed me clearly how the power of silence enhances our intuitive and telepathic abilities.

"I could see how the mind is very much like a glass of water with dirt and debris mixed in. Allow it to sit still for a while without being agitated and the debris sinks to the bottom of the glass. Then the liquid inside becomes transparent! In this same way, you can view reality more clearly through your still and purified mind, in a way that you never could before.

"Speaking greatly stirs up the mind, making it restless and directing energy outward from the fifth chakra. Thinking can also do that, but not to the same degree or in quite the same way. I have found, through many years of experience, that in order to quiet your thoughts and be more receptive, it is very helpful to remain completely silent for long periods of time."

Yudhisthira nodded in agreement and thought these words to her, "I see that you understand the importance of the fifth chakra's beneficial qualities of CALMNESS and SILENCE.

"Let's experience the power of spiritualizing our voices and the fifth chakra by chanting together now."

He teleported them to a large circular music hall, perfectly empty with its roof open to the night sky. They sat together on a small platform in the center of the building. Yudhisthira asked her to close her eyes and listen carefully to what she might hear behind the silence. As she did, she could hear a whooshing sound that resembled wind blowing through the tops of tall pine trees or the sound of a distant waterfall. She recognized it as the "baby AUM-sound" of the fifth chakra. It was beautiful and sounded like a softer version of the full oceanic sound of AUM. She allowed herself to be absorbed into it.

Behind her half-closed and uplifted eyes, she saw swirling patterns of smoke with tiny silver specks of light floating throughout it. She recognized these patterns as the fifth chakra's unique inner colors and shapes. She let herself become absorbed in these phenomena and offered the lovely sounds and lights inward and upward to the spiritual eye. Immersed in the experience, the goal of her pilgrimage seemed much closer now! What bliss!

The waterfall sounds changed into a magnificent voice. She realized that Yudhisthira was singing a chant. He transmitted to her, "Sing with me Sabella. You know this chant. You'll see how closely it matches the fifth chakra's vibrations."

They chanted together, their voices merging in perfect harmony:

I own nothing, I am free! In myself I am free.
I own no one, I am free! In myself I am free.
I need nothing, I am free! In myself I am free.
I need no one, I am free! In myself I am free.
In myself I am free! In myself I am free!
I am free, ever free! In myself I am free.
I am joyful, ever free! In myself I am free.
I am blissful ever free! In myself I am free.
I am nameless, ever free! In myself I am free.
I am formless, ever free! In myself I am free. ©

As they sang with closed eyes and open hearts, she heard several other musical instruments accompanying their chanting. She opened her eyes, curious to see who had joined them.

Sahadeva sat on a lavish cushion on the floor, a beautiful set of tabla drums in front of him. He was playing the drums with a very light and sensitive rhythm. Sabella loved how her upper body naturally swayed to the rhythm of the tablas. She looked appreciatively at the youngest Pandava brother, who winked at her and sent her a thought, "Glad you like the rhythm of this wonderful chant. Get into it, Sabella! Drum rhythms like these help to loosen the karma lodged in your spine!"

Nakula was seated to Sahadeva's right, playing a flute in a high, lilting descant to their voices. On his right sat Arjuna, lightly strumming a stringed instrument from ancient India called a *vina*.

Bhima completed the Pandava brothers' ensemble. He grinned broadly at Sabella as he enthusiastically played large finger-cymbals called *kirtals* with their chiming, bell-like sounds, staying in perfect rhythm with Sahadeva's drums. Each of the four brothers was adding a form of "his" chakra's AUM sound to their chanting session.

After an hour of chanting, she lost herself in the glory of

the music. Yudhisthira's voice was, quite simply, the finest singing voice she had ever heard. He imbued each note, word, and syllable with expansive joy. His radiant face was transfigured with light as he sang. After a time, she could no longer sing outwardly, as she was completely immersed in the chant.

The others began to play more softly, and then dropped away, one by one, until only Yudhisthira was left singing softly, then in a whisper, and then only mentally. The powerful vibrations of the chant continued to flood her consciousness with joy—joy undreamed-of! Superconscious bliss was hers to enjoy in the lingering silence, under a canopy of twinkling stars.

After a time, Yudhisthira whispered to her, "Are you ready for the concert I prepared for you, to celebrate your fifth-chakra initiation?"

She was a bit dazed as she said, "You mean that wasn't it? There's *more*?"

"That was just a warm-up. Relax and enjoy the rest of the show."

He asked her to close her eyes and repeat an invocation along with him:

> Standing at the center of the cosmos,
> Around which revolves a sphere,
> Of omnipresent, omniscient, living space,
> May our music spread like an expanding sphere.
> Directionless, everywhere!
> May silence and sound,
> Like the ether,
> Pass unobstructed through everything,
> Carrying the songs of earth, atoms, and stars,
> Into the halls of God's infinite mansions.

Afterwards, when Sabella tried to describe Yudhisthira's concert to Thomas, Issoweet, and others, she found that she was unable to convey completely all she had heard and seen, and most of all how deeply it had moved her.

At this time on earth during Ascending Treta Yuga, Sabella was recognized as a world-class musician. She had composed hundreds of pieces of music, produced concerts, and performed before large crowds worldwide. But *nothing* she had ever seen or heard could compare to this concert. She could only describe it as "the music of the spheres, accompanied by a massive chorus of angelic beings."

The musicians and chorus members were dressed in garments of radiant rainbow light, which shifted colors according to the music's tempo and mood. The music was not only heard, but seen, touched, and even smelled (rose, mint, and lavender) and tasted (sweet nectar)—these components and more were present, continuing on and on, in ever-changing patterns of exquisite beauty.

Perfectly enhancing the musical flow, the musicians and singers danced and flew about the hall in intricate patterns. As the triumphant finale completed, the angel chorus ascended into the starry night sky, singing with softer and softer voices, until the last echo of heavenly music gradually faded away.

Bhima struck the last resounding note on an immense gong that was as tall as he.

After the vibrations had finally faded into silence, Yudhisthira asked Sabella to stand and he draped her shoulders with a royal-blue cape similar to his own.

Around her neck he placed a most unusual pendant, made of transparent tubes containing swirling silver mercury, the metallic symbol of the fifth chakra. In the center was a blue lotus blossom with sixteen petals. And in the center of the lotus blossom was a cloud-shaped disc, the color of smoke, with flecks of silvery-white light twinkling over it, like tiny stars. The final center-piece was a large, deep green emerald, the astrological gemstone for this chakra. Unlike her other chakra pendants, this one seemed alive with movement.

She knelt in reverence and gratitude before King Yudhisthira, her dear friend forever.

"Sabella Lovingheart, you are now endowed with power over the Ether Element and all space. Only one obstacle remains between you and the realization of your own divinity.

"My brothers and I have given you tests, quests, gifts, and our eternal, loving friendship. We will be with you and support you at all times during the final phases of your chakra pilgrimage, for we are a part of you always.

"I have one final word of advice for you, dear one. Don't gamble with delusion, as I once gambled with King Material Desire—and lost! You must know the story. . . ."

Sabella nodded affirmatively.

"So then you know that I lost our whole kingdom. I lost my brothers, my wife, and even myself; I gambled away every-thing and was left with nothing at all. The dice were loaded, as the dice of attachment to the material world always are. Gamble with desires and delusion and you will inevitably lose.

"Fortunately, all my losses were temporary. After years of suffering, tests and trials, culminating in the great Battle of Kurukshetra, we, the Pandavas, guided by Lord Krishna, were victorious—we regained everything.

"But be careful, Sabella! Even though, like all seekers, your victory is assured in the end, and the remainder of your journey is not long now, nevertheless you will need vigilance, courage, and Divine guidance to walk the final few steps to freedom. Blessings and joy to you always!

CHAPTER THIRTY-SEVEN

Thomas enjoyed hearing about Sabella's fifth-chakra experiences, for in his heart of hearts, among all five of the Pandava brothers, he identified most closely with Yudhisthira. Sabella knew this and took great pains to recall even the smallest details of this portion of her pilgrimage. And Sabella loved transmitting the thought pictures to him. The experience of the final chanting session and concert was so rich that it was not possible to convey fully, but she did her best to express how she felt at its close.

"Thomas, I'm not sure I'll ever be able to produce another musical event. Anything I could possibly create in the future could never even *begin* to compare to Yudhisthira's concert," Sabella said, shaking her head sadly.

"On the contrary, dearest Sabella! In your future meditations, you must tune in to the essence of what you heard and saw in that concert, and with Divine guidance, you'll be able to offer to the world at least some part of the inspiration you received. I know you can do it, and I know that Yudhisthira would be pleased for you to try! The best creative endeavors, musical or otherwise, happen when we ask God to flow through us uninterruptedly."

Sabella smiled at her husband and said, "If you, God, and the Great Ones want this to happen, I'll do my part, and it *will* happen, just as it should.

"That's the spirit!" said Thomas.

The tone of her meeting with Issoweet had a very different feeling to it. After Sabella offered a much shorter review of her adventure, Issoweet nodded, indicating that what she had related was sufficient.

She asked Sabella, "You remember when King Yudhisthira said, 'Only one obstacle now remains between you and the realization of your own divinity'? Do you know what the obstacle is?"

"Why yes, of course! He was speaking of that part of the sixth chakra where the ego dwells. I know that the ego is a formidable foe, and I would be most happy to hear any advice you have for how to deal with such a powerful enemy."

Issoweet seemed unusually stern as she transmitted these words and ideas to Sabella, "Soon you'll meet Bhishma, also a great warrior—possibly the greatest, and certainly the oldest and most experienced warrior in the *Mahabharata*. He represents the ego. He was grandfather to both the Pandava brothers and their enemies and cousins, the Kauravas. Politics forced him to side with and fight for the Kauravas.

"Early in his life, he had been given the boon or divine gift to remain alive, completely invincible in battle, unable to be slain. He was virtually immortal unless he *chose* to give up his life. Can you imagine fighting against a warrior like that?"

Sabella was startled. She said, "Un-killable, you say? How could that be possible? I know that all the Great Ones have conquered their egos, merging into the higher aspect of the sixth chakra, represented by Lord Krishna. So there must be a way, right? Although to tell the truth, I'm not at all enthusiastic about having to kill Bhishma or anybody else, even if he is just a symbol."

Issoweet continued, "Then let's try to understand the ego's true nature. Like all the chakras, it is an element of the astral body. But the ego actually *forms* the physical body. It is the cause, not the effect, of physical birth and is retained after physical death. The physical body is merely an ego's projection of its astral body into the material world.

"Yogananda defined the ego as 'the soul identified with the body.' Another great saint called the ego 'a bundle of self-definitions.'

248

"The ego is a sense of selfness which has us convinced that we are the body and mind and nothing more, and that we are separate unto ourselves and not a part of everyone and everything.

"For example you might think, 'If I cut *your* arm, it doesn't hurt *me*; but if I cut my own arm, then it *does* hurt me.' Doesn't that seem perfectly reasonable? But that thought pattern is simply the LITTLE SELF's clinging to its self-identification—it has not yet expanded enough to realize its greater reality in oneness with all."

"Shouldn't we be working on knowing, understanding, and even liking ourselves—aren't these important steps along the spiritual path?" Sabella asked.

"Yes, of course! Having a healthy ego is essential. It is a major part of what deep meditation does for spiritual seekers, because it helps them to realize who and what they *really* are instead of what they only seem to be on a superficial level.

"Our egos give us the ability to function in this world in a steady and grounded way—an important asset which gives us enough stability to move into union with the Higher Self. We can't give away something which we don't fully possess!

"Unfortunately if a person has little or no sense of self, they may be mentally unstable, or at its extreme, even psychotic. You might meet someone who was suffering in that way, and say, 'Hello, I'm Sabella.' And the person might answer, looking above or to one side of you, perhaps with each eye seeming to spin in opposite directions, and say, 'Well, I'm not sure *who* I am. I think I might be an angel, or then again, I'm feeling a little devilish today, so maybe I'm the Devil. On the other hand, I think I might be a tree—yes, that's it! Hello, I'm Mr. Apple Tree. Yes, yes, that's it. Would you like to pick one of my apples?'

"I know that your heart would feel great compassion for such a person, so handicapped by being disconnected from reality. Therefore you can see that we must have self-awareness and an intact, healthy ego in order to be able to transmute the ego into its higher aspect, which is the soul.

"It's important to understand that even *having* an ego is a great accomplishment. It takes from five to eight million lifetimes lived through progressive stages of evolution, from minerals, to plants, to animals, even to inhabit a human body for the first time—a human body which, with its chakras, ego, and higher brain-centers, is fully equipped, and divinely designed to attain God-realization.

"This is all part of the great Cosmic Drama, of which everyone and everything is a part. It's also a part of the soul's *long* journey through time and space and almost countless manifestations, incarnations, and lifetimes, until it finally reaches its goal of God-realization and liberation."

Issoweet continued, "I want to remind you that it is not a matter of killing Bhishma, or destroying your ego. It is a matter of *transmutation* of energy. However, having said that, please understand that the ego is the strongest barrier which we have to overcome in the spiritual quest.

"Your ego is not an insurmountable obstacle, but it is not going to relinquish its hold on you without a struggle. In order to overcome this final obstacle, great courage and cunning will be demanded of you, in addition to every good quality you have developed.

"You must convince your own ego that it is in *its* best interests to release its grip on the 'small you' and allow you to grow into a higher aspect of yourself. It is a process reflected in the ancient legend of Peter Pan, a stubborn little boy who refused to grow up."

"I think I understand what you mean, Issoweet. I have a friend who reported that her two-year-old son, when scolded for something, was told 'Come on now; you're not a baby anymore! Don't you want to be a *big boy*?' The child replied adamantly, 'No! I *like* being a baby.'"

They both laughed at the story, and Sabella continued. "I think we all have a part of us which would prefer to be coddled and protected rather than having to overcome all the pain and trouble—whether physical, emotional, or spiritual—that we experience in our lifetimes."

Sabella thought of another question, "Issoweet, why is Bhishma depicted as being the very old grandfather of both clans?"

"In the *Mahabharata* epic, Bhishma played the part of the grandfather and eldest statesman. As such, he deserved great respect for all he had been through and accomplished. His life's experiences have much to teach us. And because both your soul and your ego are as old as you are, and in a way, as old as God, the elderliness of Bhishma is appropriate—for we have never not existed, nor will we ever cease to exist.

"Remember too, that Bhishma, even while serving as the powerful king-regent for the mightiest clans of ancient India, was one of the greatest examples of renunciation who ever lived. Complete renunciation means seeing ourselves as having nothing, wanting nothing, owning nothing, understanding that everything belongs to God. Renunciation also means that we strive to realize that we are manifestations of Divine Consciousness, and that whatever the ego relinquishes, by offering everything into to soul-consciousness, is reclaimed forever in cosmic consciousness. Nothing is ever lost!

"Paramhansa Yogananda tells a story in his *Autobiography of a Yogi* of a very great saint, Bhaduri Mahasaya.

"'Master,' said a disciple of this saint once, ardently, 'you are wonderful! You have renounced riches and comforts to seek God and teach us wisdom!' It was well-known that Bhaduri Mahasaya had forsaken great family wealth in his early childhood, when single-mindedly he entered the yogic path.

"'You are reversing the case!' The saint's face held mild rebuke. 'I have left a few paltry rupees, a few petty pleasures, for a cosmic empire of endless bliss. How then have I denied myself anything? I know the joy of sharing the treasure. Is that a sacrifice? The shortsighted worldly folk are verily the real renunciates! They relinquish an unparalleled divine possession for a poor handful of earthly toys!'"

"I love that story, Issoweet! Thank you for reminding me of it. May I ask a few more questions?"

Issoweet smiled charmingly, "That's what I'm here for, dear child."

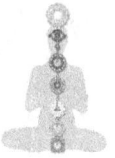

CHAPTER THIRTY-EIGHT

"The sixth chakra seems unusually complex to me. It has two symbolic characters from the *Mahabharata*, while the other chakras have only one. Bhishma represents the ego and Krishna represents the soul or God. These two entities appear to be exact opposites, and in the *Mahabharata*, they were enemies on the battlefield. What exactly does this mean?"

"First of all, Sabella, Lord Krishna was never an enemy to anyone. He had a multifaceted role to play in a very complex story. But being completely divine, he could never have had lower emotions like hatred or rage toward Bhishma or anyone else. And remember, that as that great war came to a close, Bhishma lovingly offered his life to Krishna, just as the ego eventually, when it knows the time is right, offers itself for absorption into the Higher Self, or God-Consciousness.

"It is also very important to realize that the final offering of the little self into the Higher Self cannot be made without the help, support, and purification of the first five chakras."

Sabella was satisfied with this answer, but she went on to inquire, "In the physical body, does the sixth chakra have two locations? I've heard that the area of its influence is in the lower-central part of the brain called the *medulla oblongata*, or brain-stem. Then again, I understand that the sixth chakra is also located in the area of the pre-frontal lobes of the brain, just behind the point between the eyebrows. Which location is correct?"

Issoweet answered, "It does seem to get a little complicated in this chakra. The sixth chakra's actual location is closest to the *medulla oblongata* or brain stem. Its placement here gives continuity to the straight axis of the *sushumna*, which runs up from the first chakra at the base of the spine through the center of the torso and neck, and finally up into the brain."

"Then if the *medulla* is the actual location of the sixth chakra, why don't we concentrate more there when we meditate instead of at the spiritual eye?" Sabella blurted out, unable to curb her impatience to understand this matter more fully.

"The third eye or spiritual eye has many names, such as the *Kutastha Chaitanya* or Christ Consciousness Center. It is a projection of the light of the sixth chakra shining forward from the *medulla* to the point between the eyebrows and where all our powers of concentration gather when we focus. You can see this when people knit their eyebrows together when concentrating.

"Notice also how people toss or throw back their heads, or look down their noses at others when centered in the ego, with the energy gathered at the base of the skull. It is also natural to want to bow our heads in the presence of someone or something greater than ourselves. The impulse to bow arises from wanting to unlock the small or contractive energy of our little selves and offer it into something greater.

"We don't bow our heads to meditate, because that physical position would constrict the needed inward and upward flow of *prana*. Instead we are taught to focus our attention at the spiritual eye, for it is here that we perceive the great light of God and the sound of AUM. A helpful technique is to visualize yourself in miniature form, sitting at the *medulla*, but looking slightly up and toward the light of the spiritual eye—yearning to merge into it."

"In a way," Sabella was thoughtful, "the physical distance to be traversed on the spiritual path is not very long at all—just a few inches from the *medulla*, location of the ego, to the spiritual eye, the abode of the higher, Divine Self!"

Issoweet laughed, "I suppose you could put it that way, but as we've discussed, the final few steps of your spiritual journey cannot be made until the purification of the first five chakras has been accomplished. So perhaps it is best to say that the spiritual journey is only a few feet long (the distance between the first chakra at the base of the spine and the crown chakra at the top of the head).

"Sabella, forgive me for reading your mind again, even though you have given me permission to do so, but please don't start asking me about the seventh chakra yet! We'll get to it soon enough. First, you must enter the sixth-chakra pyramid and come face to face with Bhishma, your ego, and Lord Krishna, representing your own soul. It will surely be an extraordinary experience for you!"

"Issoweet, perhaps after my successful passage through the first five pyramids, I should have more confidence, but once again I am feeling uneasy about my next adventure. To think of meeting both Bhishma and Krishna—I am in awe of them both, though in different ways. Bhishma is my final and most formidable enemy, and yet strangely enough my friend at the same time; and Krishna represents God himself. Who wouldn't have a few qualms about meeting these two?" she laughed nervously.

Issoweet remained completely serious, transmitting these thoughts to Sabella, "I know you'll be fine, my dear child. Always remember that the inner pathway to liberation is not one for cowards and weaklings! You have shown yourself to be strong and courageous, and you should never forget that you now have many powerful allies to help you!

"Before we complete our discussion today," Issoweet said, "I want to offer you a few final thoughts about the ego, which receives many disapproving comments and very few compliments, especially from those who try to explain spiritual teachings. Granted, the ego can stand in the way of mental, physical, emotional, or spiritual progress. Indeed, ego-attachment is the root cause of the spiritual diseases of pride, selfishness, aggression, doubt, and insecurity—to name only a few. Although the ego must be vanquished in the end in order to make room for superconsciousness, it is also the ego that makes it possible for us to attain the highest levels of refinement available to human beings.

"To say deprecatingly of anyone, 'Oh, that's just her ego,' is to invite the response from someone who understands these things, 'Well, of course it's her ego! What else could it be?' The cure for ego-identification is not self-suppression; it is striving to use self-awareness as an incentive for self-expansion, rather than for pride or personal power.

"The ego can also block the flow of creativity and inspiration by crying, 'I alone did this, and so the credit should be all mine!' In this case, we are like rubber tubes. If the tube is squeezed tightly at any point, the liquid passing through it may swell the tube and may even burst it—humorously suggestive of a commonly used description of egotists as people who have 'swollen heads.'

"To keep the tube from bursting, we can either release the pressure on it or turn off the flow at its source. We can release the pressure on the *medulla oblongata* by releasing the thoughts of 'I, me, and mine,' which restrict the flow of energy to the spiritual eye. When we stop taking personal credit for what we do, egotistical obstructions are removed and our creative energy flows freely toward its natural destination, the spiritual eye.

"Other ways to impede the flow of energy to the spiritual eye are to remain engrossed in physical pleasure and sense satisfaction or to accept mediocrity as a normal and natural state of being.

"Faced with the daunting task of traversing the spiritual path, many people act in a way that suggests that apathy is a sensible alternative to high aspirations. The solution which delusion often proposes is, 'Lower your energy output! You'll be more comfortable if you avoid life's challenges.' Of course this never works.

"Ridding ourselves of the many attachments created by our egos often seems impossible. We might as well try to calm the ocean's waves! It is true that it's a big task, but it isn't nearly as difficult as it seems.

"Ask yourself, 'What is it that causes the waves to rise and fall on a body of water? It is the wind. Without wind, which represents the power of delusion, the surface grows calm automatically.'

"Similarly, when the wind-storms of delusion abate in the mind, the waves of action and reaction inevitably subside. But even if the winds of delusion continue to blow causing the waves of life's circumstances to rise and fall, we can dive deep into the ocean of inner peace, wherein we cannot be affected by them.

"You should respect your ego, if only for its amazing ability to lead you ever further into delusion. Try to be fully aware of its cleverness in confusing you about the true value and meaning of life.

"Most important of all, respect your ego for its ability to reach toward higher and nobler ideals in life, as you open yourself to receive God's grace. In this way, God's promise to every soul is fulfilled: eternal, conscious, ever-new bliss in union with God.

"Love God! That is the ultimate answer. A few teachers may advise you to love yourself, first. Not so! Or rather it depends on which self you are loving. If your love is for your own ego or the little self, you are giving love to the very source of all your suffering and misery. Instead, place all your loving attention on your soul, your higher Self, which is also the presence of God within you.

"Sabella, you'll soon be entering the sub-kingdom called *samyama*, which consists of the final three aspects of Patanjali's eightfold path: *Dharana* corresponds with the *medulla* or ego aspect of the sixth chakra, *dhyana*, with the spiritual eye aspect of the sixth chakra, and *samadhi*, with the seventh or crown chakra.

"*Samyama* means a perfect state of attunement, absorption, or complete identification with whatever one perceives. It is important to realize that the highest states of meditation are in no way mind-born. They are received, not created.

"Let's briefly review Patanjali's teachings on *dharana* and *dhyana*, and see how they correspond to the sixth chakra.

"*Dharana*, the sixth limb, means concentration. A deep state of concentration implies not only a focused mind, but the rippleless first stages of superconsciousness.

"Once we come into the state of *dharana* or perfect concentration, we experience spiritual manifestations such as the light of the spiritual eye and the great sound of AUM. At this point, these perceptions are received clearly and steadily, instead of as fleeting glimpses. For example, the moon reflected in a lake's surface rarely appears as it does in the sky. What is seen are reflections of the moon, leaping, glimmering, darting here and there in a thousand ripples, with its image lacking perfect definition. Only when the surface of the lake is completely calm is the reflection of the moon true. When that occurs, the reflection appears as the moon itself.

"When *dharana* is experienced, even the thought 'I am concentrating' is a distraction, and betrays an imperfection in one's mental focus, for the ego is still present. Ego attachment cannot be affirmed into non-existence, any more than a flying bird can affirm the non-existence of air. From where else would a person begin the spiritual journey, if not from his or her sense of self, which is the ego?

"In the state of *dharana*, the ego beholds, in a state of exaltation, everything to which it has so long aspired. Clearly, now, it sees the inner lights and hears the inner sounds. Yet it is still separated from these experiences by the thought, 'I, this human being, am enjoying these experiences.'

"The next stage called *dhyana* means complete absorption and the cessation of any thought or feeling of separation from what is being perceived. It signifies a state wherein the calm and fully receptive mind loses itself in the Divine Light, or another divine attribute, and finds the ego-consciousness dissolving in what is being perceived.

"For example, when one communes with AUM, its sound vibrates the entire body and mind. The soul marvels in the realization, 'This is what I am! I am not a physical body and I am not my mind or thoughts. I am a blissful manifestation of AUM.'

"The lights that appear in deep meditation, the inner sounds that we hear, or the love or joy we feel—these experiences completely redefine our self-awareness. We recognize ourselves as a manifestation of Infinite Truth, and *dhyana* finally allows us to become absorbed in that Truth.

"In a certain way, spiritual awakening is a process of unlearning, and ultimately the sense of the Divine Remembrance. 'Ah, yes!' the soul murmurs. 'I recall everything now. This is what I am!' *Dhyana*, the seventh stage of Patanjali's eight-fold path, is the truest state of meditation. At this point the ego, contemplating the supernal reality, loses its separate identity altogether."

Sabella sent the thought to her mentor, "Everything you have told me about the sixth chakra is deeply meaningful to me, Issoweet, but if you don't mind my asking, how have you personally worked towards transforming your own ego?"

Issoweet smiled, "Well, Sabella, it is getting late, but since you have asked, I will tell you. Many years ago when I was struggling mightily to overcome my ego, I chanced upon a simple technique which worked very well for me. One of the weaknesses I was striving to overcome was my inability to get out of bed during the early morning hours—early enough to have several hours of deep meditation before I assumed my daily duties.

"At a very young age, I learned how to set my mental alarm clock; it would awaken me without fail, at the exact time I wanted to get up.

"But just as I was contemplating leaping joyfully out of my bed to begin meditation, a small voice inside me would say something like: 'Issoweet, do you realize what time it is? It is very, very early! See, it's not even light outside yet. You worked later than usual last night, and you really need a little more sleep to stay healthy. Let's roll over and snuggle up under the covers—just for another hour or so. Some additional sleep will help you be fresher for meditation and for your busy day ahead. You work very hard and deserve a proper rest! Come on now—surely your meditation can wait

259

for a little while!'

"'What or who is this sly voice speaking to me?' I'd ask sleepily.

'Silly girl, I am *you*, of course, and I am always on guard, looking out for our best interests!'"

Issoweet continued, "In the beginning and often (I refuse to say how often) I listened to that voice, gave in, and went back to sleep, believing that L.L., which was the nickname I later gave her, must know best for me, since she often told me that she and I were the same."

"L. L.? What does that stand for?" Sabella asked.

Issoweet seemed embarrassed, as she replied softly, "It is an abbreviation for 'Little Light.' As I began to understand more about what was going on, I came to call her, who is my ego, 'the Little Light that is in me.' I've never told anyone about this, Sabella. Please respect my wish that this information remain a secret between us."

"Of course. But 'L. L. or Little Light' seems to me to be a rather soft name for what we've been referring to as 'THE EGO, OUR MOST FORMIDABLE FOE.'"

"Formidable? Well, perhaps at times," Issoweet mused. "But primarily I found her to be formidably sneaky and very clever. L. L. has my number, that's for sure!"

They both laughed ruefully in understanding.

"Anyway, I soon learned to communicate successfully with L. L. in ways like this: 'Good morning, L. L.! It's nice to hear from you again.' I could almost see her, who was really me, and imagine her presence in diminutive form, sitting on my left shoulder, mischievously whispering her conspiratorial words of misplaced advice into my ear.

"'Thank you for your concern for our welfare, L. L. But you might remember that the last time I did as you suggested, things didn't turn out so well for me that day. I slept longer and meditated less; I felt diminished and un-centered all day long.'

"'Well, yes, I do remember,' L.L. grudgingly admitted.

"'And then do you remember the day after that one, when I didn't do as you suggested. Instead, we got up and had a long, deep meditation. That day was much better for us, wasn't it?'

"'Yes,' came the sheepish voice of my Little Light, 'That is what happened.'

"'L. L.,' I said, 'I know who you really are. You are my ego. I know that you mean well and think that you have our best interests in mind, but I want to make a deal with you this morning. We'll get out of bed now and meditate. As always, you'll find that you actually enjoy the process of tuning in with our soul, the big, grown-up part of us: the Higher Self. Then when our time of meditation is over, you can go back to being in charge for the rest of the day. You probably would be anyway. So can we agree to try it again this morning?'

"'Yes, I'll agree to the plan, Issoweet. But I admit that it frightens me to let go or to feel like I'm losing control of you or me or . . . something. It's confusing. Truthfully, I'm afraid I might die and I don't want to die!' L. L. sounded like a scared little girl when she talked to me like that. But at least she was finally being truthful instead of acting in her more usual duplicitous and scheming ways.

"'L. L., you can never die. It is not possible. But you can grow up and become the glorious and highest expression of who we really are. It might feel uncomfortable in the beginning, but let's try it as an experiment and perhaps continue doing it every day for a while; then we'll see how it's going for us.'

"'Before we begin our meditation today, let's say a universal prayer together. Say it with me L. L.'"

Lord, we offer up the Little Light that is in us,
Into Thy blazing light of Infinity.
Grant us the grace to know Thee,
And make us ever-increasingly,
Pure channels of Thy love to all. ©

"For many years L. L. and I have continued to say this ancient prayer composed by Swami Kriyananda in early Ascending Dwapara Yuga. It was part of an inspiring ceremony called A Festival of Light."

Sabella was stunned. "Issoweet, I feel humbled and honored that you would share with me your private experience of ego-transmutation. I will cherish this technique, and I would like to use it myself. May I have your permission to teach it to young truth-seekers; a technique like this could be a great aid to them. I would never reveal its source, but I think it is much too valuable not to pass along to others."

Issoweet nodded her head slowly, "If you think that my story can be of genuine help to others, then yes, you may share it."

"Thank you," Sabella said quietly.

"But now Issoweet, please tell me more about *samyama*. And I also want to know all about *samadhi*, the eighth limb of Patanjali's eightfold path!"

"Patience, dear one! We have discussed these topics enough for today! We'll talk more before you enter the seventh and final pyramid. But for now, I'm sure we've covered the heady sixth-chakra concepts quite enough! It is time for you to be on your way to the next pyramid. Do your best to experience these concepts instead of merely thinking about them philosophically. All my love and blessings go with you!"

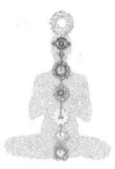

CHAPTER THIRTY-NINE

Sabella rose unusually early the next morning and kissed her sleeping life-mate goodbye. She took a moment to appreciate his aging but still handsome face, and much more than that, the depth of his virtuous character.

His God-given presence in her life kept her on an even keel and always supported her in pursuit of their mutual spiritual goals. She knew that together or apart, their bond was sure and true, for it was based in love for God, first and foremost.

Brother Solonar met her outside the sixth-chakra pyramid. He was sitting peacefully in a small courtyard, which was ablaze with sunlight, brightening the already joyful yellow, blue, and white flowers in the small garden. He offered her a delightful *amrita* drink, which she accepted gratefully and quickly drank, for her mouth was dry in anticipation of her next adventure. She thought wryly, "By the time I get used to these adventures, I'll be out of pyramids to visit!"

Solonar said, "Life is a never-ending adventure in self-awakening."

"Is there really no end to spiritual evolution?" she asked.

Solonar replied, "I will answer your question with a quote from Paramhansa Yogananda who was asked this same question by one of his disciples. He answered, 'No, you go on until you reach endlessness.'

"Sabella, it's always good to see you again, but because Issoweet has prepared you well for your visit to this sacred place, I will say nothing more, unless you have any further questions. So far, you have passed every test in your pilgrimage with flying colors, and I am confident that you'll do the same here.

"I *will* say, however, that you might find this pyramid to be very different from the ones you've visited so far. As you can see, from the outside, they all look the same—giant golden pyramids, same size, color, shape. But this one—well, it would be better for you simply to enter and continue on. My love and prayers go with you."

"Brother Solonar, I thank you. You have always been very helpful to me. Just one minor question, which I forgot to ask Issoweet. Is this chakra's correct Sanskrit name *Ajna* or *Agya*, and what is the proper pronunciation and meaning of the word?"

"It is not pronounced correctly the way it was often spelled in ancient times, which was *Ajna*. One would naturally think it was pronounced *ahj-nah*. It was one of those scholarly glitches which often happen in many languages. Just as you'll sometimes hear the word *chakra* pronounced *shah-krah* instead of its correct pronunciation: *chah-kra*, like chocolate." They laughed together.

He went on, "Correct pronunciation of words in the Sanskrit language, sometimes called the 'language of the Gods,' is very important, because the words and even individual syllables can carry seed sounds and *mantras*. So we now spell and pronounce the name of the sixth chakra as *Agya*, or '*agh-ya*,' to help us pronounce the word correctly. It literally means 'to perceive,' a meaning easy to understand, because it is with this chakra that we finally begin to perceive clearly who and what we really are."

Sabella, in a playful mood asked, "So now I must ask if there really is a chocolate chakra?"

Solonar, catching her humor, immediately played along with it, "But of course! It is located about a foot above our heads. Its color is dark brown, its sound is crunchy, and its taste is decadently sweet. So with that thought in mind to cheer you on your way, please enter the sixth pyramid."

Sabella could see a nearby section of the pyramid which was

obviously the place where she was to enter. But once inside and to her great surprise, she found herself alone, enclosed in utter darkness and absolute silence.

"Yes, so far this is a very different place." She reflected for a moment on memories of her entry into the previous five pyramids. Each time she had been met by a glorious Pandava warrior-king, who showed her the wonders of their elemental kingdoms of Earth, Water, Fire, Air, and Ether. No such greeting awaited her here.

What to do? Well, when in doubt, chant or meditate or both! It was one of her life's most helpful guidelines—she had proved its worth many times before. Even though nothing was visible in the darkness, she assumed a meditative position, levitated a few inches above the floor, closed her eyes, and began chanting:

> *Fill my body,*
> *Fill my spirit,*
> *Fill me with the sound of 'AUM.* ©

It seemed an appropriate chant for this chakra. After many repetitions of the chant, she began to hear the great oceanic-boom of AUM surging all around her. She ceased chanting and meditated on the AUM vibration, letting it absorb her completely and bring her into the higher meditative states of *dharana* and *dhyana*.

Soon the great light of the spiritual eye appeared in her forehead. When the spiritual eye is beheld perfectly, it is circular in shape and is seen as a ring of shining golden light surrounding a field or tunnel of intense, deep blue or violet. In the center of the blue-violet field shines a brilliant, five-pointed, silvery-white star.

As she began to move her consciousness through the three shining tunnels of light in the hope of not only *seeing* the light of the spiritual eye, but also *becoming* it, she heard a voice inside her head.

"Sabella, you will have an opportunity to enter the spiritual-eye tunnels later in your visit to this pyramid, but for now, please open your eyes and join me. It is time that we get to know each other a little better."

Though reluctant to do as she had been requested, she returned her consciousness from a deep state of inner absorption to find that she was no longer alone in a dark, silent place. Sitting right front of her, also levitating in a cross-legged position, was a very old, thin man with eyes that glowed like moonlight, and long, matted silvery-white hair. He was clad only in a plain white *dhoti*, the simple loincloth worn by men in ancient India.

"You must be Grandfather Bhishma. I am honored to meet you, sir."

"*Namaste*, Sabella. The honor is mine," he said politely as he bowed to her with folded palms. "Yes, I am Bhishma, but I am also *you*. Let me show you what I mean by that."

Suddenly, right before her wide-open eyes, she watched the old warrior change into an exact likeness of herself, except that it was very small—only about twelve inches high. It was a startling sight!

The miniature Sabella looked solemnly at her and said in a small girl's high-pitched voice, "Yes, I am still Bhishma, but I am also your own ego, your little self. I am here to be your friend, or not, as you so choose."

"Well, of course I'd rather be your friend!"

"Good plan!" said the little Sabella, jumping to her feet, "Let's play! Look all around you at our endless playground. I've prepared it especially for you and me to play in together. I know you'll love it, for I know you very well!"

Sabella was astonished to find herself in a place which seemed to have no beginning or end. It was full and brimming over with diversions of all kinds, like a vast amusement park with thrilling rides and attractions, including delicious food booths, parties going on everywhere, bright lights, action, music, movies, green parklands, water parks, and art museums. Her mind reeled as it tried to take it all in. She saw that everyone she knew, all her many friends, students, relatives—were there enjoying themselves greatly.

Little Sabella took her hand and the two of them skipped merrily into the middle of the overwhelming scene. L. S. sprang lightly up onto Sabella's shoulder, where she sat comfortably whispering advice into Sabella's left ear.

"Having Little Sabella with me, sitting on my left shoulder, feels somehow very familiar," she thought, but was too dazed at everything going on around her to analyze the situation clearly.

L. S. said softly, enticingly, "Call me L. S., Sabella, and tell me what you want. It is yours to have, instantly, just by wishing it so. The power to do that is ours while we are here. Don't you just love it?"

Sabella stood and looked about. She could see a concert hall nearby emanating beautiful music. She quickly realized that it was music that she, herself, had composed. It was very satisfying to hear it being played and sung so well.

She saw Thomas and her three children walking toward her with big smiles on their faces. Soon they were holding hands, laughing and dancing around her in a circle, singing her praises. How beautiful they all looked! "Mine!" she thought happily. "All this is mine and *mine alone*. What else could be more important or make me happier?"

She looked at L. S. and said, "I believe you are right! I do love everything here, and I join you in rejoicing in all the good things which are mine. And come to think of it, there may be a few things which I don't presently own, which I'd like to have in my life, and places to go, and people to meet, and. . . ."

As she began listing these items in her mind, she was amazed to see them manifested in front of her instantly: material goods, beautiful places, old friends, happy events of the past. The "few things" soon grew into an endless stream— mountains and mountains of it. All the while, little Sabella was clapping her tiny hands and laughing gleefully, for it was her greatest pleasure to please Sabella, that is, herself.

Fortunately it was not very long before Sabella became satisfied, then satiated, and then uneasily restless. She found herself becoming more and more anxious, lest any of the giant collection of her possessions be lost. Her mind roiled and churned, thinking of ways to preserve all her new belongings and keep them safe. These thoughts made her anxious and miserable.

"Wait a minute!" she thought to herself, "Something is not right here!" Her uneasiness grew stronger.

Finally she threw up her arms and shouted: "Stop! Enough of this! I do not wish to be possessed by my possessions. I can't imagine what has gotten into me, but I want it to end right now! I don't want anything else. I don't even think I want to keep what I already have!"

"Oh really, Sabella. Be honest. Of course you want more. Everybody always wants more!" Little Sabella seductively whispered into her ear, "After all, it really is *yours* by right. You deserve all this; you own it, and you should enjoy it. There is no harm in delighting in all these good things, is there?"

"But I find myself starting to worry about losing my possessions. I feel like all this stuff is beginning to *own me* and not the other way around. I am basing my happiness on having and protecting all these things. I will *not* let that happen, and I don't choose to identify with any of it!"

"How can you say that?" Little S. said disgustedly, "Look carefully at your handsome husband, your lovely home, and your three fine children. Look more closely at your eldest daughter. Isn't there something different about her?"

Sabella gazed at Lalaree fondly—but her beloved daughter *did* look different; she smiled bewitchingly back at Sabella. Then Sabella knew without a doubt that Lalaree was pregnant with Sabella's first grandchild!

"This is incredible!" she thought, "My first grandchild is coming—a tiny, newborn baby to hold and love! Wow! My very own grandchild. How long have I waited and hoped for this moment? Most of my friends have many grandchildren, and I was beginning to lose hope. And why shouldn't I have a grandchild? How thrilling this is!"

Sabella said to L. S. who was smiling smugly now, "OK, I give up. You are right, L. S! All this, and especially my new grandchild, really *is* mine. Absolutely and without question, I accept it all."

She stepped forward to embrace and congratulate Lalaree and found that her arms were holding only thin air.

"What's going on now? Where did she go?" she turned to look in dismay at Little Sabella and found herself face-to-face with Bhishma instead. Everything had disappeared into utter darkness except for Bhishma—who was her friend? Her foe? Herself?

Sabella collapsed in a heap of misery at his feet, drowning in confusion. "Oh Bhishma, I was trapped by ego attachment *again*! What am I to do? Have I failed in this sixth-chakra quest? Do I really have to try to destroy my ego—I mean—you? It's beginning to seem that I must! But you are me and all the things I love, want, and am!" she was sobbing now. "Please help me know what to do!"

Bhishma took her by the hand and gently helped her to stand up. He smiled at her compassionately and dried her tears.

He said, "Dear one, you have not failed! Do not be dismayed at your present inability to let go of your ego and every one of its self-definitions. It's a big job, but you are very, very close, for you recognize fully what is needed now. These last little ego attachments will melt away quickly in the great light of your eternal soul.

"Come, dear child, there is someone very nearby, whom you should meet—someone who will show you what to do now. Let me bring you into the presence of Lord Krishna who is your Higher Self; he also represents your soul and the Divine Presence within you."

Sabella trustingly let Bhishma lead her further into the darkness. After only three steps, a soft, warm light began to appear all around them. The light intensified until Sabella could see that they were standing at the entrance to a vast throne room of what appeared to be a magnificent palace. At the end of the room, floating a few feet above the floor, there was a large circle or halo of golden light, which surrounded a deep blue-violet tunnel. The tunnel seemed to rotate inward upon itself.

In the center of the tunnel was a man-sized, silvery-white, five-pointed star. As she gazed in awe at what she knew to be a large representation of the spiritual eye, she realized that in the central star-shape was a person, a shining God-like being, standing as still as a statue, with arms and legs outstretched to form a star-like shape—with his head, two arms, and two legs forming the five points of the star.

The great oceanic roar of AUM filled her being and everything around her.

Sabella knelt and bowed her head to the floor before Lord Krishna, for there was no mistaking what she was seeing for a mere statue. She knew who this brightest-of-all beings was, standing there in the middle of the star-shape and smiling his wondrous smile at her. He indicated that she should stand up and approach him.

Bhishma was still floating along, at her left side. She saw that Queen Draupadi had appeared, hovering at her right side. Both were holding her hands encouragingly. As the trio moved toward Lord Krishna, Sabella's heart began beating wildly in her chest.

"This is it, isn't it? Enlightenment! Am I worthy? Am I ready to do this? Ah, well, there is only one way to find out," Sabella thought.

Together they moved first into the golden tunnel and then blue-violet tunnel. They were finally absorbed into the great silvery-white light of Krishna, the Christ Consciousness, the Star in the East, the *Kutastha*, the lightless light which dispels all our darkness forever. She felt the release of Bhishma's hand, symbolic, she knew of the transmutation of her little self and all her ego-attachments into the Greater Self.

Sabella became bliss itself. She finally realized what it meant to be absorbed completely and become the divine lights and sounds, and not merely meditate on them. In an instant she knew a wholeness and oneness of which she had never dreamed.

Sabella Lovingheart joyfully surrendered her little self into her Greater Self. She realized the meaning of Paramhansa Yogananda's unusual little couplet:

> *When this I shall die,*
> *Then shall I know who am I.*

Her last conscious thought was: "I shall never be the same again!"

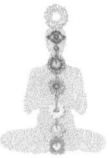

CHAPTER FORTY

Much time passed before Sabella finally emerged from her experience of enlightenment. She was wearing a long, shining garment of gold, blue, and silvery-white. She was floating in the center of the three universes, physical, astral, and causal, surrounded by joyful angelic beings of light, who were showering her with rose petals of love.

"Come child," two deep melodious voices said in unison. It was Bhishma and Krishna. They transported her to a small initiation chamber in the very peak of the sixth pyramid.

Waiting for her there were Sahadeva, Nakula, Arjuna, Bhima, Yudhisthira, and Lady Kundalini. She knelt before each of them in turn, offering her deepest gratitude. She bowed before Grandfather Bhishma too, and finally prostrated herself before Lord Krishna, who sat on a golden throne made of sunlight. She then stood before him as he first presented her with the sixth-chakra pendant and then removed his crown and placed it on her head. The crown was covered with lustrous pearls and glittering rubies—it was magnificent!

"Sabella Lovingheart, we offer you initiation into the sixth chakra. Henceforth, you possess Sight Divine. You will always see things as they really are; never again will anything be distorted or hidden by veils of delusion."

Sabella lowered her newly-crowned head in acceptance of the gift and the initiation.

She turned to express her gratitude to Queen Draupadi/ Kundalini, who had accompanied her throughout the pilgrimage and helped her conquer each obstacle that she encountered. The dark lady dropped her black veils to the floor to show herself arrayed in a brilliant white robe of energy and light.

The Goddess Kundalini spoke to Sabella, "I have a story for you, from my life as Queen Draupadi. You may remember it from the *Mahabharata*, but I want you to hear it now from my own lips.

"You have come to know me as the dark Lady Kundalini, who sleeps most of the time in Lake Kundalini at the source of the Sushumna River, rousing myself during your chakra pilgrimage, to come to your aid as needed. You also know me as the wife of each of the five Pandava brothers, for the *kundalini* power must be 'wedded' to each one of the chakras equally.

"Now I will tell you why, although I dearly love and am life-linked to these five great and wonderful warrior-kings, my heart ultimately belongs to my Lord Krishna.

"King Yudhisthira, as he humbly admitted to you, once foolishly participated in a gambling match with his archenemy, Duryodhana. The dice were loaded, and Yudhisthira lost everything: kingdoms, lands, treasures, riches, clothing, his brothers, himself, and finally, even me, his queen. We were all to become the slaves of our evil cousin.

"Duryodhana ordered one of his brothers to grab me by my long hair and drag me from the womens' quarters into the presence of the whole royal court. He then ordered my *sari* removed before this august gathering and in front of my shamed husbands—to humiliate us all. Devastated, I cried out to my five husbands to save me! But they could not, being bound by Yudhisthira's word of honor.

"Truly desperate by then, I prayed deeply to Lord Krishna, who appeared instantly before my inner sight. Immersed in the bliss of his holy presence, I saw nothing more of what happened after he came to me.

"I was later told that one of Duryodhana's wicked brothers attempted to undress me, pulling on my *sari*, laughing at me as he unwrapped it from around my body. More and more and more fabric was removed—much, much more than the usual length of fabric used in a woman's *sari*. My *sari* that day transformed into an endless piece of silk, which stood in great piles all around the royal chamber, while I remained modestly and miraculously clad in the same *sari*.

"My Lord Krishna came to save me in my time of greatest peril, of this there was no question. So since that time, even though I still love my five husbands dearly, my truest love is Lord Krishna, who saved me from humiliation, dishonor, slavery, and most likely even rape or death at the hands of Duryodhana. I am Krishna's, and he is mine through eternity. This also means that our symbolic union within you is essential for the completion of your spiritual journey. Do you understand what I am saying, Sabella?"

"Yes, my lady, I do understand," Sabella said softly. "And I am very grateful that you shared your wondrous story with me."

Lady Kundalini smiled at her and began to rotate her body in a graceful upward-moving spiral. As she ascended, she gathered up her five husbands in order, from Sahadeva to Yudhisthira, until all were encased in coils of light and energy. Whirling like a fiery white serpent, she merged them all into the shining form of Lord Krishna. Watching this amazing display, Sabella thought to herself, "That is one powerful woman! I'm glad she's my ally!"

Sabella turned to express her gratitude to Bhishma. To her surprise, her Sight Divine showed her a transformed Bhishma. He appeared, not as the grizzled old warrior-king she met at the entrance to the sixth-chakra pyramid; his body had turned silvery-white and assumed the shape of a crescent moon.

The moon-shaped being seemed to smile and wink at her, as crescent moons sometimes do. Slowly he began to ascend and move toward Krishna. She watched in awe as the crescent-moon who was Bhishma grew smaller and smaller, until it gently landed on Krishna's forehead.

It was only now that she realized Bhishma was not only

a symbol for the *little* ego, but he was also the symbol for the *transcendent* ego, which has the power to overcome all ego-attachments and merge into the Higher Self.

Finally, Lord Krishna changed into a shining sun and beamed golden rays of light into Sabella, blessing her beyond all imagination of expectancy.

Once again she melted into the sea of Oneness. But this time she was absolutely certain that all vestiges of the little, egotistical Sabella were forever gone. Ah, what bliss, what joy—too much joy, too much joy!

"Sabella!"

She felt someone sharply rapping her on the top of her head.

"Who is Sabella?" she wondered mentally.

"She is the lovely lady whom I love and with whom I am life-linked," Thomas said soothingly, and then chanted AUM-m-m-m in her right ear.

"Then why is he knocking on her head?" Sabella asked him.

"Because he wants—I mean, *I* want to talk to you, Sabella! And by the way, welcome back from the sixth-chakra pyramid. Issoweet told me that it went very well for you. I want to hear all about it."

Sabella looked at the nice man standing before her, who was speaking so kindly to her.

"Who is this person?" she wondered, "And why is he gazing at me with so much love in his eyes?"

Finally she had to ask, "Do I know you? You seem familiar to me, but. . . ."

"Uh-oh!" Thomas said to himself, simultaneously putting out an urgent call for Simeon and Issoweet to help him with Sabella's amnesia.

In an instant, Simeon appeared out of the ether with Issoweet at his side. Not even hesitating to greet Thomas, they both looked penetratingly at Sabella, reading her aura.

Issoweet touched the middle of Sabella's chest with the tip of her right index finger, and Simeon placed the tip of his right index finger midway between her eyebrows. They both closed their eyes to pray for Sabella and to act as channels for divine healing energy. Deeply concerned about his life-mate's unusual mental state, Thomas earnestly joined them in silent prayer

Sabella closed her eyes, relaxed her body, and sighed deeply.

When Simeon and Issoweet simultaneously withdrew the powerful "touch of light," Sabella trembled slightly and opened her eyes to see her husband and her mentors clustered around her.

"Hello, Thomas, Issoweet, and look, even Simeon is here with me! Why are all of you here? What is going on? Why are you all standing around me, looking at me like I might disintegrate or something?"

"She's fully back with us, I believe," said Simeon, "So I'll be on my way now, dear ones." He kissed Sabella on her cheek and vanished.

Issoweet was very relieved as she said to Sabella, who was now yawning and stretching, "Have something nourishing to eat and get some rest, Sabella. We'll talk about what happened to you soon. Everything is fine now, and we can wait for a day or so to meet."

The next day, feeling refreshed, renewed, and most importantly, feeling once more in complete possession of her mind and memory, Sabella met Issoweet back in the small chapel in the High Council Pavilion.

Sabella wasted no time in asking, "Issoweet, I want to understand what happened to me? Up to a certain point, I remember everything that I experienced in the sixth-chakra pyramid. And I love wearing my beautiful robe of initiation and my unusual sixth-chakra pendant."

Issoweet took a moment to admire the pendant perfectly positioned above the other five chakra medallions on Sabella's necklace, intertwining strands of gold and silver, studded with tiny pearls and rubies. In the center of them was a small gold, blue and white spiritual eye symbol, with two indigo petals, like wings, extending out of either side.

"Yes, my dear Sabella, you look lovely in your new finery. And your aura is shining brightly. You have been changed dramatically by your first experience of *sabikalpa samadhi*. Of course, how could you not be different after an experience of *samadhi*?"

"*Samadhi*? Yes, I thought that must be the blessed and blissful state of union I experienced. But if that is true, wouldn't I know it for certain? Something went wrong, didn't it?"

"No, not really," Issoweet replied, "You were in *sabikalpa samadhi*, which precedes *nirbikalpa samadhi*."

"Ah yes, Patanjali again," Sabella said. "The eighth 'arm' of the eight-fold path to final liberation is called *samadhi*, which literally means 'sameness' or 'oneness.'"

"Then you'll recall that there are two major levels of *samadhi*—different from each other in their manifestations. In *sabikalpa samadhi*, the meditating yogi is indeed united with his or her Higher Self. But this unity takes place only in deepest meditation; that is, in a trancelike state wherein the physical body ceases to move, having no heartbeat, no breath—almost death-like in a way, except one is able to return to waking consciousness at will. But this is a lower form of *samadhi*.

"The highest form is called *nirbikalpa samadhi*. The yogi achieves the same state of union with God, but has overcome the need to have the body remain in an unmoving, trancelike state in order to sustain that state.

"A person in *nirbikalpa samadhi* can walk, talk, teach, serve, and carry on what may seem to be a normal life. But never again does the yogi fall out of a blissful state of union with God—it is permanent and eternal.

"Most who achieve this state of final liberation merge *completely* into the great ocean of cosmic consciousness. A very few continue to exist on different planes of existence, their mission to uplift the consciousness of the whole world and especially to help sincere truth-seekers with their spiritual journeys. These few great souls are called *avatars*, saviors of mankind.

"*Avatars* are generally very few in number at any one time, but they are present in every part of the universe where sentient beings dwell.

"Naturally, your first experience of *samadhi* was the *sabikalpa* state. It is a very advanced state of consciousness, though not the most advanced state. Sometimes, as was the case with you, this experience creates major shock waves in the human psyche."

"Issoweet," Sabella asked, "Are you saying that I wasn't yet ready to experience *samadhi*? Was it too much for me to handle? Will I never experience it again? Or perhaps I have many more years or lifetimes of preparation to perfect myself, my chakras, my *nadis*—purifying them enough to be able to take it?"

Sabella felt extremely distraught as these questions arose in her mind. Her life loomed before her as being empty and useless if she were unable to attain the *samadhi* state again.

"Child, be calm. *Sabikalpa samadhi* was and is yours forever. It cannot be taken away from you. There are a few subtle refinements in your nature which need to be made to allow you to enter and exit this state with perfect ease.

"Remember how Yogananda cautioned truth-seekers about the effects of a first experience of the 'liberating shock of omnipresence.' He indicated that it might overload the nervous system in its present state of development, or that you might not be able to stand your regular life in comparison to the experience of *samadhi*.

"Your chakras pilgrimage has rapidly moved you through many levels of learning. The little time of forgetfulness, which you just experienced, was not serious, although it really frightened your poor husband. He thought for a moment that you might have damaged your mind." Issoweet smiled, "But let me reassure you again, nothing harmful has befallen you. You'll feel increasing joy and greater spiritual strength, as results of your experience."

"We'll spend most of the next few weeks together. Each day I will carefully lead you into and out of the blessed experience of *sabikalpa samadhi*, until your brain and body become accustomed to the larger reservoirs of power you are tapping into and to the higher levels of energy generated throughout the super-charged cells of your reborn being.

"And during this time, we'll thoroughly review all aspects of the higher chakras teachings. You will need to know them for your future endeavors."

"Have I or will I become an entirely new person through this process?" Sabella asked. "I certainly don't feel the same right now."

"Yes and no. No, because, in a certain way, you'll never stop being Sabella Lovingheart, or to put it more clearly, God expressing himself/herself through the unique being we all know as Sabella. Nothing of your essence will ever be lost or diminished in any way. In truth, each one of us is unique in all creation. There will never, ever be another you! God has a particular song to sing through you and through each of us. You are specializing in being *you* on behalf of all creation.

"But also yes, because one's first experience of *samadhi* feels like being reborn onto a higher spiritual plane, a place which will never cease to both thrill and comfort you.

"We all change and grow—that is what life is about. Nothing ever stays the same for very long. Life is a school! We learn our lessons, each of us in our own ways, and as a result, we evolve into the fullest expression of ourselves. Our Creator knows what he/she did and is doing, and in the end, everyone will merge back into Infinite Bliss. But *sabikalpa samadhi* is a huge leap for anyone. I am happy for what you have attained, Sabella, and I know you will never take it for granted.

"But we still have much to do now, so let's get started!"

"Issoweet, I trust your and Simeon's guidance completely,

and your help continues to be invaluable to me. I once again place myself in your hands with full confidence and love."

"My dear, you will soon be equally capable of helping others in the same ways we have helped you.

"We should start reviewing, clarifying, and thoroughly preparing you for entering the seventh pyramid. But first, do you have any questions about your most recent experiences in the sixth-chakra pyramid?"

"Only about a million," Sabella laughed, "I'm not sure where to begin!"

"Very well, please begin by giving me your impressions of Bhishma and Lord Krishna," Issoweet said kindly.

CHAPTER FORTY-ONE

Thus began for Sabella and Issoweet a time of being together for the better part of every day. Intensive reviews of all information about the chakras and the more subtle aspects of astral anatomy were thoroughly covered. An average day began with at least six hours of deep meditation. Issoweet carefully guided Sabella into and out of *sabikalpa samadhi*, until she was satisfied that Sabella could safely summon or dismiss the blissful state at will. She also wanted to make sure that Sabella's nervous system was sufficiently attuned to the state of *sabikalpa samadhi* so that no further disruptions of her memory patterns would occur.

The days and weeks flew by. They often met in the same small chapel in the High Council Pavilion, but occasionally, for variety, they teleported themselves to scenic locations in various parts of the earth or to unusual locations in other parts of the universe.

For one of their first excursions during this time, Issoweet suggested that they journey to the source of the Joyuba River, to see what it was like there and to have a picnic. Sabella was happy to comply, even though she'd visited this beautiful place several times in the past.

They sat together under towering blue spruce and incense cedar trees, which offered them comfortable shade and fresh, spicy fragrances. They listened to the burbling of several tiny springs emerging from a small hollow in the side of a nearby granite gorge. These were the headwaters of the Joyuba River. The small springs released tiny rivulets of crystal clear water, which formed themselves into intertwining streamlets.

After meditating together, they ate Issoweet's carefully

prepared herbal picnic. They agreed that even the best and freshest food tastes even better when eaten in a natural setting like this one.

When they had finished the picnic and rested for a while, Sabella thought to Issoweet, "I believe I know why you asked that we come here today."

"Ah, mind-reading again are you? Alright then, tell me why I asked that we come here today."

"The source of the Joyuba River offers us a graphic reminder of the *iḍa*, *pingala*, and *sushumna naḍis*, or *prana*-channels in the astral spine, along which the spinning whirlpools or chakras are located. I realized that we have not yet spoken in depth about these important aspects of astral anatomy. Can we do that now?" Sabella's eyes sparkled in anticipation.

"Yes, you are right, my smart mind-reader. That is what I wanted to review with you today. Do you remember from your astral anatomy courses in the Halls of Wisdom why the *medulla oblongata* is so important to our spiritual development—aside from its being the location of the ego?"

"I studied all this information a very long time ago, but I will do my best to recall what I can. I believe what you are asking has to do with the way the human body originates and is sustained."

Issoweet said, "Yes, that is correct. Please continue."

Sabella began, "The great masters of yoga teach that the *medulla oblongata* is the area of the brain where life first begins. At the moment of conception, when the sperm and ovum meet, there is a flash of light in the astral regions, where souls encased in their astral forms await reincarnation.

"It is at that moment that the soul and the energetic blueprint for the physical, astral, and causal bodies enter the *zygote*, which is the first cell formed by the union of the sperm and ovum. It immediately begins dividing again and again to form all the cells necessary for the human body.

"This origin point is in the *medulla oblongata* or brainstem, referred to by Yogananda as 'the mouth of God.' This term indicates that it continues to be an entry point for *prana* or the powerful, conscious energy that sustains us as living beings, from conception to death.

"At the time of death for the physical body, the *prana* moves inward and upward through the chakras and astral spine, into the *medulla*/spiritual eye region, at which point it exits the physical body altogether, to inhabit, once again, the astral world.

"People who have had near-death experiences often speak of a tunnel through which they passed into a great light. The tunnel they saw was the astral spine, and the great light was the light of the sixth chakra.

"We've heard the old maxim, 'You can't take it with you,' which, though true where the physical body is concerned, is definitely *not* true for the astral body, including the chakras and all the *karma* that they store.

"Because the *medulla* is where *prana* enters our bodies throughout our lives, the flow of *prana* can be strengthened when we consciously draw it in there and direct it to all parts of our bodies. This is especially true while practicing Yogananda's incomparable Energization Exercises."

Sabella continued, "When that first cell or *zygote* is created and initially divides, the *prana* shifts from the oneness of Divine Spirit into bifurcating rays of energy. This first split forms the *ida* and *pingala* energy channels, designed to transport the *prana* up and down the astral spine as well as through the chakras.

"As energy-distribution points, the chakras also move *prana* outward into the whole body. The *ida* and *pingala nadis* intertwine around the *sushumna*, just like the rivulets of the nearby spring, each one weaving its way around the astral spine. Throughout our lives and with each breath, the *prana* moves upward from the base of the spine to the *medulla* through the *ida nadi* and downward from the *medulla* to the base of the spine through the *pingala nadi*.

"As the *iḍa* and *pingala nadis* spiral around the *sushumna*, they intersect at each of the chakras. At these intersections more bifurcations occur, creating the four, six, ten, twelve, sixteen, and two lotus petals of the first six chakras, respectively, as we have spoken of earlier.

"The *sushumna* or central and most important of the *nadis* is the potential pathway for the *kundalini* energy to rise up from where it 'sleeps' at the base of the spine. But until that happens, the primary *prana* pathways in our astral bodies are through the *iḍa* and *pingala nadis*."

Sabella paused to focus her mind. The subject was complex, and she was trying to be concise in the way she explained it. "In the beginning of my study of astral anatomy, I used to wonder why the spiritually important sixth chakra would have only two petals or rays of energy, when all the other chakras have more. That was before I realized that the two petals are symbols for the *iḍa* and *pingala nadis* and the way divine consciousness enters us as a 'oneness,' and then divides itself into the opposites of *dwaita* or duality.

"When all the opposites represented in the astral body become one again, we become free from the bondage of delusion and duality. It's truly an amazing process that we all go through. Our physical bodies are a marvel in themselves, but the astral body, with the chakras, the *ida*, *pingala* and *sushumna*, the 72,000 *nadis*, the *sahasrara* or thousand-petaled lotus, *kundalini*, *prana*, and so on, is even more inspiring to contemplate!"

Issoweet smiled her approval. "Now, can you tell me about the deepest and most subtle inner channels of the *sushumna*?"

Sabella smiled, "You are giving my memory a workout today, Issoweet! Very well, here goes.

"During the deepest stages of meditation, when our *prana* moves inward, away from the *iḍa* and *pingala nadis*, it is eventually withdrawn completely into the central spine. It then passes successively through the luminous, subtle layers of the astral spine: first the *sushumna* (which is outermost), second, the *vajra*, and next, the *chitra*. After passing through the *chitra*, our *prana* enters the innermost channel, the *brahmanardi*, which is the central channel of the causal body.

It is through the *brahmanardi* channel that the soul must ascend to and through the seventh chakra at the top of the head, in order to become fully liberated. As we withdraw our energy up through this final pathway, we are finally able to offer our separate, individual consciousness into the oneness of the Divine."

"Well done, Sabella!" Issoweet said with a big smile.

Just a few days later, after consulting with Simeon and the other High Council members, Issoweet gave Sabella the long-awaited news that she would be visiting the seventh and final golden pyramid the next day. If all went well for her there, she would complete her chakras pilgrimage and receive the seventh and final chakra initiation.

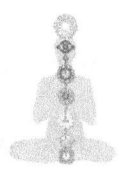

CHAPTER FORTY-TWO

Sabella was looking forward to the climax of these many weeks of intense study and adventure-filled experiences. But there was another question she felt compelled to ask Issoweet about the seventh pyramid. In truth she still had several questions, but Issoweet had insisted that all her questions would be answered after she arrived at the pyramid.

Nevertheless, she took a deep breath, and mentally projected a question to Issoweet. "Forgive me, but I have to ask just one more question. My host-guides for the first six pyramids were the five Pandava brothers, Lady Kundalini, Bhishma, and Lord Krishna. Who will be fulfilling that role in the seventh pyramid?"

Issoweet answered, "All of them will play a role in the final part of your pilgrimage, but that is all I will say about it now."

The next morning she and Brother Solonar stood gazing up at the seventh golden pyramid, which looked considerably larger than the first six pyramids she had visited. The mighty and mysterious River Sushumna appeared to flow into it but not out of it, as an ordinary river might do.

"I guess it is *not* an ordinary river, is it, Brother Solonar?"

"No, Sabella, it is not."

He turned and looked into her eyes. "This is where we must part, Sabella. No matter what happens for you from here on, I want to tell you that it has been a great joy for me to introduce you to the pyramids and their hosts. You are a dear and great soul! I know we will meet again and probably often. Thank you for your enthusiasm, your spirit of adventure, and most of all, for your friendship."

He bowed toward her, with palms folded at his heart.

Sabella returned the bow and offered him a few sincere words of gratitude for the role he had played in her pilgrimage. "Brother Solonar, I feel that this is just the beginning of our association as friends and perhaps colleagues in the training of future truth-seekers who will visit this sacred river valley. I cannot imagine a kinder or better 'gate-keeper' than you!

"So now I am finally here, ready to enter the seventh golden pyramid, representing the seventh chakra and the goal of final liberation," she thought as she looked at the pyramid's great golden doorway. Without hesitation, she entered the pyramid, with a powerful prayer in her heart and mind for divine guidance.

Sabella immediately experienced a dismaying surprise.

"What is going on?" she cried out. She thought that she must have entered the wrong pyramid by mistake, for she now found herself in the same place she had visited during the final part of her sixth-chakra experience.

She was standing in the grand throne room of Lord Krishna. But now it was empty, lonely, and full of strange echoes.

"Hello, somebody . . . is anybody here?" she said loudly, projecting her voice into the silence around her.

"Have I been sent back into the sixth pyramid for some reason?"

She hoped someone would respond to her plea. Her mind reeled with questions about where she found herself now. Had she somehow failed to graduate or refine her consciousness enough to be able to enter the seventh pyramid? Perhaps the sixth pyramid would be as far as she would be allowed to go on this pilgrimage.

In this moment of intense confusion, she felt a soft hand slip into her own. She turned to see the comforting presence of Lady Kundalini, dressed in a simple white sari. "No, my dearest Sabella, you have not failed in your quest. But surely you remember that the seventh chakra can only be approached from the sixth chakra and only when the sixth chakra is fully awakened through *sabikalpa samadhi*. That is why we must begin here."

"But I thought. . . ."

"Yes, don't worry, Sabella! As Issoweet told you, *sabikalpa samadhi* is yours forever."

"Then I don't understand. Please show me what you mean, my lady, for I am very confused."

"Issoweet told me you still have questions about the seventh chakra. I know what they are and will answer them now. What I will explain to you should dispel your confusion. You will soon understand why you are in the sixth-chakra pyramid, instead of in the seventh, as you had expected."

Lady Kundalini continued, "As you know, the seventh chakra's Sanskrit name is *Sahasrara*, which means thousand-petaled lotus of light. It is located at the top of the head. The sixth chakra is the place of enlightenment, which you have experienced, Sabella. The seventh chakra is the place of final liberation. You must first achieve enlightenment before final liberation is possible."

Sabella thought she understood a little more of what was going on. She was being offered the opportunity to ask all her questions about the mysterious seventh chakra just before she entered it.

"Very well, my lady," she began, "If the seventh chakra is our ultimate destination on the spiritual path, then why don't we pay more attention to it along the way? Why are we taught to focus our attention at the spiritual eye, especially in meditation, instead of at the top of the head?"

"Queen Draupadi, may I answer Sabella's question?" Lord Krishna had appeared before them in his shining robes of gold.

"By all means!" Draupadi said, and knelt humbly before him. Sabella quickly did the same.

"From the sixth-chakra kingdom, there is a passageway to

the seventh chakra. The seventh chakra cannot be entered successfully except through this passage. In both the astral and causal bodies, there is a corresponding channel running from the area of the sixth chakra, in the center of the skull, to the crown chakra at the top of the head.

"But it is a mistake and potentially dangerous to try to open or move *prana* through this final portion of the *sushumna* prematurely. This aspect of astral anatomy is similar to what you know about the *kundalini* power.

"To *force kundalini* to rise through the chakras from its location at the base of the spine is a mistake and can cause harmful side effects for the spiritual seeker. But rise it must, at least eventually, in order for spiritual progress and final liberation to occur. It's not a matter of if, but when it happens.

"*Kundalini* must be gradually drawn upward, not forced to move through the chakras—just as Queen Draupadi was invited, not forced to marry the five Pandava brothers—as though anyone could have forced her to do anything she didn't want to do," he laughed, and so did Draupadi.

Lady Kundalini said with a big smile on her face, "There is no safe or effective way to force me to wake up and move upward, be it through techniques or by sheer will power. I will make my way through the *sushumna* only as I am drawn by the powers of right action, right attitudes, and divine love—and most of all, through the magnetism of the great light of the spiritual eye and the help and guidance of the guru.

"This is the way I was created. To transgress this law is to face stiff consequences. Alas, some spiritual seekers have to learn the hard way, and I am sorry for that. Fortunately *everyone* eventually learns and earns their way home to final freedom. And I am always there to help them, never to hinder or hurt them, if they respect and understand my nature."

"As I have found out through my recent experiences with you, my lady," Sabella added. "I shall always be grateful for your help during this pilgrimage."

Krishna continued, "What our Queen has so eloquently

described concerning *kundalini* is analogous to the last part of one's spiritual journey. When enlightenment is fully manifested at the sixth chakra, the passageway from the sixth to the seventh chakra opens gracefully and naturally. It is then and *only then*, that the soul finds its way to God-realization.

"An ancient scripture called the *Holy Bible* speaks of this exit-point: 'After passing through this gateway, ye shall go no more out!' Final liberation means freedom from any further need for the soul to reincarnate. It means overcoming all duality and dwelling forever in blissful oneness with God."

Sabella asked, "I understand that the seventh or crown chakra is the final exit point for the soul. But are you saying that until final liberation is achieved, the soul enters and exits the physical body, not through the seventh chakra at the top of the head, but at the sixth chakra instead?"

"That is correct, Sabella," Lord Krishna said, "even though some spiritual teachers have mistakenly taught that it is a good idea to 'run energy' either into or out of the seventh chakra, this is not true. However it is important to know about this sacred gateway and its purpose. We can even see, feel, or experience its presence from time to time—this is to be expected.

"There is an interesting example of how one of Paramhansa Yogananda's earliest disciples, Dr. Minot Lewis, was shown his own crown chakra. He had just met the great master, who asked him to sit down on the floor before him, so that he could help him to calm his restless mind. After showing him the great light of the spiritual eye in his forehead, Dr. Lewis reported that Yogananda 'pressed his forehead against my forehead; it was then that I saw the great light of the thousand-rayed lotus—the most exquisite thing that can be seen, with its many, many rays of silver leaves.'"

"It is also good for us to clarify that the seventh chakra's purpose is not for sending or receiving *prana*. That function belongs primarily to the sixth chakra. The seventh chakra is, plainly and simply, the gateway to final freedom—a one-time, one-way trip," he laughed joyfully.

Krishna continued, "There is a small, but significant physical indication of the seventh chakra's presence in the human body.

"When a baby emerges from its mother's womb, there is a noticeable soft spot called the *fontanelle*, located right at the top of the baby's skull. New mothers are cautioned to take special care that this part of the baby's head is not injured until the skull-plates have had time to seal together, to protect the brain. This happens by the time a baby is about a year old."

Queen Draupadi interrupted Krishna—he didn't seem to mind. "Sabella, don't you love that word, *fontanelle*? To me it brings an image of a large fountain of light, which actually is how the crown chakra appears energetically, even though it is more often called the thousand-petaled lotus of light. Fountain? Lotus blossom? They are similar images, and they offer a good way to imagine how the seventh chakra looks, with its many, many rays of radiant energy and Divine Light."

Krishna continued, "When the *fontanelle* is closed and the baby's skull is intact, we have a perfect symbolic indicator that the crown chakra is not the soul's exit point—at least not yet. It will open when the time is right. Let me again emphasize that the seventh chakra should not be forced open prematurely before the spiritual seeker is truly ready."

Out of curiosity, Sabella chose this moment to briskly rap on the top of her head with her fist. "You're right," she said ruefully. "The top of my skull seems solidly closed."

Krishna chuckled, "No holes in the top of your head, Sabella? Well, I did say that a newborn baby's open *fontanelle* is primarily symbolic! There is another interesting story about the crown chakra.

"Back in the early years of Ascending Dwapara Yuga, one of Paramhansa Yogananda's most advanced disciples was Sister Gyanamata. Yogananda asked several of his disciples to enter the room where she had just passed away a short time before, instructing them, 'Touch her feet and feel the cold temperature there, which indicates that her life force is departing quickly from most of her physical body.' They did this and found what he said to be true.

"'Now touch the top of her head,' he said. The top of her head felt as hot as fire.

"'The intense heat in her crown chakra,' Yogananda explained, 'shows that she departed her body in a state of *nirbikalpa samadhi*. Her soul left her body through the thousand-petaled lotus. She has achieved the state of *moksha* or final liberation. She is free; she has no need, ever again, to reincarnate.'"

Lord Krishna looked very intently at Sabella as he transmitted this thought to her, "Sabella, first we will take you to the beginning of the passageway from the sixth to the seventh chakra. Entering and passing into and through the crown chakra will, at that point, be your choice—yours alone to make. At that time and if you are ready, you will experience *nirbikalpa samadhi* as the final step of your spiritual journey."

Sabella said solemnly, "Please, Lord Krishna, I need to meditate now and call upon my *sat-guru* to guide me and to help me to know what to do. I cannot take the final steps in my spiritual journey without doing this first."

"So be it!" Krishna said, as if smiling.

Sabella sat down, right where she was and prayed deeply for guidance. She soon entered the blissful state of *sabikalpa samadhi*. She was no longer breathing, her heart was not beating, and her mind was completely still.

Soon a glowing tunnel appeared before her inner vision. She intuitively knew that it was the final passageway from the sixth to the seventh chakra, which would take her from enlightenment to final liberation.

Many years passed in Sabella's life, during which she often relived the memory of these sacred moments and wondered if she had made the right decision. At these times of doubt, she received inspiration from the words of a great saint who had lived in Ascending Dwapara Yuga, for they reflected her own feelings closely. He said, "I have not yet experienced *nirbikalpa samadhi,* but I can't help thinking that, were I in that state, I wouldn't have anything like the strong urge I feel to help others."

How enticing it was to contemplate the short passageway to final liberation—it pulled on her soul with an intense magnetism. But in that moment, she knew without question, that it was not yet her time to enter it. She had been offered an important mission to accomplish on earth. Still she knew that even as far as she had come and as much as she had accomplished on her pilgrimage, she must stay where she was, with her husband, her mentors, and all the Great Ones she met during this pilgrimage. They would give her the power she would need to move successfully through the next phase of her life.

Lord Krishna spoke softly into her right ear, "Sabella, please return to us now."

When she had returned from her *sabikalpa* state, he spoke again, "Stand up and look carefully into the passageway before you. Although you have chosen not to enter it now, it will remain there inside you, waiting for you to enter, when the time is right.

"But you have earned the right to observe, in vision, what will happen for you someday soon, when you do travel through this final tunnel into the seventh chakra, thereby achieving *nirbikalpa samadhi.*"

Sabella did as she was told and gazed unblinkingly into the shining tunnel. The light grew brighter and brighter, absorbing her into it. The great booming sound of AUM filled her with ceaseless, ever-new joy.

In a vision, she saw herself years later, at this same entrance to the tunnel. Sahadeva met her there and merged his form into hers. Nakula, Arjuna, Bhima, Yudhisthira, Bhishma, and Lord Krishna, did the same. Her aura expanded to infinity, and all her chakras were filled with colorful shapes, dazzling lights, and the cosmic sounds of AUM.

Lady Kundalini appeared, holding the shining cords of *iḍa* and *pingala* in her left and right hands. Similar to Sabella's earlier experience in cosmic consciousness, she saw the lady began to whirl like a cyclone, causing the *naḍis* to merge first into the lady herself and then into Sabella's own *sushumna*, propelling both of them deeper and deeper through its last subtle layers.

Her vision showed massive amounts of divine energy flooding her being, dissolving all remaining vestiges of her physical, astral, and causal bodies and burning away any last remnants of *karma*.

Finally, she saw her soul pause briefly in her crown chakra. She realized that the seventh chakra, like the seventh pyramid, has no need for any kind of physical form. It was simply the gateway to *satchidananda*, ever-existing, ever-conscious, ever-new bliss.

There was no one there to meet her—she knew that there was no need for that sort of help any more. She had *become* everyone and everything. Indeed, she realized that there was no "there" in which to be. It was all a great oneness, with no boundaries, no forms, no beginnings, or endings. Her vision immersed her in . . . what could she name it? She found out later that she was completely unable to describe this part of her sacred pilgrimage. Thereafter, she always held it in her heart as a private treasure.

What she did feel she could share with others was that in the final moments of her vision, she clearly heard a passage from Yogananda's poem "Samadhi," resounding throughout eternity:

> *Four veils of solid, liquid, vapor, light,*
> *Lift aright,*
> *Myself in everything,*
> *Enters the great Myself.*

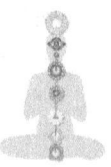

294

CHAPTER FORTY-THREE

"What happened?" Thomas asked Sabella when she materialized at home the next day. "Have you successfully completed
your chakras pilgrimage? Did you graduate with honors? How
did you feel when you were in the seventh-chakra pyramid?
Where is your new robe and pendant?"

"Thomas, please! Give me time to accustom myself to this
world. I will tell you all that I can, but some of it. . . . I'm not
sure I'm capable of describing my experiences in words or
even mind-pictures. Please be assured, dearest one that I will
do my very best to share with you everything that I can. But
I am here now, and all is well with me. I love you!"

Sabella eventually did tell Thomas as much as she felt
inwardly guided to reveal. He understood, as we all should,
that our deepest spiritual experiences are best left hidden
and cherished inside our hearts.

Two weeks later, Issoweet, Simeon, and the rest of the High
Council members received Sabella in the main pavilion, to
hear her tell of her pilgrimage through the seven golden
pyramids. She wore her sixth-chakra robe of blue, gold, and
white, and her beautiful six-chakra-pendant necklace.

She did not wear the spectacular pearl and ruby crown, which
Lord Krishna had given her, feeling that this was not the
proper setting. She couldn't imagine what a proper setting
for her to wear it would be. For now, it remained displayed
in a place of honor in her home.

The Council members were delighted to hear that she had
already begun formulating ideas for the new "Chakras

Paradigm/Advanced and Experiential Course of Study," for the Hall of Wisdom.

As she began to make her report she asked the Council members, "How much detail would you like to hear from me right now? I have not yet had the time to complete my plans, but I don't think it will take very long. I feel so much inspiration, excitement, and energy for the project, to say the least!"

Simeon transmitted these thoughts to her on behalf of the High Council members: "Sabella Lovingheart, you have done very, very well! Sharing with us just a few highlights of your pilgrimage will be sufficient for today. We all offer you our congratulations and our love. Take whatever time you need to reveal your future plans. Issoweet will work with you and you can offer us more details when you feel ready. We have complete confidence in your ability to create an 'Advanced Chakras Course of Study,' as we have asked you to do."

Before they left the High Council pavilion, Issoweet asked to speak with Sabella in private. Sitting together in the small pyramid-chapel where all of Sabella's chakra adventures had begun, Issoweet said to her, "There is no need for me to tell you of my deep love for you, Sabella. I know you feel it in your heart, and I know that we will continue to work together in harmony for many years to come. To ease any misgivings you may have about not yet choosing to enter the seventh-chakra pyramid, I'd like to tell you a story.

"Once there were three friends who lived in a village in the forest. They had heard rumors of a giant wall somewhere deep within the forest, beyond which was a place of great mystery and surpassing beauty. Together they decided to try to find the wall. After many days of searching, they stumbled upon it.

Immediately they saw that it was much too tall to climb over. Still they had a great desire to scale the wall and see what was on the other side. They decided to form a kind of 'human ladder' by standing one atop the others' shoulders. In that way they hoped that the person at the top could see over the wall and report what she saw there.

"Their plan worked well, but when the woman on top finally was able to see what was on the other side, she cried out with great happiness, clapped her hands together, and leaped over the wall before revealing what she had seen.

"The two remaining friends naturally were disappointed, but they decided to persevere and find another way to climb the wall. After some exploration they found a place where they could roll some large boulders together to form a mound next to the wall, thus making a platform upon which to stand. Thus in a similar way to their first attempt, one could stand on top of the shoulders of the other and reach the top of the wall.

"Once again, as soon as the woman on top saw what was on the other side of the wall, she shouted with delight, forgot her promise to her companion, and disappeared over the wall.

"With sadness in her heart, the final woman found herself alone. Being a determined soul, she resolved to find a way to climb the wall. It took her a very long time, but with great effort she was finally able to build a tall platform which allowed her to boost herself to the top of the wall.

As she stood there on top, she saw before her the most beautiful garden-like setting that can be imagined. The sight of it filled her heart with divine light, peace, joy, and an overwhelming desire to enter the gardens immediately and dwell there forever.

"Just as she was about to do exactly as her friends had done before her and leap joyfully into this inexpressibly lovely place, she remembered all the people who were back in the village where she lived. If she entered the gardens now, the villagers might never know about this place or make the effort to come here and climb over such a high wall. She knew she must go back to share the good news of its existence and to guide them here. So that is what she did."

"Oh, Issoweet, thank you, and I do understand! Your inspiring story has helped to heal my heart," Sabella said as she knelt at her mentor's feet for a blessing, which Issoweet willingly gave her.

CHAPTER FORTY-FOUR

Happy months sped by as Issoweet and Sabella clarified the details of what soon would become a world-famous feature of the Halls of Wisdom.

The "Chakras Paradigm/Advanced and Experiential Course of Study" (CP/AECS for short) was in great demand, as soon as it became available for graduate students to enroll in its various seminars. Drawing together the brightest, best, and most spiritually advanced students—only ten of them for the first session—Sabella was thrilled at how well it was received by everyone: students, other faculty members, and the High Council members.

Of the ten students who completed the course, three of those students, the best of the best, were guided by Sabella and Brother Solonar through their own chakras pilgrimage in the valley of the seven golden chakra pyramids.

Sabella knew it was important for the students to gain a greater appreciation for their own chakras by making good friends with them, understanding their importance in every aspect of their lives. This was especially true for those who would go on to become instructors of advanced chakras-studies in other places, or even on other planets or other sectors of the universe.

One interesting and unexpected idea was born during the development of the new courses. Sabella realized that to truly grasp this material, there needed to be a personal chakras healing and purification phase of each student's experience. The idea became so magnetic, that it quickly changed from being only a small part of the curriculum for the CP/AECS program in the Halls of Wisdom, into a worldwide movement.

As the years went by, Chakras Healing Clinics began springing up like wildfire all over the earth. All were facilitated by
graduates of the CP/AECS.

Anyone could seek healing or rejuvenation at a Chakras
Healing Clinic. Clients were welcomed by the clinic's director and shown around the beautiful grounds, which were
always amply populated by colorful, fragrant flowers.
Extensive flower gardens played an essential role in the
healing process—their harmonious and uplifting vibrations
and fragrances supported rapid healing.

Within the grounds were seven carefully placed pyramids,
each about thirty feet tall and made of brightly colored,
transparent glass—red, orange, golden-yellow, green, blue,
indigo, and violet.

New guests would spend time inside each of the pyramids,
but only after completion of a basic chakras orientation
program and several experiential practices. This program
included a thorough introduction about what the chakras
are, how they function, as well as exercises, such as chanting, meditation, visualization, Energization Exercises, and
yoga postures.

The diet for a guest's stay included primarily fresh fruits
and vegetables. As a central part of the meals and to support
the chakra being focused on that day, one particular food
or beverage was highlighted. For example, beets for the
first chakra (red in color and a root vegetable, perfect for
the root chakra), or orange juice for the second chakra
(liquid, bright orange, and very sweet, and reflective of
this chakra's Sanskrit name, *swadisthana*, which literally
means "sweetness'), and so on through each of the seven
chakras.

A minimum stay of two weeks at a clinic was generally
required, though many guests liked it so much, they stayed
longer. A reasonable amount of energy credits were charged
to a visitor's Universal Energy Account, but no one was
turned away for any reason, even if they didn't have enough
credits to cover a visit to the clinic.

The success rate for the numerous and often miraculous healings which occurred at the clinics was astonishing! They soon became extraordinarily popular all over the world. And why not? They were extremely effective in creating an optimal environment for healing to occur. Many guests returned again and again for a "chakras tune-up," with some happy visitors making it an essential part of any vacation time they had.

Soon it became clear that Chakras Healing Clinics could benefit children also, if the programs were carefully modified to meet the requirements of a child in need of healing. It did not take long to see that even healthy children loved to visit the "Chakra Wonderland Parks," as they came to be known.

One bright graduate of CP/AECS branched off to create Chakras Healing Clinics for Animals, which initiated a world-wide debate as to whether or not animals have chakras. In any case, Animal Chakras Clinics soon became wildly successful as well. Animals may or may not have chakras in the same way human beings do, but they certainly responded amazingly well to energy-healing and divine love.

Sabella Lovingheart's "Seven-Point Plan for Understanding, Experiencing, and Healing the Chakras" became the primary foundation for teachers' curriculums and for directors of the healing clinics, providing clarity for the complex, but ever-fascinating subject of the chakras. It explained as simply as possible how the chakras function and how they affect a person's life, health, and well-being on every level.

A Seven-Point Plan for Understanding, Experiencing, and Healing the Chakras

1) The chakras are a part of our astral/energy anatomy and should be worked with *holistically*—that is, we should never focus only on one or two of the chakras for exclusive or special emphasis, while neglecting the others. Even if a part of the body is obviously malfunctioning, we cannot be certain that the nearest chakra is the one needing attention. It might be another chakra, or more

likely, *all* of them which need purification. Therefore, it is best to work with the chakras as a *whole system*, using many or all of the tools offered below. The most powerful of these tools are meditation techniques such as Kriya Yoga, which direct energy through all the chakras, while magnetizing and purifying the astral spine gradually, but powerfully.

2) There is no such thing as a "blocked chakra." *Prana* is pouring into and through all the chakras at all times, and is constantly being distributed by the chakras into the body's 72,000 *prana* channels or *nadis*—otherwise no life in the human body would be possible. However, when the energy flowing through them becomes impeded or partially "clogged" with the debris or *vrittis* of past karma, "leakages" occur in the form of strong attachments, bad habits, and likes and dislikes. In this state (which is generally the human condition!) perfect health of body, mind, emotions, and spirit is not possible.

3) It is not advantageous to ask someone else to "fix your chakras" for you. So-called "chakras healers" may claim that they can clear, balance, or heal your chakras through massage, pendulums, or other esoteric techniques. This might be fun and inter-esting; it may even offer some temporary relief. But true and permanent healing can be done *only* by the individual, with the inward and divine help of God and gurus. Working effectively with the chakras primarily involves *interior* work and cannot come from outside. No one else except you made you into the person you are right now, so you are the one who must fix yourself. Places such as the Chakras Healing Clinics provide an excellent environment for healing to take place. But even in such places, a person's own efforts are always needed.

4) Learning from and being in tune with a true guru or qualified spiritual teacher are essential components in working with the chakras. They can guide you in creating a more perfect inner environment in which the chakras can be purified and healed. They can instruct you in

the most important tools for purifying the chakras; the techniques of meditation, Kriya Yoga, and listening to the AUM sounds of each chakra. They can also help you with shifting attitudes—letting go of harmful mindsets and cultivating helpful ones in each chakra—which is almost equal to deep meditation as a tool for clearing the chakras. In addition to these two most important ways of working with the chakras, there are a few more very efficient ways to achieve enlightenment and final liberation: chanting, AUM-ing the chakras with specific musical tones, listening to uplifting music, positive affirmations, visualizations, Energization Exercises, and yoga postures. There are other ways to work with the chakras, using colors, astrology, gemstones, and so on, but they are of secondary importance. To re-emphasize this point, the two *most* effective ways to purify the chakras are practicing the techniques of yoga and meditation and shifting one's attitudes, from harmful to beneficial.

5) Reading about the chakras and taking classes and courses are very helpful. However, what is most important for a teacher to strive to do is to find ways to help students to experience the chakras' presence within themselves. If you are teaching people about the chakras, remember that a person's *personal experiences* of the chakras are a hundred times more effective than merely talking or reading about them.

6) When teaching the subject of the chakras, it is always best not to use the format of discussing every aspect of the first chakra before moving on to the second chakra, then on to the third, and so on. It is much more effective to discuss the various qualities of all the chakras, progressively, going from the first to the seventh chakra. For example, explain the chakra Elements of Earth, Water, Fire, Air and Ether, then the attitudes or qualities (both positive and negative) of the chakras, from bottom to top, then the sounds of the chakras, bottom to top, next the colors, then the gemstones—and so on, through the many aspects of the chakras.

7) We should have fun while tuning in to our chakras. They are a part of us all, waiting for us to awaken them by *being interested in them.* Make friends with your chakras, for they can fill your life with great joy!

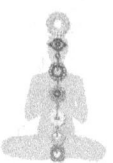

CHAPTER FORTY-FIVE

Rivers seek passage,
Unhindered by rock or tree,
So may our lives flow,
Steadfast toward the sea. ©

Many gloriously productive years passed, and Sabella thrived in her new field of service. She coordinated CP/AECS in the Halls of Wisdom and elsewhere, led individuals or groups of pilgrims through the valley of the seven golden pyramids, and went wherever she was needed for consultations with students or teachers on the subject of the chakras and astral anatomy.

She and Thomas still found time to collaborate on increasingly inspiring musical presentations, most of which were based on what she had learned and experienced during her chakra pilgrimage.

Sabella also enjoyed spending time with her grandchildren and great-grandchildren; there was quite a large flock of them now, and they all adored their famous grandmother, who, busy as she was, spent as much time as possible with them. She told them stories about fabulous adventures and showed them many wondrous things about themselves.

One late afternoon, she took her youngest great-granddaughter, Sabellina, age twelve, down to the beach on the Joyuba River. Sabella hoped that Sabellina would enjoy twilight by the river as much as she always did.

After sitting quietly for a while, Sabellina exclaimed, "Great-Gramma, I hear voices, music, and other sounds too—they seem to be coming from the river. Are they real or am I imagining them?"

"Rivers do that, my little darling, especially this one," Sabella sent her thought waves to the obviously sensitive child, who looked very much like she had at that age.

"Listen carefully and you will hear beautiful melodies. If you like, I'll teach you how to mentally record the melodies; then we can play and sing them together. Would you like that?"

"Yes, thank you! I would like that very much!"

"Then let's sit quietly for a little longer and see what we can hear."

As it began to grow darker, the fireflies began their joyous, nightly air-dances.

"Great-Gramma, is it alright if I ask you a question?"

Sabella said, "Of course!"

"Why are you so happy all the time? Is it because you are famous and have such a nice Great-Grampa for your life-mate, a large family who loves you, and plenty of good friends? Are these the things which make you happy?

"Those are big questions for a little girl, but they are very good questions! My greatest happiness comes from none of the things you have mentioned, though I am very happy to have all of them in my life—including you, Sabellina.

"Happiness, or true joy, as I like to call it, comes only from inside us. Nothing outside of ourselves will bring it to us. The kingdom of heaven is within us, but we have to search for it. If you really look for it, Sabellina, you will surely find it!"

"But how do I do that, Great-Gramma? Where do I start looking?" Sabellina sincerely asked, looking cute with her little brow knitted in an expression of serious concern.

"Well, dearest, I'm very pleased that you are asking me that question. I can show you a map which will lead you to your own highest happiness, which is within yourself. And I can introduce you to many friends and guides who can help you along your way. Would you like that?"

"Yes!" excitement blazed in Sabellina's intelligent, blue-green eyes, so like her great-grandmother's eyes.

"Then I think the best way to introduce you to this magical map to perfect joy is to begin by telling you a story—a true story of a woman who traveled along a river. No, it was not this small river." She had caught Sabellina's thought-question.

"It was the giant and mighty River Sushumna, which flows in a far-away place called the Valley of the Seven Golden Pyramids."

Sabellina grinned up at Sabella Lovingheart and snuggled closer to her. She said softly, "Great-Gramma, I'd *love* to hear that story—every single word of it!"

The two of them sat together for many happy evenings, during which Sabella's stories of her amazing adventures flowed on and on, like the shining river quietly gliding along beside them—a river not unlike the river which flows inside us all—moving forever onward to the great ocean of bliss.

THE END

ADDITIONAL INFORMATION

Chakras Chart

English Name/ Location	Sanskrit Name & *Literal Meaning*	Body Parts Influenced	Physical, Mental, or Spiritual Functions	Musical Note for "AUM-ing" Chakras	Ashtanga Yoga & *Spiritual Aspects*
Crown chakra, 1,000-Petaled Lotus, Seat of Liberation	Sahasrara *Thousand-fold*	Top Part of the Brain	Seat of the soul; site of final liberation		Samadhi & *Liberation*
3rd/Spiritual eye, point between the eyebrows, enlightenment, Christ center	Agya (positive pole of the Agya chakra) *To Perceive*	From the base of the skull to the point eyebrow area (eyes, ears, nose, mouth)	Enlighten-ment site, concentra-tion, will-power; the senses	G (above middle C)	Dhyana & *Divine Joy, Enlighten-ment*
Medulla oblongata, "Mouth of God"	(negative pole of the Agya chakra)	Medulla oblongata, brain stem, back of head close to neck	Entry point of life-force, regulates breath & heartbeat	F	Dharana & *Ego (self-offering)*
Cervical Center (Throat/Neck)	Bishuddha *To Purify*	Neck, throat, vocal cords, thyroid glands	Speaking, singing, swallowing	E♭ (E flat)	Pratyahara & *Calmness, expansion*
Dorsal Center (Heart)	Anahata *Un-struck*	Heart, lungs, diaphragm; shoulders, arms, hands	Breathing, Blood circulation; Manual dexterity	D	Pranayama & *Divine Love*
Lumbar Center (Navel)	Manipura *Lustrous Jewel*	Stomach, intestines; liver, many other organs of digestion	Digestion; Assimilation Human Power Center	B♭ (B flat)	Asana & *Fiery Self-Control*
Sacral Center (Sex Organs)	Swadisthana *Sweetness*	Sexual organs, reproductive system	The Creative Impulse; Procreation; Sexuality	A	Niyama & *Ability to follow Niyamas*
Coccyx Center (Base of Spine)	Muladhara *Root or Support*	Anus, rectum; hips, legs, and feet, the ability to walk	Elimination; Ambulatory power; Survival	G (below middle C)	Yama & *Ability to follow Yamas*

Beneficial Qualities and Attitudes	Harmful Qualities and Attitudes	Inner AUM Sounds	Maha-bharata Characters		Tastes
Beyond duality, harmony, free, omnipresent, omniscient, samadhi bliss.					
Divine attunement, radiant joy, Solution-consciousness, will power.	Coldly-rational, too intellectual	AUM (Om); like the roar of a great, bursting sea	Krishna		Very Sweet, Divine Nectar, "Amrita"
Selfless service, divine surrender;	Ego-involved, proud, vain, "I, Me, Mine"		Bhishma		
Expansive, deeply calm, enjoying silence	Restless, spacey, bored, mercurial	Wind through the trees, waterfall	Yudhisthira		Extremely Bitter
Devotion, unconditional love, compassion;	Attachments, harmful emotions	Deep bell, gong (or higher bell sound)	Bhima	Satya	Sour
Fiery self-control, joyful zest for life, enthusiasm, self-acceptance	Ruthlessness, abusive, manipulative, guilt-ridden	Harp, vina, plucked string instrument	Arjuna	Treta	Bitter
Flexible, open-minded, willing, intuitive	Wishy-washy, ungrounded, indecisive	Flute (crickets, trickling water)	Nakula	Dwapara	Mildly Bitter
Steadfastness, courage, loyalty, determination, grounded	Stubbornness, bigoted, stuck, heavy-minded	Bumble-bee (rumbling motor)	Sahadeva	Kali	Sweet Juice

311

Chakra Colors and Other Vibrational Aspects

ENGLISH NAME & LOCATION	SANSKRIT NAME & LITERAL TRANSLATION	ELEMENT	TRADITIONAL OUTER COLOR RAINBOW SPECTRUM	INNER COLOR & SHAPE	ARCHITECTURAL SHAPE	PETALS OF RAYS OF ENERGY	VEDIC ASTROLOGICAL RULINGS SIGN & RISING PLANET	PRIMARY GEMSTONE	SUBSTITUTE STONE	METAL	COLOR FOR EACH DAY OF THE WEEK
Crown Chakra 1,000 Petal Lotus Seat of Liberation Top of the Head	**SAHASRARA** "Thousandfold"		VIOLET	LOTUS BLOSSOM MANY PETALS		1000					SUNDAY (SUN'S DAY) RED
Spiritual Eye, 3rd Eye Seat of Enlightenment, Point Between the Eyebrows	**AGYA** Positive Pole of the 6th Chakra "To Perceive"	SUPER ETHER	INDIGO	SPIRITUAL EYE GOLD, BLUE, WHITE		2	LEO (+) SUN	RED RUBY	GARNET	GOLD	
Medulla Oblongata Seat of the Ego Brain-Stem	Negative or Receptive Pole of the 6th Chakra						CANCER (-) MOON	PEARL	MOONSTONE	SILVER	MONDAY (MOON'S DAY) PEARL WHITE
Cervical Center Throat, Neck	**VISHUDDHA** "Purification"	ETHER	BLUE	SMOKE WITH CHECKS OF LIGHT		16	GEMINI (+) VIRGO (-) MERCURY	GREEN EMERALD	GREEN TOURMALINE PERIDOT GREEN JADE	MERCURY	WEDNESDAY (MERCURY'S DAY) GREEN
Dorsal Center Heart Area	**ANAHATA** "Unstruck"	AIR	GREEN	BLUE SPHERE	SPHERE OR GLOBE	12	LIBRA (+) TAURUS (-) VENUS	WHITE DIAMOND	WHITE SAPPHIRE WHITE AQUAMARINE WHITE TOPAZ WHITE CRYSTAL	COPPER	FRIDAY (VENUS'S DAY) BRIGHT WHITE
Lumbar Center Navel, Solar Plexus	**MANIPURA** "Lustrous Jewel"	FIRE	YELLOW	BLOOD-RED TRIANGLE	PYRAMID	10	ARES (+) SCORPIO (-) MARS	RED CORAL	CARNELIAN	IRON	TUESDAY (MARS' DAY) RED
Sacral Center Sexual Organs	**SWADISTHANA** "Sweetness"	WATER	ORANGE	WHITE HALF-MOON	DOME	6	SAGITTARIUS (+) PISCES (-) JUPITER	YELLOW SAPPHIRE	YELLOW TOPAZ CITRINE	TIN	THURSDAY (JUPITER'S DAY) YELLOW
Coccyx Center Base of the Spine	**MULADHARA** "Root or Support"	EARTH	RED	YELLOW 4-SIDED FIGURE	SQUARE OR RECTANGULAR BOX	4	AQUARIUS (+) CAPRICORN (-) SATURN	BLUE SAPPHIRE	AMETHYST LAPIS LAZULI	LEAD	SATURDAY (SATURN'S DAY) BLUE

HESSONITE OR CINNAMON GARNET
CHRYSOBERYL OR CAT'S EYE OR TIGER'S EYE

IDA – UPWARD FLOW – RIGHT
PINGALA – DOWNWARD FLOW – LEFT

WHAT IS A YUGA?

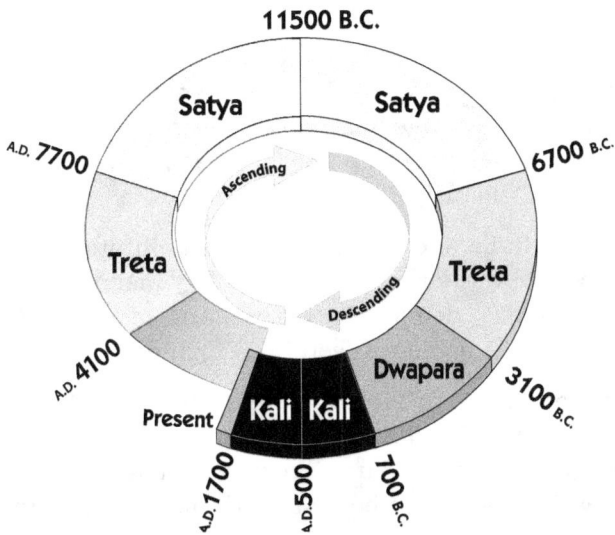

Yuga is a Sanskrit word which means an eon or extremely long period of time.

In India, and particularly in the teachings of yoga, time is described as moving through cycles, rather than in a linear fashion. The yuga theory explains that there have been in the past, and will be in the future, both "higher" and "lower" ages, manifesting in cyclic patterns.

Just as our planet's seasons move through summer, autumn, winter, and spring, each yuga involves stages of gradual change, through which the earth and the consciousness of human beings, as a whole, either progresses or regresses.

Toward the end of the 19th century, a man with exceptional credentials as a scholar wrote a book called *The Holy Science*. Swami Sri Yukteswar (1855-1936) of Serampore, Bengal, was a master of great wisdom, deeply learned in the ancient lore of India. In his book he stated that, according to a system of chronology that was established by astronomers in ancient times, our planet moves through great cycles of time called yugas.

The Holy Science appeared in 1894. In it Sri Yukteswar described this ancient chronology in detail, and corrected certain misinterpretations of that chronology, which had crept in over recent centuries. He announced that the earth actually left the lowest age of *Kali Yuga* recently and entered the next and higher age of *Dwapara Yuga*. This was contrary to a current belief that our planet still had more than 400,000 years of Kali Yuga left.

Long ago in India and in other ancient civilization, different names were given for four ages. The Egyptians called them the ages of gods, demi-gods, heroes, and men. The Greeks named them the golden, silver, bronze, and iron ages.

The ages described in the yuga theory are four: *Satya Yuga*, the spiritual age; *Treta Yuga*, the mental age; *Dwapara Yuga*, the energy age; and Kali Yuga, the dark or materially-oriented age. *Kali Yuga* is said to be an age of spiritual ignorance.

According to Sri Yukteswar, a full yuga cycle takes 24,000 years to complete and includes two major divisions: 12,000 years of *ascending* consciousness and 12,000 years of *descending* consciousness.

Looking at this system from an astronomer's point of view, the ascending cycle of the yugas represents a progression from the time when our solar system is the farthest from the center of our galaxy to the time when it is closest to that center.

The scientific explanation given for the progression of the yugas is that our sun has a dual star, and that these two stars revolve around each other. Because of this revolution, our sun with its planets moves in a great elliptical orbit toward, then away from, the center of our galaxy, which is a tremendous vortex of energy.

The yogic teachings say that rays of spiritual energy are emitted at the galactic center, and that the closer our solar system comes to this center, the more energy floods our planet. As the level of energy increases, human consciousness becomes correspondingly more enlightened and aware.

As our solar system moves away from the source of these energy rays, human consciousness becomes duller, that is, less able to understand things as they truly are. Spiritual progress becomes much more difficult.

Our solar system reached the point farthest away from the galactic center in roughly 500 AD, during the heart of the Dark Age or Kali Yuga.

We are now moving back again toward the galactic center; consequently, human beings are more able to understand the more subtle truths of life. People have begun to recognize, for example, that matter is not essentially solid, but is really energy. In fact, it is only because we've moved into the more enlightened age of Ascending Dwapara Yuga that mankind is able to understand the concept of the yuga cycle.

The two lower yugas are Dwapara Yuga, "The Age of Energy," and Kali Yuga, "The Material Age."

Since 1900 AD, our planet has been in Ascending Dwapara Yuga, and we find, amazingly, just in one century, how much we have advanced. Everything we know of modern times— airplanes, cars, electronics, radios, television, computers— started after 1900. And we're just at the beginning of this new "Age of Energy." The discoveries that lie ahead of us are enormous, and all will be based on an awareness of energy as the underlying reality of matter.

A very different kind of world and universe will open up as we advance into this new era. Before the end of Ascending Dwapara Yuga in 4100 AD we will have learned to bypass the limitations of the speed of light, and will conquer the delusion of space and distance; we will realize that the most distant galaxy is as easy to visit as are our present surroundings.

The two higher ages are Treta Yuga, "The Mental Age," and Satya Yuga, "The Spiritual Age."

Beginning in 4100 AD (Ascending Treta Yuga), people will understand that consciousness engenders energy and that with their own minds they can direct energy to accomplish their goals. As mankind's mental control, intuition, and knowledge of the universe evolve, mental telepathy will occur naturally. This understanding will be the hallmark of Treta Yuga.

Treta Yuga will also be an age marked by human beings' ability to overcome all limitations of time. In Treta Yuga, most people will understand that time, like space, is a delusion, and that the most ancient civilizations exist, not in the distant past, but right now, in the eternal present.

This novel, *Through the Chakras: A Tale of Adventure in the Seven Golden Pyramids*, begins in Treta Yuga about 3,900 years from the present time.

In a certain sense, it does not matter which yuga we find ourselves in on this earth or on any other planet (Paramhansa Yogananda said there are many inhabited planets). For as we reincarnate from life to life, through *many* lifetimes, the best way to live is to tune in to the highest octave of the time in which we find ourselves, and to use it for our own, and all others' highest possible good.

The yoga sciences teach that the goal of life is self-realization and oneness with all that is. That goal is possible for us during any lifetime and in any yuga.

If you would like more information about the yuga theory and its explanation of the history of our planet, including its interesting ways of predicting the future, we highly recommend *The Yugas*, by Joseph Selbie and David Steinmetz, published by Crystal Clarity Publishers, *crystalclarity.com*. This is, without question, the best book ever written on the subject.

In friendship,
Nayaswami Savitri Simpson
Ananda Village, California, USA

The yuga diagram and information about the yugas is taken, in part, and with thanks, from the article, "The Higher Yugas and the Unfolding of Human Potential," by Swami Kriyananda, in Ananda Sangha's *Clarity Magazine Online* (Fall, 2010).

THE MAHABHARATA AND THE PANDAVA BROTHERS

Several of the characters in this novel have their origins in the longest epic in the world, the *Mahabharata*. The Holy Scripture known as the *Bhagavad Gita* is the central and most important section of the *Mahabharata*. The *Gita*, which is very short by comparison to the whole *Mahabharata*, clearly outlines the essence of the yogic sciences and explains how a sincere truth-seeker may walk his or her inner pathway to self-realization, as easily and efficiently as possible.

The *Mahabharata*, if read without spiritual guidance, may be seen to be a chronicle of entertaining adventures and intense warfare. Much of the action appears on first reading to be more political than spiritual. However, great masters of yoga have explained that it is deeply allegorical, offering a unique look at the kingdom of our minds. The characters represent our many different psychological traits, each of which has a life of its own.

Within our consciousness, we may recognize these different sorts of mental citizens—some of them noble, some of them ignoble, some altruistic, some selfish, some looking for spiritual truths, and some thinking of how they can get out of having to look for truth—all of this clearly revealing our constant inward struggle between darkness and light.

On the surface, the *Mahabharata* is an account of a civil war, the conflict and deceit which led to the great battle of Kurukshetra, and the destruction of the Kshatriyas (the warrior class of India) in that war, which actually occurred about 700 BCE.

The primary characters are the rulers and members of two royal houses which lay claim to the same lands and possessions: the Kauravas, those committed primarily to seeking power and influence, and the Pandavas, who seek to live by spiritual principles. They grew up together as cousins and fellow-students, but were violently split apart due to the Kauravas' hatred, jealousy, and intense desire to rule the kingdom without the Pandavas' participation.

The Pandava leaders were five brothers, Sahadeva, Nakula, Arjuna, Bhima, and Yudhisthira. They symbolize beneficial attitudes associated with the first five chakras.

The Kauravas were led by Duryodhana or "King Material Desire" and the powerful grandfather of both clans, Bhishma, who represents ego. Duryodhana had 99 brothers, who represent harmful mental attitudes. Seemingly outnumbered, the Pandavas still prevailed, primarily because of their reliance on the guidance of Lord Krishna, who represents God or the Higher Self.

War casualties were massive. Most of the kings and greatest warriors of that time were killed, including Duryodhana, Bishma, and most of the Kauravas.

But allegorically speaking, it was necessary that the Pandavas, the forces of right action, win the war—for the power of righteousness within us is always victorious eventually.

I have taken the liberty of taking a few of the main characters and stories from this ancient epic, and placing them in *Through the Chakras*.

I bow in gratitude to all the characters, gods, and goddesses of the *Mahabharata*. I ask for their forgiveness if I've misrepresented them in any way or not shown them proper respect. But in my heart I feel that they had as much fun as I did through retelling a few of their stories in a new format.

GLOSSARY

Sanskrit and Other Terms

agya Sanskrit name for sixth chakra, the ego center in the medulla oblongata, literally means "to perceive," sometimes spelled ajna

amrita Also called soma, the "blissful nectar of the Gods or immortality," a life-sustaining liquid or very sweet taste which is experienced in the deepest states of meditation.

anahata Sanskrit name for fourth chakra, literally means "unstruck"

asana Third "limb" of Patanjali's eight-fold path, right posture and the ability to sit completely still

ashtanga yoga Patanjali's exposition of the eight-fold path, or the eight aspects of enlightenment

astral body The body of light and energy

AUM The vibrational sound of the cosmos

avatar A liberated soul who returns into manifested existence to help those still wandering in delusion

bishuddha Sanskrit name for fifth chakra, cervical center, literally means "purification," sometimes spelled vishuddha

brahmanadi The central channel of the causal body; the final channel through which one ascends into superconscious union with God

causal body The ideational body, or innermost body composed of thoughts and ideas

chakras Plexuses or centers through which energy flows into the astral body, helps to animate and sustain the physical body

chitra Third of the luminous, subtle layers of the astral spine

dharana Sixth "limb" of Patanjali's eight-fold path, one-pointed concentration

dharma Righteousness or right action

dhyana Seventh "limb" of Patanjali's eight-fold path, absorption in deep meditation

dwaita Duality, opposites

guru Dispeller of darkness, teacher, spiritual savior

homa A small ceremonial fire, into which one may symbolically cast away past bad karma or darkness and cleanse oneself with light

ida One of the two superficial energy channels in the astral spine, ida begins and ends on the left side of the spine; the energy passing upward through it causes inhalation

karma Literally means action; the law of karma involves action and reaction

kriya yoga Ancient yogic science of meditation used to magnetize the astral spine and direct life-force to the brain

kundalini Located below the base of the spine, where the outward-flowing energy of the astral spine becomes 'locked' in its downward pull. Kundalini awakening occurs when the outward flow of energy gradually relaxes its grip and begins to return upward, in the direction of its source in Divine Consciousness.

kutastha The spiritual eye, the third eye, the seat of enlightenment, located midway between the eyebrows, it is the projected light of the sixth chakra. It is also called the *Kutastha Chaitanya* or Christ Consciousness Center. It is a projection of the light of the sixth chakra shining forward from the medulla oblongata to the point between the eyebrows and where all our powers of concentration gather when we focus.

loka Location

manipura Sanskrit name for third chakra, lumbar center, literally means "shining jewel"

mantra Words with special sounds, vibrations, and powers

medulla oblongata The section of the brain or brain-stem closest to location of the sixth chakra; sometimes called "the mouth of God." It is the place where prana enters the body

moksha Final liberation, union with God

mudra Positions of the body used to evoke power or stimulate certain inner energy flows

muladhara Sanskrit name for first chakra, coccyx center, literally means "root or support"

nadi Prana channels in the astral body; there are 72,000 of them, including the ida, pingala, and sushumna

nirbikalpa samadhi Permanent and unconditional state of ecstasy and union with God

niyamas Second limb of Patanjali's eight-limbed or eight-fold path, the five "do's" of the spiritual path

pingala One of the two superficial energy channels in the astral spine; pingala begins and ends on the right side of the spine, the energy passing downward through it causes exhalation

prana Conscious cosmic energy, life-force, that which animates the body and makes life possible

pranayama Fourth "limb" of Patanjali's eight-fold path, control of energy or life-force

pratyahara Fifth "limb" of Patanjali's eight-fold path, interiorization of the mind

sabikalpa samadhi Impermanent, conditional ecstasy, sustainable only in a trance-like state

sadhu Holy man

sahasrara Sanskrit name for seventh or crown chakra, literally means thousand-petaled lotus

samadhi Superconscious union with the Divine

samyama A perfect state of attunement, absorption, or complete identification with what one perceives, the final three "limbs" of Patanjali's eight-fold path

satchidananda A description of God as ever-existing, ever-conscious, ever-new bliss

sat-guru One's true guru designated by God, an eternal relationship

sushumna The deep astral spine through which Kundalini ascends toward enlightenment, also outermost of the luminous, subtle layers of the astral spine

swadisthana Sanskrit name for second chakra, sacral center, literally means "sweetness"

vajra Second of the luminous, subtle layers of the astral spine

vritti One tiny whirlpool of feelings or committed attachments lodged in the astral spine

yamas First limb of Patanjali's eight-limbed or eight-fold path, the five "don't's" of the spiritual path

yoga One of the three main systems of Indian thought, it teaches the sincere seeker how to escape delusion and merge with God, literally means yoke or union

yugas Ages or cycles of time, vast eons of time, includes Kali Yuga (dark age), Dwapara Yuga (second age, or age of energy), Treta Yuga (third age, or age of mental powers), and Satya Yuga (highest age of spiritual consciousness, also called Krita Yuga)

Proper Names

Arjuna Third of the Pandava brothers, son of the god Indra, represents 3rd chakra, asana in Patanjali's eight-fold path, and fiery self-control

Ashwini Kumaras Twin gods of healing and knowledge, fathers of Sahadeva and Nakula

Bhagavad Gita The short but important central portion of the *Mahabharata* which explains the path of yoga

Bhima Fourth of the Pandava brothers, son of the god Vayu, represents 4th chakra, pranayama in Patanjali's eight-fold path, and the power of vitality

Bhishma Represents the transcended ego, grandfather to the Kauravas and the Pandavas

Dharma God of righteousness and truthfulness, father of Yudhisthira

Draupadi Wife of all five Pandava brothers, represents kundalini

Dronacharya The young Kauravas' and Pandavas' instructor in archery and other warrior skills, represents habit

Duryodhana King material desire

Indra King of the Gods, ruler of the heavenly realms, the god of the rain, and the father of Arjuna

Kauravas Evil cousins and enemies of the Pandavas, represent negative tendencies

Kunti Mother of the three oldest Pandava brothers, eldest wife of Pandu, represents the power of dispassion

Kurukshetra The body, the field of action, or battlefield upon which the great battle in the Mahabharata took place

Lord Krishna Represents the Divine Essence, the soul, or the Higher Self

Madri Mother of the two youngest Pandava brothers, youngest wife of Pandu, represents the power of attachment to dispassion

Mahabharata The longest epic in the world, deeply allegorical

Nakula Second-youngest Pandava brother, twin to Sahadeva, son of the twin gods called the Ashwini Kumaras, represents 2nd chakra, the niyamas of Patanjali's eight-fold path, and the power to adhere to virtue

Pandavas Sons of Pandu, the forces of righteousness, represents positive tendencies

Pandu Husband of Kunti and Madri, human father of the Pandava brothers

Sahadeva Youngest Pandava brother, twin to Nakula, son of the Ashwini Kumaras, represents 1st chakra, the yamas of Patanjali's eight-fold path, and the power to stay away from evil

Vayu God of the winds, father of Bhima

Yudhisthira Fifth of the Pandava brothers, son of the god Dharma, represents 5th chakra in Patanjali's eight-fold path, and calmness in psychological battle

RECOMMENDED BIBLIOGRAPHY

Available through Crystal Clarity Publishers,
Nevada City, CA USA,
crystalclarity.com

A Pilgrimage to Guadalupe [a novel], Swami Kriyananda, 2013

Autobiography of a Yogi, First Edition, Paramhansa Yogananda, 1946

Chakras for Starters, (book and audio CD), Savitri Simpson, 2002

Demystifying Patanjali, Swami Kriyananda, 2012

Karma and Reincarnation: Wisdom of Yogananda Series, Paramhansa Yogananda, 2007

Love Perfected, Life Divine [a novel], Swami Kriyananda, 2013

Paramhansa Yogananda: A Biography: With Personal Reflections & Reminiscences, Swami Kriyananda, 2011

The Art and Science of Raja Yoga, Swami Kriyananda, 2002

The Essence of Self-Realization, Swami Kriyananda, 2009

The Essence of the Bhagavad Gita, Swami Kriyananda, 2006

The Meaning of Dreaming, Savitri Simpson, 2016

The New Path, Swami Kriyananda, 2009

The Time Tunnel [a novel], Swami Kriyananda, 2012

The Yugas: Keys to Understanding Our Hidden Past, Emerging Energy Age, and Enlightened Future, Joseph Selbie & David Steinmetz, 2010

Through Many Lives: A Tale of Time Travel Through the Yugas, Savitri Simpson, 2011